Trusted

By

Kerry Barnes

Trusted by Kerry Barnes ISBN – 978-1-8380440-6-0

This is a work of fiction. Names, characters, places, and incidents either are the product of the author's imagination or are used fictitiously. Any resemblance to actual persons, living or dead, events, or locales is entirely coincidental.

Trusted by Kerry Barnes ISBN – 978-1-8380440-6-0

For more information, address: kerrybarnes999@gmail.com.

First paperback edition October 2021

Publishers Once Upon A Book

www.authorkerrybarnes.co.uk

Warning

This book contains graphic details of murder, kidnapping and violence.

Other works by Kerry Barnes

Ruthless

Ruby's Palace

Raw Justice

The Hunted

The Rules

The Choice

Deceit

Cruel Secrets

Wicked Lies

Ugly Truth

Raising A Gangster

Outcast

Voice of Reason

Voice of Rage

Dedication

To my mum for her endless support and kindness.

Chapter One

Kera stared into the small mirror that hung from her bland bedroom wall. Her eyes were red from crying and she wondered if her life would get any easier. Her heart literally felt as though it had been ripped from her chest. She had only been hugging her mum to say goodbye. It was the end of the visit and the spiteful screw had no right to physically tear them apart. It was obvious that the officer didn't like her mother. So, in Kera's eyes, the screw deserved the backhander, and she didn't regret it. Except, now she was banned from the next visit. She only hoped that the officer wouldn't give her mum a hard time over it.

Judith's high-pitched voice rang through her ears like an air raid siren.

'Kera Anne, your food will get cold if you don't hop to it!'

Feeling utterly sick at having to leave her mother behind in that shithole of a prison, Kera sat at the table, but, really, she didn't want to eat or speak. She was well aware that Judith found her reluctant to have a conversation with them – a mark of rudeness – and knew that this meal would end in a row.

'That is a good piece of gammon right there.' Judith pointed with her knife, before morphing into a mannequin with a shrill voice. 'You know, Kera Anne, that I will not see good food go to waste. Now, come along, and eat it up.'

'Best do as she says, Kera Anne. We don't want our Judith upset, now, do we?' said Nigel, in his attempt at an authoritative voice.

However, to Kera, he sounded like Mr Bean.

Glancing up at her foster mother, Kera saw how she was smiling at Nigel, smug in the fact that her husband was backing her. She shivered in disgust at their pathetic behaviour. It was completely removed from what she'd been used to. Her own parents had been lively and louder, and their jokes had always left her with a real bellyache from laughing. *They would never have made her eat tasteless food or act like their shit didn't stink*, thought Kera, as she pushed another soggy cabbage leaf around the plate.

'I'm really not hungry, and please can you stop calling me Kera Anne! It's just Kera. Only my dad ever called me Kera Anne, and he always said it in a really sweet way. So it's kind of personal to me.'

Judith's lips tightened. 'Are you suggesting I am saying it incorrectly? Kera Anne is your name, is it not?' She wiped the corners of her mouth with the linen serviette and glared at her husband for him to stick up for her again.

Kera wanted to slap the spiteful look off Judith's face. She hated everything about the woman. The way she sat up straight with her eyes peering down her long pointed nose was a wind-up in itself, let alone the woman's thin, tight lips that curled into a smirk. Yet, worse, she hated her high-pitched voice. Everything about Judith and Nigel was irritating. She grinned inwardly, thinking how much the couple, who were in their mid-forties, looked so much like brother and sister. They both had strawberry-blonde hair and pasty complexions; he had a couple of moles on his face, and so did she. They wore clothes that were so plain, they blended into the magnolia wallpaper. To anyone else, they were kind, sweet people, and in the main, they probably were. But to Kera, they were posh, passive-aggressive snobs living in a council house.

Nigel, 'the knob', as Kera mentally referred to him, had worked for the civil service until he took early retirement, but she guessed he'd been fired. Judith had never told anyone what exactly she did for a living. Only to say she had a little part-time job in the offices; however, she left out the part that she was the cleaner. Their primary income was from fostering. Although

Judith and Nigel had fostered in the past, they had never adopted, and so they were only allowed to foster teenagers. The home was a far cry from what she'd been used to, and she found it impossible to fit in with their ways. The endless rules over being tidy, even in her own room, were simply too much. She tried to block out the tuts and the wag of the finger, but what Kera hated the most was Judith shaking her head. 'Now, Kera, we don't do that, do we? Nice young ladies sit up straight at the table. Classy young ladies don't wear earphones and certainly don't chew chewing gum. It's a filthy habit.'

Sometimes Kera found it amusing to blow a bubble with bubblegum in Judith's face, just to see her head almost twist off its neck in revulsion.

Kera knew the Leonards had their own issues, and being religious too, they consoled themselves with the idea that they were doing good. So they could walk around with their noses in the air believing they were better than anyone else. And she had sussed that out a year ago, merely by the way they spoke in such a condescending manner to anyone who would listen. Smiling with their humourless lips, they truly believed they were a cut above everyone else.

Kera had taken a lot of their digs about her mother and father with a pinch of salt, but today, Judith was really pushing her buttons.

Before there was an argument, Kera stood up to leave, but she was snapped at by Nigel. 'Sit down and don't you be so rude, Kera Anne. Judith has cooked a delicious meal for you, yet it seems we have this insolence every time you go and visit your mother! Well, young lady, it's not going to continue! You are only fourteen years old and in our care, and so you will do as we say.'

Retaking her seat, Kera glared at Nigel. 'What do you mean by "it's not going to continue"?' She sensed something was going on because of the way the two strawberry heads looked at each other.

Judith wiped her mouth again with the serviette as if she were the Queen. 'You are so defiant when you come back from your visit, and may I say despondent, and, Kera Anne, it's not good. We are here to look after your well-being, and, quite frankly, we feel that these visits are not helping you at all.'

Feeling incensed, Kera began to tap her foot like a drummer and bite her lip to fight the urge to let rip. She was so much like her own mother – like two peas in a pod, people would say – and she was proud of being so and of her temper as well, for that matter. 'You dare try to stop me seeing my mother! For fuck's sake, my mother shouldn't even be in that stinking, poxy place.'

'Kera Anne!' shouted Nigel. 'I will not have that language at my table. Now, you apologise to Judith this minute.'

'And you, ya ginger prick, can fuck off!'

Judith grabbed Kera's arm and squeezed it hard. 'As much as you think your mother is a good person, a jury of twelve found her guilty of murder. Now, finish your food. Can't you see! This is what happens when you visit your mother. You come back obviously with an appalling attitude and a mouth filled with expletives. You don't want to end up like her, but you will do, the way you are carrying on.' Judith's voice became so high-pitched that it was like scraping nails down a chalkboard. 'And I am going to speak to your social worker about your visitation rights with your mother. I will insist for your own good, Kera Anne, you stop *all* visits.'

Those words were like a red rag to a bull. Kera ripped her arm away from Judith's clutches and snatched her fork. With an uncontrollable urge, she rammed it into Judith's upper arm. The force behind it was so hard that Judith toppled off the chair, dragging the tablecloth down with her.

As soon as Kera realised what she had done, she knew she had to get out of the way. As she looked down at Judith, she was shocked to see the carnage on the floor. Plates of wet cabbage and the contents of a gravy boat had covered the woman. But, far worse, Judith was screaming while clutching her bleeding arm.

Kera recognised that she had done some serious damage from the amount of claret everywhere. Clasping her hands over her mouth in shock, all she could think of doing was to scarper. So, leaving Nigel to help his screaming wife, she hurtled out of the kitchen and up the stairs into her room and slammed the door shut behind her. Her breathing intensified as her throat tightened with emotion.

Even with the door closed, she could hear Judith wailing like a baby and Nigel fussing over her. They would no doubt call the social services, and she would go to the children's home. It was at that point, Kera knew she had to get away. However, she was intelligent enough to know that she couldn't live on the streets; she hadn't come from that life. Her father had once been a very successful businessman, and she was the only child, *her father's princess*. They had lived in a five-bedroom detached house with an indoor pool, and as far as she was aware, they still had a holiday home in Cyprus. They'd once had two Labradors. God knows where the dogs went after the social services had got involved.

She felt the tears welling up and blinked them away. She missed her father, and, of course, her mother, who was convicted of killing her dad. But she knew her mum had not murdered him. Reading the papers and listening to her mother's side, she was all too familiar with the case. Her so-called Uncle Calvin, her father's business partner, was a creep; she had never liked him, but he had wormed his way into her mother's affections, and they'd had a fling, albeit only a couple of times. Her mother, Madeleine, had always been a straight-up woman and had never lied about the short-lived affair. It was Calvin's statement in court that day that had made the jury think she was guilty. She was accused of shooting dead her husband, but the truth was, as Kera understood it, her mother hadn't killed him at all. A man dressed in black had come in through the door that her mother had stupidly left open and shot Nicolas, her father, in the chest. The shooting was at such close range that her mother was also coated in the blood and the ballistics residue. The gunman threw the gun at her mother, who instinctively caught it. The intruder then ran through the back door. At that point, her mother fell to the floor to see if she could revive her husband, but it was too late: he had been shot through the heart.

By the time Kera had arrived home from school, the house was swarming with police and an ambulancc standing at the ready. It would be the two worst moments of her life. First, seeing her mother covered in claret and her father zipped up inside a black body bag. And second, hearing eventually that her mother had been found guilty of her father's murder.

Nicolas's business partner, Calvin Stuart, had admitted in court that he had been sleeping with her mother when her father was in Spain on business. He had also told the police that he wouldn't marry and take on her daughter as his own unless she got divorced. But he knew she wouldn't do that because she could lose all the money invested in the business as well as their two homes. Her mother was livid about the lies because she had not wanted to marry Calvin at all. They'd only had sex twice, and she'd regretted it the second time and vowed not to drink too much when he was around. However, her angry outburst in court, where she jumped up screaming and shouting at him, did her no favours at all. She also had a few previous convictions for violence, albeit in her very much younger days, and so by the time the jury left the courtroom to deliberate, it was practically a forgone conclusion that she would receive a guilty verdict.

Kera had cried for a week, feeling so desolate. And with no other family members to live with, she was put into the social services system.

As Kera sat on the end of her bed, she could hear sirens. Her first thought was that Nigel had called the police and she would be carted away. Then, as she got up and stared out of the window, she saw an ambulance. *Surely the wound wasn't that bad, was it?* she asked herself. Watching as the paramedics helped Judith into the ambulance, she clocked Nigel looking up at her. His eyes darkened, and an evil grin began to spread across his face. She shuddered at the thought of being alone in the house with knobhead Nigel.

The ambulance left without the flashing blue lights, so Kera assumed that Judith was merely being dramatic; she wasn't to know, though, that Judith was taking warfarin, and so the bleeding wouldn't stop.

The house was now very quiet as Kera stared out of the window to the home across the road. She saw two little girls in the window. They were dancing and laughing. Then she saw their daddy run into the room and join in the dancing. Tears unexpectedly cascaded down her cheeks; she missed her father so much. He was from Lebanon, and he had worked hard to build his storage and shipping business, determined to make a good go of it. Something happened, though. He was killed in cold blood; she had her suspicions, but she dared not air them, not until she was old enough to be believed.

Sitting back on the bed, she opened her laptop and stared at the screen saver; there were her parents and her in the middle. It was the day they had gone to see *Lion King* at the theatre. She remembered her parents were approached by model scouts interested in her. She recalled how excited she had felt that day. Still, her parents had flatly refused to entertain the idea, with her father saying that she must concentrate on getting an excellent job because her good looks would eventually wear off, and besides, she was only twelve years old. Although she was tall and looked older, she was, to him, still a baby.

Now at fourteen, it crossed her mind that perhaps she could do modelling and get out of this suffocating, oppressive house. Her bedroom was the box room, which was the size of her walk-in wardrobe at her parents' home. Not that she minded the fact that she'd had to downsize. Of course, she missed the luxury, but what outweighed all of that was missing her parents. And the Leonards were the complete opposite of her own loving mum and dad.

As she clicked on to her social media account, she felt a surge of excitement; there was the agent again. She thought he was very handsome himself for an agent. Her heart beat faster when she saw a few private messages, and, to her surprise, the photos of herself that she had sent to him. He had managed to edit them to look like she belonged on the cover of *Vogue* magazine. She did indeed look so grown up, and even more thrilling was that he had implied she could earn thousands from just one photo shoot. The last message was the most exciting; he had a photo shoot coming up and wanted to meet with her to fill out the forms and get her registered. The payment would be twenty thousand pounds.

Right away, she messaged back, but as she attempted to type, she remembered she would have to get permission from her foster family, and there was no way they would allow it. Her heart sank and a lump lodged in her throat. Slowly, she typed.

Kera: I would love to have the opportunity to go to the photo shoot, but my foster carers would never allow it.

Waiting with anticipation, she bit her nails, hoping he would reply and not just drop her like a hot brick.

As the minutes passed away, she became desperate and contemplated just going to the shoot, maybe faking a letter from Judith, if, of course, she wasn't arrested first, after this evening's attack on her.

Agent: Hi, Kera, that's a shame because Chanel really wanted to have you on their books, and, more importantly, in this year's fashion week. I wish you well.

Kera: Chanel?

Agent: Yes, Chanel.

Kera convinced herself that she would take up this opportunity and believed that she wasn't breaking any rules if she didn't ask permission. In her mind, she was desperate to be a model and even more determined to model for Chanel. She was simply eager to have a goal in mind. Her schoolwork had gone to pot after her father's death, and nothing seemed to interest her except this idea right now. She decided to lie.

Kera: I have asked my foster carers, and they said it's okay. What do I need?

Agent: That's excellent news, Kera. So, this Chanel range has not been shown yet, so everything about this photo shoot

is very much under wraps, which means you have to sign a top-secret contract. So do not contact anyone on social media or tell a single soul what you will be doing. Once your photo is in all the magazines and on all the billboards, then you can show it to your friends.

Kera felt her stomach doing backflips with excitement.

Kera: Oh no, I won't say anything to anyone.

As Kera typed those words, she thought how proud her mother would be that she was modelling for none other than Chanel. It was her mother's favourite brand of perfume and handbag. She wondered if she would get free samples. If so, she could send them to her.

Agent: Right, Miss Future Face of Chanel, I need to get these contracts signed ASAP before Chanel decide to go with another model they have in mind.

The thought that this new dream could be whipped away from her made her panic.

Kera: I am ready now.

Agent: Okay, you mentioned you live in Bromley. Can you get to our premises in Central London?

Kera: If you give me directions or a postcode, I am sure I can.

She once again felt anxious because she had never been to London alone. However, she wanted the job and had to come across as mature.

Agent: I will send a cab to collect you and bring you to the offices. Is that easier for you?

The relief was immense.

Kera: Yes, please! she typed, followed by her address.

Dragging a small suitcase from beneath her bed, she threw in her laptop, a pair of jeans, a Disney sweatshirt, and her make-up bag, along with a few hundred pounds in savings. She had no intention of returning to the Leonards or going to a children's home. She just hoped that the cab would arrive before the foster carers returned.

Within minutes, a black BMW with tinted windows pulled up directly outside the house. Kera felt the adrenaline coursing through her veins as she jumped down the stairs. Not wanting to draw attention, she quietly closed the door behind her. The truth was she didn't want the nosey neighbours to tell the Leonards anything.

As she walked to the car, she saw a smartly dressed man look back.

'Cab for Kera?'

Kera grinned, nodded, and clambered in.

As they pulled away, she noticed how hot it was inside the car and pressed the switch to open the window, but it wouldn't work.

'It's warm, isn't it,' she said to the driver, hoping he would put the air con on or do something to cool the car down.

'Here,' he said, as he handed her a bottle of water.

All the excitement had left her mouth dry, so she gratefully took the drink. Removing the lid, she gulped a few mouthfuls of the cold water. Instantly, it cooled her down, and so she sipped the rest until it was gone. The gentle motion of the car sent her into a light sleep. She tried to wake herself up a few times, but her eyelids felt so heavy. The hot feeling left her, and a sense of relaxation took its place. Even though she was dozing, she felt the car come to a halt. But as she opened her eyes, her surroundings seemed obscure. Then she realised she couldn't see or hear properly. Terror struck. She'd been drugged. Even the fear didn't have her sitting bolt upright. No matter how hard she wrestled for control, she had no real influence over her body; she felt paralysed and totally helpless.

The door opened, and two men dragged her from the car and carried her to a van. Inside, Kera thought she could see a coffin, and she tried so hard to clear her blurred vision, but she couldn't. The sounds of the men were muffled, but she sensed an accent, perhaps Eastern European. Then, for a moment, her eyes focused, and yes, it was a coffin. Alarmed by the mere thought of being inside a wooden box, let alone being buried alive, was agonisingly petrifying. It was worse than anything that her imagination could manufacture. This was a real live horror story where she was screaming, and yet no sound left her lips. A warm sensation crept over her lower half, and she knew then she had wet herself.

Too weak to fight her kidnappers, she could not stop them from throwing her into the coffin. All she could do was to stare with begging and pleading eyes, her mind filled with dread. As the lid was slowly put in place, she lay there in the terrifying pitch-black.

The only words she managed to say were 'Help me, Mum.'

Chapter Two

June 2011

The heavy clanking sound as the doors slid open was one of the many stark reminders of where Harper had spent the last twelve years. She certainly wouldn't miss the noise of chains rattling or the smell of metal, sweat, and overdone carrots. And definitely not the lack of her liberty. In nervous anticipation, she sat on the edge of her bed, with her bag packed, waiting for the officer to lead her to reception to sign her out. Out to the big wide world, to the fresh air, the sounds of birds, fast flowing rivers, and the leaves rustling in the breeze. She smiled to herself. As if she would be going to such a pretty country paradise. No, she would have to go home initially to the council house in the middle of St Mary Cray, where she had spent all her life growing up. She only hoped that the authorities wouldn't have any grounds to change their minds and keep her locked up.

Pulled from her thoughts as her cell door opened, she jumped up – a usual habit. Standing in the doorway was Madeleine Hanna, a woman in her forties, who usually wore confidence like a diamond encrusted crown. Even when she stuttered, she held a glare that invited a fight. However, today, her eyes seemed heavy with fatigue. Her face was gaunt and only a sad smile tugged at her mouth.

'So, you're oh-oh-off, then.'

Harper smiled. 'I won't miss this place, Maddie, not one bit, but I will miss you. Not so much the fights but the banter and the friendship.'

Madeleine, for the first time ever, blushed. 'You go and see your boy and give him a h-h-hug from me.'

'I will, Maddie.'

'Please, Harper, try and find her for me.' Her tone turned serious as she held up a photo of a man from a newspaper clipping – Calvin Stuart.

'I will do me best, but, Maddie, I will do it when I can. It won't be my top priority. You do understand, don't you?'

'I do, but . . .' Madeleine looked around her and leaned in to whisper into Harper's ear. 'I can't trust a fucking living soul, except you. I need you to do this for me, Harper. You know there is money in it for you, and believe me, girl, you will need it out there. No bastard will give you stuff for free. And I can't see you flipping burgers at McDonald's.'

Harper nodded. 'Like I said, Maddie, I will do my best, but I need to sort out my little boy first. Then I will look for her and see what I can find out about this Calvin Stuart geezer.'

Madeleine uncharacteristically threw her arms around Harper and hugged her. 'It's gonna be a right fucking dull place with you gone. But fingers crossed, if that twat of a lawyer finds any evidence that shows I wasn't the killer, then I could be out too, and I won't stop until I find my girl.'

Harper pulled away and looked at the dark, almost black, eyes staring back at her. 'I know, mate, and I will do my best to help.'

Hearing those words gave Madeleine a glimmer of hope, but as Harper left the cell, she didn't follow her. She struggled as emotion punched her hard in the chest and a sob lodged in her throat.

She could only have served her time pain-free if she was safe in the knowledge that her daughter was being cared for. However, the social services had told her that Kera had gone missing after a vicious attack on her foster carer. They assumed she had run off because she thought she would be in trouble. So the media gave the situation no attention. The police had her down as a missing person. They more or less expected they would come across her one day probably selling herself or maybe having overdosed in some crack house.

Madeleine knew that her daughter was very green behind the ears; she would never survive on the streets. She prayed that she was still alive. However, she feared the worst because by hook or by crook, Kera would have sent a letter to the prison by now, to let her know she was safe.

Harper glanced back. 'Maddie, I will promise you this: when I have me own drum, my door will always be open to you.' She looked away because she could see Madeleine was crying. They had been close. Madeleine had arrived only a year ago, and yet they had struck up a bond after a few fights. The news that her own little girl had gone missing had ripped Madeleine's heart out. And Harper knew that now she was leaving, Madeleine would find serving her time even tougher. She wished so much that she could take her too.

***

A line of women stood along the landing, all saying their goodbyes, as Harper nodded and acknowledged each one. She remained on the heels of the officer who was leading her away to freedom.

Lucy Hubble was the most spiteful officer on the wing, and she'd had it in for Harper the minute she'd stepped foot in the prison, but all that didn't matter now. She was getting out and couldn't wait to hear the last slam of a metal door behind her. Once she reached reception, she was greeted by the number one governor, who shook her hand and politely said she never wanted to see her again.

The fresh air and bright sunshine were perfect for making her own way home. A cab had been called because she knew that no one would be at the gate waiting for her, although, inside, she hoped that someone would be there holding her little boy's hand, and he would run to her with a huge hug. Again, she smiled to herself because she guessed that wouldn't happen either. That was the one thing she'd had time to do – daydream.

As the car swung into the entrance, Harper was surprised at the design. So much had changed in all those years that she didn't recognise any new motor. The inside smelled of leather, and the ride itself was smooth.

'So, home sweet home, is it?' asked the driver.

Not wanting to talk, Harper ignored him. She tried to take in the blue sky, the cherry blossom, and the quietness except for the humming of the car engine.

'Sorry, love, I'll let you have your ride in peace,' he said, knowing that there were two types of prisoners: those who were overexcited and could rabbit for England and those who were absorbing the reality. He guessed this tall attractive woman fitted the latter type.

***

Delores stared at her daughter's stern face and unexpectedly felt uneasy. Fingering the deep scar that ran from her eye to her chin, a cold shiver shot up her spine. The pounding in her temples was like bongo drums. 'So you're home, then!' she spat, in an acid tone. Seeing the lack of emotion on Harper's face, Delores wanted to square up to her to show her that she was still the family's matriarch. However, the last few years had been cruel. Her knees creaked, and she'd practically had to do a warm-up before she could even walk across the room these days. The middle-aged spread hadn't helped matters either, and forty fags a day was playing havoc with her lungs. If it had been only a few years ago, she might have leaped from her chair and grabbed Harper around the throat, with a gentle squeeze to warn her who was the boss. The trouble was, though, Harper was a lot like she had been in her younger days; she wouldn't take too much shit from anyone; well, at least that was what she liked to think. She continued to stare at her daughter. In many ways, she admired the girl, except the problem was she hated her too. That don't-give-a-rat's-arse look on Harper's face told Delores that she was better off not pushing her daughter too far.

Harper held up the clear plastic bag that contained the last twelve years of her belongings. 'Yes, Delores, I'm home.'

‘Nothing’s changed, has it? Always either Mother or Delores. You never did like calling me Mum, did ya?’ Delores huffed. ‘And let’s get everything clear. You ain’t staying long, Harper. So don’t get too bleeding comfortable. I don’t want you here any longer than you probably even wanna be yaself.’

Harper was thirty-four years old, tall and toned, with short spiky mousy hair that enhanced her high cheek bones. Her eyes, very catlike, were an unusual mix of greens. As much as she had always been considered attractive, she didn’t feel it. Today, standing in a pair of Primark jeans and a Glam rock T-shirt, she felt even less so. Her sister Lexi had been kind enough to send her a few bits, including the trainers that were a size too big, but Harper was grateful; it was more than her own mother had done for her. Still, she hadn’t expected a penny or a visit from the woman anyway.

Scanning the room, Harper noticed how it was more or less as she had remembered, the night the police had dragged her away. The three-piece suite had faded, and the cushions had come away from the solid frame. The carpet had obviously been replaced. It would have been impossible to remove the bloodstains out of the original one.

Harper was surprised that the authorities hadn’t offered to move her mother and sisters after the incident. She had even wondered how she would feel stepping back inside this house after all this time, but, really, she felt nothing, except sadness, maybe. The room was dismal. The woodchip wallpaper was peeling off up by the ceiling. And all the yellowing woodwork was flaky, probably from her mother’s chain-smoking. She clocked muted colours of the old photos, still in their original frames. They were of her and her sisters when they were kids. The sideboard was laid out just as it was, with the photo frames, the two china bunnies, and a small vase with faded dried flowers. Yet, everything was thick with dust.

The house used to smell of peaches and cream when she lived there, but that was only because she had kept the place spotless while her mother was doing what she wanted to do.

'If you think I'm gonna jump up and hug ya, think again, Harper. You ruined me, you did. You fucking ruined me.' She felt her cheek again before she sat up straight and snatched the packet of cigarettes from the side and lit one up. Leaning back into the threadbare armchair by the fireplace, she stared at her daughter. 'I ain't offering you a fag, Harper, 'cos I want you to understand this. You are here temporarily, and only 'cos I was in a good mood when your probation officer asked me. A nice woman she is. She's smart, speaks nice, and loves her dear ol' mum.' She took another drag on her cigarette and flicked the ash against the heavily weighted glass ashtray. 'Takes her mother flowers every Sunday.'

Harper smirked, and her thin lips curled at the edges as she nodded her head. 'Yeah, her mother's a nice woman.'

'And what the hell is that supposed to mean?'

Harper looked her mother over and shook her head. 'You, Mother, are a nasty, selfish piece of work. I would only buy you fucking flowers to put on your grave. Now, I'm going to my room. I'll keep out of your way, and as soon as I get me own digs, I'll be gone. Don't worry on that score.'

Delores had been completely on her own for the last two weeks because no one had been by. The weather had been too bleak even to stand outside and have a gossip with the neighbours. The thieves had stopped calling because she hadn't paid them for the last lot of meat they'd got for her. The corner shop refused to serve her any more vodka because she still owed them for the previous seven bottles. Still, Harper was back, and knowing her eldest daughter, she probably had a bob or two stashed away. 'Harper,' she called out. 'Seeing as you're 'ere, I'll put the kettle on. Maybe we should chat. There's no need to be at loggerheads now, is there? We oughta make the best of the situation.'

Harper was halfway up the stairs when she heard her mother's change of tone. 'If you're after money, dream on. I hardly had a proper job inside that paid a weekly wage to put any savings aside. So forget trying to be nice. Besides, it really doesn't suit you.'

'Oh, fuck off, then!' Delores screamed back.

The upstairs of the three-bedroom semi was just as dirty. The landing carpet probably hadn't seen a Hoover in twelve years. And as Harper passed her mother's bedroom, she got the distinct whiff of sweat, piss, and marijuana. She cringed and headed to the box room ahead of her. That had always been her room, and the bedroom next door had belonged to her three sisters. Stopping in the doorway, she glanced around the four small walls and smiled to herself. It was probably the same size as her prison cell and not much more homely either. Sitting on the end of her lumpy bed, she sighed to herself.

Although she believed that Delores owed her at least the use of her old bedroom, she was grateful because her mother could have said 'no' to the probation officer. And then she would have been put into a temporary shelter where the clocking in and out would be monitored, and it would have been like prison all over again. She didn't want that at all. She needed some freedom after being cooped up for so long.

Her eyes drifted to the bathroom, and a sudden warm feeling enveloped her. A nice long hot bath seemed so appealing compared to the communal showers in the prison.

As she ventured into the bathroom, she heard her mother shout up the stairs, 'If you wanna 'ave a bath, you'd best leave a couple of quid to pay for the leccy. I ain't made of money!'

Harper rolled her eyes and turned the taps on before bellowing back, 'You will have your money, don't worry!'

She listened to her mother's grunts and mumbles before she closed the bathroom door and removed her clothes. In twelve years, she hadn't seen a full-length mirror, and the sudden sight of herself made her eyes widen. She wasn't the same woman who went away all those years ago – not in mind, personality, or body. Her skin wasn't so soft and polished. It was pure white through lack of sunlight, and around her knees there were wrinkles. She gently ran her hands over her stomach and allowed her fingertips to feel each indented tiger stripe. The stretch marks would always remind her of her pain. There had never been a day when she hadn't thought of him.

Easing herself into the hot bath, she lay back and enjoyed the heat as it warmed up her bones. She closed her eyes, and, unexpectedly, Teddy Ryder's face came to mind. A lump lodged in her throat, and tears sprang to her eyes. She rarely cried; maybe it was too overwhelming coming home, back to this house, back to face the past.

***

Harper had dozed in the bath for an hour when the creaking of the floorboards woke her up. She had learned to sleep with one eye open if the cell door wasn't shut for the night. The only decent sleep she got was when the lights went out. Sitting up straight, she listened and heard the sounds of slow footsteps of someone making their way back down the stairs. Instantly, she stood up, grabbed a towel from the radiator, flung it around her, and opened the bathroom door. As soon as she glanced into her bedroom, she noticed her bag was on the bed, but not where she had left it. Her heart sank. Delores, the mother from hell, had obviously rifled through it.

The only money she had in that bag was from saving every measly penny from her ironing job inside. She had saved it up for a special gift. In a fit of rage, she tore down the stairs, just as Delores slipped her feet into a pair of shoes. With a swift snatch of her mother's hair, Harper pulled her back and whispered in her ear, 'Steal my money, and I'll fucking kill ya. Now, hand it over.'

She let go of Delores's hair and watched as her mother turned around.

'Don't you threaten me, Harper Kane, or I'll be on the phone quick fucking sharp to your probation officer.' She smirked and placed her hands on her hips. 'Threats to kill, Harper, eh? You ever threaten to murder me again, and I'll have your sorry arse back inside for good, this time.'

'Don't you fucking try me, Delores.'

'I tell you now, it won't take much for me to call your probation officer, and I know how it works. You, girl, are on a life licence, and any nonsense, and you go back inside for the rest of your foreseeable,' spat Delores, with a nasty sneer that showed her stained teeth. 'So, no more threatening to kill me, or else.'

Harper stared into the woman's eyes, the one human being who was supposed to love and protect her children, but all that glared back was spite. Instantly, Harper grabbed Delores's wrist, pulled it to her face, and stared at the five-pound notes sticking out of her mother's clenched fist. 'You really are the scum of the earth, aren't you, Delores. Years, it took me to save that money.'

Delores let the money drop to the floor. '*Have* your money, but you so much as make yourself a cup of fucking tea, then you, my girl, will have to pay for it.'

Harper pulled the towel tighter around her before she bent down and scooped up the money. For a moment, it felt like she was back inside again, fighting for what was hers. Not that many girls had tried to take her on. She had always been able to handle herself and would often find herself down the block after a ruck.

As she returned to her bedroom, she rummaged through the belongings, mainly clothes. Some of them had been handed in by her sister Lexi; most were her cast-offs. Not that it mattered. They were the same size. She knew that although Hasad Boz, Lexi's fella, was loaded, he wouldn't give Lexi so much as the bones off his arse. Even so, while Lexi didn't have much, she had a big heart. She only wished she could say the same about Erin, the sister who was a year younger than her. Lexi was two years younger at thirty-two, and then there was Charley, the 'baby' she called her, although now she would be twenty-six.

She laid her clothes on her bed and glared at them. They were old and faded, but as tempting as it was to buy herself a new rig-out, she had saved that money for her boy.

Sliding into the blue jeans that she'd worn earlier, she pulled on a pink checked shirt, allowing it to hang loose. Her hair was practically dry; it was so short now. She smoothed it down with her fingers and thought back to the days when she was proud of her long blonde hair, when it was thick and it had kept its lustre. Teddy had loved it. He would make her take it out of a bun or a ponytail just so that he could see it hanging loose. She wondered if part of the reason for practically chopping it all off was to make a point when she saw him again. However, as it turned out, she had cut off her nose to spite her face and regretted the decision.

Delores's high-pitched yelling pulled Harper from her thoughts.

'Harper, there's someone here to see you!'

Peering out of her bedroom window, Harper tried to see if she could catch a glimpse of whoever was at the door. It was probably her probation officer calling. With a last-minute glance in the long mirror, Harper slipped her feet into her trainers and headed downstairs. She guessed right away the visitor wasn't her probation officer when she saw her mother standing in the doorway to the living room and wearing a smug grin on her face.

Delores flicked her head. 'Teddy wants a word.'

Harper felt her body burn up with embarrassment. Her heart was hammering as she swallowed to unglue her tongue from the roof of her mouth. It was bound to happen sooner or later. So it was best that she met him now before ultimately moving on with her life.

Delores stepped aside and sniggered as Harper slid past her into the living room.

Teddy had his back to her, staring out of the window. His physique hadn't changed in twelve years. There were a couple of strands of grey that mingled with the fair colouring of his wavy hair. It was cut into his neck and was left a little longer on the top. The smell of his leather box jacket told her it was new, and his aftershave was strong.

Suddenly, she felt old and ugly. There was nothing attractive about her, not right now. For a split second, she wanted to run back upstairs, so that he couldn't see what she looked like.

But it was too late. He spun around.

His green eyes were piercing. They always had been, ever since she and Teddy were thirteen when they'd had that very first kiss. She had fallen head over heels in love with him.

He tilted his head and looked up through his lashes, his hands resting on his hips. 'All right, Harper?'

She could see he felt awkward, and he had every reason to be.

'Yeah.'

'You look good, girl.'

'Oh, fuck off, Ted. I look like shit because for twelve stinking years I was inside, where there are no boutiques, hairdressers, sunbeds, or Botox clinics to go to.'

He sighed, knowing that she was referring to her sister Erin, who'd had everything done – even a boob job.

'You don't need it, Harps. I always said you were a natural beauty.'

Many moons ago, she could have fallen into his arms with a comment like that, but not today. Today she focused on keeping her eyes dry. 'Say what you need to say and then leave.'

'Aw, come on, Harps. It was a long time. I would have waited, but *twelve years*. You must understand, babe.'

Harper chewed the inside of her cheek and stared, not moving a muscle. 'I never once asked you to wait, Ted. I asked you to do the right thing. I never wanted you to stay single. Surely, you knew me better than that? But, Ted, this ain't about you and her. You two, I really don't give a shit about. It's *my* boy *I'm* concerned about.'

Teddy shuffled about, moving a bit of fluff around with his shoe. He couldn't look her in the eye. 'We've been good parents to that boy.'

A rush of anger gripped Harper around the throat. 'That *boy*? You mean *our* son, *our* boy,' she huffed. 'You can't bring yourself to say it, though, can you, Ted?'

'Erin's brought him up for eleven years. She loves the boy. *I* love him.'

Harper lunged forward, her eyes wild with hate. '*I* love him. He is *my* son. You never even let me be a mum. You took that right away from me when you shacked up with my own whore of a sister.'

Teddy didn't move. He knew that Harper had a terrible temper and could easily crack him one.

'Every fucking night, I cried myself to sleep in that poxy cell wondering what my baby was doing – what he was like – and none of you brought him to see me. A few photos, and that was my fucking lot.'

'It was best for the boy. Dragging him up to the nick is no life for a little one. You must see that, Harps.'

She stepped back and ran her hands through her hair. 'You and her stopped him from knowing me. He never even had the choice, did he? Anyway, where is Erin?'

Teddy rubbed the back of his neck. 'She was a bit nervous about coming over.'

'Yeah, I bet she fucking was.'

Their eyes met, and the same attraction was pulling them together, like a magnetic force.

Harper stepped back. 'I can't forgive her or you.'

'It wasn't planned. We got the house for Little Eddie. He kinda brought us together. I wasn't—'

'Like I said, I don't give a shit about you two. I only care about my boy, and I'm fucking livid that you kept me out of his life for all those years. Well, anyway, where is he now? Is he at school, or . . .?'

'Er . . . Harper, it's probably better all round if you don't see him. He doesn't know who you are.'

'Well, that's fine. I will be telling him, Teddy. He will know that I love him and that I'm his mother.'

Teddy shook his head. 'Harper, he calls Erin "Mum".'

The anger and hurt were like a bolt of lightning shooting through her heart. She screamed in pain and swiped his face, leaving a deep claw mark. The minute she looked at the fleshy cut, she gasped for breath. She hadn't meant to hurt him; but she wanted to hurt her sister, though.

Teddy clutched his face and then looked at the blood on his hand. 'I guess, I deserved that.'

Remaining silent, Harper glared, her head all over the place. And now she had just done it. They would never let her see her son now, surely.

'Listen, Harper, Eddie is doing well. He has good grades at school. He is in the football team. Just let him be.' He paused and looked her over before pulling out a wad of twenty-pound notes. ''Ere, take this.'

Her tears were ready to fall, but she took a deep breath and shook her head. 'I don't want your money or your damn pity. I just want my son!'

'I don't pity you, Harps. I've never pitied you. I just thought . . . well, maybe you could treat yourself.'

'You really are something, aren't you! You tell me we will be together when I get out, then I hand my baby over to you, only for you to shack up with my sister, and then you come here with money, like a buyoff.'

'Aw, babe, it's not like that. Come on, please.'

He put his arms out to hug her, but she pushed him back. 'Just leave, and take your guilt money with you. And tell my backstabbing sister that I will be seeing my son, and I will tell him the truth.'

A flicker of fury slithered its way across his face. 'And what would you say? Oh, I'm Harper Kane, your mother, who served twelve years inside for murder. It's better if you just stay away.'

'That, Teddy Ryder, is never going to happen. So swivel on your size ten fancy Italian leather shoes and fuck off.'

‘Harps, listen, my scrapyard business is doing well. Eddie is doing well. I can offer him everything he needs.’ He held up his palms. ‘Come on, my treacle. You’ve got to understand that so much has changed. Little Eddie has a nice home, decent clothes, and money for college if he wants to go.’

‘You bastard, Teddy! It isn’t all about money. It’s about love as well.’

‘Love don’t pay the bills, my little stocking top.’ He lowered his tone, in an attempt to sound compassionate.

‘You’re a cruel man, Teddy, and Erin is an evil bitch. But Eddie is still my flesh and blood, not *hers*!’ she bellowed, while visibly shaking with absolute rage.

He said no more but looked her up and down before storming from the room.

Harper flinched at the sound of the door slamming shut. Her shoulders dropped and a dry sob caught in her throat. Years of unspent tears built up behind her eyes, but she would wait until she was in the privacy of her own bedroom before she would allow a single one to fall.

Teddy’s words had completely knocked Harper sideways. So much so, that she almost didn’t see Delores leaning against the kitchen door frame, with her arms folded and a satisfied grin on her face.

The anger instantly dried up Harper’s tears. ‘You love it, don’t you, Delores. My sister, bringing up my son and shagging Teddy. It must be a real tonic for you.’

Suddenly Delores’s face lost its smirk, and her eyes looked down. ‘Actually, Harper, as much as we both know you ain’t my favourite daughter, I did feel that Erin had done you a wrongdoing by taking the relationship with Teddy further than she should have.’

Harper raised her brow. For a brief moment, she thought perhaps her mother would be her ally.

‘Still, Harper, Erin and Teddy do make a good pair, and my grandson is in good hands.’

With a feeling that her heart had been completely ripped from her chest, Harper walked away, climbed the stairs, and once inside the box room, she pulled a pillow to her face and sobbed into it. She tried not to make a noise. She didn’t want to give her mother the satisfaction, but the sob was stuck in her throat, and she had to cough to cover it up. He was right. She had nothing to offer her son. But Teddy hadn’t kept his promise to ensure her needs were taken care of when she got out; he was with her sister now. It was no secret that Teddy was doing well for himself. He had promised her a nice home, driving lessons, a decent car, and a completely new wardrobe for the day she was released. In the beginning, when he didn’t miss a single visit, she’d believed him. She remembered him crying when he took the baby and those words through his tears. ‘I will bring him up here for every visit and send photos every day. He will know his mother. I promise you that, Harps, and we will have the biggest white wedding you’ll ever see.’

What a huge let-down. She would have to get her act together and fast. Now Teddy hadn’t fulfilled his promise, she would have to do it all alone. Anger spurred her on to the day when she would show Teddy Ryder that she could have it all. However, she knew in her heart that it would be almost impossible to get custody of her son. How could she when she had nothing to offer him. For a start, no one would employ her, and she would be fortunate if the council gave her a bedsit, even in Catford.

She would have to earn some decent money, and to her mind, there was no legal way of doing it – not unless she had a long-lost aunt somewhere who had left her a ton of money in her will.

***

Kera looked down at her shackled ankle and noticed the sore was oozing pus. She really didn’t want to ask the huge ugly man for a plaster or a tablet because the way he licked his lips when he ogled her breasts made her feel sick with dread. And the thought that she may have to return a favour set her heart beating like a jackhammer.

The heat was relentless. She guessed this was because of the huge overhead water pipes. Wherever this place was, it was clear that neither she nor the other girls could be heard. They had even tried to scream at the same time; it had been her idea, but no one came. It was getting late, and they were all hungry and desperate to go to the toilet. The only bucket in the room was full and the contents now stank to high heaven. It was hardly surprising: the food was like eating shit and the terror of being kidnapped had given all the girls diarrhoea.

The only consolation right now was that she hadn't been buried alive. She had realised soon after her entrapment that the coffin had been used just for transport. And, of course, it had meant that she had no idea where she had been taken.

Looking at the girls now, she only wished that they would stop crying and help her with a plan. They were pretty, all around her age, but not one of them seemed to have the gumption she knew she had. She wasn't her mother's girl for nothing.

Chapter Three

As Harper sat on the end of her bed, she heard a knock at the front door. Right now, though, she didn't care much for visitors; she wanted to be left well alone until she had a plan in place to get out of this house and have money under her belt to make a life for her and her son.

She could hear a mumbling, and then by the way her mother put on a posh voice calling her down, she assumed it was the probation officer.

Harper looked in the mirror at her tear-stained cheeks and quickly hurried to the bathroom to wash her face before walking downstairs to meet Vanessa Capshore, who was standing in the living room.

She was a tall woman, much like herself. Her hair was cut into a neat bob, and she wore only a hint of make-up. Harper guessed she was in her mid-thirties, but her dewy complexion gave her a younger appearance.

'Ah, there you are, Harper. Great. Can I get you to sign a few more papers? We can have a quick chat, and I'll be gone and leave you in peace to see family and friends. It will be hard at first, but we have already discussed this, so take your time getting to grips with the changes, especially with the technology – phones, computers. You know what I mean.'

Harper wondered if she actually intimidated Vanessa because the woman was speaking fast and seemed a little flustered. The inmates had said to Harper that she had a sour face and a hard look about her. But that hadn't been the case at all; she had always felt so alone.

'Yes, of course. Er, can we speak privately?' asked Harper, as she glared at her mother.

Vanessa nodded and turned to face Harper's mother. 'I know this is your home, Ms Kane, but would you mind if we have this room to ourselves for a few moments?'

Delores suddenly felt awkward. It was the manner in which Vanessa spoke, and it didn't really take much for her to feel self-conscious when a classy, educated woman was around.

As soon as Delores left, Harper sat in an armchair and Vanessa went over to the sofa where she looked at it with distaste before perching herself on the edge.

'What is it?' asked the probation officer.

'I need my own pad. I know it was good of my mum to give me a place to stay but . . .' She fought to maintain a semblance of control and pointed to the floor. 'I just can't stay here. The memories of what happened are all in this house.'

'Oh!' Vanessa paused. 'That's a difficult one, Harper. We tend to organise your initial accommodation and then it's up to you. But I do understand your predicament, and I will look into it as soon as I get back to the office.'

The loud ringtone from Vanessa's phone made the probation officer stare at the number before she got up. Placing her hand over the mouthpiece, she said, 'Sorry, Harper, but I must take this.'

Watching Vanessa walk over to the window and whisper into the phone, Harper guessed it was about her. The telltale sign was the look that Vanessa gave her before she ended the call.

'So that was my boss, Harper. It seems that Erin has called the office. She is concerned that you will contact Eddie.' She stopped and waited for Harper to respond.

'Sorry, Vanessa, I'm not sure why Erin has contacted your office. You see, Eddie was only living with my sister and his father while I was in prison.'

Vanessa sat down and stared for a moment while chewing her lip. 'I'm not sure how to tell you this, but, quite frankly, I am stunned that you are not aware of the fact that your sister and her partner have a residential order on Eddie.'

With her eyes narrowed, Harper inclined her head. 'What does that mean?' Her words came out slowly, with an edge of concern.

Vanessa sighed. 'It means that the court has given Ted and Erin parental rights for Eddie to live permanently with them. You would have to fight for custody, and I have to be honest with you, Harper. If he has lived with them for eleven years, I can't see the courts letting you have custody. You might, however, get access, but for now, I must insist that you stay away.'

Harper jumped to her feet. 'Stay away? But he is my son. I didn't go to prison because I hurt or harmed him. It wasn't supposed to be this way. Teddy was going to look after him until I came home. That was the deal.'

Vanessa was nodding, quickly trying to agree, to calm Harper down. She instantly realised that this was going to be why Harper would end up back inside. 'I understand, Harper, but you listen to me and listen good. You will never see him if you go back to prison, will you? So, for now, you must stay well away and . . .' She paused and sucked in a sharp intake of air. 'I will see what I can do to help, but believe me, Harper, you go anywhere near him, and you'll be back behind bars.'

With a look that could strip paint, Harper held her tongue before she said something that she would regret. The feeling of suppressing her anger drove her to tears, and she couldn't contain them as they ran down her cheeks, finding the creases in her face.

The sight was unexpected, and Vanessa wasn't sure how to handle it. She couldn't hug a probationer. Quickly, she delved into her Louis Vuitton tote bag and found a tissue. 'Here you are, Harper.' She handed it to her and then went on. 'I know it must be painful but . . .'

'*Painful?* You don't have kids, do you? I mean, you could never understand the love between a mother and her child.'

Vanessa nodded in agreement. 'No, you're right, Harper, but my job is to make sure you stay on the outside with all your needs met to prevent you going back to prison. So just stay away. Please.'

After wiping her wet cheeks and sniffling a few times, Harper stopped the tears. 'Where is this paperwork you need me to sign?'

Vanessa slid out the file from her bag and flipped it open. 'Just there and there.' She pointed to the dots. 'It's only to say that you are living here for the time being. Also, you must remember that any changes to your circumstances have to be run by me first. And you must report to me regularly. I know it seems a lot, but once you are settled, the visits will be less sporadic and more of a regular nature.'

Harper was so distraught over the residential order for her son that she forgot to push the issue of moving out of her mother's home to digs of her own.

By the time the front door closed for the second time, Harper was ready to punch the sneer off her mother's smug face. 'And you heard all of that, I suppose?'

Delores nodded. 'Yeah, and she is right. Leave the boy be. He's happy enough. He knows he has an Aunt Harper.'

Those words had Harper snatching her mother by her hair and slamming her face against the wall. 'You are a fucking evil woman. You really are. And I fucking dare you to chase after my probation officer and tell her what I just did.' She let go of her mother's hair and stormed off upstairs.

Delores knew that her daughter, if she had wanted to, could have pushed her head right through the wall, but she must have held back that force, which meant that she was in control. Still, it had hurt.

Thirty minutes later, with Harper still trying to come to terms with the fact that her chances of getting her son back were almost impossible, there was a knock at her bedroom door. 'Harper, I've made you a cup of tea. Can I come in?'

'If you must.'

Delores used her elbow to open the door while she held two cups of piping hot tea. Seeing her daughter's face, she almost had to look twice. There was no doubt that of all her children, Harper was the double of her younger self.

'I think we should talk. I know we don't like each other, but we will be under the same roof, so I guess we had better make a decent job of it.' She handed Harper the drink. 'Two sugars.'

Harper gently took the cup and sipped the strong brew. It was nice to have a decent cup of tea, and her mother could at least make a good one, except for the fact that she'd added a huge amount of sugar.

'I appreciate you putting me up, but I will be gone the minute I have the chance.'

'I can't say as I will miss ya, but like I always say, better to be honest than a snake in the grass.'

Harper felt her blood boiling again because of all people Delores *was* a snake. In fact, she was so much worse. She would deny what was going on right under her nose just to have what she wanted. Before Harper went to prison, she'd had to do something to protect her sisters from the string of sex-starved men that Delores seemed to attract. Harper took a deep breath and sipped another mouthful of tea to calm her burning rage. She glanced at the scar on her mother's face and felt guilty. But it only lasted a second before she was angry again.

'So, then, what will you do for a bit of money?' asked Delores, totally oblivious to Harper's flaring nostrils.

'Go to the jobcentre, of course.'

Delores laughed. 'Oh, leave off, girl. Who in their right mind will give you a job? Don't think it's the same now. You need qualifications as long as your arm to work at the Tip Top bakeries these days.'

The smell of doughnuts filled the streets of the Crays from the Allied Bakeries, commonly known by its previous name Tip Top. Half of the Cray either worked there or at one of the other factories, but Harper knew she wouldn't get a job there. It would have to be a smaller concern, perhaps a family-run one, where they would give her a go. However, she was also aware that she needed a lot of money if she wanted her boy back. How she was going to compete with Teddy's wealth, she had no idea.

Harper turned to face her mother. 'Well, I don't know yet, so leave off about work.'

'All right, Harper, there's no need to look at me as if I pissed on your chips. I'm only trying to help.'

Harper jumped up and slammed the cup down on the nightstand. 'No, Delores, you are not trying to help. You are getting off on rubbing my nose in the fact that I am now an ex-con with no prospects and a boy I can't even fucking visit. I'll save you the time in dragging the pain out of me. I'm hurting more than you could ever imagine. There!'

Delores stood up and hurried from the room. She paused at the doorway and looked back at her daughter, and for a moment, she felt something. Was it guilt, possibly, shame, maybe, or love? Whatever it was, she didn't like it and looked away.

***

It was past eleven o'clock by the time Teddy put his key in the lock of his front door. Erin almost ripped it open when she heard him. 'What is the point in you having a fucking phone, Teddy? I might have guessed why you turned the fucking thing off, you dirty, rotten bastard. I knew it. I fucking well knew it—'

'Oi, now, shut your mouth, Erin. I don't want the boy woken up by your foul bleedin' gob.'

'Oh, is that right? Well, maybe he needs to hear what his father's been up to, eh?'

Teddy stormed past her and into the lounge where he walked over to the bar and poured himself a whisky. 'Go to bed, Erin,' he said, quietly, before he sank into the heavily cushioned armchair.

Pulling the scatter cushions from behind him, he threw them onto the floor.

Erin was still dressed in her bright-pink tracksuit, her hair pulled up in a messy bun, and her skin more fake-tanned than usual. Teddy guessed she had been indulging in another spray tan. And when he looked closer at her, he saw that her lips were plumper and her eyebrows darker. His mind instantly went to Harper, who looked beautiful in his eyes without any make-up.

Erin leaned against the door frame, bouncing her leg in fury. 'Well, I thought at least you could have come home and let me know how it went today, but, oh no, you obviously had so much more to talk about than handing her the money and telling her to stay away. Gagging for it, was she? I mean, twelve years and no cock. I bet she handed it to you on a plate, eh?'

Teddy stared, and then slowly, he shook his head. 'You don't know what you are on about, Erin. I left Harps—'

'*Harps?* Harps, is it?'

Teddy was trying to hold back his temper, but having spent most of the day drinking down the pub, he was less inclined to keep his cool. Everyone knew he was a nutter when he lost it – even Erin. Not that he would ever hurt her.

'I said, go to bed.'

Erin sensed the cold tone in his voice and decided to change her own manner. 'Look, I understand that you and her had a thing all those years ago, so, of course, I'm gonna worry. You would if the boot was on the other foot.'

Teddy glared before he jumped up to pour another drink. 'I offered her money, and she refused it. I said that the boy was okay, and he didn't need her in his life.'

Erin smirked. 'Did you?' she asked excitedly. 'Then, what did she say? I bet she was fucking livid. Still, she can't just come home and pick up where she left off. Life has changed. We have Eddie and each other.'

Teddy sensed the cockiness in her words. He spun around and gave her his trademark glare. It was a look that told most men who knew him to get out of his way.

'What?' asked Erin, pretending to act dumb.

'She's your fucking sister. She's never hurt you, has she?' He stepped forward.

Erin frowned. 'What? Well, she is a convict, a murderer.'

'No, no, no, Erin. She is a woman who protected her sisters, and you, Erin Kane, are one of them. And now, I see you gloating in the fact that you have her son and her ex. Me!' He poked himself in the chest. 'She has nothing, Erin, absolutely nothing. And I can see on your face that you're pleased about that.'

Erin stepped back, the tears in her eyes welling up. 'What is this about, Teddy? I thought we were happy. We have this lovely home and our boy. But now, you're turning on me. Why?'

Teddy felt the anger burning his throat. So rather than hit Erin, he launched the crystal glass and its contents across the room. 'But Eddie is *not* our boy. He is *her* boy, and you, Erin, wanted to stop her from seeing him. Why, Erin? Tell me why?'

Seeing the emotion in Teddy's eyes, she knew then that he still loved Harper. He probably always had. She could never compete, and she hated it. She detested always playing second fiddle to her eldest sister, the beautiful sister, the sister who was taller, stronger, and harder, and the sister who, in her eyes, still had the man she so desperately wanted for herself.

Her mind flashed back. They were young teenagers. Harper was thirteen, and she would have been twelve years old when they'd met Teddy and his friends. They were sitting on the bench by the boating pool on Sevenoaks Way. Teddy was fourteen then, and she recalled saying to Harper, 'I am gonna marry that one. You watch. I want first dibs on him.'

Erin often wondered if all those years ago when Harper had said 'Yeah, sure, Erin, go for it. But I think he is seeing Candy's sister, Rhea', she was teasing her. Either that or she had actually meant her to make a play for Teddy.

And at first, Teddy had taken a shine to her. That was until Harper had dug her claws in, and that was it: she had the boy. Like the way she got everything. Even when they secured the Saturday jobs in the chip shop on Marion Crescent, Harper was always offered the extra shifts after school because the owner fancied her. She often found herself cursing when she tagged along with Harper, and there were many days when she just wished she had stayed at home. When they were at The Glades Shopping Centre, it was Harper who was approached by the modelling agency. The agent was even rude to her, stating that Harper was naturally beautiful, whereas she wasn't so much. She seemed to have been living in Harper's shadow her whole life, even if they were out and about meeting up with friends. It was Harper who everyone greeted first, while she would be lucky if she received an acknowledging nod.

How life had changed. She had Teddy and Little Eddie, as they called him, her son now, not Harper's, and she would make sure that her sister stayed well away.

'Ted, I'm not pleased that my sister went to prison and I was left holding the fucking baby, literally, but for almost twelve years, I've brought up Eddie and loved him as my own, so she should be grateful.'

Teddy tilted his head to the side, shocked. 'Are you fucking deluded, Erin? All of you should be grateful to *her*. It's as if you've forgotten why she went to prison in the first place. And you have the fucking audacity to treat this situation as if it's us against her. Well, Erin Kane, I'm not against Harper. She is the mother of my child.'

Those words hit her like a kick in the guts, and her temper erupted like a volcano.

'*Mother of your child*!' she screamed, as she stepped forward. '*I* am the mother of your child. *I* cleaned his shitty arse. *I* taught him to read, to write, to swim! And you dare say she is the mother of your child!'

Teddy threw his hands in the air. 'Ah, I fucking knew it, Erin. This ain't about the boy. It's about me. You don't want Harper to have me. That's right, ain't it?'

The truth of what he'd just said slapped her in the face, and her eyes widened. 'Don't be stupid,' was all she could say.

Teddy took a few deep breaths and sighed. 'If you must know, after I left Harper, I had a meeting with Richard Newbury.' He turned his back on Erin and walked to the bar, where he poured himself another drink.

'Richard Newbury? Why?'

Teddy gulped a large mouthful of whisky. 'Because he has put a fucking great bounty on your sister's head, that's why.'

Erin hardly thought it over before opening her mouth. 'And what's that got to do with you?'

Teddy didn't turn to face her, this time. 'You really must have a deep hatred for your sister. I don't know why, and I really don't give a flying fuck why, but know this, Erin: if I hear you say one more thing against her – see the front door – I sure as fucking hell will launch you through it. And you will kiss all of this goodbye. Now, shut up about Harper. You have what you wanted, so don't gloat about it. And another thing. You say nothing about Richard Newbury. That's *my* business.'

Erin could tell from that tone that she should now shut her mouth and perhaps talk again in the morning. She left and headed upstairs, with hurt and jealousy weighing heavily on her mind.

As she sat at the dressing table, gently removing her make-up, Teddy entered the room. He was unbuttoning his shirt. She watched him in the mirror as he walked over and stood behind her. He leaned down towards her face, and she could feel his warm breath on her neck. She assumed he was going to kiss her, and they would spend the late hours making love. However, she couldn't have been more wrong. She was stung again by the words that he whispered in her ear. 'You didn't even ask me if Richard Newbury will remove the bounty on your sister's head.'

Erin looked down at her trembling hands as she tried to think of what to say. 'I just assumed that you would have sorted something out.'

As he stood up straight, Erin glanced at his reflection, and her heart skipped a beat. She loved him so much that the fear of losing him to Harper worried the life out of her.

He glared back at her before parting with a cruel remark.

'Do you know how different you look when you take that shit off your face? Is it too late to look more like the face you were born with?'

Erin didn't answer. She lowered her gaze and held back the tears. But she winced when he slammed the door behind him. So there would be no lovemaking or sweet words. It would be a sleepless night of tossing and turning.

Chapter Four

Richard Newbury was fifty-one years old. His heavy weight made him look much older. He couldn't be bothered with the gym or watching what he ate or drank because he was vain. To him, having money and a reputation meant he had it all. He had plenty of money, and he could buy any bit of skirt he fancied. His wife Peggy had learned to turn a blind eye to his life outside the marital home and even knew that he was financing a London flat for Felicity, or Fliss for short, his regular tart on the side.

Richard sat behind his office desk and stared at the photo of his brother Nathanial, his dead brother, who would have celebrated his fifty-fifth birthday if he hadn't been murdered. He'd always looked up to Nathanial and had never believed the rumours. Nat, as he had been called, had been a big man, with honey-blond hair and green eyes. He had set up the family pornography business in South-West London and was raking it in long before Richard took over. From videos to live sex shows, Nathanial knew how to make money, and he had been on the verge of making it big before he was murdered.

The Newbury name was well known in and around South-West London and even parts of South London. They kept their business out of South-East London and Kent because there were a few bigwigs running the manors there, and he couldn't be bothered with the grief.

Harper Kane was out of prison and there was a score to settle. The likes of Teddy Ryder and his little posse wouldn't stop him – no one would. He leaned forward and picked up the photo in its frame and smiled at the picture. 'I'll get revenge, my brother, that much I promise you.'

He replaced the photo and then stared at the holdall with the fifty grand inside. Shaking his head, he laughed; it caused his large belly to bounce up and down.

The tap at the door pulled him away from his satisfied musings. 'Come in.'

It was Peggy, who was holding a mug of coffee. Richard looked her over. He had to admit that for a fifty-year-old woman, she was still attractive. She had managed to keep her petite figure and her deep-red hair, although she could have been dyeing it for all these years. 'Put it on the coaster,' he said, in a cold tone.

She did as he said and offered a smile. 'So, what are you up to today, Richard? Only, I was hoping to get off down to the caravan for a few days.'

Richard raised his eyebrows. 'Why don't you go off to Spain? We've got a fucking lovely villa with the pool, and yet you would rather scoot off to that poxy caravan park in fucking Winchelsea. What is it, eh? Got some geezer giving you one, have ya?'

Peggy hated her husband's vile mouth, which was emphasised by his deep hoarse voice. 'Oh, stop it, Richard. The girls are celebrating Melissa's fiftieth, and I thought it would be nice to join them. You don't mind, do you?' She smiled again. And then a cheeky expression adorned her face. 'Or have you got something special planned for us this weekend?'

His eyes darkened because he realised that it would be harder to get over to Fliss's if Peggy was under his feet. 'Do what you want. I don't care.'

'No,' she replied with a sigh. 'You never really have.'

Richard would have launched the mug of coffee at her head, but he'd become less keen to throw things at her, ever since he'd nearly killed her last year by launching a glass fruit bowl and knocking her clean off her feet.

As soon as she closed the door behind her, Richard got on the phone to his younger brother Larry. It rang for what seemed like ages, which raised Richard's temper. By the time Larry answered, Richard bellowed down the phone, 'Fucking answer the damn phone, you silly little prick!'

'I was in the shower. What is it that's got your goat, Rich?'

'Listen, Larry, I want you over at mine in ten minutes. Daft boy Teddy Ryder has dropped off fifty large, and I need it out of the office.'

'But—'

'No buts. Just get here.'

'Richard, what the fuck was Teddy doing at yours giving you fifty grand?'

'The silly boy must have heard about the threat to have Harper Kane blown away, so he came by to pay me fifty thousand smackeroonies not to kill her.'

'So, he bought her life, and you took the dough. Well, fuck me, Bruv, I really thought you had—'

'Hold up, Larry. Before you piss ya knickers . . . I took the money, and I did say I wouldn't kill her, but . . . Larry, are you there?'

There was no response and Richard realised that his brother's phone had either lost signal or the battery was low. He redialled, but it went to voicemail, and so Richard decided to leave a message. 'As I was saying, I took the money from silly bollocks, and I did promise I wouldn't kill Harper, but I didn't say I wouldn't touch her boy. She will wish I killed *her* when she hears what I'll do to the kid. I swear, I'll string the scrawny boy up by his ankles and bleed the fucker out until there ain't a drop of blood left in him. I guarantee the bitch will turn inside out when she sees his dead body, and a fucking good job, an' all. Anyway, I wanna know about this client you have. I hope you ain't been treading on the Russian's toes. Call me.'

***

While Delores was snoring her head off, Harper was searching for anything that would tell her where her son went to school or where he even lived. All she wanted was to see him. Carefully trying not to make a noise, she opened the drawers in the living room. Right away, she spotted a clue – the school photo. It was one that she hadn't seen. As she stared at her son's huge round eyes and his cheeky grin, tears fell like a waterfall down her cheeks, and her throat felt as if she was choking on a tennis ball. 'Ah, my little Eddie,' she whispered, as she stroked the photo. Then, her eyes were drawn to the badge on his blazer, and her heart skipped a beat. *St Olave's Grammar School.* So, her little boy was a clever child. She knew St Olave's only took the brainy kids. The school wasn't far at all, on Goddington Lane in Orpington. She could hop on to a bus and wait, just to see him in the flesh. Sliding the photo into her jeans pocket, she smiled to herself at the fact that of all the Kanes, her little Eddie would be the one to make something of himself.

Before she closed the drawer, she spotted another photo, one of her little sister Charley. She looked so innocent. Her eyes were round and pretty, unlike her other sisters, including herself. She had only been fourteen years old the last time she'd seen her. Her terrified expression, her skin white like a porcelain cup, and her pleading for help would permanently be imprinted on her mind. It was the reason she had felt compelled to do what she'd done. Every night as she lay in that prison cell, she saw little Charley's terrified face, and she told herself that it had been the right thing to do. Another tear trickled down her cheek. 'Where are you, Charley?' she whispered.

'Well away from this madhouse, and I don't blame her.'

Harper turned to find her mother in the doorway, still in her rotten dressing gown. Her hair was sticking up in all directions, and her face was filled with creases from sleep. Looking at the clock, Harper sighed; it was ten o'clock in the morning. Her mother obviously hadn't changed; she had always been a lazy cow.

'Are you not bothered what happened to her?' asked Harper, as she quickly wiped away her tears.

Delores ignored her and shuffled barefoot into the kitchen.

Harper placed the photo back into the drawer before closing it. She listened to her mother making a hot drink and then heard the spoon stirring two cups. *Two cups.* Taking a seat in the armchair, Harper gazed around the room. The morning light shone in through the window, and the dirt and dust became even more evident. The filth irritated her. She couldn't live like that, so she jumped up to find the cleaning equipment. She stopped when she saw Delores carrying two cups of coffee, a cigarette dangling from her lips.

Relieving her mother of one cup, Harper returned to her chair. 'Did you ever hear from her, like a Christmas card? Anything at all?'

Delores shook her head, placed her cup of coffee on the side table next to her armchair, and removed the cigarette from her lips, before blowing a huge plume of smoke into the air. 'Social services said that it was in Charley's best interests to relinquish all contact with me. In fact, all of us. The psychiatrist recommended that she should not visit you either, for the sake of her mental health, whatever the fuck that meant. And, apparently, it was what that kid wanted as well. And the stuck-up prick of a judge said he respected her wishes because as far as he was concerned, I was an appalling mum. The cheeky old bastard, what the hell did he know.'

'You should have fought for her, Delores. She was the baby.'

Taking another deep drag, Delores replied, 'She was a fucking little liar and a troublemaker. The shit she said about me flowed out of her ugly gob like diarrhoea. So, if her new foster parents could put up with her, then great. Good riddance, is what I say. 'Cos she ain't ever welcome back here.'

Holding the cup of hot coffee, Harper took a deep breath to stop herself from launching it at her mother. In her head, she counted to ten, to suppress her anger, which was fast escalating out of control.

'Charley was a sweet kid, an innocent kid. The trouble with you was that you wanted all your girls to run around after you to kiss your feet, while you turned a blind eye to what was really going on in this house.'

Delores acted as though she hadn't heard those words and sipped her coffee before puffing on her cigarette again.

Deciding not to argue over the facts of the past, Harper changed the subject. 'And where is Lexi? I thought she would have popped over to see me. She sent me in some clothes. I thought . . .'

'Hmm, yeah, well, she can't fucking move unless her fella says so, the Turkish wanker. I've a good mind to use me savings to have that little prick done in. I mean, who is he to say Baby Yosef can't call me Grandma. He won't let me babysit, you know. I fucking hate him.'

'So if he is that bad, why is our Lexi still with him?'

'She is shit-scared of him, and you wanna know why she cancelled on your visits half the time? Well, it was because she didn't want to turn up with bruises on her face.'

Harper sat up straight. '*What?* He *beats* her?'

'Yeah. I told her to leave him, but she said if she did, he'll take the boy out of the country, and she will never see him again, so she suffers the abuse.'

'Fuck me, I never knew he hit her. I could tell she wasn't happy, but *abusing* her! Does he hit the boy?'

Delores looked away. 'I wouldn't like to say. He is just one big bully, and his family are much the same. They're all mouths and knives.'

'Please, Delores, don't tell me he *cuts* her?'

'No, not that I am aware of. But that Boz family – his father, uncles, brothers, and cousins – own all the kebab shops, the fish and chip shops, the barbers, and the garages. She is watched by all of them.' She sighed. 'She can't leave him unless she wants to say goodbye to Yosef, for good.'

Harper tutted and shook her head.

'What?' snapped Delores, noticing her daughter's disappointment. 'Don't look down your fucking nose at me. You have no idea.'

Staring intently, Harper raised one well-defined brow.

'Everything and I mean every fucking thing went to shit when you got banged up,' snapped Delores. 'I had social services in and out like Piccadilly Circus over Charley. And then Lexi thought she could do as she bloody liked by staying out all hours mixing with the scumbags up the road. What was I supposed to do, eh? I was all over the place, what with your court case, police, solicitors, and nosey fucking reporters, and then Erin, suddenly spending money she didn't have on hairdos, make-up, sunbeds, in fact the lot. You can imagine what I thought she was up to.'

'What do you mean?'

'Well, I wouldn't be surprised if she was selling her arse for cash.'

Harper rolled her eyes. 'Well, it's obvious to me that you gave up on the girls. Because if you had been a good role model then . . .' – she tutted again – 'who knows? Anyway, Delores, I haven't got the time to sit around drinking coffee and smoking all day. I'm off to try and find a job.'

Delores took another drag on her cigarette. 'Good luck with that. There's fuck all out there and nothing for a jailbird.'

***

As soon as Harper closed the door behind her, she felt her shoulders tighten. Twelve years with only a couple of town visits before leaving prison had in no way helped her to prepare fully for the outside. It was 1999 when she was banged up. The height of fashion was anything the Spice Girls wore. She was young enough back then to wear crop tops and loose combat-style trousers. Being tall and slim, she could get away with most styles, but Teddy had liked to see her midriff, especially when she was tanned.

Today though, there would be no midriff showing or long hair flowing. She wore plain straight jeans and a black shirt. She had nothing. Even her make-up, which she had stuffed away in the drawer in her room, was dry and cracked, so there wasn't even a little bit of lipstick to coat her lips. She sighed to herself; she must stop allowing her thoughts to turn to Teddy. He was now her sister's fella, and that was all there was to it.

The morning was fresh but not too cold. She could walk to the jobcentre and fill out the relevant paperwork so that her probation officer wouldn't be on her back. As she marched along the road, she noticed how everywhere seemed tidier; the gardens were better kept, and a few of the neighbours had new front doors – all in the same style but with different colours. *The council must have done the rounds*, she thought.

In the distance, Harper could see a woman in a tight figure-hugging dress and a massive mountain of Afro hair. At first, she didn't recognise her and the woman obviously likewise until they were a few feet away from each other.

'Fuck me, Harper, you're home!' screeched Candy Jefferies, in a high-pitched voice. She held out her arms for a hug.

Harper preferred not to be tactile. Her prison days saw to that. But she'd known Candy since she was six years old, and so she hugged her back. It was a warm embrace, and she could feel tears welling up. She hadn't experienced anything warm and affectionate for so long, apart from the sad farewell to Madeleine.

As they pulled away, Candy looked Harper over. 'You ain't changed, girl, 'ave ya?'

Harper shrugged her shoulders. 'A few wrinkles here and there.'

Candy gave Harper a sorrowful expression. 'Well, girl, they ain't laughter lines, are they? Anyway, how are you doing? I never wrote. Ya know me. A lazy bitch.'

Harper chuckled. 'It's fine. I was having too much of a ball to read anyway.'

Candy looked around. 'Where are you off to?'

'The jobcentre. I need to get some money together, Candy. I need to get a home and a life for my boy.'

Candy raised her brow. 'I never agreed with it, Harper. I can't even talk to your sister now, and as for Teddy, you're better off away from him. I couldn't believe what they did, the minute you were inside.'

Harper held up her hand to stop Candy from saying any more. 'It is what it is, and now I'm home, I need to get my life in order, if I'm to get my little Eddie back.'

'The sooner the better.'

Harper frowned. 'What do you mean?'

Without thinking, Candy blurted out, 'Well, we all know that Erin only took on your son to get her claws into Teddy.' The second she realised what she had said, she threw her hand over her mouth. 'Shit! Sorry, Harper. None of my business.' Changing the subject, she said, 'What do you reckon your chances of getting a job are?'

Harper shrugged her shoulders again. 'I don't know until I get in that jobcentre.'

'Well, I'll tell ya, girl. Fuck all.' She looked around again. 'Harper, I might have something for you, though.'

'I know you mean well, Candy, but I cannot do anything illegal on probation. One wrong move, and I'm back serving time.'

'No, no, nothing like that. It's all straight up. My sister manages a club. Granted, it's a bit seedy, but the owner needs staff.'

Harper gave a false laugh. 'I never have and I never will show my fanny for a fiver.'

Candy shook her head. 'No, it's bar work. The owner, Vadim, likes a good-looking woman, and you're certainly no ugly bird, are you? I mean, with a bit of make-up and your hair styled, you could be strutting your stuff on one of those catwalks.'

Harper searched Candy's face for any signs she was pulling a fast one. Then she recalled Candy's elder sister Rhea and how much of a hard-nosed bitch she was. Five years older, and with a neck like a giraffe, with high cheekbones and a smirk instead of a smile. 'Your sister and I never really saw eye to eye.'

Candy laughed. 'She's mellowed. Besides, all that was years ago. Everyone has moved on, Harper. Rhea's thirty-nine years old, not a teenager, and you, Harper, you may still have your rep for a decent ruck, but you've got a kid now . . .' She paused when she clocked the sadness on Harper's face. 'Anyway, Harper, if you're interested, go to the club. It's called The Click. It's behind the electric shop at Bromley North, near the station. Ask for Vadim.'

Harper chuckled. 'Is he Eastern European?'

'He's Russian, but he's okay. He's good to me sister. No joking, she has it all. A nice motor, a flash place, and he pays his staff well. And Rhea did say to me that when you came out of the nick, she wanted you to call her.'

Harper nodded. 'I'll think about it, but thank you, Candy. I do appreciate it. I must be off. I need to get this jobcentre interview over and done with. I can't fuck it up and go back to that shithole.'

Before Harper walked on, she gave Candy a hug. It was the first time she felt human again.

'Don't forget, Harper, if you want to earn good money, go there tonight at seven o'clock. I'll let me sister know.'

***

No sooner had she reached Bromley High Street than people were glancing her way. Feeling very self-conscious, Harper walked on with her head down. Not in shame but so that she wouldn't get so pissed off that she would belt someone. Outside the jobcentre, there were a few of the old pissheads. She was surprised to see them still staggering. She assumed they would have died years ago. A couple of people she knew from the Cray said ‘hello’ but they didn’t stop to chat. Harper guessed they were off, ready to start the gossip.

Inside the jobcentre, there were seats filled with people in some kind of queuing system. Unsure of how it worked, she walked over to the counter where the woman behind the Perspex screen was on the phone. Waiting patiently, Harper could sense the people behind her mumbling, but she ignored them. She knew there would be scandalmongering.

The woman finished her conversation and glared at Harper.

‘Sorry to bother you. I don’t know what I’m supposed to do. Like the process.’

The stocky middle-aged woman huffed. ‘Take a ticket and wait for your number.’ She pointed to a machine on the wall.

At that moment, Harper wanted to walk out, but that nagging voice at the back of her head said ‘*Just get on with it*’. Taking a ticket and then a seat, Harper noticed that so many people were on their phones texting; she didn’t have a phone and had never texted in her life. The number of people waiting dwindled down until the doors closed and there were only her and a couple of young lads left. Once she was sitting up at the desk with the plastic partition, the million awkward questions began. After an hour of cringing and suffering the snotty woman’s glee at putting her down, she was relieved when the woman finally said, ‘There is a cleaning job in the offices – part-time, ten hours a week, five pounds and ninety-three pence an hour.’

‘Less than sixty quid a week! I can’t live on that,’ said Harper, almost choking on her words.

The woman behind the Perspex screen shrugged and looked over Harper’s shoulder to call the next person.

The idea of working in a bar was becoming more appealing by the minute, so by the time Harper left the jobcentre, she had convinced herself that it was the right move. Fingering the money in her pocket, she decided that hiding behind a bush to have a quick glimpse of her son could probably wait for a few days. She wanted to be presentable and face her little boy when she was dressed in decent clothes, so that he would be proud to call her Mum. If she was to achieve any of it, she would take the job in the bar, if this Vadim would have her.

First things first, she needed a decent outfit. Fashions had changed, and she tried to have a look at the young women without being caught, but there were so many styles, so she decided to simply pop into the nearest clothes shop. She didn't look up to see which shop it was, but as she scanned the racks and clocked the young women browsing, she noticed the clothes weren't too expensive. Armed with a few bits and pieces, Harper entered the changing room. Years ago, she would have collected her wages and then headed off to buy the latest fashionable clothes for the weekend. It was so different then; she had her friends waiting outside the changing rooms to whistle or tell her she looked great. They were fun times – the clothes, the parties, the clubs, and Teddy. But now she was alone.

By the time Harper returned home, Delores was asleep in the armchair, her hand still gripping a glass of cider. Not bothering to disturb her, Harper headed for her bedroom, where she laid out her clothes and placed the few bits of make-up on the small dressing table. A quick bath, a little gel to smooth down her hair, and a slap of lipstick, and she was beginning to look like her old self. A pair of black jeans and a blouse, which was edged in a few sparkles, looked good on her. They were professional but fun. She had managed to purchase a pair of high wedges to finish off the outfit.

Just as she was admiring herself in the mirror, she heard shouting and screaming outside the house. At first, she didn't pay attention to the din, but when she heard a man's deep voice shout, 'Lexi, I swear to God, I will fucking annihilate you!' her blood ran cold. Darting to the window, she saw a man across the road, and below, at the garden gate, was Lexi, clutching a baby.

It took her back to when a boy much older than Lexi had chased her sister home and slapped her face right outside the front door. Harper remembered feeling like a raging bull fired up to cause havoc. The lad at the time hadn't expected her to fly out of the front door, leapfrog the garden wall, and deck him. The sensation from a rising anger that was ready to eat her insides out was back.

She guessed the man who was shouting insults was Hasad Boz. He was big, dark, and vicious looking, but worse, he was slowly walking towards her house, checking around to see if anyone could see him. *The sly bastard*, she thought, before she flew out of her room and down the stairs, almost ripping the front door off its hinges. Her sister was gripping the child, but Harper could see Lexi had taken a beating. Her milky-white arm had purple marks, where he had obviously been grabbing her, and her left cheek and left eye were puffy and an angry red colour. Seeing the state of Lexi, the sister who shied away from trouble, somehow sent Harper over the edge of any sense of responsibility. Without saying a word, she grabbed Lexi and pulled her inside before she stepped forward to confront the man.

Hasad beckoned her. 'Oh yeah, and who's this?' He looked her up and down and laughed. 'Come on, then, you fucking silly tart.'

She instantly hated him, with his narrow eyes closed together and his oversized mouth shaped into a mocking smirk. 'You'd better fuck off before I'm nicked for a second murder!' she yelled, as she marched towards him.

The man laughed, taunting her. 'Think you're hard? I know all about you, Harper, "the big I am" Kane. You're nuffin but a piece of ex-con shit. But I'll be back, and I will take my son and burn down your shit pit of a house. So watch your back, Harper, and tell Lexi I am not done with her either.'

'You know nothing about me. Now, fuck off, before I call the police.'

Feeling an arm tugging her, she turned her head to see the beaten face of her sister pleading with her to come back inside. The vision reminded her of Charley and the look of terror on her face before the police arrived. There was something deep-seated inside her that compelled her to protect her sisters.

But the minute she spun around to go back to the house, he screamed at her.

'See, you're all just silly slappers with big gobs and no idea!'

However, he hadn't realised that Harper wasn't walking away through fear. She was removing a loose brick from their garden wall.

Now livid, she gripped the brick and headed for him. 'Silly slappers, are we?' Her voice went up an octave, her eyes turned dark, and her face tightened. 'Well, watch this silly tart, you ugly fat bastard.'

Hasad was in no way as nimble and fast as Harper. He was overweight, and the only reason he ever went to the gym was to collect monies owed. All he could do was to put his hands up to protect himself before Harper smashed the brick over his fingers that were shielding his head. He screamed, and she struck him again.

'Now, fuck off, and if you ever come back, I will annihilate *you*, and every member of your family. You won't have a chip shop, kebab shop, or a fucking school tuck shop left.'

Sliding his good hand into his back pocket, he pulled out a knife. He pressed a button releasing the blade, and suddenly he grew a pair of balls. As he waved the blade in front of her, he yelled, 'I'll cut your face open!'

Harper stepped back and laughed. 'You fucking twat. You couldn't slice an apple. Look at you, you greasy lard-arse wanker.'

Fuming that this woman, who was also his girlfriend's sister, was belittling him in the street, and now with an audience cheering her on, he wanted to kill her. But as he swiped the blade in front of her face again, she lobbed the brick so fast it hit him on the bridge of his nose, knocking him backwards. Stupidly, he dropped the knife to clutch his face.

Morris Baker, a man who lived across the street and who had come out of his house to witness what was going on, pulled out his handkerchief and picked up the knife. As if he were some kind of forensic pathologist, he looked at it. 'Evidence, with your prints on.'

However, Hasad wasn't listening. He was staggering back to his flash BMW, which was parked haphazardly in the street.

The other neighbours, who had joined the audience, clapped when he drove away, but Harper wasn't looking for a pat on the back. She was still incensed about the fat bastard beating up her sister. So the practice of counting to ten and taking deep breaths, which she'd learned in anger management, went clean out of the window. It must have been a natural reaction that was built in. If anyone hurt her sisters, she would go for them, and with everything she had.

Sucking in air, Harper calmed her rage and merely watched until Hasad's electric-blue coloured motor was out of sight.

'Harper, would you come in mine for a minute, love.'

Harper looked at Mr Baker. He had seriously aged; his once muscular frame was now bony. She would have said 'no', but she recognised the sadness in his eyes. He was probably in his sixties but he looked seventy-five. The death of his wife followed by his daughter would have sucked any form of happiness right out of him.

Harper held up five fingers, indicating to her sister, who was standing in the hallway, that she would be five minutes, before she followed him into his home, which had an identical layout to her mother's. She winced when she spotted his backbone protruding through his shirt. Closing the door behind her, she followed him through to the kitchen, which still consisted of the original council cabinets. They were green with metal strip handles. The stove was an old free-standing version with the grill at eye level. Against the wall, there was a small table and two chairs, and on the table, there was a brown teapot covered in a crochet teapot warmer. Nothing had changed since she was a kid.

'I won't keep you, Harper. You've probably got a million people to see and lots to catch up on.'

He coughed and had to take a seat.

'Hey, Mr Baker, are you okay, love?'

He nodded. 'Of all the sympathy cards, your letter, which arrived the morning of my little Gayle's funeral, meant the most to me, ya know.'

Harper reached across and stroked his bony hand. 'She was me mate, and I was inside that stinking prison when I should have been by her side. Did she really go peacefully, Mr Baker?'

Morris nodded. 'She spoke of you, all the laughs you had, and the naughty antics too, but yes, she died in her sleep, at the finish.'

Harper felt a lump in her throat; she was heartbroken. She had received the news that her friend, whom she really saw as just another sister, was terminal, so all she could do was talk to her on the phone.

'Now then, I don't have much. We weren't a rich family but there are some things that mean more than money. I know how you saved my Gayle from getting beaten that day, and you took the beating. If it had been my Gayle, well, put it this way, the poor little beggar would have died back then.'

'Oh, I dunno, Mr Baker. She was a tough one too.'

He shook his head. 'I've watched you since you were a kiddie looking after your sisters, and barely out of nappies yourself. Every morning, you were checking they were dressed properly, adjusting their hats and scarves, and ushering them up the road.' He laughed. 'I remember when Lexi had a thin jacket, and you got as far as the end of the road, and then you took her jacket and gave her your thick coat. I wouldn't slate your mother, but she *was* useless back then – still is, I suppose – and I often wonder what in God's name would have happened to your sisters, if they hadn't had you.'

Harper smiled, but her eyes were sad. 'I didn't have a choice. Delores was an old tart, and that, I'm afraid, Mr Baker, was the hand my sisters and I were dealt.'

He stood up and opened a cabinet door and removed a deep cake tin. 'I couldn't believe they locked you up, Harper. It should have been your mother.' He placed the tin on the table and sat back down. 'Anyway, every month you were inside, I put a little bit of money in this here tin. Anything I had over from my bills and food. I was never one for holidays or a fancy motor, so Harper, this, my girl, is for you.'

The shock was written all over her face. Her mouth dropped open, and her eyes nearly popped out of her head. '*What?* No.'

'Oh, don't go all daft on me, girl. It's no fortune.'

She watched as he opened the lid, the tears pricking her eyes. 'It's not the amount, Mr Baker. It's the thought.'

'Well, I reckon there's probably two and a bit thousand pounds, and I know me little missus, Gawd rest her, and my Gayle, love her, they would want me to give this to you.'

Harper stared at the money with her hand over her mouth. Tears were now streaming down her face. 'I can't take this. I don't deserve it.'

'Harper, you listen to me. I know what you did, and as far as I'm concerned, you did what most men wouldn't have the flaming balls to do. You probably did society a big favour. Now then, you take the money, and you do what you must to get your boy back.'

The mention of her son suddenly stunned her. 'Why would you say that?'

Morris sighed heavily. 'I listen to the chat, and even though I am older and less active, I still get out and about, and I'll tell you this. Erin is nothing like you. She never has been. Never will be. She has too much of her mother in her, and by Christ, kid, she was so jealous of you. My Gayle used to tell me, and, of course, she couldn't tell you because everyone knew no one could bad-mouth any of your sisters.'

Feeling concerned, Harper wiped a tear that was tickling her nose. 'She wouldn't hurt my son, though, would she?'

Morris shrugged his shoulders. 'Probably not physically, but she doesn't love him like you would, or do, I mean.'

‘I can’t thank you enough for the money, Mr Baker. I promise I will put it to good use and use it to get my boy back. Can I leave it here, though, for safekeeping?’

He nodded. ‘Yeah, of course, you can. I suppose Delores would be sticking her fingers in the cake tin, if she knew about the cash in there.’

Harper smiled, stroked his hand again, and rose to leave.

‘And you remember this. No matter, whatever happens, you have always got this place if you need to lay your head down.’ He winked and walked her to the door.

Harper held out her arms to hug him. She wanted to cry again when she felt the lack of muscles on his bones.

***

The shit bucket had now become a sick bucket. Although the whimpering had stopped, the sound of retching, followed by a whoosh of fluid, forced Kera to put her hands over her ears. The twelve mattresses on the floor were almost swimming in sick. This was hell, surely. She had given up with prayers. In fact, *none* of the girls prayed anymore. Maybe they had simply lost hope. Then, even with her hands covering her ears, she could hear a thumping sound. The ugly brute was on his way. What did he have for them now, apart from a wandering hand?

The door opened, and there he was, the six-foot muscle-popping beast. He held a paper bag and a crate of bottled water. He dished out tablets, and without question, the other girls took them and drank the water. The last time she drank the bottled water, she was out cold. Perhaps it wasn’t such a bad idea. At least she would be free for a moment from the smell, the whining, and the pains in her infected ankle.

He knelt down beside her mattress on the floor and offered her a tablet and the water. ‘You must take this medicine. You are all sick, and you must get well.’

‘Actually, I would rather die, if you don’t mind.’

No sooner had she got the words out of her mouth than he grabbed her hair, yanked her head back, and forced the tablet down her throat.

She lay down on the pillow and closed her eyes, hoping to visualise her mum's smiling face. However, all she could see was the beast's crooked teeth behind an evil smile and his intense stare boring into her.

Chapter Five

Lexi had Baby Yosef cradled in her arms as she sat in the armchair, tears rolling down her red and bruised face.

Harper could hear her mother in the kitchen and assumed she was making tea. She wondered if this was a regular thing.

'Well, that was a welcome home,' said Harper, trying to make light of the situation, although inside, she was still shaking, and in the back of her mind, she wondered if the police would rock up and take her away.

'I would've come and seen you more when you were inside, but I couldn't, Harper. He wouldn't let me even come over today. So I snuck out. His cousin drove past me and obviously called Hasad. He then chased me here in the car and . . .' She paused, choking on her words. 'He beat me, in front of Yosef, poor Yosef.' She stopped again to clear her throat before she broke into sobs. 'He tried to literally rip him from my arms.' She looked down at her baby, who was asleep but still dry sobbing.

Harper stared at Yosef and noticed how much he actually looked like Eddie. He was a little darker, but he was not as dark as his father.

Whereas both Lexi and Harper were slim and tall, Erin was shorter and had a more voluptuous figure. Although Lexi was younger than Erin, she looked older. Her frame was tiny compared to when she was a vibrant-looking teenager. Her hair was long and scraped back in a ponytail, but it was so thin that it looked like she was going bald in parts. Her nails were bitten down to the quick, and where her earrings should have been, there were scars, obviously from her earrings being ripped from her ears.

Harper noticed a few other white scars; there was one on her lip and another on her cheek. Her blood was boiling. That bastard had stripped her sister, who was once a pretty girl, down to nothing but a battered and scarred skinny wreck.

'Look, Harper, I didn't want to bring trouble here. I just wanted to see you and let you see your nephew.' She smiled down at the baby.

Getting down on the floor, Harper knelt beside the armchair and stroked the baby's cheeks. 'Ahh, love him, he is beautiful, like his mummy.'

Lexi's heart ached, seeing how Harper was so motherly and gentle with Yosef. Erin had Harper's little boy, and that should never have happened – ever.

'I will have to go back, Harper. He'll kill me if I don't.'

Harper could see that heartbreaking expression. It was Charley all over again. 'No, Lexi, you're gonna stay here. Me and Delores will look after you.'

''Ere, fucking bossy boots, who made you in charge? I'm the fucking queen of this castle.'

Getting up on her feet, Harper stood with her hands on her hips. 'So, what do you suggest, Delores?'

Waving her hands, Delores sighed. 'Lexi will do what Lexi does. She'll go running back begging for forgiveness—'

'I've never had a choice, Mother. You have told me point-blank I can't stay here with the baby.'

Harper glared at her mother. 'Are you for fucking real? How could you turn your back on her? Look at the fucking state of her face!'

She stopped when Baby Yosef stirred, lowering her voice. She carried on, the second Yosef was back to sleep. 'Do you get kicks out of seeing us lot suffer?'

Delores huffed. 'Don't be stupid, but at my time of life, I can't have half the Turkish community smashing my door down. That Boz family own every takeaway from here to Timbuktu, and the garages down in Catford. A dangerous lot they are. We all know they ain't legit, either. And I'm too bloody old to be getting involved.'

Harper shook her head. 'No, you'd rather throw your own kids to the wolves. She is staying here tonight, and as soon as I can, she will be living with me, as far away from here as possible.'

Delores knew that look and that tone and decided not to argue. Instead, she played the doting grandmother and scooped Baby Yosef up and took him off upstairs to lay him in her bed.

'Do you mean it, Harps?'

'Yeah. When have I ever said something I didn't mean?'

Lexi nodded. 'He will be back, though, and he'll bring backup.'

Harper tilted her head to the side. 'So you're quite sure he won't call the Ol' Bill, then?'

'Nah. He would be shamed by his brothers and cousins if he did that.'

Harper paced the floor in thought. 'Listen, Lex, I have to go to Bromley tonight, to see a man about a job. Will you be okay?'

Lexi looked up and nodded. However, her face was so bruised her left eye was practically closing up.

'He should be buried for beating you. Why you ever went with a nasty piece of work like that, I'll never know.'

Lexi got up from the armchair and stood awkwardly with her hands buried in the back pockets of her jeans. 'He was all hearts and flowers in the beginning, and then, when I got pregnant, everything changed. I felt like I was the property of his whole bleedin' family. But, Harps, he will be back because I have his son, and no way will he let me bring the baby up on my own. He'll kill me first.'

'Jesus, Lex, Yosef is your son too. You'll be safe here, surely? But I have to go out. I need money to get a life for us.' She pointed up. 'I need to get away from her.'

Unexpectedly, Lexi flung her arms around her big sister and cried. 'It's so good to have you home. I've missed you so much. Nothing was ever the same after you got locked away. My life went to shit.' She pulled away and wiped her cheeks. 'Sorry about that. I just really missed you.'

Harper gently ran her hand down her sister's bruised cheek. 'Yeah, I wished I'd never got banged up. Things would have been so different. And I would have my little Eddie, and you, Lex, wouldn't have a fucking great shiner. Your eye is swelling up quite bad. Go and put some ice on it.'

Lexi smiled and left the room to get ice from the freezer. All she found was a bag of peas, a dried-up box of ice cream, and two frozen loaves of bread. That was one thing they were never short of in her own home – food. She looked out into the garden and saw the dumped mattress covered in green mould and the grass looking like a jungle. She couldn't let Yosef play outside. It would be like throwing him into the lion's den. *Is this how she would end up living if she went it alone?* she wondered. For as much as Hasad was a bully and a controlling freak, her son would never go without. He had everything he wanted. She started to question whether she could really give her son the best life if she seriously decided to leave Hasad and his family.

Chapter Six

It was close to getting dark by the time Harper stepped off the bus. The air had a chill to it, and it would have been fine if she had worn a jacket, but she didn't own one. She walked with care in her wedges since she had been out of practice wearing heels.

The club itself sat back from the street. To the right of the building was an alley wide enough for cars to drive into. To the left appeared to be an old cottage attached to the main building. She wondered if it was one of those houses that for whatever reason the property developers couldn't purchase, so it was left there to stick out like a sore thumb. Without the place lit up or the ropes surrounding the entrance or even the presence of big burly bouncers, it looked pretty low-key. The enormous industrial bins seemed to be overflowing, and a general whiff of stale beer floated beneath her nostrils.

Clutching an old but clean black handbag, she knocked loudly at the entrance door. It seemed so large that she wondered if her thumping would even be heard. To her surprise, the door opened, and a less than polite heavily built man stood there looking her up and down. 'What!' was all he said, but his voice had an accent. Maybe it was Russian or Eastern European; she wasn't sure.

'Harper Kane, to see Vadim,' she said, holding her head high. The one thing she did was to try not to look as though she was being intimidated.

He stepped aside, and with a sharp move, he flicked his head in the direction of the entertainment area of the club. Slowly, she walked forward until she heard him lock the door behind her. He then marched ahead, indicating that she should follow.

The dance area was surrounded by small glass panels separating seating areas, all VIP drinking sections. The bar ran the entire length of the main room, and to the right, there was a platform for the pole dancers. It wasn't as seedy as she had imagined it to be. She continued walking across the room until the man stopped at a door behind the stage and knocked.

'Come!' came a deep guttural voice, with a hint of an accent.

The stocky man opened the door and nodded for Harper to enter.

She was surprised to see a younger man. She pictured him being a lot older, from his husky voice. He was sitting at his desk working, so all she could see was his white shirt casually worn with the top button undone. His hair was fair and cut neatly into a short back-and-sides. As he looked up, Harper noticed the ice-blue colour of his large dewy eyes and was taken aback by how handsome he was. Not that she had actually visualised him before entering the room. All the same, he was strikingly good looking.

'Vadim, this is Harper Kane, to see you.'

'Sit!' he demanded, as he continued arranging some paperwork.

Harper took the seat opposite and watched as he gathered up some files and placed them in a filing cabinet. He then returned to his seat, picked up a packet of foreign cigarettes, and offered her one. Gratefully, she slid one from the packet and leaned forward for him to light it for her. Next, he poured two glasses of something amber in colour. Again, she gratefully accepted the drink.

It had been a while since a spirit had touched her lips. This was a good one. It was smooth and didn't make her cough as it slid its way down.

'So, I guess you are here about a job?'

'Yes, my friend Candy mentioned that you were looking for bar staff.'

Vadim looked her over. 'Stand up for me.' His accent wasn't very strong, but there was no mistaking it was Russian.

She didn't quibble but got up and took a drag of the cigarette.

Again, he looked her over. 'Sit, thank you.'

She retook her seat.

'You have very long beautiful legs. You could make so much money, not pouring drinks but artistically showing yourself off. You could easily make five hundred pounds a night.'

Harper wondered if Vadim had seen her eyes widen. Five hundred was a small fortune and enough to have her own place. She shook her head. 'I was hoping for some bar work.'

Vadim chuckled like a girl, which momentarily startled Harper.

'You girls are all the same. If we men had what you have between your legs, we would make a fortune.' He sighed. 'So, bar work. Do you have experience?'

'Yeah, yeah, sure,' she said, knowing full well she had none, but how hard could it be to pour a gin and tonic?

'We have a uniform here. All the girls have to wear a short black skirt and a shirt tied below the boobs. You understand, yeah?'

Taking a larger swig of her drink, she then nodded, all the while thinking of the money. It had to be better than five pounds and ninety-three pence an hour offered at the jobcentre. 'What are the rates?'

'I decide that when I see how you work. You see, I like my girls to flirt to get the men spending money. This club is about the idea of sex. The punters want to be treated like handsome princes. Can you do that?'

She nodded but cringed inside. 'Yeah, sure. So what's your highest earner and your lowest?' she quizzed, wanting to know the rough rate of pay.

'Yes, very good,' he said, now grinning. 'My top girl, she earns a hundred to a hundred and twenty. The others earn about eighty.'

'Okay, very fair.'

‘You can start tonight, but you must change and maybe’ – he pointed to her face – ‘put some make-up on. You are a very unusual-looking woman. I think the punters will like you.’

She wasn’t really into lots of make-up, but if it was going to earn her decent money, then she would cake it on with a trowel, if need be.

‘Go to the changing room where the dancers get ready. And on the rail will be your uniform. Get changed, and then, Harper, I want to see how you pour me a drink.’

He stared for longer than she would have expected. However, she held his gaze, although perhaps she shouldn’t have. The realisation that she hadn’t had a man for so long caused her to look away. Surmising to herself that she was finding him sexually attractive, she was well aware that this wasn’t like her. Teddy had been the only man she’d ever loved. He had been her rock and the one she’d planned to grow old with.

Rising from his seat, Vadim stood in front of Harper. He smiled warmly and blushed before he gently ran his finger down her cheek. ‘You are very beautiful. But you know that, eh?’

Harper’s eyes narrowed. ‘Please, I just want to work. I need the money.’ She could have kicked herself when she’d said that. She was a proud woman, and even in desperation, she would never let her pride slip. The beatings she’d suffered when she had first gone to prison had not been enough to reduce her to tears. The experience had given her an edge and made the inmates back off. She had been forced to act like a woman made of steel, and she felt until now, she had perfected it.

‘I understand. Please forgive me. I find you so . . . what is the word . . . unusually attractive.’

Harper took a step back and almost lost her footing, but he quickly grabbed her arm to steady her. ‘I’ll wait in the bar. Come when you are ready.’

She said nothing and watched him leave the room. Once the door closed behind her, she glanced in the mirror and saw that her cheeks were flushed. That was a first: she’d never blushed before.

As soon as she was in the girls' changing room, she searched through the rack of clothes. It didn't take long to find a uniform that fitted. She imagined what the room would be like when all the dancers were excitedly getting ready. A row of girls sitting at the bench putting on lipstick while looking into the mirrors outlined with bright lights. She peered at the make-up bags and boxes and found foundation and some bright-red lipstick. After applying as much as possible, she added eyeliner and enhanced her catlike features before she tied the shirt in a knot above her belly button. For extra measure, she unbuttoned the shirt to reveal a little cleavage and left the room.

With confident strides and an added wiggle, she headed to where Vadim was at the bar. He turned on his stool and looked her up and down.

Harper clocked his eyes widen and the slight smile that creased the corners of his mouth. His eyes drew her in, sending a tingle of goosebumps up her arms. Vadim was a looker, no question.

'Yes, yes, perfect. Please go to the other side of the bar and pour me a vodka on the rocks.'

Piece of piss, thought Harper.

As she placed the drink in front of him, he instantly grabbed her hand and looked at her fingernails, which were short and chipped. 'You must have these manicured. Fake nails, please.'

Harper felt instantly ugly and self-conscious. Again, it was not like her.

He stepped down off the stool, walked around to the other side of the bar, and opened the till. After sliding out a few ten-pound notes, he slapped them on the bar. 'Take the money. Call it expenses.' His voice had softened, and again he touched her face. 'You are very beautiful, so you have the job if you want it. You will start at eighty pounds. How does that sound?'

Harper nodded. 'Can I work tonight?'

'Yes, but tomorrow, you must get your nails done. All the girls have to have lovely nails, and they all have fake ones.'

‘Oh, do they?’ she asked, feeling a little better about herself.

‘Yes, and they all want to look their best, and it’s a bit of a competition, although they will be very jealous of you because you will be the prettiest girl in the club.’

Harper wanted to laugh at his flattery. She was drawn to his eyes. They opened slowly and sucked her in.

He stared again but leaned closer, waiting. There was a pause as his head was tilted at an angle, ready to kiss her.

All she had to do was to move just that little bit closer, but . . . she hesitated.

Vadim gently placed his hand at the nape of her neck and slowly pulled her closer until their lips met. Feeling his breath so close, and now with his lips pressed against hers, she returned the kiss. The sexual attraction was like a million rubber bands pinging. While his tongue searched her mouth, his hand slid around to her left breast. Gently, he caressed her. Unbuttoning her blouse, he looked down. Harper could sense he liked what he saw, and she enjoyed how she felt. It was the first time in years that she actually felt alive and beautiful. His hand touching every inch of her body, had obviously aroused him, because she could feel his erection building between her legs. The second she unzipped his trousers, she was giving him her consent. And she was desperate to feel him inside her. As her hands reached down and she unclasped his belt, he took control. Removing her underwear, he lifted her onto the bar, pulled her legs apart, and entered her. At first, she felt pain but then ecstasy. As he thrust deeper and harder, she wanted more, so she moved back and forth, enjoying every stroke, until, finally, she felt her legs turn to jelly as she rode the longest orgasm in her life. She didn’t know if he had ejaculated or not until he pulled her down from the bar, turned her around, and entered her again. Suddenly, she felt sore. He was going for some time. The urge for gratification had left, and her feeling of regret had taken its place. He groaned and finally stopped before removing himself.

As Harper turned around and straightened herself, she saw someone in the shadows and then heard a slow but loud clap.

Rhea Jefferies stepped closer until she was in the light.

Feeling totally humiliated, Harper looked down in shame.

'You, Vadim, are a fucking bastard, and as for you, Harper Kane, I didn't take you for a slut. I was fixing you up for a job, not to steal me boyfriend.'

Harper looked up and met Rhea's dark, spiteful eyes. Slim and immaculately dressed in a white tailored suit with her hair straightened and her large plump lips coated and defined in a deep-red lipstick, Rhea held her hands firmly on her hips and sneered. The gold around her neck and the two earrings, shaped like seahorses, were obviously statement pieces.

'What the fuck are you doing in here hiding and watching?' snapped Vadim.

'Lucky I did, Vadim, or I wouldn't have caught you in the fucking act, you dirty bastard.'

Feeling totally ashamed, Harper pushed past Vadim and tried to make her way to the door, but Rhea had other ideas. She stepped in front of Harper, blocking her way. 'You fucked me over, years ago. You humiliated me in front of my friends, and now, after you're out of the nick a fucking day, you're screwing my fella.'

Harper felt her stomach churning because she assumed that this would end in a physical ruck. 'Rhea, it was years ago. We had a stupid street fight, and it just so happened that day you came off worst. I'm sorry about your fella. I didn't know. I'll go.'

'No, you will not go!' shouted Vadim, before he grabbed Rhea's arm to pull her away. 'And you, Rhea, have no claim over me. We made it very clear that you are *not* my girlfriend. And sneaking in here, you're like a stalker. I am not your *anything*. Let's get that very straight.'

Rhea shot a look his way. 'Oh, really? So why were you in my bed this morning, you wanker?'

Vadim rolled his eyes. 'You, Rhea, are just a friend with benefits, but the way you are now, it's really very irritating, like a mosquito buzzing around and annoying the hell out of me. It's time you found yourself another job.'

'*What?* Are you kidding me? Seriously, Vadim, I have run this club for years, and you wanna just kick me out?' She shot Harper a glare. 'I suppose you want this slapper to run it for you. I guess she is a better shag, but then, she would be good, what with all that pent-up frustration of years behind bars.'

Disgusted with herself, Harper shook her head, feeling her world collapsing around her. 'Look, I'll go. I'm sorry.'

But Vadim held his hand up. 'No, actually, Harper, you have done nothing wrong. She has pissed me off for the final time. She has fucked off so many good girls because of her jealousy that I am now going to kick her out. I was going to this morning, but we did, as she said, end up shagging. Anyway . . .' He waved his hand at Rhea. 'It's time for you to go. I want you out of the flat by tomorrow afternoon. Claude will help you pack. Come back next Friday, and I will have your wages and a little extra for you, and by that, I mean money.'

'Oh, come on, Vadim. Let's talk privately. Not in front of her. Maybe in your office.'

Vadim smirked. 'No, I don't think so. Now go.' He waved his hand.

Rhea showed in her curled lip that she wasn't holding Vadim responsible for what had just happened. That was down to Harper.

'This is you all over, Harper. You want what's not yours, but still, you fucking take it. First Teddy, now this Russian prick.'

Harper would accept responsibility for all her wrongdoings. And she would speak up when she was being accused of something she hadn't done. She hadn't taken Teddy from Rhea. Even as a kid, back then, Rhea had pretended she was Teddy's girlfriend, but Teddy had been a free agent. At the time, they were kids, and so it wasn't as if she'd stolen someone's husband. As far as she was concerned, merely stating you have an interest in someone didn't make a relationship official. Harper even remembered Erin saying she liked Teddy. She sighed inwardly because Erin now had the man. 'Teddy was a free lad to date who he wanted. You were a bully, Rhea, and the fact is you tried to fucking bully me, and it didn't work, did it? A second ago, I was prepared to apologise to you, but I don't think you're angry with me through anything I have done but more for the woman I am. I guess, you're jealous, and that's a horrible trait.'

Rhea's nostrils flared with every word that Harper slung her way, but, worse, those words were valid. She had always secretly hated Harper because she had it all – the figure, the looks, and Teddy.

'Jealous? Ha! What, of a skanky jailbird like you? They even took your kid off you. I ain't jealous, darling. You can have this prick and crack on. I'm off.' She stormed past Harper, nudging her shoulder as she went. Just before she reached the door, she turned to face them both. 'And you, Vadim, I have so fucking much on you, you'd better watch your back, or, with one drink too many, I will let my mouth run away with me and . . .' She shrugged her shoulders dramatically. 'Who knows, Vad, I might just sing like a pretty yellow canary.'

'So now, Rhea, you have just shown me what you are really all about. You think the police are interested in what I do in my club? Ha! They come along themselves to buy a few drugs, so go ahead: tell the police and then see what happens.' His accent had suddenly become thick and intimidating.

He casually took his glass from the bar and downed the last of the vodka, his expression now very different from the soft, attractive man that Harper had just had sex with. He literally sent a chill up her spine.

Rhea glared again, this time with a knowing smirk. 'And you, Harper, I hope someone has the balls to take the fifty grand.'

Harper frowned, totally confused. '*What?* What are you talking about? Fifty grand?'

Rhea looked down. She'd said too much and hurried through the main door into the alley.

Facing Vadim, Harper asked, 'Do you know what she's talking about?'

Vadim rubbed his bristly chin and then hurried from the bar, back to his office.

Harper decided this situation was way out of control and wondered if perhaps she should have taken the cleaning job after all, but then she heard Vadim talking very fast and angrily on the phone. Of course, she couldn't understand a word of it because the conversation wasn't in her mother tongue.

She was about to head back to the changing room when Vadim returned from his office. 'You wait here. I will find out what she means. And, by the way, she is not my girlfriend and never has been. Yes, we have slept together, but that is all.'

Harper wondered if she was now in the same category as Rhea – *friends with benefits* and concluded she probably was.

The main door to the club suddenly flew open, and there, with a nasty mark on her face, was Rhea, who was being dragged back inside by the stocky man who had let Harper into the club.

Harper was shocked to see that Rhea was in a bit of a state: her white suit was covered in dust, her hair was a mess, and she was crying. All in the space of two or three minutes, Rhea had gone from glam to trash. Feeling her throat tighten up, Harper realised that she was dealing with a very dangerous man.

'What did you mean, fifty thousand pounds? What is this?'

Rhea tried to snatch her arm away, but the stocky man, obviously a bouncer, held her tight. He was like a machine just standing there.

'Get your hands off me, Claude, you Cossack cunt, or, I swear, I will bite your fingers off.'

Harper gasped when the man backhanded Rhea.

'Oi, what the fuck are you doing? Let her go!' yelled Harper.

It was clear that Rhea was dazed from the vicious slap.

'I said, let her fucking go!' she yelled again.

But Claude merely looked at Vadim for clarification.

Harper glanced at Vadim, her eyebrows knitted together. 'What the fuck is this? I only asked if you knew what she was on about. There's no need to have her bashed up. Jesus!'

Vadim ignored Harper and stepped closer to Rhea. 'You called me a Russian prick and a wanker, and I said nothing because I assumed you were hurt, but then you made threats – very dangerous threats. Never mind Harper, I want to know what this fifty grand is about.'

Rhea appeared visibly shaken; her confident look was replaced by a look of terror. Her eyes darted from Harper to Vadim. 'Nothing. I just heard a rumour that there was a fifty-grand contract on her head, that's all.'

'Liar!' roared Vadim, as he slapped her face hard.

Harper jumped at the noise. She could almost feel the pain herself.

'Leave off. I don't care what she meant. Fucking leave her alone!'

'This has nothing to do with you, Harper. Keep out of it.'

The expression on Rhea's face was enough to tell Harper that this man was going to hurt her badly. In an instant, she grabbed the vodka bottle that was on the bar. Gripping the bottle by its neck, she lifted it high in the air and smashed it down on the bar. The result was a savage, deadly weapon. All three looked to see what had caused that almighty bang.

Vadim put his hands up. 'Put that down before someone gets hurt.'

'Oh, believe me, Vadim, someone will get hurt if you and that big fucker don't let her go. I swear to God, mate, I will carve you both up if you so much as touch a hair on her head.'

Vadim chuckled. The anger on his face disappeared, and he smiled gently. 'Okay, I wasn't going to hurt her, but, Harper, you are a big girl. You must understand. This woman is behaving very stupidly. I pay for her home, her car, even that designer suit she is wearing, and I expect loyalty and respect. And look at her. She is annoyed because I like you, and so she makes threats. This is not the way it works. But I won't hurt her.' He turned back to Rhea. 'You are biting the hand that feeds you. This is not good, Rhea. Now, tell me, what is this fifty-grand business?'

Harper could see that the tension had relaxed a touch, but she still gripped her makeshift weapon.

'Richard Newbury has a fifty thousand-pound contract on her head.'

Vadim stepped away from Rhea. 'Hmm, Richard Newbury.' He looked at Harper. 'Does this man mean anything to you?'

Harper nodded. 'Yeah, actually he does. He is the brother of the man I served twelve fucking years over.'

'Can I go now?' asked Rhea, nervously.

'Go? Oh, you mean run to this Richard and tell him that you fucked up, eh?'

Harper was confused now, but she listened, intrigued.

'I wondered why you were so keen to have Harper work here. I should laugh, but this demonstrates to me, Rhea, that you are an evil woman. Harper . . .' he said, as he looked at the broken bottle in Harper's hand, 'was going to fight to protect you, and yet you were prepared to set her up to be murdered.'

Harper sensed what was happening and twisted her head in shock. '*What?* Were you really, Rhea?'

Suddenly taking on a cocky stance, Rhea shook her head. 'No, I wasn't. Don't be fucking silly.'

'I know you, Rhea, you sly bitch. You very definitely set her up. You wanted her here so that you could be her manager and know her every move.'

'No, no,' said Rhea, now talking very fast. 'I just heard some guy in the club talking about it, that's all. I swear to God.'

Vadim was slowly nodding his head. 'You take me for a fool – big mistake. No one would talk freely about a contract killing and in *my* club. I know what you have done because I know how it operates, and you, Rhea, you fell for an old trick, you silly, silly girl.'

Harper felt her heart beating so fast. Once again, someone she thought she could perhaps trust had betrayed her. Rhea had played on the fact that she guessed she would need a decent job, and so she had sent her little sister to get the ball rolling.

'No, Vadim, that's not it at all. I promise.'

'I know when you are lying. You always chew your bottom lip. Over the years, I have let you get away with the odd grand here and there going missing. I have watched the way you have bullied the girls you see as a threat to you. Even the younger girls, who, by the way, I didn't believe were old enough to work here. They never even lasted the night because of your stinking attitude. And now I find,' he said, in a voice that was becoming louder by the minute, 'you planned to have a contract killer come here, to my club! What the fuck would that do to my business, eh!' he bellowed, stepping forward and grabbing her by her hair, pulling her ear close to his mouth.

Harper couldn't hear what he was saying, but she saw the blood drain from Rhea's face. She contemplated intervening, but the thought that Rhea was instigating an execution *on her*, which was troublesome enough, now made her wonder if there was actually anyone she *could* trust. Inside prison, it was dog eat dog, but outside, it seemed, it was far worse.

Harper looked at Claude and saw a knowing look as if he had received instructions. She clocked Vadim nod, but Harper was now overwhelmed by the situation and wondered if she was dreaming up the idea that these two Russians would kill Rhea off.

Claude marched Rhea to the door and gave her a last shove over the threshold to see her on her way.

Letting out a sigh of relief, Harper placed the bottle – what was left of it – on the bar. 'I should leave. This is not the life I wanted, and it also seems that I have a contract on my head for fifty thousand pounds.'

Vadim stepped around the broken glass, walked to the other side of the bar, and poured himself another vodka. 'Do you want one?'

Harper shook her head. Her muscles were tight, and her stomach felt as though it had been turned inside out.

'I can sort out this fifty thousand-pound contract. In my country, everyone has a contract on them.' He laughed. 'In this country, very few carry it out. I don't know this man, so, to me, he is a nobody. But, Harper, he is a nobody who would happily use my club to have you drawn in to monitor your movements in preparation for you to be executed at a time of his choosing. I am not happy about this at all.'

Harper said nothing but listened.

'I will have Claude pay him a visit and tell him that you work for me, and if anything were to happen to you, I will take his head and feed it to my Komodo dragons.'

'And why do you think he will be afraid of you?'

Vadim raised his eyebrow. 'You have been inside for a long time, Harper. I have a lot of influence in this part of the country. He will not tread on my toes, or he'll know the consequences.'

'But why would you do that for me? I'm a nobody to you.'

He swigged the last of his vodka and poured another. 'You are not Rhea. I like you. A lot.'

'But you don't know me.'

Vadim grinned like a boy and his eyes lit up. 'But I do. You have more balls than my men. You are modest, not flashy, and you are the most natural woman I have ever met.'

Harper blushed and looked at the floor. 'Please, Vadim, although your compliments make me feel good and even attractive, I think I know I'm not beautiful. Unusual, yeah, but stop with the flattery. You've already shagged me, so let's be straight with each other.'

Vadim chuckled. 'See, that's another reason I like you because you are so upfront. There's nothing false about you.'

'I'm a jailbird. I have nothing except the clothes I came here in. I'll work hard, but never fuck me over for wages. I have a son, you see, who lives with his father, and I want my boy back, so I need to earn enough to get him and me a home. I heard you say about Rhea having a place, so if you have a flat, a bedsit, or anything at all that I could afford, then great.' She looked up and saw his smile and knew it was genuine. She blushed. 'Look, Vadim, we had sex, and I'll admit it was good. You aren't an ugly monster. We both have needs, so sex could be on the cards, if you could find your way to seeing me okay.' She looked down again, feeling a tad ashamed.

He slammed the glass on the bar top. '*No!* I didn't fuck you because I saw you as an easy shag.' He lowered his tone. 'I like you, Harper. I mean it. And yes, I have a flat for you. Rhea will have to get her own place now, but she knows this. The management job comes with the flat. She is no longer the manager, so it's yours, for you and your boy.'

Harper could feel her heart racing with excitement, and since she was on a winning streak, she decided it was now or never to push her luck. 'So, this management position. Does it pay well?'

Vadim stared at her for a while before he kissed her, and she wondered if he was contemplating having a second go at the goods, because she had to be honest with herself, she was probably his goods for now.

'Two hundred pounds a night. The flat, except the bills. I don't deal with those kinds of things. The job isn't easy. You will have to order the drinks, make sure we never run low, and the girls must be sober, pretty, and working hard. You hire, and you fire them.'

It was a lot to take in, but all that money and a free flat were enough to do whatever it took.

Chapter Seven

Relieved that Rhea had gone, Harper settled her nerves and waited to greet the staff. She was surprised at the girls when they arrived. Vadim wasn't wrong when he said he liked his staff looking immaculate. They were all beautiful, and, as he'd said, their nails were manicured. The dancers made their way to the changing room, but they didn't seem as lively and chatty as the bar staff. They looked sluggish and glum. The DJ tested the sound systems and the lights. Harper gained a sense of what the club would look like once it was in full swing.

She tried to appear confident, but inside, she was shrinking, wondering if she was up to the job.

Vadim clapped his hands, and the girls stopped talking, almost standing to attention.

'Harper is now your manager. You do as *she* says, or you leave.'

A tall blonde with long hair extensions, called Roxy, raised her hand as if she were in school. 'Where is Rhea?'

'I don't know, and I don't care. She no longer works here.' His tone was sharp, and Roxy said no more.

Harper looked for an ally among her new colleagues, someone who would show her the ropes, but it was Vadim who came to the rescue. He must have guessed.

'Harper is going to watch you girls tonight, so all of you be on your best behaviour.' He shot his eyes to the camera that scanned the bar. It was a broad hint that they could be seen.

As soon as Vadim walked back to his office, Harper asked the girls if they knew where the dustpan and brush were kept to clean up the mess she had made on the floor before any punter had an injury.

Roxy frowned. 'As the manager, that ain't your job, Harper. Vadim would go bonkers if you cleaned up while we watched.'

Frenchy, a shorter girl with a wide black fringed short bob, huffed. 'Stop sucking up, Roxy. If Harper wants to manage the club, then she can learn like the rest of us, or be out on her ear.'

Roxy shook her head. 'You're a spiteful, jealous cow, Frenchy. I suppose you were hoping for the manager's job yourself.'

Frenchy looked Harper up and down. 'Where did you work before? Are you even up to it?'

Harper didn't like her tone or her cocky stance, but she had dealt with women like her inside. She knew that as much as they acted hard, it was always a front. 'So your name's Frenchy, is it? Then, Frenchy, as I'm not working for you, love, but working for Vadim, you can go and fetch the dustpan and brush yourself and clear up the mess.'

'You *what*? That's not my job.'

'Oh, darling, it fucking is now. You see, I have a hell of a lot of experience with birds like you, and trust me, your attitude doesn't bode well with me. I asked Roxy for the dustpan and brush because I would do it myself and muck in with you all, but see, you, you've just fucked that up. Now, clean up that mess or leave.'

While Frenchy stormed from the bar, Harper looked around. A woman wandered in who was obviously late, but she didn't appear the slightest bit bothered. Like Roxy, this woman had very long hair, but it was a deep red. She also had an air of confidence about her.

Frenchy, now distracted from fetching the dustpan and brush, whispered into the tall redhead's ear. Instantly, the redhead shot a look at Harper.

Harper smiled at her and waved her over. She expected the woman to hurry, but she didn't. She sauntered over as if she had all the time in the world. Frenchy was by her side. For a moment, Harper was stumped by the dynamics.

'This is Pixie, Claude's better half,' said Frenchy, as if she was introducing some major player in the club.

'Great. Hi, Pixie. Nice to meet you. I'm Harper, the new manager. Are you bar staff or one of the dancers?'

'Bar staff,' Pixie replied.

Pixie's slightly foreign accent was one that Harper didn't recognise. The club was filling up, so Harper left Pixie to it.

As the evening went on, Harper got to know the girls, apart from Frenchy, who was still sulking. The others were kind and friendly and in the same boat. They all needed money and would flirt outrageously with the men. Roxy explained that as some of the punters would take the flirting as a real come-on, the girls stayed behind for an extra hour with the bouncers, to wait until it was safe to leave.

While Harper kept one eye on the bar, she was clocking Vadim with the other, hoping to catch a reassuring smile. Then she saw him hand Claude a set of keys. Claude was a big man, but he was the smallest compared to the other men on the door.

The whole evening was an eye-opener. The dancers, who had arrived earlier looking either fed up or hung-over, now appeared on the poles looking entirely different. With their made-up faces and their sexiest of moves, the entire transformation was something that Harper could not have visualised. However, when she entered the changing room, she realised why. They were all snorting cocaine before it was their turn to work the floors.

The dancers were different from the bar girls. They were there to do a job and not to socialise. Some were Eastern European, and a couple were English. They acknowledged Harper with a nod or a half-smile. Harper soon realised that there was very little to manage. The system seemed to run itself.

Watching how the club operated, she concluded that the dancers were raking it in, just as Vadim had said. The money stuffed into their knicker elastic was plentiful. However, Harper knew she couldn't do it, and a flat along with two hundred pounds a night were sufficient rewards for her.

As Harper leaned against the wall, she didn't notice a man, probably in his fifties, staring at her, until he climbed down from the stool and waved his glass under her nose. 'A Jack Daniel's, darling, and make it a double.'

Roxy instantly stopped what she was doing and took the glass. 'I'll get that for you, sweetheart,' she said.

The man, who was dressed in a smart blue suit and white shirt, snatched the glass back. 'I said, get me a Jack Daniel's.' He kept his eyes firmly locked on Harper's.

Harper glanced at Roxy and smiled. 'It's okay. I'll get this.'

'Good girl. Now then, three ice cubes, and fill it to the brim, and have one yourself.'

Harper did as he asked, but when she asked for the money, she was rudely interrupted. 'You should have been told that I don't pay. I am surprised that Vadim hasn't mentioned me. Never mind, so who are you?'

'Lula, Mr Cox. She's new,' said Roxy, before Harper even had a chance to tell him herself.

Harper then guessed that Roxy was probably not her real name, and, for whatever reason, the girls were keeping who they really were close to their chest.

'Well, Lula, best you remember that I don't pay for fuck all in here.'

Harper nodded politely. As soon as he walked over to the pole dancers' arena, Harper sighed. 'So Vadim allows the filth in here.'

'You guessed he was the police, then. No, they don't come here, except that prick. I think Vadim lets him in because the guy is as bent as a nine-bob note, but the club never gets raided. Well, not a proper raid. We have had a couple of coppers come in and escort a few of the younger girls out. Rhea was warned a million times to check the girls' IDs but she was a know-it-all. Occasionally, though, word would get out that underage girls were serving or on the pole, and then they would get taken off to social services or wherever. That's when Vadim used to argue with Rhea. I guess, she could round up the young and desperate and pay them peanuts and then pocket the rest of their wages for herself.'

'That's bloody wicked. I didn't realise that the Rhea I knew back in the day could be so ruthless. Just goes to show you can't trust anyone, eh.'

'No, you can't, and see that Mr Cox. Watch him, Harper. He will want to have a piece of you, that's for sure.'

'I'll cut his dick off before he ever touches me, the ugly bastard.'

Roxy chuckled and carried on serving the next punter.

Feeling uneasy, Harper tried to tell herself that she wasn't doing anything wrong. After all, she had every right to work in a club. But then she clocked Frenchy with a tray in her hand and a glass filled to the brim. She placed the tray on the table next to Cox and whispered something to him. That was when she realised that Frenchy was talking about her because he shot around and glared her way before a delighted grin spread across his face.

'Roxy, come here a minute.'

Roxy apologised to her customer and stood in front of Harper. 'What's up?'

'Tell me, was Frenchy friends with Rhea?'

Roxy nodded. 'Yeah, they were close. Why?'

'Did she tell you girls that I may be working here and where I had come from?'

Roxy nodded again. 'She said you were just out of prison and that she wanted to give you a job. So I guess that's why Frenchy had the right hump because she has always wanted the management position. You wanna watch her. She is forever sucking up to people. I reckon she thought you did the dirty on her.' She shrugged her shoulders. 'Me, I don't care who's who, as long as I get paid and live a peaceful life, and to be honest, Rhea was a right fucking bitch to work for. Anyway, why d'you ask?'

Harper flicked her eyes to Cox. 'I think she just told him about me.'

'What a fucking skanky whore.'

'Never mind. It is what it is, and I'll have to deal with it, one way or another.'

Harper thought back to the worry over the fifty grand on her head. Surely no man in their right mind would kill her in the club in front of everyone, including a bent copper? She hoped that the flat would be a safe place until she could meet this Richard and talk to him, so he could hear her side of the story.

It wasn't long before Cox was back at the bar. His smarmy smile and the one eye that moved out of sync with the other demonstrated to Harper that he was pissed.

'I'll have another one, and you, Lula, or Harper, or whatever you prefer to be called, can bring it over and keep me company.'

Feeling her throat tighten, she held back from wanting to clump him one. She hated men like him. But she needed this job, so, politely, she said, 'I will have Frenchy bring your drink over.'

Livid, as well as drunk, Cox slammed his hand on the bar. 'I said, I want *you* to bring me over the drink and to keep me company, or shall I tell Vadim that you're a dangerous bird to have around? Or, of course, I could always pay your probation officer a little visit.'

'Mr Cox, what about *my* company? We never actually sat together and talked,' said Roxy, as she moved along the bar, practically pushing Harper out of the way.

'No, you are not my type, but you' – he poked Harper in the chest – 'are right up my street . . . for now, that is.'

Harper couldn't comprehend that this copper could be so cocksure that any one of the girls in the club would do as he said, but on the other hand, she was pretty sure he had Vadim's backing, or else he indeed would have been bounced clean out of the club.

'Sorry, Mr, er . . . Who are you, exactly?' she replied, as she stepped from around the bar and looked Cox over, staring at his shoes.

Cox unexpectedly felt self-conscious. He also peered down at his shoes, wondering what it was she was looking at. He then shuffled, but his awkwardness was replaced by one of annoyance. 'Don't look at me like you're fucking better than me, you cheeky brass.'

A couple of the other girls could hear him over the loud dance music and stared his way.

'Go and sit down, Mr Cox, and I'll bring you over a special cocktail . . . my treat,' said Pixie, trying to intervene.

This time it worked, and Cox walked back to his seat where he slouched and pretended to be interested in the dancers.

Harper noticed Pixie pouring several spirits into a tall glass, and then she popped out a capsule from just inside the elastic of her skirt. She glanced around and then made sure the glass was under the counter before she handled the powder with the intentions of hiding it from view of the CCTV cameras. As soon as her eyes met Harper's, she winked, and Harper returned a grateful smile.

Harper watched Pixie hand Cox the tall drink and chat to him while he took gulps. By the time the glass was almost empty, Harper could literally see the man slide further down in the chair. She chuckled to herself for a moment until she saw Frenchy staring at her.

'I want a word with you.'

Frenchy raised her brow. 'I ain't done anything wrong. Just what I'm paid to do. So what's your problem?'

With an exaggerated grin, followed by a laugh, Harper placed her hands on her hips and said, 'I know what you did, you sly fucking trollop. You told that geezer who I really am, and manager or not, I don't take too kindly to little snakes like you. So let me give you a word of warning. You ever think of crossing me again and I will rip your pretty little face clean off. I have done worse to birds a lot bigger and harder than fucking you, so don't try me. Got it?'

Frenchy shrank into herself. She could see Harper wasn't playing at being tough; she was definitely the real deal. Just her words had a force behind them.

'I said, got it?'

Frenchy nodded. 'Yeah.'

'Good. Go and collect the glasses and take that sour look off your face.'

Frenchy didn't argue. She sloped off and busied herself returning the glasses. She hated that job because the men watching the dancers always felt they had the right to smack her backside or get a quick grope.

As the punters started to leave the premises, Vadim appeared. He glanced over at Cox and laughed. 'I take it Mr Cox was pushing the girls too far again.' He grinned at Pixie.

'I see the first night with your new manager went very well, then?' He directed the question to Frenchy, who suddenly turned bright red.

***

Vadim asked Harper to stay behind. He handed the girls their wages and gave Roxy an extra twenty quid and a wink. It was the first time in years that Harper actually felt a twinge of jealousy. She had wanted him to wink her way. But she needed to focus and not get carried away; besides, she wanted that flat and the job.

The club was empty. Once the bouncers had left, Vadim took Harper to the back room used for storage and refrigeration.

‘Now that you will be my new manager, you must remember that as soon as you use the keys to get in, you must tap three sixes followed by three nines into that device on the wall. Now, I have changed the code because of Rhea’s departure. Only Claude, you, the cleaner, and I know it. The CCTV is only for me to watch the girls. It doesn’t record, so there’s no need to worry about changing tapes.’

Gently, he slipped his arm around her shoulders. ‘Come with me,’ he said, as he walked back towards the office. To her surprise, he slid aside a bookshelf to reveal a door. Removing keys from his pocket, he unlocked it.

‘This is the back door. It connects to the little cottage on the side. I use it when I don’t want to go through the main entrance. You know how it is. Someone ready to fight. Everyone has a grudge. Everyone is nosey, but not you, eh?’

Harper shrugged her shoulders. ‘I have enough in my old life to deal with. I don’t need to worry about anyone else’s business.’

When the door was opened, it was clear that this was once a two-up two-down cottage that for some reason hadn’t been knocked down when the club was built. It was, however, being used. This connecting door was proof of that. To the left, she saw a small living room-cum-office, with the front door leading to the outside, and to the right, there was a small kitchen. Directly in front of her, there was a steep staircase possibly leading to a separate flat or a couple of bedrooms.

‘Is this the flat that comes with the job?’ she asked, hoping it wasn’t but only because the place was joined to the club and the noise would be horrific.

‘No, it’s my main office.’ He then pointed to the front door. ‘And my escape route.’ He laughed, insinuating it was a joke, but she wondered if, in fact, it was.

Before he opened the front door, they heard a knock.

‘Who is it?’ called out Vadim, but the reply was in Russian. Although Harper had no idea what was said, she recognised the person speaking. It was Claude.

Vadim opened the door, and Claude held up a set of keys; they exchanged a few words in Russian before Claude left.

'So tomorrow, come back, and I will show you how to manage the stock and general admin stuff.'

Harper smiled shyly because she found herself in limbo. Was there to be a romantic relationship or had he just wanted a manager and a shag? Deciding not to question it, she stepped down from the doorstep and began walking away from the cottage.

'Harper, wait. Where are you going?'

She stopped and felt a tinge of excitement. 'Oh, I was going to find a cab and go home.'

'No, I'll make sure you get home safe, not by cab, and you haven't taken your wages.'

As much as Harper was a confident woman, she had moments when she felt awkward, and this was one of them.

He pulled a wad of cash out of his jeans pocket. She guessed that there was probably a few hundred quid there and expected him to count it, but he didn't. He handed it to her.

'Take this, for now. Get some decent clothes and your nails done and come back. I will also show you your new flat.'

A black car pulled into a parking space by the club and reversed up to a foot away from them. 'Claude will take you home.' His Russian tone became gentle. 'You will come back tomorrow, won't you?'

She nodded. 'Yes, I will.'

As if she were a high-class lady, Vadim opened the rear door of the Mercedes S Class for her and kissed her gently on the lips. 'I will see you tomorrow.'

Gratefully, Harper sat back, breathed in the smell of new leather, and enjoyed the ambience of the interior.

'What is your postcode?' asked Claude, who was staring through the rear-view mirror.

Harper reeled it off. She had forgotten about a satnav device. She was still getting used to all the mod cons on the outside.

***

A few hundred yards before she reached her mother's front door, she decided to ask Claude to stop. She didn't want anyone knowing her business. And pulling up at three in the morning and getting out of a flash motor would certainly have tongues wagging.

Stepping out, she quietly closed the door behind her and nodded a 'thank you' to Claude. The night air was cool and helped clear her mind. So much had happened in the last few hours compared to being stuck in a prison cell for hours on end doing sod all. Reliving the sexual encounter, she couldn't help but compare Vadim to Teddy. Perhaps they had been too young because she really couldn't remember Teddy being that good. She shook off her thoughts and cursed out loud. She mustn't think of Teddy again. He was with her sister now, and considering how he and Erin had betrayed her, she would block him from her mind completely. Hopefully, her life was now on the up. And the likes of Teddy and the people from the past would stay exactly that – in the past.

Totally oblivious to her surroundings, Harper didn't see Erin across the road watching her until she heard footsteps running towards her. The second she spun around, now aware that there was a fifty-grand contract on her, she was shocked to see her sister with a claw hammer in her hand ready to impale it in her head. In a flash, Harper grabbed Erin's wrist and bent her hand back until she dropped the tool.

'What the fuck are you *doing*?'

Erin was out of breath through anger and the fact that she had just attempted to cause Harper serious harm. For so long, she had allowed her jealousy and anger of her sister to spiral, and now she was out of prison, she was convinced that her sister would claim her old life back.

'You just couldn't let me have him, could ya!' she screamed.

'What are you on about?' replied Harper, backing away from Erin, who was clearly fired up and ready to fight.

'Spent all night shagging him, did you? Well, did you?'

Harper knew Erin was talking about Teddy, and so she could easily have wound her sister up even more. But she decided it was late, and she really didn't want to draw attention to herself and have the probation service recalling her licence and slamming her back in prison.

'Erin, I haven't been with Teddy. I've been to work.'

'You liar. I saw you get out of his Mercedes.'

Harper shook her head. 'You saw me get out of *a* Mercedes but not Teddy's. Why didn't you ask him, Erin?'

'Because he was with you. He's not at home, but I bet he fucking is now, now he's dropped you off.'

'You fucking what? So who is looking after Eddie, if you're here and you thought he was with me?'

Suddenly, Erin's face changed, and her skin seemed milky white. 'He is fine. He's fucking eleven. Not that it's got anything to do with you.'

'So, is my boy indoors on his own at three in the fucking morning?'

'Oh, shut up, Harper, it's not your business.'

Seeing a flash of red mist descending, Harper grabbed her sister by the throat and pulled her close to her face. 'Have you left my boy *alone*?'

Erin, coughing and panting, now desperate to pull Harper's fingers away from her windpipe, dropped her phone.

Unexpectedly, Erin's phone rang, and Harper let loose her grip.

It was Teddy. Harper spotted his name flashing on the screen. Instantly, she reached down and snatched the phone while Erin continued to cough and tried to catch her breath.

‘Teddy, this is Harper. What the hell is going on? Erin is outside my house, and with you gone all night, my little boy was home alone.’

‘Harps, no, she was here. I . . . er . . . I only popped out.’

Hearing the stutter in his voice, Harper was fuming. ‘You think I was born yesterday! My sister is here because she thought you were out all night with me, and it’s now three-fifteen, and this stupid bitch has been lurking like a fucking stalker waiting for me to get home. So my boy was left alone.’

‘Keep your hair on, Harps. He is fine. He is in his room, soundo . . .’

Harper heard Teddy climbing the stairs, but she waited anxiously, her heart now in her mouth, as she had a bad feeling about this.

‘Eddie, are you in the bathroom?’ she heard Teddy calling, and then she heard his voice get louder with an alarmed tone to it.

‘Teddy, Teddy, answer me. Is Eddie there? What’s going on? Teddy!’

Erin was now breathing okay, and she tried to take back her phone. ‘Give it to me, Harper.’

But Harper held the phone tightly to her ear as she backhanded Erin clean around the mouth.

‘Teddy, fucking answer me! Is my boy *there*?’

A voice, barely audible, said, ‘No, Harper, he’s not here. Look, ask Erin. She’s probably dropped him at a mate’s.’

Harper glared at her sister. The blood was seeping from a corner of her sister’s mouth. ‘Here, tell Teddy where Eddie is.’

Taking the phone from her sister, Erin frowned as if Harper was speaking another language. ‘*What?* He was in bed.’

It took a few minutes before the realisation hit them both. Eddie was not there.

Delores, hearing the shouting and screaming, ushered her two daughters inside. 'For fuck's sake, why do you always have to make a fucking show of me? You'll wake up the whole street. Get inside, before the police turn up an' all. That's all I fucking need,' she said, practically yanking Erin into the hallway.

Harper took the phone from Erin, who was now looking very sheepish.

'Teddy, where is he?' Her voice cracked in fear.

'I don't know, Harper. His bed has not even been slept in.'

Harper glared again at Erin. 'Where is *my boy*?'

'I swear I don't know. He was upstairs. He likes his room. I only popped out.'

'His bed hasn't been slept in. You left him alone.'

Erin's fear turned to anger. 'Don't be so dramatic. He is an eleven-year-old boy. He is not a baby.'

'He is *my* baby. I swear to God, if anything has happened to him, I will kill you, Erin. With my bare hands, I will murder you.'

'If you hadn't got locked up, then you would have brought the kid up yourself. But now, after eleven years of me seeing to his every need, you wanna lay into me and judge me.'

'You weren't supposed to stop him from seeing me. You took my baby and kept him for yourself, and you took my fella. You even took my life, Erin.' She poked herself in the chest. 'My fucking life.'

'No, Harper, you ruined all of ours.'

Lexi was standing on the middle tread of the stairs. 'Shut up, Erin. She didn't ruin our lives. We did that all by ourselves. Now, what's this about Little Eddie?'

Harper looked at her sister dressed in a thin nightie, and it was then that she could see just how frail she actually was. With a bruised face and her thin and straggly hair, she appeared the polar opposite to Erin, who had it all – the perfect skin, mountains of thick hair, and a tracksuit that would have cost a pretty penny.

‘He’s gone missing. This bitch assumed I was seeing Teddy because he didn’t go home. But she’s left my boy home alone. And now Teddy’s home but Eddie’s missing.’

The phone rang again. Harper, in all the shouting, must have cut Teddy off. ‘Have you got him?’

‘No. I’m calling the police. Tell Erin to get home. They will want to talk to her.’

Delores was still trying to close the front door, but with arms flailing and everyone seeming to be shouting at once, she gave up and stepped back.

‘Get off home, Erin,’ growled Delores. ‘I bet the lad’s having a sleepover and forgot to tell you.’

Erin barged past Harper, knocking her arm as a statement. But she didn’t expect Harper to snatch her by the hair and pull her back. ‘I warn you, Erin, if my boy is hurt, you’re fucking dead.’

The hair extension suddenly came off in Harper’s hand. She looked Erin up and down. ‘You really are a fake bitch, aren’t you?’

‘Piss off, you loser,’ hissed Erin, as she snatched the hairpiece and stormed out of the door and along the street.

‘Let her go, Harper. You don’t want to end up back inside over her,’ said Lexi.

As soon as the door slammed shut, Harper fell to her knees, placed her hands over her face, and sobbed – the cry getting caught in her throat.

Lexi was shocked. She had never witnessed her sister shed a single tear. She was the tough one, the one who never felt pain.

But it was Delores who helped her daughter up on to her feet. ‘Come on, girl. Sit yaself down in the living room. I’ll make you a coffee.’

Guiding Harper to the living room, Delores could feel the weight of emotion. As her daughter tried to wipe her eyes, Delores, for the first time in her life, actually felt the girl’s pain and could feel her own eyes welling up with tears. 'I'll go and make that coffee,' she said, before she shouted up the stairs, 'Lexi, bring your sister a fag, will ya, and I'll have one, an' all!'

Lexi, who had run up the stairs to check on her baby, hurried back down. 'Mum, don't shout. You will wake Yosef.' She handed her mother a cigarette and then rushed over to her sister. ''Ere, Sis, take this. It'll calm your nerves. Little Eddie will be okay. He has lots of mates. I bet he's gone to theirs.'

Delores entered the room and sat in her armchair. 'Lex, finish off making the coffee, will ya? The kettle has just boiled.'

Lexi followed her mother's instruction, knowing she obviously wanted a private word.

With Lexi in the kitchen, Delores handed Harper a tissue from a toilet roll on the side. 'A lot has changed since you went away, and I know I ain't been the best of mothers, but don't push your sisters away. We are family. We should stick together.'

Harper laughed. 'I know you probably mean well, but come on, Delores, you don't know the meaning of the words "stick together". Where is Charley? 'Cos you didn't fight to keep her as part of the family, did you? And you didn't discourage Erin from taking my life.'

Delores puffed on her cigarette. 'She *didn't* take your life. She just ended up bringing up your son and living with your ex.'

'They were my life, Delores. They were my whole fucking world.'

Lexi came into the room with a mug of coffee. ''Ere you are, Sis. Maybe you should try to rest, and as soon as Erin or Teddy have any news, they will be on the phone. Kids especially his age go off and do foolish things. They have ideas of running away because they didn't get an ice cream for afters. They are back home the next morning.'

Harper wiped her face with the tissue and noticed it was covered in black mascara. She took the mug and slowly sipped the coffee. It was really sweet. She wasn't used to so much sugar, although before she was sent to prison, she took three heaped spoonfuls in her coffee.

'Cheers, Lex. It's just how I like it.'

Lexi smiled. 'I remembered, Sis.'

Out of the blue, Lexi leaned forward and kissed Harper's forehead. 'I really missed you, Sis.'

Harper nodded. 'And I missed you too, Lex. In fact, all of ya.'

'He'll be okay.'

Harper wiped her face again. 'What is he like, Lex? Is he a good boy, polite? Or is he a little man's man, all cars and wrestling?'

Lexi sat on the floor beside her sister. 'He is a real sweetie. He is so caring and polite. He's a little nervy, sometimes, but he is just a little lad. He is so sweet with my Yosef. He plays really nicely and gently with him. He is one of those little boys that will melt your heart as soon as you lay eyes on him.'

Harper was smiling and crying at the same time. 'Is he like Teddy?'

Lexi shook her head. 'No, Harps, he is like you. He's your double, only cuter.'

Delores took herself off to bed, leaving Lexi curled on the sofa and Harper in the armchair staring off into space. There wasn't much else she could do, and sitting drinking coffee and smoking Lexi's fags wouldn't close the bridge between Harper and herself. That bond was broken for good. In fact, she thought to herself, there had never been a bond. Erin was the only child she'd ever had any time for. She didn't have anything in common with the others, who were nothing like her side of the family.

Chapter Eight

The landline phone rang, which almost made Harper jump out of her skin.

Lexi rubbed her eyes. Suddenly realising what was happening, she straightened herself up.

Harper flew across the room and held the phone to her ear. Her heart was thumping so fast she thought she wouldn't be able to hear anything over the powerful drumming of her pulse.

Teddy's voice sounded confident. 'He is fine, safe and sound. I just thought you should know.'

A belt of rage cracked like a whip. 'You just thought I should fucking *know*?' Her voice was on the verge of waking up the whole street. 'Where was he?'

'He must have gone sleepwalking. The police found him under the willow tree in the garden, wrapped up in a blanket fast asleep. So, calm down. He is fine.'

'*Calm down?* Are you fucking delusional? I won't calm down, Teddy. You and my senseless bitch of a sister left my son alone, and he went sleepwalking. What if he had gone sleepwalking in the road and got killed, eh?'

'Listen, Harper, your sister's having a tough time, at the moment. Cut her some slack, will you.'

'*A tough time!* What the fucking hell do you think I was doing for twelve years? Having a party with the happy fairies? You lily-livered tosser of a man. I will fight you for him, Teddy, so get ready to man up, because, believe me, I will get my boy back.'

With that, she slammed down the receiver. 'What a fucking arsehole, and as for my sister, the evil bitch, what did I ever do to her?'

Lexi looked down as if she was actually hiding something.

'Lex, what's going on? If you know something, tell me! What was I supposed to have done to her to make her detest me?'

'I suppose you might as well know. Erin was making out with Ted when you were on remand. She got pregnant. And 'cos you were having a baby, Teddy told her to have an abortion. Anyway, the abortion went wrong, and they had to remove her womb, so she can't have kids, and she blames you for that. She said that if you hadn't always got your own way, then she would have a family of her own with her own child.'

Harper threw her hands to her mouth in shock.

'But you know what? I blame Erin. I do, really. She was throwing herself at Teddy and pretending to comfort him when you got nicked, but, all the while, she was enticing him into her bed. Everyone could see what she was doing except him. Then, when he turned to drink, of course, one thing led to another, and before you were even convicted and sentenced, she had his pants off. When you told us you were expecting, Teddy pushed her away and felt guilty, but, then, *she* dropped the biggest bombshell by saying she too was pregnant.'

'I didn't tell Teddy I was expecting right away because I didn't even know myself, what with getting nicked and then going to prison. I was at least four months before I realised, so I could never have had an abortion – not that I would've anyway, even if Teddy had begged me. But, Lex, having an abortion is shocking. She must have been so upset when Teddy asked her to get rid of it. And by Christ, she must have loved him to go through with it because I wouldn't have.' She sighed. 'But why did he though, really?' asked Harper.

Lexi sighed. 'The lawyers told him that at some point you would have to hand the baby out and obviously to him, since he is the father. He knew you so well, Harps, because he guessed you wouldn't *want* to keep the child in a place like that. Erin, with all her fake promises, vowed to help, but really it was a ploy to suck him in. But he said he couldn't have two babies the same age. It wouldn't work out.'

'Couples have twins.'

Lexi shook her head. 'No, he meant she would favour her own child. So, anyway, she had the termination, but, as I said, she can't have kids now, so she blames you.'

'That's stupid, and I don't believe that's the real reason she fucking hates me so much.'

'She hates you, Harps, because she has always been second best. And that's not your fault either. Everyone likes you, but they just tolerate her. Even me, 'cos, Harps, she can be spiteful. She wants to hurt you because she had to bring up Eddie and not her own child, but she took it that Teddy wanted your kid and not hers.'

Harper took a deep breath and forcefully exhaled. 'Well, watch me, Lex. I will get my boy back and . . .'

'And the man?' said Lexi, finishing her sister's sentence.

'No, Lex, not the man. She can have that prick. I wouldn't go back with him, not now he's been with me sister, but I might just fuck him to piss her off.'

Lexi giggled, and her eyes, which were apart from being swollen, lit up.

'Never mind all that, Lex, I need to get you somewhere safe, and I might just have a place.'

'Really? What, a secret place?'

Harper nodded. 'I've got myself a job, and it comes with a flat. I'm off to work later, and, hopefully, I will have the keys. You, me, and the baby can move in then, and soon, I will have my boy as well. Imagine it, Lex. It will be great. You can watch Eddie while I work, and I can watch the baby during the day while you do whatever it is you want.'

Lexi clapped her hands together like a kid.

It pleased Harper, and she smiled from ear to ear before she placed her finger over her lips. 'Trust not a soul.'

Lexi smiled and nodded, realising that as much as everyone had said prison would change her sister, she was relieved to discover it hadn't. Harper was still the mothering soul she had always been.

***

Harper called Vanessa to check in but left out the fact that she had a job. She didn't want the probation officer to deny her the right to work in a bar, although the crime for which she was convicted wasn't alcohol-related. Still, she didn't want to take that risk, not until she had secured the flat and everything was going okay.

After a few hours of sleep, Harper went to Bromley where she had her nails manicured and took in some dress shopping. She had the money and would use it to get herself shipshape. By the time she jumped on the bus, it was reaching three o'clock. She felt so much better after having a few highlights put in her short hair, her eyebrows tinted, and her nails given a French manicure. And with the sunglasses and plain black sleeveless summer dress set off by a pair of slingback sandals, her confidence was through the roof. She noticed a few young men look her way and give her a second glance. This was new. She hadn't sensed she was attractive before she went to prison, but now it was as if she'd had a facelift. And she wondered what the difference was. The only thing she could think of was the short hair. Perhaps it suited her more than she'd first thought.

With a large black bag slung over her shoulder filled with gifts, Harper put the key in the lock and headed inside her mother's house.

Delores stood with her mouth open. 'Fuck me, did you win the lottery? Or have you found yourself some sheikh to sell your arse to?'

'You have to lower the tone every fucking time. If you must know, I went to work last night. I was promoted to manager, and the club owner gave me an advance to have a brush-up. So I did.'

Delores looked her daughter over and curled her lip. 'Think you're special, I suppose.'

Harper ignored her mother's gibes and fished inside her bag for a black shopping bag. ''Ere.' She handed it to her mother.

'What's this?'

'Just a present for letting me stay here. Because the truth is, you didn't have to, did you?'

Delores's face changed. Seemingly looking a little awkward, she nervously removed the dress from the bag. It was long and flowy and had a beautiful tropical print with a fringe along the hem.

Holding it up against herself, she replied, 'This must have cost a pretty penny. You didn't have to, but thanks.' Still embarrassed, Delores hurried up the stairs to try it on.

Lexi was feeding Yosef some cheesy-smelling concoction from a jar. 'Wow, wit-woo, Harper. You look like a celebrity.'

Harper smiled and rolled her eyes. 'I wanted to look my best for work tonight,' she said, as she placed the bag on the sofa. Again, she fished inside for the other presents and handed them to Lexi. 'A tracky for you, and a couple of T-shirts. Oh, and there are a few bits for the baby.'

Lexi looked up with the spoon in her hand. 'For *me*? Blimey, it's been a long time since anyone treated me. Thanks, Sis.'

Harper felt the sadness in Lexi's voice, and it cut her to the core to think she had given a man a beautiful baby, and yet he couldn't even treat her to a decent rig-out. She'd noticed the lack of passable clobber on Lexi when she came to see her on a prison visit.

The rest of the day seemed to drag for Harper before she left to go to work. All the way to the club, she thought of Vadim and wondered if he was full of shit or the genuine article. Obviously, she hoped for the latter.

Claude's Mercedes was parked by the entrance along with a couple of other cars that she didn't recognise. The club seemed more inviting this evening. She thought that perhaps it was because she felt less self-conscious and happier that she had a job that came with a bit of power, and, of course, a man who showed her attention and made her feel special.

After a couple of knocks, Claude opened the door. He looked a little tired with stubble on his chin and the top button of his shirt undone. Glancing her over, he frowned because initially he didn't recognise her. Then he raised his eyebrows. 'Come in, Harper, and no smashing bottles tonight, especially vodka bottles.'

Harper sensed he was trying to be funny, but his stern face had her questioning whether he was or not.

Forcing a smile, she stepped inside. 'Is Vadim here?'

Claude flicked his head for her to follow him. 'Yes, come, Harper. He was hoping you would come back.'

Sensing the urgency and the speed at which Claude marched towards the office, Harper formed the impression she was to become part of something important. She soon found out that she wasn't wrong.

Vadim, who was sitting behind his desk, wasn't alone. Three men were also present. The office was stuffy, and she clocked the men's sweaty faces and crumpled clothes. Phones were laid out on the desk, and she also spotted an empty bottle of vodka on the side.

Vadim looked up, and the second he saw Harper, his eyes brightened. Swiftly jumping to his feet, he waved his hands. 'Please, gentlemen, leave us.'

There was no discussion. The three businessmen and Claude left the office, closing the door behind them.

'You look, um . . . I think the word is striking. I would say very Russian, but you may not take that as a compliment.'

Harper shrugged. 'Words should only be taken as compliments if they are meant that way.'

'Sit, sit.' He waved his hand, indicating that she should take the chair opposite him.

Gracefully, she sat and waited.

'Something has come up, and I must leave the country for a few days. Some business of mine needs my urgent attention.'

She nodded. 'And?'

'And so I need someone I can trust. Now, Harper, I know you probably think that we have only just met, so why, you may be thinking, should I trust you? But I am an excellent judge of character. I know you are honest and fair, and you are not the type to, er . . . what's the saying, again?' He paused; then he laughed. 'Yes, you won't bite the hand that feeds you.'

Harper smiled. 'You do good by me, Vadim, and I will return the favour. You must know I spent many years inside, and I learned a lot, including what loyalty means.'

He opened the top left-hand drawer of his desk and frowned. 'Claude must have the keys to your flat. It's not far from here. He will show you where it is. Now, while I am away, please make sure the girls do their jobs. Don't tell them that I am out of the country. In fact, don't tell *anyone* my business or yours at all.'

'I won't. I'm not one for gossip.'

He smiled and winked, which made her legs feel like jelly. She was attracted to him – she was sure of that now.

'Pay each of the girls a hundred pounds a night. Any nonsense from any one of them, then just fire them. There are plenty of girls willing to work for that kind of money. If the punters get out of hand, call for Claude, and he will throw them out. All the money at the end of the night, you can put in the safe, but please keep a record – for the taxman, you see. And take whatever you need.'

'You are very generous, and yes, Vadim, very trusting. I don't understand why.'

There was a long pause as Vadim looked her over. His eyes appeared tired. 'Indeed, there are not many people I can trust, but there is something about you. You were prepared to fight to protect Rhea when she was ready to set you up. You are a strong woman, and a kind woman, and . . .' He laughed. 'I like you very much.'

He rose from his seat and walked around the desk where he leaned down and kissed her lips. 'You are so beautiful and yet you don't even know it yourself. But I do.'

Harper felt her cheeks burning.

'I must go.' He kissed her again, and then he looked at his watch.

She sensed his urgency and decided not to hold him up.

He held the door open, and as soon as she walked out, he locked the door, and handed her the keys to the club. 'Having these will give you authority. Yet . . .' He laughed. 'I think the girls respect you already. Take care, Harper.'

He was gone before Harper even had a chance to take it all in. But she wasn't about to look a gift horse in the mouth. She told herself that this would be an opportunity to prove to Vadim that she was trustworthy.

Somehow, the club seemed huge as she wandered around.

Unexpectedly, Claude appeared. He'd been bending down behind the bar.

'Is everything okay?'

She didn't expect his look of disdain.

'Yes. Why?'

'I wondered what you were doing, that's all.'

'Looking for a phone I lost. Anyway, it's not there,' he growled.

His attitude was a bit off, making Harper think that perhaps he didn't care too much for her. Not that she was worried. After all, Vadim was her boss, not Claude.

***

Richard slipped into Fliss's bed and made her jump when his cold hands grabbed her breasts.

'Richard, really, do you have to be so sodding rough. Boobs are meant to be caressed, not fucking groped and squeezed. It doesn't give me pleasure. It fucking hurts.'

Richard was not in the best of moods since his brother hadn't turned up to collect the money and Rhea wasn't returning his calls. He hated it when a woman wouldn't jump to his attention. The only one who could partially get away with it was his wife, and that was because she kept a clean home, ignored his indiscretions, and didn't stick her nose into his business affairs. His father was his idol, and his mother was a bitch, so he had no time for women, apart from using them for his own needs.

'If I want a bloody squeeze, I'll have one.'

Fliss sensed the tension in his voice and knew not to antagonise him. She was due on soon, and her breasts were swollen and still very painful. Yet one of his backhanders would be worse.

'Get your drawers off, Fliss. I ain't got time to mess about. I'm a busy man.'

Fliss was having second thoughts about their relationship. She certainly wasn't finding him attractive anymore. In fact, she was beginning to despise him. And the worst of it was, the more she froze up and used excuses not to have sex, the rougher he got. The only real reason she stayed as his mistress was for the flat, the car, and everything else that he paid for. She would lose the lot if she fucked him off. So, with nowhere else to go, she stayed and suffered. It had crossed her mind that if he pushed her too far, she would go to the cops, and, hopefully, they would put her in a safe house. The only issue would be if they didn't believe her or if they saw her as his long-standing bit on the side who wanted to do him wrong. The worrying part was that if it went pear-shaped, he would kill her, for sure.

'Come on, girl, I'm in a rush,' he said, now annoyed. 'If you don't want to give me a good fuck then I will kick you out of this flat and replace you with a younger bird.'

Fliss's eyes widened. 'What? Like a teenager?' No sooner were the words out than she wished she had shut her mouth. His temper was brutal and getting worse by the month.

Pushing himself up and off the bed, in one fluid movement, he grabbed the mattress and tipped her out of bed and onto the polished tiled floor. Winded, she gasped for breath and felt every bone in her body vibrate in pain. But she had to get away before he could do some severe damage. However, as she attempted to get up, she found she couldn't move her leg, and the fear of being paralysed sent her into a blind panic.

Screaming in such a high-pitched deafening voice made Richard stop dead in his tracks. He'd never heard her scream like that.

'Oh, no, no! I can't move my leg!'

Richard saw her face drain of any colour and knew she wasn't playing games.

'What have you done, you silly cow?'

Fliss, in her satin slip and blonde curls, which hung damp with sweat around her face, was struggling to breathe. She couldn't answer. It was apparent she was in agonising pain.

But all that ran through Richard's mind was the aggro this would cause. If she accused him of breaking her back or hip, or whatever it was she'd done, then the police would have grounds to get him down to the station and pin all sorts on him. And right now, he had a very lucrative deal that needed his attention. He couldn't mess this up, or he would have the nastiest Russian stringing him up KGB-style, whatever that meant.

He glanced at his watch. It was eight o'clock. He had to be at the meeting point in two hours. He couldn't stay here to see to Fliss.

'Help me, Richard. Call an ambulance. I can't move my leg . . . and the pain. Oh, Richard, please do something. Help me.' Her face was now a greyish colour.

Richard straightened the mattress and then attempted to help her on to the bed. She screamed out, and he stopped. 'Shut up. I need to move ya, you silly bloody woman.'

'Oh, Richard, the pain is unbearable. What's happened to me?'

Bending down again, he tried to scoop her up, but she squealed so loudly, he felt his eardrums almost bursting. Regardless, he carried on until he managed to lay her on top of the bed. Grabbing a pillow from the floor, he put it under her head. 'There, is that better? I've got to go. But I'll be back.'

Fliss grabbed his arm. 'No, Richard, please don't leave me. I feel weird. I don't feel good at all. Call an ambulance, will you? I think I've really hurt myself.'

Richard looked at his watch again. He didn't have time to do anything except button his shirt and force his feet into his shoes.

'Please, Rich . . .'

Not bothering to answer, he left the room quietly, closing the front door behind him. He would sort her out when he returned.

***

Once he was inside his car, he called Rhea again, but it went straight to voicemail, like the hundred calls before. His temper was now raging, and if he could get his hands on her, he would take her head off her shoulders. She was paid well to do as she was told. He wondered if Rhea was getting too big for her boots. Working for Vadim gave her some protection, and he would never step on Vadim's turf, but Vadim was nothing compared to the Russian he was dealing with. Although he hadn't met him face to face, there was enough evidence to suggest that he was a very dangerous and violent man. He was also extremely rich, and Richard wanted to be a bigger part of his business. He had supplied the main Russian with the goods via Rhea, right under Vadim's nose. And no one had suspected a thing. The Russian's contacts had told him that there were others in the club ensuring that the deals were successful, and so, up until now, all was hunky-dory. No one had reported back to the Russian anything that would upset their financial arrangement, so far as he was aware.

'Damn!' He banged the steering wheel when Rhea's phone went straight to voicemail once more.

Anger mixed with anxiety made Richard twitchy. He looked in his rear-view mirror a million times to check no one was following him. He then banged the steering wheel again, the second Fliss popped into his head. 'Why did you have to fucking wind me up!' he shouted to himself.

Dead on ten o'clock, he drove down a country lane and took the long drive that was almost a closed tunnel where the green bushes and trees bowed across it. Finally, he arrived at the huge house. The garage attached to the side of the building was open, and he could see two cars inside. There was also a black van, which he knew was used by funeral directors. It made him shudder and reminded him of the day they had carried his father away, in the very same type of vehicle. He'd only been thirteen, and at the time, he couldn't quite understand why his father was being taken away in a plain black van with no urgency about it, instead of in an ambulance with flashing blue lights. It was the last impression he'd been left with.

As he stepped out on to the crunchy gravel, he saw the helicopter in the field at the back. He then clocked one of the foot soldiers guarding the side of the building. The Russians were always so ready for an attack that they guarded the place like they were protecting the Russian president. This was serious, heavy stuff.

His brow was now laced in beads of sweat. He hated feeling so uneasy. Rhea was supposed to have sent photos of the girls, so that he could forward them on, but although she had promised him two girls, she still wasn't answering her phone, and neither was she sending through the photos. He had to believe she would carry out her job, as she had done a hundred times before, and that on this one occasion, she had simply misplaced her phone.

Two dark terrifying thoughts shot through him. What if the police had arrested her? What if the Russian already knew? He swallowed hard as his stomach sounded like an orchestra. There were suddenly so many what-ifs, it was leaving him feeling as though he was balancing on a cliff edge in a strong wind.

He had been told earlier by his contact that he would meet the elusive Russian by the name of Zavid. Judging by the signs of excessive security, he guessed they were telling the truth – that the main man they all feared was indeed in the building. Another frightening thought popped into his head. If something had gone terribly wrong with the deal, he could be executed, bagged up, and thrown into one of the coffins inside that black van.

The front door of the house opened, and there in black army clothes and carrying a gun was one of the guards; he pointed the gun and flicked his thumb over his shoulder, indicating that Richard should go inside.

Taking a deep breath, Richard wiped his brow and took confident strides along the hallway to the largest of the rooms to the right.

Surrounding the main man were four soldiers.

Richard felt his mouth dry up and his throat tighten.

'Come in,' said Zavid, the Russian, a slim man, who was dressed surprisingly in a pair of jeans and a white linen shirt.

Richard stepped forward and held out his hand.

Zavid dismissed his offer of a handshake. 'I have my best customer going into the club tonight expecting to see two young girls you arranged for me, but I have not received their photos.'

Richard attempted to explain himself but was instantly silenced by Zavid raising his hand.

‘This client is a very dear friend and one who I really would not want to upset. You were given the details: blonde, blue eyes, slim, with budding breasts, and you said that you would have your people find such specimens and have them brought to the club to work so that my client could see them with smiles on their faces,’ he said, as his head twitched sharply to the side.

Richard could now feel his face burning. If he ever got out of the place alive, he would kill Rhea.

‘I have gone to great lengths to arrange this. You see, Vadim knows my client, and I couldn’t risk him recognising the man. So, I have, let’s just say, caused chaos in Russia for Vadim, and he has gone back to make good the mess. All of this has cost me greatly, so, as you can imagine, I cannot lose the money my client was willing to pay for the girls, and I cannot lose face with my client either, because he, let’s just say, ensures my life in the UK is safe and secure. So, Richard, I have empowered you with what is a very big deal for me.’

With every word that Zavid spoke, Richard felt his heart beating faster and faster. He wondered if he was going to have a heart attack on the spot. He waited until Zavid had finished speaking before making a feeble attempt at reassuring the man that everything was in hand.

‘Don’t worry. The two girls will be at the club tonight.’ He realised his voice was making a cracking sound because he was so nervous.

‘They are no doubt there already pouring drinks and looking pretty. As promised, there are two of them, both blonde and aged fourteen.’

Zavid looked up through his eyelashes. ‘And you are sure these girls are not older?’

Richard showed the palms of his hands. ‘My source has never been wrong before. She is as good as having a catalogue to order from. Have I ever let you down?’ He tried to sound assertive, considering he was talking to a younger man and one not in a business suit.

Watching Zavid look at the men standing directly on either side of him, Richard felt his stomach churn. They were smirking.

'You think I care about past business?' Zavid shook his head. 'I don't. It means nothing to me.'

Richard suddenly felt the measure of the man and he coughed. 'Uh, sorry, yes, I was just saying—'

Zavid held up his hand to shut Richard up.

'Hmmm, so where are the photos of these girls? You were supposed to send them to me, and I have nothing.' He held up his phone and waved it about.

'Sorry, but believe me, the girls are very pretty, and, as I said, very young, and they will be at the club ready for your client to view. I promise you that.'

Zavid laughed. 'Oh. I hope you didn't think I would just let you walk away and accept your feeble promise. No, you can be a special guest of mine here at the house until my client has chosen his goods.'

Richard felt his tongue become glued to the roof of his mouth. He had no idea if Rhea had managed to secure the two girls because she wasn't answering her bloody phone. 'I won't let you down.'

When Zavid smirked, Richard sensed the cold darkness behind that cruel grin. It was the first time that he wished he had never got involved. Yet, the money was not to be sniffed at. He felt as if he had shot up to the next level. His business had grown, and although his goods were young girls, and he could serve a very long time if caught for human trafficking, he mentally justified the dosh against the potential loss. He had secured a lifestyle that he'd longed for, and he wouldn't jeopardise that. He also assumed that being part of what was known as the 'Seahorse Club' would offer him some protection. However, he was quickly grasping the fact that there was no joining of forces. He worked for this man – nothing more.

'Richard, you must have been told some things about me. If you are a clever businessman, you would have done some homework to understand that I do not take risks and never give second chances. Even if you are loyal for fifty years, my men will tell you that the one time you let me down, I will kill you. You, Richard, have been merely a business client. You have your own people to source the product, and you get paid, but when you fuck up, you die.'

He looked down at his shoes and sucked in air through his gritted teeth. 'I cannot afford to upset my best clients. And, Richard, you are easily replaceable. There are many men out there like you, so think hard about that. I have put a lot of faith in you, and, of course, trust, but, again, I give no second chances. You can wait here. I will pay you, but only once my client is happy. And know this: you die, if he is *not* happy.'

Richard could now hear his stomach contents swishing about and wondered if his bowels would tighten and stop him from shitting himself. He now realised that his portion of the drug dealings and prostitute rackets in South London was nothing in comparison. This was international business and on a whole other level. He had to admit he was probably in way over his head.

***

The vomiting seemed to have subsided, and the other girls were sleeping better. Kera looked at her ankle; it appeared to have improved. At least the swelling had gone down a bit. A distant clip-clop sound, like a woman walking in high-heeled shoes, pulled Kera from her thoughts. 'Hey, girls, listen. A woman is coming. I can hear her.'

The other girls sat up and were deathly quiet. Then Coral, the youngest, at only thirteen, suddenly clapped her hands. 'Yes! Yes! We're being rescued.'

As the footsteps approached, they could also hear a padding sound, possibly from men's leather soled boots.

The girls got up and jumped on their mattresses. 'We are saved!' they cried.

Kera was hoping that they were right.

The door opened, and there wearing a check Chanel suit, her hair in an elegant bob, stood a woman. Beside her were two men dressed entirely in black.

Kera knew then that they weren't the police. They looked just like the men who had bundled her into the coffin.

'Girls!' she said, quietening the excitable racket.

'Quick, please help us before that awful man comes back,' said Lauren, the posh girl whose parents had died in a yachting accident.

'No one is going anywhere. Now then, I have fresh nightwear and that area over there,' she pointed with a perfectly manicured finger to the tiled corner of the room where there was a pipe protruding from the top of the wall, 'is, in fact, a shower. So I want you each, in turn, to get undressed and have a thorough washdown.'

The silence said it all. The girls' hopes of being rescued were utterly dashed, and now more shocking was a woman making demands.

A woman? *How could she?* thought Kera.

Kera knew the purpose of being locked up. They were to be sold as sex slaves; yet the other girls, in their innocence, refused to believe it.

The woman beckoned Kera over. 'Strip!' she demanded.

But Kera glanced at 'the beast' as she called him. He was ogling her breasts again, licking his lips as if he had severe learning difficulties.

'No, I won't. He is staring at me.'

'Larsen, leave!' the woman bellowed, before she turned to Kera. 'He wouldn't interfere with you. It would be the last thing he would do because he knows your virginity must remain intact. Or you are worthless to me.'

Instantly, Kera replied, 'Well, you may as well let me go because I am no virgin, lady.'

The woman smirked. ‘Ah, well, in that case, Larsen may as well have you. Because he doesn’t care if you are a virgin or not. He will use every orifice in your body for his own amusement.’

Kera’s eyes widened in horror. ‘Okay, missus. Listen, I *am* a virgin. Really, I am.’

The woman nodded to the other guard to cut loose the girl’s tracksuit bottoms.

Kera couldn’t stop the tears falling as the woman allowed the humiliation to take place. Naked and vulnerable, she stood helpless under the cold shower. The woman demanded that Kera lathered every inch of her body, even in front of the man.

Chapter Nine

Although Saturday night was bound to be the busiest evening, Harper took her time to get to grips with the running of the club by going through the ordering system, checking where all the stock was kept, and completely familiarising herself with the place. The girls began to arrive and to take their positions behind the bar. The dancers sauntered in; some were as high as kites, others looked the worse for wear, but Harper knew that they would be good to go once they'd popped a few uppers and slapped on the make-up.

The lights came on and lit up various club areas, leaving some of the VIP sections subtly lit; she assumed this arrangement was done for the benefit of the shadier clients. All the tables were reserved for regular punters.

When Frenchy arrived, Harper noticed how different she seemed. With a smile, Frenchy offered to make Harper a coffee. However, Harper wasn't that stupid. No one's character changes overnight. She returned the smile and shook her head. 'No thanks, Frenchy, and why the sudden personality transplant?'

Frenchy laughed. 'Oh, come on, Harper, every new girl gets initiated.'

With a puckered brow and a death stare, Harper retaliated. 'Initiation? Really? I think you took an instant dislike to me, and since then and now, something has made you become more pleasant. Either that, Frenchy, or you planned to put some sleeping pills in my coffee. And, Frenchy, let's get something straight, shall we? I'm not the new *girl*. I'm the new *manager*.'

Frenchy's face flushed with humiliation and anger. But she kept her lips curved in a smile and unclenched her fists. She couldn't afford to be thrown out tonight. But inside, she was boiling because there was something about Harper that made her uneasy. Perhaps it was her fear of her, or, more likely, the fact that the woman seemed to command attention and could potentially change the dynamics in the club. Disturbingly, Harper could mess up everything she had worked so hard towards. Before Harper had arrived as manager, she was getting somewhere. She had a good relationship with Rhea and things were going well. Now, literally overnight, all that had changed. The most crucial task this evening was to take care of the two young girls, who were due to arrive at any time, without Harper causing a problem. But with Rhea's phone still off, it would be pot luck if those kids arrived or not. All she had to do was to keep the girls behind the bar until the nod was given, and then they would be escorted out via the back door.

A hot feeling ran from her neck to her forehead; it always happened when she felt anxious. And this evening was probably the most apprehensive she had ever felt.

'All right, so to be honest, Harper, I was a little bit peeved because Vadim always said I was deputy manager, and if Rhea ever left, I was next in line. But then, you showed up, and you were straight in, and you don't even know the club.' She looked down as if she was genuinely upset.

'Okay, Frenchy, fair enough. I suppose I would've been pretty pissed off too, but no hard feelings, eh? Me and you will get on just fine.'

Frenchy peered up at Harper and gave her a partial smile, intending to come across as friendlier. She laughed. 'One thing, though. I'm not a cleaner.'

Harper laughed along with her. 'Yeah, all right, Frenchy. Anyway, new beginnings.'

Just as Frenchy walked towards the bar, she stopped. 'Oh yeah, before I forget, did Vadim tell you about the two new girls starting tonight?'

Harper shook her head. 'No, he didn't mention it.'

‘Yeah, he wanted me to train up a couple of girls, apparently, because he is opening a new bar up town.’

Feeling uncomfortable, Harper could only nod. She wished, however, that Vadim had said something to her. The place was now so busy that the punters were two deep at the bar. ‘Frenchy, where is Pixie? Isn’t she supposed to be here tonight?’

Frenchy shrugged her shoulders. ‘Pixie only works part-time. She comes and goes as she pleases ’cos she’s Claude’s bird. So there aren’t any strict rules for her.’ She hurried away before Harper questioned her further about the new girls.

As the punters started to arrive, Harper noticed that there seemed to be a different clientele. Many of the men were younger, and they were ordering bottles of champagne and acting showy, loud, and brash. Then it dawned on her: it was an ideal place for a stag do. Before she had a chance to blink, the place was packed, the girls were on the poles, and the bar staff seemed to be rushed off their feet. She couldn’t stand by and just watch; she decided to muck in and serve. Then she noticed that Frenchy wasn’t behind the bar or serving drinks at the tables, and Pixie still hadn’t turned up for work. Her thoughts turned to Vadim; he wouldn’t be too impressed with her first night as manager. The customers were becoming impatient.

Turning up the speed, Harper got stuck in and lined up six shot glasses, filling each one with a Jägermeister, ready to pop into the glasses of Coke. The demands for drinks were deafening. Then, there was a moment of relief: she saw Frenchy wave.

‘Harper, we have the new helpers just in time, wouldn’t you say?’ she shouted, above the music.

But Harper was being pulled in so many different directions, she didn’t initially clock the two new girls.

Roxy had dropped one of the glasses and was on her hands and knees picking up the fragments. However, she was making a mess because she had managed to cut her finger, which was dripping blood everywhere.

With his tie loose and jacket open, a young man was shouting to the bar staff to line up more Jägers and bring them over. He wanted the bill put on his tab, but he was refusing to hand over a credit card.

Then there was Frenchy, who was ushering two new girls across the room to the changing area.

'Come on, love. Hurry up. I'm dying of thirst 'ere.'

Harper was staring at the girls following Frenchy. They seemed very young and appeared a little lost.

'Love, shall I fucking get 'em meself?' bellowed the young man.

'What? Oh, sorry. Go back to your table. I'll have them brought over.'

The young man huffed and walked away.

As her adrenaline began to rush around her body, Harper turned her speed up another notch and quickly lined up the next six shot glasses, and in seconds, she had them filled with vodka. After balancing them on the tray, she hurried over to where the gobby young man and all his loud mates were sitting on a horseshoe sofa and placed the drinks down on the low table.

As she did, one of the men, a large man with a beard and bushy brows, ran his hand up her skirt and pinched her backside.

Her instant reaction had her swiftly punching him in the face. The other men looked on, horrified, and the bearded man was so embarrassed he could only laugh and grab her breasts. 'I love a tough bird,' he said, loudly enough for everyone in the group to hear him.

Harper stepped back and glared. 'Touch me again, and you'll be fucking barred. I'm not a piece of meat. I'm the manager here.'

'And I'm a paying customer,' growled the bearded man, 'and the customer is always right.' The smile left his face. His tone became serious as he got to his feet and poked her hard in the shoulder. 'And you are nothing but a dirty whore, so back off, bitch.'

The younger man, who'd initially ordered the drinks, tried to get his friend to sit down by tugging at the tails of his jacket. 'Leave it to me, mate. She's probably on the blob.'

'I'm no whore,' Harper fired back, as she marched towards the front door.

Claude saw her and frowned. 'Everything okay, Harper?'

'Chuck out the men on table fourteen. They are way out of hand and one of them called me a whore.'

Claude smiled, mockingly. 'Is that all, Harper? All the girls get called names. It goes with the job, or are you blind?'

'I'm not blind, Claude, or naïve, but the geezer didn't *just* call me a whore. He also grabbed me arse and then me tits.'

Harper glanced over at the security guards checking the punters' pockets and she also clocked the line of thirsty customers outside, all hoping to get in.

Claude, who was keeping one eye on the queuing punters and the other on her, in between huffs and tuts, made Harper feel petty-minded.

'Are they spending good money?' he asked, as he patted down a small weasel-looking man.

Holding back her fury, Harper felt her face glowing. 'Will you throw them out, Claude, or shall I?'

'I'm not sure why Vadim hired you as manager, but there are a few things you have to learn. Being touched-up goes with the territory. Anything more than that is not acceptable. Some customers we don't argue with.' He tutted again and shook his head. 'This club is selling the idea of sex, not cream teas and home-made lemonade, love.'

'Well, that may be so, Claude, but I ain't for fucking sale,' she snapped, before pressing her lips into a thin white line.

Claude stopped what he was doing, straightened up, and stared her straight in the eyes. ‘Everyone has a price,’ he stated, as he bared his teeth like a Rottweiler.

She felt a sudden spike of unease from his cold words and strange expression. ‘So, what’s *that* supposed to mean?’

‘Nothing.’ He glared with darkening eyes, and then his voice became slow and threatening. ‘But throwing out one of our regulars is a very bad move.’

Determined not to feel intimidated by Claude, Harper shrugged her shoulders. With all intentions of storming off, she paused when she caught sight of an unusually attractive man. He was probably in his forties, very sleek, and dressed in a tailored black suit. He was sporting a large gold and diamond watch – probably a Rolex, she surmised. His dark hair was long and slicked back leaving the ends in curls. He was so familiar, yet she couldn’t place him. Her first thought was that he was a celebrity because she was almost certain she had seen his face either on the TV or in the newspapers. She could tell that the two men with him weren’t buddies all out for a jolly. They looked more like his security.

Stepping away from Claude, she watched for a moment. The sleek man approached the front of the queue. He was accompanied now by an olive-skinned gentleman, and both were immediately let in. Claude then acknowledged the two sidekicks, before shaking the main man’s hand. Harper noticed how different Claude was. She thought for a moment he almost bowed.

Heading back to the bar, Harper caught sight of the two new starters. They were dressed in short black skirts and skimpy white shirts. With their faces caked in make-up, they resembled rag dolls. Harper immediately wondered if they were even old enough to be out and about alone. They certainly couldn’t apply their make-up very well. She watched as Frenchy showed them how to pour a drink. Something wasn’t sitting right.

‘Frenchy, a word please,’ said Harper, clicking her fingers.

With an over-the-top smile, Frenchy skipped around the two girls. 'Everything all right, Boss?'

Harper shook her head. 'Please don't call me "Boss".' She pointed to the two girls. 'Those girls over there. How old are they?'

Frenchy waved her hand. 'I don't know, but Vadim must have seen their IDs, so they must be old enough.'

'For fuck's sake, anyone can pull a fake ID out of their arse. They look too young to be here.'

'No, they don't, Harper. The trouble is, you've spent years inside, and so everyone is gonna look young to you.'

Harper glared. 'Watch your mouth, Frenchy. And I wasn't born fucking yesterday. They don't look old enough. In fact, they barely look sixteen.'

Frenchy looked around her. 'You don't understand, do you?' She tilted her head to the side and glared. 'You *really* don't understand.'

'Understand what?' snapped Harper, now confused by the serious expression on Frenchy's face.

'Just leave well alone. You do your job and I'll do mine.'

Harper stepped back. 'What are you prattling on about?'

'Those girls are streetwalkers. This is safe for them. They can earn a bit of money without having to sell their fannies for a tenner.'

Harper could tell that Frenchy was on edge. Her little yarn she had just spun was totally unconvincing.

She looked over Frenchy's shoulder. 'Really? That's bollocks, Frenchy. They look like they've just stepped out of school to me.'

'Yes, well, they're off the streets before they get hooked on heroin, sleeping in doorways, and sucking dicks for a score.'

'This place will get closed down if the police discover that kids work here, and I'm not having any part of it. Frenchy, get them out.'

Before Frenchy said another word, the man who Harper was still trying to put a name to at the bar was now demanding the blonder of the two girls pour him a drink.

Harper watched as the youngster glanced at Frenchy for approval.

Frenchy nodded.

The looks on the kids' faces said it all. They were way too young to be in a bar.

Harper went over to Frenchy and whispered into her ear. 'I said, get them out, Frenchy. There are fucking sleazy ol' men in here. I can see they are ogling them, and I can also see the girls are barely out of nappies. Now, get them out before I remove them myself.'

'We are short-staffed and need all the help we can get.'

When the well-groomed man with the flash Rolex watch ran his hands down the very blonde girl's face, it instantly sent Harper into a rage. It was reminiscent of the predicament her little sister Charley had faced all those years ago. That innocence and fear that had burned in her eyes. Harper pushed past Frenchy and moved the two girls along the bar.

'Sorry, sir, what can I get you?'

'Mr Rolex' frowned. He looked from Frenchy to Harper and remained silently intimidating.

But it wasn't so much this man who concerned Harper but Frenchy. Her wide eyes and pale face suggested that she was terrified. *But why?* Harper wondered.

Without a word, the same customer flicked his hand dismissively and pointed a finger at Frenchy. 'You serve me.'

Awkward and hesitant, Harper grabbed the blonde girl's wrist. 'Come with me, and you too,' she said to the other girl.

As the youngsters were removed out to the back of the bar, where all the fridges and bins were kept, one of them protested. 'No, wait. I want to work here. The money is good, and I need it for my holiday. Please give me a chance.'

Harper let go of her wrist. 'What's your name?'

The girl looked down. 'Bethany.'

'And you?' Harper asked, looking at the other girl.

'Victoria.'

Harper recognised that their names and their accents were a far cry from this area. 'How old are you both?'

Before the girls could answer, Frenchy appeared in the room. 'I told you. They are old enough. Now, what's your fucking problem, Harper?'

'You, Frenchy, are my fucking problem!'

'We're run off our feet. I've got punters three deep at the bar. I need those girls where I can see them serving fucking cocktails.'

'You are not the manager, Frenchy, *I* am. And I don't want this place shut down because we're using underage girls.'

'You have no idea, do you? It won't get closed down because Vadim has a couple of Ol' Bill in here drinking and shagging for free. So, Miss Know-It-All, just let the club run itself, and you make sure you look pretty for Vadim. 'Cos let's be honest, Harper, you only got the job because you are his next conquest.'

'Regardless of what you say, Frenchy, I want these kids out of here.'

Harper could tell that Frenchy was starting to panic, and so she knew then that there was more to this. So she decided to dig her heels in. 'Go back to the bar, Frenchy, and do what you're paid to do.'

Frenchy shook her head, looking around the room. 'You will be sorry, Harper. I promise you that.'

As soon as Frenchy was out of sight, Harper said to the girls, 'Please wait here while I get some money from the bar for you. I'll pay you tonight's wages, but you can't stay here. Go back to your parents, or anyone you know who will take you in. Don't stay on the streets. It's a cruel place, or . . .'

Bethany looked confused. 'I am going home to my mum. I just really need the money for my holiday. There are a few of us going.'

Victoria giggled. 'Yes, we are going to Africa to look after the orphaned elephants.'

Harper glanced from one girl to the other and clocked that they were genuinely well-looked-after girls. Both were posh and pretty, with fair skin and not a tattoo, a piercing, or a dyed lock in sight.

Back at the bar, she saw Frenchy looking very uneasy. She was talking to 'Mr Rolex'.

Keeping one eye on him, Harper opened the till and grabbed a few notes before hurrying to the back room. But the girls had vanished. Quickly, she opened the rear entrance door that led directly to the alley, but there was no one there at all. It was odd. Why would they disappear, when it seemed they had wanted money for a trip and were prepared to work in a seedy club to pay for it? And why did Frenchy tell her an out-and-out lie that they were street girls? They most certainly weren't street kids. In fact, they probably had some royal blood running through their veins. They were decent girls, desperate for holiday money.

Just before Harper closed the door, she heard a voice shouting for her to hold it open. It was Pixie. She was running and seemed to be flustered.

'Some bastard slashed my tyres. I couldn't get a cab either. Sorry, I'm so late, Harper.'

Harper waved her in before she closed the door behind her. 'Did you happen to see two young girls with blonde hair?'

Pixie was still catching her breath. 'No. Why?'

Harper waved her hand. 'Oh, nothing, I guess.'

'You look good, Harper. Had your hair done?'

'Yeah, yeah, I thought I should spruce myself up.'

'Oh yeah? And what does Vadim think?' She winked.

'He's not here. He's left me in charge. Madness, because I've only been here five minutes.'

Pixie was already in her uniform, so she got to work behind the bar right away.

Feeling thirsty, Harper helped herself to a glass of water and glanced around the club. She saw that Frenchy was walking 'Mr Rolex' and the olive-skinned man to the main entrance. The two security men were following. Unexpectedly, as if he had eyes in the back of his head, 'Mr Rolex' spun around and glared at Harper before disappearing into the night air.

Suddenly, she recalled where she had seen him before. It was in a newspaper. That was it! He was in the newspaper clipping that Madeleine had shoved under her nose before she herself had left prison. Of all the places, he happened to have walked into the club she was working at. Madeleine had never mentioned that he waltzed around with security. Although she suspected this would be possible since Madeleine's husband and his business partner were loaded. *Who owns a shipping company without being rich?*

She looked at the clock and willed the time away, just as she had done in prison.

Her head was pounding from the noise and the constant thinking and watching. Frenchy was beginning to really annoy her. Seeing her hurry back to the bar with a satisfied grin on her face riled up Harper even more.

She stood in front of the bar flap preventing Frenchy's entrance.

'How do you know Calvin Stuart?'

Frenchy stopped dead in her tracks. 'Who?'

'That man with his two security guards who just left the club.'

Harper could see the intrigue written all over Frenchy's face, but it was short-lived. 'Don't know what you're on about. Let me pass. Where are the girls?'

Harper hated being taken for a fool. 'Never mind the girls, I asked you who you were talking to.'

'Harper, move out of my way. I need to see those girls.'

'They've gone, Frenchy, back to their nice homes with nice parents.'

Frenchy's eyes widened. '*What?*'

'Yes, nice homes. They were never fucking streetwalkers. You may think I'm stupid but I'm not. Why would you encourage kids to work here, for fuck's sake?'

Before Frenchy answered, Harper looked around and realised there were too many people within earshot.

'Go out to the back room, and we can talk there, or else get your bag and leave.'

Acting like a petulant child, Frenchy stormed towards Harper, forcing her to move sideways, to avoid being cannoned into, and headed for the back door. She almost ripped it off its hinges before stepping out into the alleyway. She looked left and right. 'Where are they, Harper? I have to find them!'

'Never mind the girls. They've gone home. Right, that man with the dark hair combed back and dressed in a black suit. You were talking to him.'

With the corner of her lips turned down and her arms folded, Frenchy shook her head. 'I don't know what you're on about. I was serving the punters.'

'You were escorting him out of the building. I fucking *saw* you.'

Frenchy shook her head. 'You're seeing things, Harper, that are not there. I didn't escort any man out of the club. I went to see if Claude or the others wanted a drink. I always do. It's part of the job, to keep the security plied with cold drinks.'

Harper decided not to push it. Something was obviously going on, but she would bide her time and pretend she believed Frenchy's pathetic explanation.

The evening dragged on, and Harper was almost dead on her feet by the time it was over. The doors were shut, and the girls were having a couple of drinks while they waited for all the customers outside to leave. Any found loitering were moved on by the security staff.

Each girl said goodbye to Harper and left, leaving her alone with Claude. He seemed cold and menacing compared to yesterday. Something was not right. She watched him as he continuously checked his phone. Then he tapped in his passcode - all the sixes. She wanted to laugh; it would have been fitting if it had been three sixes.

Eager to leave, Harper stood with her bag over her shoulder and her hand out. 'Vadim said you have a set of keys for me.'

Claude looked her over. She could see his expression was deadpan. He rolled his tongue over his top teeth, and his eyes glared.

She felt uneasy. Claude was a lump of a man, with hands like shovels and no neck. His muscular body was ripped with bulges under his shirt. She knew that one clout from him, and she would be waking up next week. Pushing the thought from her mind, she told herself he was just a moody bastard.

'The keys?'

He chuckled. 'Oh yeah. Sure. Vadim said I have to take you to the flat.'

'Is that a problem?' asked Harper, defensively.

'No.' He laughed. 'Quite the opposite, in fact.'

His threatening tone and his spiteful eyes gave Harper cause for concern. 'The keys!' Again, she held out her hand.

Claude reached inside his jacket and pulled out a set of keys with a key ring that looked like a seahorse. She remembered Rhea's earrings and assumed they were part of a matching set.

He held them up. 'Come on, then. I'll drive you to the flat.'

Harper shook her head. 'No, I'm okay to go alone. What's the address, Claude? I'll go there later because I need to go to my mother's house first.'

'Vadim insisted that I take you home.' His voice was viperous, like a predator luring her into his den. She snapped out of her paranoid thoughts.

'Claude, Vadim isn't my husband or my father, so just hand over the keys, and I'll be on me way.'

She stepped forward to take them, but he stepped back as if he was playing a silly game.

Her nerves were being rattled, and in response, she flared her nostrils. 'Don't fuck about, Claude. It's late and I want to get home and put me feet up.'

'But Vadim wanted me to drive you home.'

'Like I said, Vadim isn't me husband, and the last time I checked, he left me in charge.'

A sudden laugh made Harper flinch.

'Hmmm, yes, and Vadim thinks he is the boss, but he isn't.' He looked around the room. 'He owns this building, and, yes, the business, but he doesn't own us and the *real* business. Harper, it is not run by Vadim but by someone else.'

Not wanting to believe the big brute, she laughed back at him. 'It is usually little men who have the big ideas, but it seems you are a big man with little ideas. A fool who said out loud his mental thoughts. Now, Claude, hand over the keys and step aside. I am leaving as the manager and not as a figment of your imagination.'

'Vadim doesn't know you from Adam. He is an idiot, a wealthy one, but an idiot all the same. All he knows is you are easy on the eye and probably a good fuck. But you could have him over a barrel, as you people say. There is money in this club. A lot. You are an ex-con, after all.'

Harper felt her blood boiling. 'I was inside for fucking murder, not petty theft. Look, Claude.' She lowered her voice to appeal to his better nature. 'I need this job, and I want to do it well. I need to start a new life for me and my—'

'Son!' interrupted Claude.

Harper thought back to whether she had mentioned her son in his presence. She decided she hadn't. She raised a questioning eyebrow. 'How do you know about my boy?'

'I know so much about you, Harper Kane. I know who you killed. I know where you live. *And* I know where your little boy lives.'

She knew then that those cold words were menacing. He wasn't merely interested in her life. He had gained knowledge regarding her family for a purpose. Instantly, she felt her blood run cold.

He laughed. 'Handsome lad. Likes his sleep.'

The hairs on the back of her neck stood on end. 'You *what*!' she whispered. Her heart was pumping so fast that she felt she was going into temper mode. She had to control it. This man was huge and was capable of anything. *Was his intention to do her harm*? she wondered. She was a few feet away from the bar with no weapon to hand.

'What the fuck do you mean?' she hissed, through gritted teeth.

But he didn't answer. He grinned like a satisfied glutton who had just eaten the last cream cake.

A voice from behind her spoke up. 'He means it was a piece of piss removing your little boy from his bed and placing him under the tree in the garden.'

Harper spun around to see Pixie standing there, with a cigarette in her hand. She looked so different. Now, with her wig removed, her natural hair was short and dark. She had no make-up on and wore black faux leather trousers and a plain white T-shirt. Harper wanted to gasp because the transformation was unbelievable. If she hadn't recognised her voice, she would never have guessed it was Pixie.

'What the fuck is going on?'

Pixie moved closer to Harper but kept a safe distance. 'Rhea told me all about you. Laughing at you, she was. Personally, I think she enjoyed seeing you on your downers. What she hadn't banked on was that I was taking in every tiny detail because that's what I do. And you, Harper, were such easy pickings.' She held up her hand and pinched each finger as she unveiled her knowledge. 'First, a jailbird on a life licence; second, desperate to get her kid back; and third, desperate for money and a place away from her mother's, and so on and so on.'

Harper could only stare at them both. Drowning in confusion, she tried to claw her way through recent events to understand what was going on, but her mind was all over the place.

'The operative word there, Harper, is *desperate*. You've been to prison, so you know how it works. You don't want to go back there, do you?'

Still glaring, Harper remained silent.

'No, of course, you don't, and you want to protect the ones you love because, Harper, you have done that your whole life, haven't you? I heard that your sister Lexi is at your mother's because you bricked her abusive boyfriend.'

It was evident that Pixie had done her homework and sussed out her vulnerabilities. She guessed then that they would ask her to do something for them. Right now, she was clueless. She had no idea who they were and what they were all about. However, now, when Pixie spoke, she sounded like she had too much saliva in her mouth, demonstrating her true accent. To Harper, it validated this set-up as a front for something that was probably so much more sinister than a few horny men getting their kicks out of half-naked pole dancers. This was no seedy club, run by a well-meaning Russian. It was obvious to her that the club was a front for a type of crime that she would never be part of. So she decided to walk away.

Claude blocked her exit without laying a hand on her.

Her attempts to walk around him failed when he grabbed her arms to hold her still. Not being too pleased with being held against her will, she pulled her head back and butted him clean across the bridge of his nose. It hurt her head so much that she assumed she'd inflicted a serious injury on him.

He let go of her arms, but his reaction was unexpected. He moved with speed as he pulled back his fist and smashed her hard on the chin. The power behind the blow knocked her back, and she staggered in shock before falling down.

The room was spinning, and her eyes wouldn't focus, but she could make out Claude and Pixie reaching down and grabbing her arms. Her legs simply wouldn't hold her up. She knew what it was to be knocked out. The only woman ever to have done that before was Madeleine when she had first arrived at the prison. Madeleine had hammered her with an industrial pan after a row in the kitchen, literally knocking her off her feet. Strangely, that was the beginning of their friendship; however, she could imagine Pixie and Claude being best buddies. The room was getting darker, and she was gripped by fear, knowing she was losing complete consciousness, and, worse, powerless to do anything to stop it.

Chapter Ten

Unaware of how long she had been unconscious or where the hell she was, Harper tried to take a deep breath, but something was stopping her. Her chest felt so tight that all she could muster were shallow breaths like a panting dog.

Blinking furiously, she strained to open her eyes and face the bright light. It was clearly day time. Her head was banging with every pulse, her mouth was as dry as a bone, and her stomach was on the verge of expelling its contents. She felt as if she was suffering the worst dry white wine hangover. But, of course, she hadn't been drinking. In fact, she hadn't been drunk in over a decade.

Slowly, she managed to focus and realised she had been tied to a chair. As she peered down at her hands, one of them had a cannula taped to it. *What the fuck!* Her jaw was throbbing, and gradually she recalled receiving a full-on blow from Claude. Suddenly, fear oozed from every pore. Fear of being tortured, fear of never seeing her son again, and fear of the unknown.

Forcing her brain into gear, Harper had to think straight. She was still alive, so whoever had tied her to the chair wanted something from her. The fact that she owned sweet fuck all led her to the conclusion it had to be information.

'Good morning, Harper. It is my pleasure to finally meet you.'

After staring at the expensive leather shoes and the dark blue jeans, Harper lifted her head to face the man with an accent, even though he spoke excellent English. He wasn't as big as the soldiers around him. He was, however, striking. With his short dark hair cut close to his head and his eyes very catlike, similar to her own, she could be fooled into thinking he had Italian blood; yet he spoke very much like Pixie and Claude. He appeared harmless, soft in fact. His tone most definitely wasn't deep, harsh, or intimidating. Her fear disappeared as quickly as it had arrived. Perhaps it was his smile or the fact that he looked quite charming.

With a slow smirk weaving its way across her face, Harper shook her head. 'I don't know you, but if you'd really wanted to meet me, you could've visited. I have had the same address for the last twelve years.'

'Oh, I see. You think you are funny, eh? Well, I don't have time for jokes or games.'

Harper felt her heart race, the second his tone changed. His smile had left his face. She didn't try to wriggle free or curse or even scream. She knew damn well there was no point. This man was surrounded by his own gun-wielding army.

'Untie her!' he demanded, as he waved his hand at the man standing to her right.

The guard removed an evil-looking knife from his wide belt, and, in a fluid movement, he cut her ties.

The relief was immense, and Harper fell forward as she took a deep breath. Ripping the cannula from the back of her hand, Harper held it up and dangled it. She tried to make light of the sudden cold atmosphere that bounced off every wall.

'I personally wouldn't use this as a formal invitation.'

'Ah, so you *are* the comedian, I see.'

Harper stood up, allowing the pins and needles sensation to leave her body slowly and painfully.

Harper guessed from his excellent English that he'd either had a very gifted teacher or had spent a chunk of his life in the UK. She'd been inside with a Russian, who had been caught with a heavy amount of cocaine, and she was one hard cow, but for some reason, the woman had taken a liking to her, and so having always had a thirst for knowledge, she had learned a lot about the Russians. Such as, there were no equivalent words for 'a' or 'the', so most Russians would slip up if they pretended to be English.

'So, if I'm your guest, can I ask for a glass of water, please, Mr, er . . . ?' She smiled, almost sarcastically.

‘Get Harper a drink,’ he said, pointing to one of his guards. He turned back to her. ‘Call me Zavid.’

‘Zavid what?’

He snorted. ‘You will never know that. You simply call me Zavid.’

While the guard did as he was ordered, another placed his hand on her shoulder and pushed her roughly back onto the wooden chair.

She glared. ‘You only need to ask me to take a seat. There is no need for brute fucking force.’

Zavid laughed. ‘So you think you are here of your own free will?’

She shook her head. ‘Sorry, mate, but that is a stupid question. A punch on the chin and a fucking needle in my arm, which I didn’t put there, is hardly a pleasant invitation. But I’m in your company now. Since to my knowledge I have never crossed your path before, I am not sure how the hell I could have pissed you off, considering I spent so many years behind bars. So I assumed you would be a gentleman and treat me with some kind of respect.’

The guard returned with a large glass of water and shoved it in her hand. She stared for a moment before offering it to Zavid. ‘Go on, put my mind at ease.’

Zavid took the glass and sipped the water. ‘Satisfied? Now, we must talk.’

Harper enjoyed every mouthful of the cold liquid, which soothed her burning throat and held the nauseating feeling at bay.

She finished the drink and looked back at Zavid, who was now smirking at her.

‘That was rather pointless. I could have filled your syringe with poison if I had wanted to kill you, but you know that.’

She lifted her chin and grinned.

‘I must give you credit, Harper. You were testing the level of power you possibly have over me. You want to know how much I am prepared to respect you.’

Raising a confident eyebrow, Harper replied, ‘Something like that.’

As much as the Russian wasn’t particularly tall or big, like his foot soldiers, his mere presence dominated the room.

‘So you are bright, and that’s good because that means you will understand my proposal.’ He paused and paced a few steps. ‘You will continue to work at the club—’

‘I’m not sure that I want to. Money isn’t everything to me.’

He nodded. ‘No, I believe you, but your family is.’

Harper’s eyes widened in anger.

‘Yeah, see, the mention of your family, and you are ready to go in for the kill.’

Harper stood up, and before the henchman attempted to push her down again, she turned to face him. ‘Touch me, and you will have to fucking kill me. I will not be manhandled by a bully. Now, back the fuck off.’

Zavid nodded for the guard to do as she said.

‘Look, stop trying to make some kind of impression. I am, as you said, not stupid. You have clout.’ She looked the Russian up and down. ‘And a man who has a flaming army for support and who owns all of this’ – she pointed around the room – ‘is either a wealthy Russian politician or part of the Russian mafia. So, Zavid, I get you’re a powerful man, and I ain’t no big shot, so just let me go,’ she spat, with a face full of fury.

‘I can see why Vadim likes you.’

‘Flattery bores the fuck out of me.’ She folded her arms and rolled her eyes.

‘You are to continue to manage the bar. Pasha will give you your orders.’

'*Pasha?*'

'You know her as Pixie.'

Harper nonchalantly shrugged her shoulders. She needed to get away, and right now, all she could do was to promise to go along with their plan until she could think straight. 'Sure, fine. Now, can someone take me home?'

'You do understand, if you don't do as Pasha says, your family—'

'Shut the fuck up about my family, and I swear with everything I have, if you hurt any one of them, I will hunt you down and burn you alive.'

Zavid saw the fury in her eyes and felt her passion. He knew then that he could control her. 'Yes, Harper, I do believe you would.'

Her face twisted in rage as she pointed at him. 'Seriously, you fucking prick, get on with the details. I need to be elsewhere.'

Zavid began pacing the floor again until he stopped abruptly, and his whole head began to twitch as though he had some affliction. 'Have you ever seen a man burned alive?'

The actual thought of it made her mouth go dry. 'No, but you could always be the first.'

'I have. You see, it's an unusual threat for a woman to make. It is a cruel way to die . . . but life is very cruel, and there is no place for compassion.'

Harper tapped her foot on the marble floor.

'Okay, let's discuss business. Did you know that there is fifty thousand pounds on offer for your head on a silver platter with an apple shoved in your mouth?'

Harper's ears pricked, and she stopped tapping her foot. 'I did hear that was the case.'

Zavid slowly shook his head. 'The threat is genuine.'

Nonchalantly, Harper replied, 'Well, I have been out for a couple of days now, and I'm still alive.'

'Yes, you are still alive because the man who wanted you dead now wants to hurt you even more, so he has retracted the fifty thousand-pound contract on your head, and now, it hangs over your son's.'

The sudden realisation hit her like a ton of bricks, and her face drained of blood as she swooned.

'You have to let me go. I need to get my son away.' She tried to run to the door, but one of the guards pulled her back.

Zavid held up the palm of his hand. 'Wait! Your son is safe.'

He could see she was suspicious and anxious to get away. He flicked his hands for the henchman to leave the room. 'He is safe, I promise you.' Pulling a phone from his pocket, he dialled a number and began talking, but it was all just foreign to her.

Ending the call, Zavid stared at the screen.

'Here, see, this is your son, no?'

Harper snatched the phone from him and stared at the photo. Eddie was in the garden kicking a football, and there was Teddy sitting at the table reading the Sunday newspaper. She zoomed in on the paper and could see it was today's edition.

'Why do you have someone following my son?'

'I want you to know that one bad move from you and he is just an expendable commodity to me.'

Those words were like shards of ice piercing her heart. It made her realise how fragile life was. No one was invincible.

'I am baffled by all of this. Tell me what you want from me, and then perhaps we can have a discussion.'

Zavid laughed. 'I am not the man who has put a fifty thousand-pound contract on your son's head.'

Now angry, Harper felt hot tears building up, and her voice quivered for a moment. 'How could anyone want to kill a child?'

She stiffened and took a deep breath. 'I have a bloody good idea who it is.'

'Richard Newbury.'

He paused and waited for a reaction, but he could see she remained stone-faced.

'I see, you have plans for him yourself. I am not surprised, Harper. People like you are like the lioness putting her own life in danger for her cubs. You killed his brother, didn't you?'

'I'm tired, I'm hungry, and I want to know for sure that my little boy is okay, so please stop playing with your words. You don't need to intimidate me. I am already.'

'Okay, Harper, I can protect your son.'

She poked herself in the chest. 'Let me go, Mr Wise Guy. I can protect my own son myself.'

He shook his head. 'There is only one man who Richard is afraid of, and that's me, so I can make sure your son stays alive while you do what I want.'

She waved her hand. 'Like I said, I don't need your help. Thanks but no thanks.'

'You don't understand, but let me show you. You said you would burn me alive if I hurt your child, but, really, you meant you would burn anyone alive who would touch your son. Correct?'

Harper nodded, wondering where this was leading. She knew she was acting confidently, but, inside, she was afraid of the Russian and the power he had. The photo of her son playing happily in the garden made her feel sick with worry for him. He was so innocent. He was just a little boy kicking a ball, probably believing he was David Beckham.

She nodded again.

He smiled and flicked his head, indicating that she should go with him.

She was desperate to get out of the place, and so, now relieved, she followed him from the room. She soon realised that it was a beautiful large building, a manor house. Catching a glimpse of the rooms as they passed, she noticed they were filled with large statement sculptures and grand pieces of eclectic furniture. One room had a wall completely covered in a beautiful mosaic of a seahorse. The windows were huge, and the frames were made of thick stone; some were arched. She looked out. All she could see was countryside. So even if she managed to leg it, where would she go? They were in the middle of nowhere.

She followed him through a few doors, each room grander than the last. An armed guard stood at each doorway. Finally, they were outside, and it was at that point she realised how vast the landscape actually was. Then she noticed the luxurious cars and a black van. *Surely, he wasn't into the funeral service game?*

Eventually, they entered a large carport. And as the three guards, who were standing in front of the Russian, parted, there tied to a chair was a big man. She wasn't surprised to see that it was Richard Newbury. He looked reasonably smart except for the fact he was sweating profusely. He had a wet stain on his trousers. He'd clearly pissed himself and had what looked and smelled like vomit down his shirt.

His head was flopping so that his chin touched his chest. He looked up, and his eyes flicked from Zavid to Harper. 'What is this all about?' he hissed.

'Surely, you know her, Richard? This is Harper Kane.'

'I fucking know who she is. What I want to know is why she is here, and why I am tied up.'

Harper looked Richard over. She knew what he was thinking. Yet to her, he was nothing. She had conjured up a vision of a big and fit man with a look about him that said 'Don't fuck with me.' But, however big Richard might be, there was also something pathetic about him. His fat blubber lips? The way his eyes drooped? Or was it the way he spoke, which had a very nasal whine to it? In a nutshell, he was a slob in an expensive suit.

Zavid clicked his fingers, and two foot soldiers began to set up a table; they then brought in what looked like a rolled-up tool belt, a blowtorch, and a can of petrol.

Richard's eyes almost bulged out of his head. 'What the fuck are you doing?' he yelled, as he tried to break free of the ropes that bound him to the chair. 'Come on, please, what's going on? I did everything you said. The girls—'

'Shut up, Richard.'

With his eyes darting from Zavid to Harper, Richard hoped for a laugh or at the very least a tiny chuckle that would suggest it was all a joke, but, instead, they both just stared straight at him.

'Look, you can have the money back. All of it. Please, my car, take my car.'

The Russian shook his head.

'Okay, okay, listen, please. You can have everything. My villa in Spain, it's beautiful, mate. It's got a pool. Take it, it's yours. Please, just let me go.' Desperately trying to break free, Richard whimpered, 'Oh God, no! No, please!' he cried, as he looked at the weapons placed meticulously on the table. Sweat trickled down his grey face, and his eyes were now bloodshot.

'Harper, this is the man who was going to have your son murdered.'

The last time she saw Richard, he was in the courtroom gallery. He was younger and slimmer then. She very quickly concluded that he had spent the last decade filling his face, and by the purple thread veins across his nose, it looked as though he liked a good drink too. She started to enjoy the terror on his face as his eyes darted around the carport. The smell of petrol lingered, so she knew Richard would be terrified. Just the mere thought of being burned alive would have his guts twisting in panic.

'What is this? What is going on? I don't understand.' His pleading eyes searched Zavid's face for answers.

'You made a lot of money through our arrangement.'

Richard nodded. 'Yes, and I have never let you down, so why this?'

'You became lazy and cocky and didn't pay enough attention.'

'I don't understand.' Fear gurgled in Richard's voice.

'You see, your niece was more interested in fucking Vadim than taking care of business.'

Harper was listening, and as the cogs turned, it suddenly struck her. Rhea and Candy, his nieces? Surely not. Of all the people she trusted most, she would never have believed Candy would screw her over. Anger laced with sadness spurred her to jump in.

'You planned to have me murdered, and your two spineless nieces were helping to set me up! Is that right, Richard?'

His eyes shot to Harper's, but seeing her standing there with a major hard-nosed attitude pushed him to switch to being incensed. 'You murdered my brother, and you think you would get out after serving only twelve years and walk free? Fuck off, darling. My Rhea loved her uncle, and yeah, she got you in the club to have you exactly where she wanted you and right where my contract killer would know your movements. I wanted you dead, Harper Whore Kane.' His dark eyes lost their fear as he glared with hate.

'Perhaps it was Rhea's quest to avenge her uncle's murder or her infatuation for Vadim that caused your niece to fuck up, and fuck up very badly,' said the Russian, taking back control of the conversation.

Fear returned to Richard's voice. 'What? No, I mean, I had no idea,' he bumbled.

'No, you are right, you had no idea, and you were paid highly to know everything that goes on. But you left it to Rhea, the stupid woman with the big mouth, to take care of the girls, but when she fucked up, it nearly cost me a big client. That is why you are no good to me. You are too much of a liability.'

‘Please, no, listen. Rhea did find the two blonde girls, as you instructed. I know she did. She made the arrangements. They were eager to start work. It was all organised. Please, believe me.’

All the while Richard was fumbling for words and pleading his case, the Russian just nodded.

‘The girls disappeared, Richard. Poof! Into fucking thin air. So tell me, Richard, do you have a higher bidder?’ he bellowed.

Harper jumped at hearing the shrill tone in the Russian’s voice, but as she listened, she then realised precisely what was going on. For the first time in her life, she felt totally helpless, let alone overwhelmed. This was seriously heavy shit that she was now caught up in the middle of. All she wanted to do was to put her hands over her ears, so she didn’t have to listen to the actual crimes they were all involved in and run from the place. Even the thought of going back to prison would be a pleasure compared to this. The area was surrounded by what now looked like an army, and it was apparent that Zavid was one very dangerous man. She assumed then that he was head of the Russian mafia or some other organisation just as influential. However, she knew he had her right where he wanted her, to do as he asked. The feeling of guilt that would consume her if she could even contemplate assisting human trafficking was immense, but the risk of losing her son was immeasurable. It had all become self-evident that for the moment, she was caught in a no-win situation with just her position as bar manager keeping her alive. But what would be asked of her in return for her life and that of her son was something she just didn’t want to know.

Zavid laughed, and Harper noticed once again how he twitched as though he had an unruly nerve that literally moved his whole head.

‘So, Richard, Harper is going to hear what exactly you said you would do to her little boy – her little eleven-year-old son, her innocent, sweet boy.’

Richard looked at Harper and clocked how the dynamics were odd. Harper wasn’t cuffed and tied to a chair. She was standing freely, side by side with the Russian. 'I wasn't going to hurt your little boy. It was just a threat.' He laughed nervously. 'Come on, Harper, I was going to give you a slap when I saw you because you killed my brother, but that's all.'

The words 'little boy' circled Harper's mind, and her emotions changed from fear to anger. As if someone had flicked a switch, her eyes glared with deadly intensity.

'Seriously, Harper, I wouldn't have hurt your son.'

Zavid giggled, like a girl. 'Go on, Richard, be a man, and tell Harper what you told your brother. Go on.'

'What? I never said—'

'That you would string him up by his ankles?'

Richard knew that Zavid had been told precisely what he had said to Larry, and he wondered if his own brother had turned against him. God forbid, his brother. He stared – speechless.

'I bet you are wondering how I knew,' said Zavid, as he held out his hand and clicked his fingers. One of the henchmen handed him a phone.

Richard stared, his heart pumping furiously. The stupid shark phone case was Larry's. No question. No one else had that case. He was either dead or someone else had tied him up. His mind returned to the message he'd left on his brother's phone.

Zavid pressed 'voicemail'.

Richard knew then he was fucked. Because there as clear as day was his voice saying how he would hang the kid up and bleed him out.

He looked from Harper and back to Zavid. Both pairs of eyes told him what he knew already; now, all that faced him was the way in which he would die. Judging by the array of tools on the table, he guessed these Russians had plenty of options.

Chapter Eleven

Harper knew that Richard only had a few minutes to live. She needed information now or it would be too late.

Pivoting, her eyes paused on Richard in anger. 'Tell me, why did you want my son murdered instead of me? Is it that you're a real sick and twisted son of a bitch, like your ugly perverted brother was, or what?'

Resigned to the notion that they would murder him anyway, Richard sucked the phlegm from around his mouth and gobbed. The slimy content landed by her feet.

'You hate me so much that you would have taken great pleasure in seeing my head on a platter, so someone must have paid you handsomely to stop you having me killed. Who was it?'

'Fuck off, you cocksucking slut!'

Zavid nodded to one of the henchmen. He picked up the can of petrol and began dowsing Richard.

'No!' he screamed, when he realised he was going to be set alight. The fuel burned his eyes and stung his nose.

But Richard's hysterical pleas to stop what was happening to him had no effect.

The henchman continued to empty the petrol can.

'All right, please,' he choked.

The henchman held the canister above Richard's head but stopped pouring.

'Okay, it was Teddy Ryder, the fucking wanker. He paid the fifty grand to keep you alive, but God knows why, when he has your prettier fuckable sister on hand to suck on his cock.'

Richard could see that Harper's facial shrug, followed by a broad grin, was clearly aimed at teasing him, and he could sense the pure loathing in her eyes. However, reality slapped him in the face when he felt the petrol run down his back.

'What? Seriously, no, come on, please.'

Harper turned to walk away. This wasn't her call to make, and Zavid was right; she had never seen a man burn alive, and she really didn't want to, either.

The whooshing sound as the guard lit the petrol, followed by the guttural screams, compelled Harper to hold down her stomach contents. Whatever forced her to look back, she would never know. It may have been morbid curiosity or disbelief. But whatever it was, she wished she hadn't witnessed what happened to Richard. The horrific scene was dominated so much by the smell of burning flesh that it made her gag. She clenched her jaw tighter. The man, who was still writhing around in agony, was now black, and his skin had bubbled to the extent that it resembled paint being stripped from a wooden door. Then the screams stopped, and apart from the dancing flames, nothing else was moving – Richard was clearly dead.

Gone was one dangerous man she wouldn't have to deal with again. She turned to the Russian and wondered what on earth her life would be like now with this mafia man – unthinkable, probably.

'Now you have witnessed a man burn alive. You must be pleased because it was what you wished for, Harper.'

She gazed in a trance, musing over Zavid's unperturbed face. Maybe twelve years ago, people would have viewed her as cold and callous as Zavid, but she had her reasons for going to jail. Perhaps Zavid had his reasons for killing Richard the way he had.

However, what was more believable was the idea that he was making a point to frighten her, simply because she had threatened to burn him alive. The thought of being beholden to the man troubled her severely.

'So, you may go and do what you have to do, but on Tuesday night, the club will be open, and you will be there as manager, like before. Pasha will tell you what you are to do. Do we understand each other? Oh, and you will be watched all the time.'

Harper realised that in the meantime, she would have to play along. 'Yes, fine. Please would someone drive me home?'

He nodded, but as he leaned into her, he whispered, 'Please don't do anything silly because I have your little boy in my eyeline. I will do what I have to, if you go against me. You do understand, don't you?'

'Why me?' she asked, genuinely baffled.

'Some things in life are coincidences, and some are not. When Pasha told me that Vadim made you manager and that there was also this, as we say, bounty on your head, by a man I personally have done business with, it raised a few questions. Pasha, you see, leaves no stone unturned, and it is apparent that you have also served time with someone I know very well, and Pasha spoke with her about you. It appears that you have the qualities we want to manage the club for us. Vadim is so struck by you that you will be able to distract him, shall we say. You will be paid very well, but, equally, you will be punished very severely . . .' he said, as he looked back over his shoulder, 'as others have been, if you dare to cross me.'

Taking back some dignity, Harper said, 'If I am to work with you—'

'*With* me?' he interrupted. 'No, Harper, you will work *for* me, but what were you going to ask me?'

'Your surname.'

He smiled stiffly. 'That, you will never know, but some call me "The Serpent".' The boastful gleam in his eyes diminished along with his smile. 'Now, you must leave.'

Shocked at his schizophrenic change of tone, Harper nodded sharply, and followed the guard to a car. However, in front of her, being held up under his arms, was a man who had clearly been smashed to a pulp. Moving her eyes, not her head, as she passed him, she clocked who it was – Larry Newbury, Richard's brother. He had taken a serious beating. Then her eyes looked down to the man's handless wrists. She wanted to scream and run, but she acted as if she wasn't bothered, even though she felt as though she was about to turn her insides out. And while the muscles in her legs had already turned to mush, it was now her pulse that was beating madly in her neck as a hot flush swept through her. She really couldn't afford to mess about. This gang of Russian mafia – all lunatics – literally took no prisoners, unless they happened to be young girls. She shuddered.

***

The soldier – bodyguard – henchman, or whatever he was, guided her to a car. As she climbed into the back, she found that she couldn't see anything outside because the front of the car was blocked from view by a bulletproof screen and the rear windows were all blacked out. Powerless, she rested her head on the cushioned arm of the back seat, closed her eyes, and drifted into a light sleep.

Finally, she awoke when she felt the car spin around. Her senses told her that something was wrong. After a few sharp turns that caused her to slide along the seat, the car came to an abrupt stop. She tried to open the door, but it wouldn't budge. So she waited and listened. The driver opened the rear door for her. Without his black padded jacket and his gun belt, which he must have taken off in the car, he seemed so much smaller. Dressed in a black T-shirt and combat trousers, he merely resembled a workman.

Harper climbed out, and instantly, she felt the heat of the midday sun. It was in stark contrast to the air conditioning inside the car. Taking a moment to get her bearings, she realised she wasn't outside her mother's house but a few hundred metres away. The smell of fire lingered in the air, and for a moment, she assumed it was from her clothes. Then she glanced at the soldier, who appeared uneasy, as, with a sad and almost sympathetic expression, he gently pushed her in the back to guide her along the street.

'What is it? What's going on?'

'My English not good, your address, police, and firemen.'

The word 'firemen' hit her like a sixteen-pound bowling ball. She ran like the clappers, praying to God that her family were safe. As she turned the corner, she could see the fire was already out, but the place was overrun with police and a special fire crew. They were the investigation unit. Harper stopped at the corner of the road. The fear, the emotion, and the run made her almost collapse breathless.

The soldier grabbed her arm. 'Please, Harper, be at the club, as he says.'

She turned to face the genuine look of concern on the soldier's face. She nodded. 'I will be. This isn't his doing, is it? Please, I must know.'

He frowned. 'No, this is not us. We do not need to do this. You understand?'

She nodded, caught her breath, and tore away from him, desperate to know if her family were safe.

As she approached the house, or what was left of it, she saw her probation officer standing there and running her hands through her hair.

'Vanessa, are my family okay? Please tell me they are.'

Vanessa's expression was filled with such a sorry-for-your-loss look that Harper found herself collapsing to her knees and covering her face with her hands. All the fear, the pent-up anger, and frustration over the last twelve hours or so had taken its toll. Her tough-guy act had vanished completely. Now, she was an emotional wreck and trembling so violently, she felt she would have a fit at any moment.

Vanessa bent down and placed her arm around Harper's shoulders. 'Your mother is fine. They told me that your sister Lexiana is in the hospital.'

Harper listened, waiting for news of the baby. But Vanessa didn't mention his name. Trying in vain to compose herself, she took a deep breath and looked at Vanessa. 'And Yosef?' she managed to speak, although she was choking on a sob.

'He is missing.'

'*Missing?*' Her voice was high-pitched, in disbelief.

'Not missing in the fire, Harper. He wasn't in the house. Look, they called me because you weren't here, and now, they want to haul you in for questioning. Is there anything you want to tell me?'

With an annoyed frown, Harper got to her feet. She wiped her cheeks. 'Like fucking what?'

Vanessa stepped back. 'Where have you been?'

In her effort to think straight, she snapped back, 'I've been to work.'

The probation officer raised her brow in scepticism. '*Work?*' She exaggerated her disbelief by tilting her head.

'Yes, fucking work, Vanessa,' replied Harper, followed by a glare of fury.

Vanessa shuffled from foot to foot and straightened the designer bag that hung from her shoulder. 'It's just that you haven't mentioned anything about work, and you know you are supposed to tell me about changes like that.'

'Yes, well, I only started on Friday. It was a trial run. I didn't say anything to you because I didn't know if the boss would keep me on. Does that really matter, right now? What's going on? Where the hell is Yosef? And is my sister okay? Where did they take her?'

Sensing the urgency and anger rising in Harper's voice, Vanessa knew then she had probably overstepped the mark, considering she had just informed the woman that the paramedics had taken her sister to the hospital.

'By all accounts, Lexiana suffered some burns, but they are not life-threatening. And . . .' she hastened to add, 'there was some smoke inhalation. Your mother is okay. She's at your other sister's, but the police think that someone, possibly you, Harper, went into the house around 1 a.m., when both Lexiana and your mother were asleep, and removed the baby and *then* started a fire.'

'Me!' she gasped. 'Why would I do that, for Christ's sake?'

Vanessa gave Harper a leave-it-with-me wink. 'It's because you were not around, but if you were at work, then you have a cut-and-dried alibi. So, what does this job entail?'

'I work in a bar, as a general dogsbody and cleaner. So where did they take my sister?'

'She's at the Princess Royal University Hospital in Orpington. Look, Harper, the police want to speak to you. Let's get that over with, and then, I'll take you to see her.'

Wiping her face again, Harper nodded. 'Okay, and do they have Hasad, her fella, in custody?'

Vanessa shook her head. 'Apparently, he's not in the country. He's in Turkey, visiting a sick relative.'

A feeling of fury mixed with heartache ripped right through Harper. 'He *isn't* in Turkey. He must have taken Yosef. Vanessa, trust me, that bastard kidnapped the baby and fucking burned my mother's house down.'

'Why would you say that?'

Shaking her head, Harper scowled in absolute frustration. 'Honestly, how the hell did you become a probation officer? You are so damn naïve, aren't you.'

Vanessa pursed her lips. 'I have a degree—'

‘Not in the psyche of abusive husbands, I bet. Look, Hasad is the epitome of a first-class bully. Why do you think my sister was staying at my mother’s house, eh? Did you not ask yourself that?’

Vanessa didn’t answer but called the detective over. ‘Harper, tell the detective, not me. My job is to make sure you’re not taken back to the prison.’

Detective Antony Barrows, forty-six years old, bowled over, with his pen at the ready.

He was a large man, and Harper thought he possessed a level of confidence that probably surpassed even Zavid’s.

Feeling exhausted and irritated, Harper, nevertheless, tried to wear a smile. She answered his questions as to her whereabouts over the past twelve hours or so, obviously leaving out the meeting with Zavid. And since the club closed at 1.30 a.m., she had a checkable alibi, and so she was free to go. But she didn’t appreciate his lack of enthusiasm or urgency to find her nephew.

‘Is that *it*? A few questions, an okay from my probation officer, and now we’re done? What’s happening about my missing nephew? Christ!’ She threw her hands in the air. ‘The house has burned to the ground, my sister’s in hospital, no one knows where the baby is, and you scribble a few fucking notes. Is that it?’

‘No! Ms Kane, that’s not it. We are doing everything we can at the moment to find your nephew and catch whoever is responsible for this arson attack.’

‘I *know* who it is, and it’s someone in Hasad’s family. In fact, he threatened to do it.’

Barrows pulled a handkerchief from his inside pocket and wiped his brow.

The weather was so muggy that Harper could feel the sweat trickling down her back.

‘We believe Hasad is in Turkey, and his brothers have alibis too.’

'Yeah? Are you sure? Have you checked? And I bet none of them seemed concerned about Yosef, did they? No, of course they fucking didn't because *they* have the baby.'

The detective glanced at Vanessa and then at Harper, and with a glimmer of a devilish grin, he leaned into her ear. 'I am doing more than you think. Believe me, love, just so you know.'

His words seemed to imply more than just a semblance of trivial information.

Harper felt the warning tone in his voice. *Did he think she would go after the family, and were the police watching them?* she wondered.

'Do many kids in this area go missing?' asked Harper.

'Usually teenagers. Not babies, so that's why I have every confidence we will find him soon.' He glanced at Vanessa. 'That's something your department occasionally deals with.'

'What? Oh, yes, sorry, missing teenagers. Well, not my department so much, unless a teenager is on probation. It's more the social services. It's usually the troubled ones who go missing, not tiny babies.'

'Your ol' man, Peter. Is he still in social services?' enquired the detective.

Vanessa replied with a nod and a painted-on smile.

'Yes, nice guy, Peter. You both work in the same building, opposite each other, don't you?'

Vanessa nodded again and bit her bottom lip as if she was just about to burst into tears. 'Yes, we do. Right, Harper, I can take you to the hospital. Hopefully, it will put your mind at ease,' she replied, changing the subject.

Then Barrows turned to Harper. 'Er, before you leave, would you mind telling me how you got that bruise on your chin? It looks a little swollen to me.'

Harper fingered her lump and chuckled. 'I got a touch of heat stroke and toppled over, bashing my face on the sideboard.'

The detective nodded and wiped his sweaty brow one more time.

Harper was now exhausted, but she followed Vanessa over to her Mercedes.

'Very nice, Vanessa,' she said, as she admired the car. She'd already clocked the Louis Vuitton bag hanging from her shoulder. 'Probation pays well.'

Vanessa blushed. 'I am a stickler for a savings account.'

Harper chuckled again. 'Your own or someone else's?'

At first, Vanessa didn't get the joke. Then she offered a faint laugh before pressing the fob on her key ring.

A flash of something shiny sparkled and it caught Harper's attention. The key ring was designed in the shape of a seahorse just like the one on the key ring attached to the flat keys promised to her. Harper's mind then returned to Zavid; specifically, the mosaic on one of the walls they had passed when he marched her through the house. It was also designed to represent a seahorse.

***

It was 1 p.m. by the time they arrived at the hospital. Harper didn't wait for Vanessa, who strode off to purchase a car park ticket. Marching straight into the building, Harper made enquiries as to her sister's whereabouts.

The ward had four beds to a unit, and there in the corner with her hands bandaged and her face red and sore was Lexi.

Ignoring the fact that she was probably not adhering to the strict visiting times, Harper hurried over to her sister and threw her arms around her. 'Jesus Christ, Lex, what happened? I nearly had fucking kittens when I saw the house burned down.'

Lexi's eyes filled with tears, and like a stream, they tumbled down her cheeks. 'Yosef was asleep in Mum's room. I was asleep in my old room. It was the smoke that woke me up.' She stopped to catch her breath. Her hands were shaking and her eyes were streaming. 'I ran to Mum's room, but she was all over the place, swaying and staggering. Oh my God, Harps, the heat, it was so bad. The room was so dark, I couldn't see him. I searched on the bed, under the bed, but I couldn't . . .' She paused to stop the crack in her voice. 'I thought he might have crawled out of the room, so I searched everywhere upstairs. Mum ran downstairs and managed to get out of the house. I crawled along the floor. Remember how they taught us in school? But, Sis, it was so hot, the flames – they were up the bannisters, and they caught your bedroom door frame alight. I tried to get into your room to see if he was hiding under your bed, but I couldn't do it, Harps. I couldn't get in there. I was so terrified that he would burn to death, but the flames, the heat.' She stopped and buried her face in her hands and sobbed like a baby.

'Lex, he wasn't in the fire. Someone took him.'

She stopped crying, wiped her face, and nodded. 'I know that now. The detective asked me questions, but he was kind enough to tell me that Yosef may well be alive. It's just the thought that I couldn't get to my baby. I couldn't help him. It will never leave me, Sis, will it – that fear?'

Harper rolled her eyes, listening to her sister. She was too sweet for her own good at times. 'The detective was kind enough, you say, eh, Sis? Well, they can have praise when they fucking well find him.'

Lexi looked a little dazed. 'It's my fault. I shouldn't have left him to sleep in Mum's bedroom. But, really, I should have stayed put at Hasad's place. Then, I would still have my baby and Mum's house would still be standing.'

Harper wiped the hair away from her sister's sore face. 'Are you hurting, Lex?'

'Only inside, I am. I knew he would come for Yosef. I knew I could never really get away. He is probably in Turkey by now.'

'We will get Yosef back, Lex. I promise you, we will.'

With an accepting smile, Lexi closed her eyes.

A nurse tapped Harper on the shoulder somewhat abruptly. 'We have very sick people on this ward, and Sunday visiting hours are from 2 p.m. until 8 p.m., so I am asking you politely to leave and come back later.'

Harper spun around and gave the nurse a death stare before getting up from the bed. 'Don't ever touch me again, love.'

The middle-aged Irish nurse was stunned, but she didn't want to upset the woman any more than she had, so she offered her a hesitant smile and walked away.

'Lex, tell me, how come Mother didn't see or hear anyone coming into the house?'

Lexi kept her stinging eyes closed. 'A box of wine arrived for her earlier. She was drunk by nine o'clock. Oh God, I wished I'd had Yosef in bed with me, not hers. Well, never again. Why do I trust her, Harper? Every time, she lets me down.'

Harper gently stroked her sister's hair. 'Sis, I promise you this. I will get your boy back, even if I die trying.'

'Where will I go? I can't stay at Erin's. We don't get on.'

Her voice was faint and weary. Harper guessed they had given her morphine.

'I told you. I have a place. It comes with the job.' She stopped, her mind shooting back to Zavid. How could she take the accommodation, knowing that it was linked to the Russian? Biting her nails, she watched as her sister fell into a drug induced sleep.

***

Vanessa was in her car and busy on her phone. She almost jumped out of her skin when Harper nudged her arm.

'Sorry I marched off. Anyway, thanks for the lift. Look, since you've seen me today, do you mind if I skip Monday? As you can imagine, I have a lot to do.'

Vanessa still looked startled.

'Are you okay, Vanessa?'

'Yes, yes, you made me jump, that's all. I'm not used to people creeping up behind me when I am having a private conversation.' Her tone sounded defensive.

Harper shrugged her shoulders. 'You're in a bloody public car park. So?' she said, glaring as she waited for an answer.

'Er, what? Er, no, it's fine. I will expect you in my office on Tuesday, though, at 11 a.m. sharp.'

A sudden feeling of overwhelming exhaustion gripped Harper. 'Vanessa, you couldn't do me a favour, could you, and take me to work? I have a few bits I need to finish off before the club opens again.'

It was evident that Vanessa was distracted by something, but she nodded to Harper to get in.

Again, Harper clambered into the front seat and was about to give Vanessa directions when she stopped and stared at the seahorse catching the light as it swayed with the movement of the car.

While Vanessa drove, Harper noticed the probation officer's hands: they were clearly trembling.

'Everything all right, Vanessa?'

'What? Oh yeah. Everything's fine.'

As Vanessa headed towards Bromley North, Harper felt uneasy herself. How in the world did Vanessa know where she worked? She had not even told her. With her mind in turmoil, Harper tried to recall if she had mentioned the place, but she was damn sure she hadn't. Glancing at the seahorse, a disturbing thought crossed her mind. *Was her probation officer involved in this evil crime?* A cold unnerving feeling swept over her. She shook her head and blinked a few times to regain her composure. She had to question if her suspicions were becoming absurd. As far as she was aware, her probation officer was an upstanding member of society. Then, she recalled mentioning something to the detective. Perhaps she *had* named the club; yes, that would be it.

Vanessa's phone buzzed loudly, and it nearly caused an accident, with a cyclist forced up on to the pavement.

'Hey, Vanessa, are you sure you're okay? You don't half seem on edge.'

Vanessa drove into the street that led to the club. 'Will this be okay?' she said, without answering Harper's question.

'Yeah, sure, thank you.' Slowly, Harper got out of the car and found it odd that Vanessa didn't say another word. Instead, she nervously smiled before tearing off.

Once the car was out of sight, Harper banged on the door. She hoped that the cleaners would be there, but there was silence. 'Damn!' she shouted, as she realised there were no cars. She was now stranded, with no home to go to, and no money, but worse, she had no bag, which contained her keys to enter the club. Rubbing her bruised chin, she sighed. Her only hope was to get inside the club. She thought about the ladies' toilets and wondered if the small window was open. *Surely not. Claude would have made sure it was all locked up, wouldn't he?*

As soon as she made her way behind the club and looked through the window, she noticed that it was closed but not locked. Grabbing the corner of the window, she managed to tug it open. It was a small opening, and so if she had been a few pounds heavier, she wouldn't have managed to slither in like an adder. She had to go in head first, but Lady Luck was on her side because she spotted a table just below her, so her outstretched arms didn't have to break her fall from any great height, and she managed to get down with nothing impeding her except for her shoe, which became caught on the latch. It was dark inside the club. Worryingly, the sensor lights hadn't come on. She wondered if the security system had been deliberately turned off. Finally, she found the light switch. Nevertheless, she still couldn't shake off her nerves. The place seemed so very spooky. *Get a grip.* With her senses on full alert and her skin alive with goosebumps, she needed to focus on locating her bag and finding a hotel for the night.

When she entered the bar, which opened into a back room, she was relieved to find some ambient lighting still switched on. She looked behind the bar, but there was nothing. Certainly no bag. Moving quickly into the back room, she felt as if eyes were watching her. *Where was the sodding bag?* She was almost at the point of desperation when she clocked what she was looking for. There by the back door beside the fridge was her bag. *Of course! She'd had it with her when she'd butted Claude; it must have fallen off her when they dragged her to the car to meet Zavid.*

She did a quick check of the rooms and was relieved to find she was alone. Instantly, the adrenaline rush, which she'd had when she arrived, dissipated. Now she felt tired, and she needed some energy to keep going. Thinking a Coke would liven her up a bit, she walked back to the bar, where she prised the lid off a Coke bottle. She drank as quickly as she could and belched loudly. Then she chuckled to herself. She needn't have worried about sneaking into the club like that. No one was around to hear her animal noises. She popped open another bottle and glanced at the cutting board used for lemon slicing. The knife glistened under the fluorescent strip that ran under the glass shelving.

She needed sleep urgently. Remembering Vadim showing her a secret entrance to the cottage next door to his office, she finished her drink, popped the knife into her bag, and approached his office. Using the set of keys that Vadim had given her, she let herself in, locking the office door behind her. Then, she slid the bookcase aside before venturing into the adjacent building. Alone, she had the chance to take a closer look. It reminded her of her granny's house. The staircase was narrow and steep and it had a carpet runner going up the middle. It even smelled like her granny's place.

Her legs felt as though they were weighted down by lead socks, but once she reached the top, she found a bedroom and a bathroom; both were small but clean. The bedroom was certainly adequate to catch forty winks. The room was cool, a relief from the muggy weather. It comprised a double bed, which had a quilt covered in a white duvet slip and a basic pine wardrobe with a matching cabinet. The long Victorian sash window was dressed with a wooden blind. On the bedside cabinet there was a clock and a plain black lamp. The only décor in the room that was feminine was a ballerina picture, hung over the bed.

After kicking off her shoes, Harper placed the bag on the floor, and the knife under her pillow, before she lay down on top of the bed. It was now late afternoon on Sunday. It meant she hadn't slept properly since Friday night. She was hungry, but she was too tired to eat, so within seconds, she fell into a deep sleep.

Chapter Twelve

It was 3 a.m. on Monday when Harper stirred. The room was almost completely dark except for misty shards of moonlight. Her brain slowly moved into gear before realising where she was. *Had something woken her up?* As her eyes began to adjust to the darkness, she felt a cold shiver run up her spine. Because standing in the corner of the room was an ominous shadow of a man, a big man. Like a child, she stared and prayed for the shadowy figure to disappear into the blackness and not touch her. But when she heard the gentle hiss of breathing, she felt her hair stand on end. Holding her own breath for a moment, she could still hear it. He wasn't moving, merely standing there. Naïvely, she hoped all the while she was looking at him, he wouldn't move.

She was wrong. When he stepped out of the darkness, the moonlight shone a streak of milky light through the blind. It caught a strip of his face that highlighted his crooked grin and dog-snarl teeth.

He took up the gap between the bed and the door.

Harper assessed her options. She realised it would be futile to attempt to dash past him. But she wasn't going to give in, even though he had hurt her once already. So she rose to her feet, knowing this would be one hell of a fight.

'Fuck off, Claude!'

He didn't answer; he just stared, licking his lips in anticipation.

'If you so much as touch me with your fat fingers, I swear to God, I will create mayhem, be it with your boss or the police.'

'You won't do that, Harper Kane, will you?' he smirked. 'Because you know what we will do to your family. We own you now.' His chuckle was cruel and menacing. 'It's how it works.'

Harper thought of how terrified the young girls would be, to be faced with someone like Claude, with his deep threatening voice and powerful build. She knew what it was like to be petrified of a man. To fear his hands touching her.

'I ain't one of your little girls you took off the street, you fucking great oaf. You know that if you batter me, your boss will be shitting hot bricks because it may just tip me over the edge and give me no choice but to go to the police.'

Claude began unbuttoning his shirt.

Panic rose in her voice. 'What do you think you're doing?'

'You work for us now, and I am going to sample the merchandise.'

'I don't work for you, you cunt. I just manage the bar and turn a blind eye, so fuck off, Claude. I'm warning you.'

He continued to remove his shirt and belt while Harper trembled with fury. It was one of those moments where she was supposed to count to ten and think of something fluffy, but right now, all she could think of was murder. His. As he bent down to remove his shoes, she lunged forward to make a run for it, but he was fast and grabbed her waist, before literally catapulting her onto the bed. He wasn't only fast. He was forceful too. So much so that her head smashed against the wall, momentarily stunning her. A feeling that her brains were rattling inside her head and her nose being pricked by pins and needles stopped her from lunging at him again.

'You are going nowhere!' he hissed, through his gnarly teeth, as he continued to remove his shoes.

Pushing herself up the bed, Harper was afraid; it brought back dark memories of men in the past who had tried it on with her. She was scared and angry. No man had the right to help himself. All her life, she'd had to fight. She had fought for her virginity, for her sisters' safety, and for her own sanity, and she would be damned if this great ugly Russian was going to take what wasn't his.

Desperate to think of a way out before he hit her again, Harper stared at the door.

He chuckled and leaned down to turn on the light. He was completely naked and standing to attention. Having the room illuminated suddenly made it more real.

Her stomach churned, and her hands shook. He was a big man, with bulging biceps and arms like the branches of an oak tree. And his manhood was enormous. But she wasn't going to lie back and let him rape her. Never.

Unexpectedly, he grabbed her by her short hair and pulled her face towards his penis. She tried to tear away, but he had the strength of a gorilla.

The knife! The knife! She remembered she'd put it under the pillow before falling asleep. With one hand, she tried to hold him back, and with the other, she frantically searched under the pillow. Panic gripped her around the chest like a tightening tourniquet. It was not there. She must have moved the knife in her sleep. Her arm was shaking and aching from the resistance. He was forcing her lips to touch his disgusting, stinking dick.

'No, slut? You don't want to satisfy me?' He shook her head and then violently slapped her face.

It stung like a million bees. Her eyes widened when he slapped her a second time and then a third. The pain was immense. She felt her nose pop and knew he had probably broken it with the force behind the backhander.

She removed her hand from beneath the pillow to protect her face, but he was so powerful, she was like a kitten fighting a lion.

He grabbed her around the throat with one hand and almost lifted her off the bed. She couldn't breathe and was desperate to rip his hand away. Finally, he threw her back down and laughed, as though he was enjoying her struggle. His laugh took her to the past. To the man who had tried to rape her when she was a kid. He'd laughed too, before he'd received a swift kick in the bollocks. He didn't laugh after that. In fact, he didn't visit their mother again.

She slid her hand under the pillow once more, as she finally managed to sit upright, but to no avail. While her mind was on finding the knife, his was obviously on getting her knickers off. But she kicked and kicked. One hard kick landed between his legs.

He stopped and groaned, his features contorted into an anguished grimace. Holding himself, he hopped and moaned.

She had clearly caught him with a good one.

But it only intensified his fury, and instead of a slap, he threw a punch.

Harper moved quickly enough to dodge the full force of his fist.

Bingo! She felt the cold handle of the knife. It was now in her hand. As he came at her again, she lifted the weapon and stabbed him right through his knuckle.

The shock at first compelled him to back off and investigate the damage.

Harper leaped from the bed, clutching the weapon to threaten him.

'Get out of my way, Claude, or I will cut you up and put your balls on a plate.'

Claude's lips tightened; his eyes then narrowed before he pulled back his fist to really belt her one. He was big, but he wasn't swift enough. He had clearly filled his boots with copious amounts of vodka and was probably not as fast as he thought he was.

Harper managed to dodge his clumsy punch and viciously stabbed his side. She assumed he would fall like a sack of shit, but he didn't.

He went at her again as if the wound was a pinprick. His punch caught the side of her head.

She wobbled, and that's when he attacked again. Clutching his punctured side with his damaged hand, he used his other one to crack her in the ribs.

Although it hurt like hell, Harper wasn't ready to die just yet. With all the strength she had, she screamed, 'Turn it in, you vile bastard!' as she plunged the knife into his chest again and again. Fury and fear were a cocktail that had never agreed with her, and so she continued plunging the knife into his chest until she was out of breath. The series of frenzied blows were decorating the room in speckles of claret.

Claude himself was in a pool of blood – a lifeless mess on the floor.

Breathless and shaking all over, she collapsed on the bed, gasping for air until she could calm down, gather her senses, and process the carnage she had created.

Think, Harper, think!

It was still reasonably dark. If she could drag his body outside, then it would look like a street attack, she told herself. She remembered Alicia, one of the girls in prison, who had tried to dispose of the body of her abusive husband. She'd wrapped him in cling film to contain the blood before she'd carried him to the boot of her car.

Cling film! Cling film!

She remembered there was a roll of it in the back room, where the fridges were. Treading carefully around him, she ran down the stairs, through the office, and into the club. Along with the cling film, she grabbed some black sacks. Searching the cleaner's closet for household products, she found a bag of salt, rubber gloves, and a large container labelled 'bloodstain removal solution'. With a deep frown, she stared at it, wondering why there would be an industrial cleaner for blood, and then she realised it was a club, and with alcohol came fights, and with fights came claret.

With her arms full, she hurried back to the bedroom and carefully laid everything on the bed. Her heart was racing, and her back was dripping with sweat, but she had to get the man outside. She couldn't leave any evidence of Claude's demise in the cottage. She stared at the gruesome mess and particularly his face; it was still showing the large dog-like teeth. He stank of vodka, sweat, and now – she sniffed the air – of shit. *Oh God, the bastard had shit himself.* She could handle blood, but shit was a whole other thing. Still, it had to be done. Pulling a long strip of the cling film, she laid it across his chest and then attempted to roll the man over. The issues were twofold: firstly, she couldn't budge him because he was a dead weight, and secondly, he was wedged between the bed that was already positioned up tight against the two walls and the wardrobe.

'Damn! Damn! Jesus, Alicia, did you make your story up? Your abusive husband must have been a skinny rake of a man,' she mumbled to herself.

There was only one way she could dispose of him, and that was to cut him into sections. *Oh, fuck me!*

She sat contemplating actually cutting the man up. *Could she do it? Was there any other alternative?* No, there wasn't, apart from confessing, and, really, that would simply send her back to prison, self-defence or not. And how could she plead self-defence or rape? She had no stab wounds or any of his semen on her body.

She had to get this situation sorted soon. What if Vadim returned? Her pulse drummed in her temples. Tearing back to the club, she searched for a saw, although she thought it was probably hopeless. After a good twenty minutes of frantically searching, she leaned against the bar and sighed. Then she saw a set of car keys, Claude's car keys. She could drive. It had been a while, but, no doubt, it would naturally come back to her. The only issue now was time. She had to wait until the shops were open.

Having paced the floor of the bedroom for hours, she finally removed her clothes, washed the blood off her hands and face, and hurried to the changing room. In a bag in the corner, she found one of the pole dancers' tracksuits. She quickly slipped it on, then rifled through the wigs. By the time she left the changing room, she was a new person, what with the long red hair, oversized sunglasses, and rapper-style silver tracksuit. And wearing one of the girls' flip-flops and a full face of make-up, she was ready to go. Taking a few twenties from the till, she had money to buy what she needed.

Luckily, she had recalled how Claude drove the car. Fascinated by its luxury, she had watched how he had put his foot on the brake to start it. She managed to move slowly from the kerb and along the main road. The drive was smooth, and the power steering made it a doddle.

She hadn't a clue about the opening times of the store, but she had no choice. If it was shut, she would have to wait. Getting used to the powerful car now, she lowered the driver's window a little. The breeze was enough to soothe her chaotic mind. How could so much have happened in such a short space of time? It was as if she had been drugged and was living in some crazy, fantastical dreamworld.

Her thoughts turned to prison and a reminder of when she had counted down the days before her release. Every day away from her boy had been painful. It still was. She had accepted the advice from Teddy that her little Eddie shouldn't be visiting a nick as often as he was. He was always so clean and smart. It wasn't right that he sat on a plastic chair surrounded by officers and inmates. Some of the latter were high on drugs, with scabby lips and skeletal faces. They were enough to give *her* nightmares, let alone a toddler. That was the last time she saw her son. He was three, with a mop of blond curls, eyes like moonstones, and a smile that would melt anyone's heart.

She would never forget that day. He was dressed in an Aran knitted jumper, a pair of beige trousers, and a little baseball cap. He had waved so sweetly as his father carried him out of the visiting room. She smiled that day, although her heart was breaking. Her eyes were stinging with tears ready to fall the moment he was out of sight. And tumble they did. She cried herself to sleep for weeks. Then, she realised that she had to toughen up. A long bird was hard enough, but she was on a wing with the evil, the insane, and the outright violent inmates. It was do or die.

She couldn't return to prison now. She had to get her son back and honour the promises to Madeleine and her sister Lexi. If the police ever got a whiff that she was involved in Claude's death, self-defence or not, she would be right back inside and serving the rest of her life behind bars. She pushed the thought away.

Her mind flicked to the baby, Baby Yosef. She knew he was with Hasad or with his family, so he was safe; she felt it in her bones. But guilt consumed her. If she hadn't bricked Hasad, then perhaps he wouldn't have burned the house down, as he'd threatened, and Lexi would still be cradling her son.

What a fucking mess!

The B & Q signage was the same as it was all those years ago. The store was open. She could see customers wheeling their trollies inside. Parking the car, she got out, lowering her head before making her way into the superstore. Trying not to make eye contact with anyone, she found the tools section and grabbed three hacksaws of varying tooth sizes, a small axe, and some heavy-duty rubble sacks, along with nylon rope. Her eyes were drawn to the soft furnishings section, and in particular, a range of duvets and covers. That was a thought. She grabbed two pillows and a white duvet set.

The cashier hardly looked up as she scanned the items and held out her hand for the money. 'Got your ol' man busy today?'

'Yeah, cutting up some bits that are in the way,' Harper replied, slapping the twenties into the cashier's palm. Once she was back in the car, she was careful to keep to the speed limit. She didn't want the police stopping her.

It was 11 a.m., by the time she returned to the bedroom. Placing her outer clothes in a bag, she left on her underwear. Then, pulling on a pair of rubber gloves, she stared at Claude's face and decided she couldn't bear to look at it anymore.

Although she hated the man, she could only dismember him if she visualised cutting up a lump of meat.

Unravelling the black sacks, Harper placed one over Claude's head. She then lifted his shoulders and put another sack underneath to catch the blood, regardless of the fact that it shouldn't be pumping because he was dead. Gripping one of the hacksaws tightly in her hands, she knelt down beside the dead man. With her nostrils flared, she took a deep breath, as if she were about to dive into a swimming pool.

Gently placing the teeth of the hacksaw onto his shoulder joint, she closed her eyes and began to saw. She had to do this slowly at first because she could feel the blade slip as it attempted to cut through the muscle. In frustration, but not getting anywhere fast, she pushed and pulled the saw vigorously. *This was not the right way.* The hacksaw seemed to chew the flesh away, rather than cut it.

A longer sharp knife.

Jumping to her feet, Harper hurried to the bathroom and washed her hands, still with her rubber gloves on, and went in search of a longer knife. She could feel the sweat running down her back. The small kitchen downstairs in the cottage had practically no cutlery and only one long knife. *That will do.*

Wasting no time, she got back to work, until, finally, she felt the density of the bone. Sweat dripped from her forehead and her top lip. It was hot and thirsty work, but she had to carry on, to get him out of the room. After stopping for a breather, she took the small axe, lifted it above her head, and plunged it down right on the joint. The squelch and thud, as the axe chopped through his shoulder, made her gag. She had become a butcher.

A sudden feeling filled her mind with a sense of dreaded reality. *What the hell was she really doing?*

She had focused on the severed arm. She had done it. Claude's arm was now detached from his body. Hurriedly, she tore off another black sack from the heavy-duty roll, opened it, and placed the arm inside. The hand was popping out, and she noticed a ring, an ID giveaway, if ever there was one. Sliding the ring from his finger, she put it on the bed and decided to give it some thought later.

It was a long and arduous process; it was taking all her strength and stamina to remove his limbs, leaving just a torso with the head still attached. She wondered if, after all this, she would be suitable for the mental health hospital and labelled as deranged. Still, as mad as this whole ordeal was, she suddenly felt very much in control and perfectly sane.

There was no point in leaving his butchered body parts out on the streets because it would look like more than a simple street brawl that had ended in murder. Instead, it would suggest a retribution killing or send out a message to the Russian mafia, or whoever they were. And with that kind of attention, the police would be swarming all over the place.

She had been meticulously careful and had used every tip learned from spending years inside with killers. She had parked his car in the alley that ran alongside the club. It was pretty well hidden from passers-by. She carried each bag through the club and out to the back, where she placed his body parts in the boot. Each time, she scanned the surroundings first.

Finally, she was left with the main bulk of his body, with his head still attached. Although he was heavy, she could deal with the weight. Wrapping him in cling film took a while, but once she'd finished, she bagged him up in the heavy-duty sacks before she tied the nylon rope around the covered head. There was still some mess in the room, even though she had used black sacks to cover the floor, but she guessed cleaning products would remove most of the blood.

Feeling sticky from sweat and bursting for a pee, she hurried across the small landing to the bathroom. After using the toilet, she ran the shower, stripped off, and cooled herself under the gentle spray. Emerging with a small towel, she quickly dried herself. Then, cupping her hands under the tap, she drank voraciously to quench her thirst. Slipping back into the silver tracksuit and putting on her rubber gloves, she felt ready to put the remaining part of Claude's body into the boot of his car. As she hauled him down the stairs, there was a loud thud as he hit each tread.

It had been eerie when she had arrived at the club. Now, with the nylon biting into her hands, and it rubbing against her shoulder, and the incessant sound from hauling a dead body, she realised she was living a real-life horror film in which she was playing the lead role.

As she reached the bar, she heard a noise coming from the back door. She glanced around. *Where the hell would she hide what was left of the body? And who was trying to get in?* Sweat covered her brow as her breathing intensified. She prayed to God that whoever was trying to enter the club was merely hankering after a drink. Lifting the hatch, she used all her strength to haul the torso behind the bar. It proved exhausting: her arms were shaking as though she had been at the gym for hours lifting weights.

Scanning the area, she checked for any signs of blood. There were none. Then she removed her rubber gloves and hid them under the bar counter along with the car keys.

Before she had a chance to think what to do next, the back door opened and there in clear view of the bar stood Pixie, who was dressed in a black catsuit.

Instantly, she caught sight of Harper and marched towards her.

But Harper needed to meet Pixie well away from where she had hidden the body.

Opening the hatch, Harper frowned. 'What do you want me to do, Pixie? Only, Zavid said you would have instructions for me.'

Pixie waved her hand dismissively. 'Nothing. Where is Claude?' She appeared preoccupied.

Harper hoped that Pixie couldn't see the faint blush in her cheeks or the sweat curls at the nape of her neck. 'Er, he was here earlier looking for a phone.'

Pixie stood defiantly with her hands on her hips. 'He came back for a phone?'

Harper nodded. 'Something about an important call he needed to make. He asked me to help him find his mobile. He seemed a bit pissed off or anxious. I don't know. Anyway, he found it.'

'Did he speak to anyone?'

Harper nodded.

Pixie's frown deepened in disgruntled surprise. 'Who?' she demanded.

Harper sucked in air through her teeth. 'Er, not sure. Er, I think I heard him say Clive or was it Clayton? No, maybe it was Calvin. I'm not sure. I could be wrong.'

'Calvin?' Her voice was brittle.

Harper shrugged. 'Possibly.'

'You said he sounded annoyed?'

Harper nodded. 'Kinda grumpy. I just got out of his way. I wasn't going to take another clump from him.'

Pixie was gazing around. Clearly, something was bothering her, and Harper knew then she had set the cat among some dangerous gun-wielding pigeons by mentioning Calvin. Yet Calvin wasn't here to dispute what she'd said, and Claude was hardly in a position to call her a liar.

'Are you sure he was talking to a man called Calvin? Because if you are lying to me, you will suffer badly. You understand?'

Harper was on to a winner; she would stir up a hornet's nest. Now, seeing the frustration, or possibly concern on Pixie's face, it told Harper that it *was* Calvin Stuart who was in the club last night. Calvin wasn't a common name. She guessed he was a bigwig among this circle of evil criminals.

'Look, Pixie, or whatever the fuck your name is, your boss has a hold over me by using my son as a guarantee, and I agreed to go along with whatever, but don't fucking push it. I'm not a punching bag, or a silly bit of a kid, for that matter. I'm like you, a grown woman, so fuck right off with the threats. I said I thought he was talking to a man called Calvin. It's none of my business, and I couldn't give a fuck who he was arguing with.'

Pixie lifted her chin. 'You are a hard bitch, aren't you, Harper?'

'No, Pixie, I'm just a woman who doesn't take shit for no reason. So, if he comes back, what shall I tell him?'

Looking Harper up and down, Pixie frowned. It was Monday and the club wouldn't be open until Tuesday. 'What the hell are you doing here?'

'I was checking the stock and seeing to the accounts, like Vadim asked me to.'

Pixie glanced around the room again before pulling a phone from her bag.

Harper felt her heart sink. If Pixie called Claude, his phone would almost certainly ring somewhere in the cottage next door. She only hoped that the walls were soundproof.

She watched anxiously as Pixie held the phone to her ear while tapping her foot. 'Fucking answer!'

Gradually, as they waited for the call to be answered, Harper felt her body relax.

'Why is his car outside if he is not here?'

Harper shrugged her shoulders. 'He may have gone off with the man who pulled up a few minutes ago.'

'What man?'

'I don't know.'

Pixie's face was now glowing red in anger. 'Harper, don't fuck with me. What man? What car?'

'He was arguing on the phone outside the club. Later, when I put the rubbish outside, I saw a man in a flash car. I don't know what make, just a black one. The man had longish hair. That's all I know.'

Harper clocked Pixie grit her teeth and mumble 'Calvin' under her breath.

She spun around. 'When Claude comes back, tell him he must call me urgently.'

'Yeah, sure. Oh, Pixie, what's the address of my flat? Claude gave me the keys but forgot to tell me the address.'

'251B, Rodway Road,' she called, over her shoulder.

'What, here in Bromley?'

'Yes.'

For a brief moment, Harper felt a twinge of excitement. Rodway Road was a lovely street – posh, in fact.

Harper watched Pixie march through the back room and push through the rear door, obviously with the bit between her teeth. She waited until she heard a car start up before letting out a heavy sigh, and then she continued with the disposal of Claude's body and cleaning the mess in the bedroom.

Chapter Thirteen

By early Monday evening, Harper had cleaned the bedroom to a professional standard. Luckily for her, the walls were painted with washable paint and the industrial cleaning liquid worked like magic. Checking that there was nothing incriminating on the camera footage, she discovered that Vadim was being truthful when he had said the cameras didn't actually record: they were only live. Finally, she eyeballed every inch of the route she had used to drag the body parts, ensuring there were no traces of blood.

Wearing her wig and oversized glasses, Harper drove Claude's car to Hasad's garage, part of the Boz family's business. She had learned in prison that many main roads were fitted with ANPR cameras, so she avoided those and stuck to the side streets. Reaching the garage after closing time, she searched for any CCTV cameras. It wasn't worth taking any chances, so she circled the area a few times, before she parked the car directly in front of the premises.

The first part of her plan was in place. So far, so good.

After thoroughly wiping the interior of the car clean of potential DNA, she stuffed the wig, her sunglasses, and the silver tracksuit top inside a plastic bag, leaving just the tracksuit bottoms and a black T-shirt on before she turned the corner and headed to the bus stop to catch a bus back to Bromley, to her new place. She threw the plastic bag into a large communal bin, near to a block of flats, before she sprinted to catch the bus.

***

The flat was Victorian. Harper could tell just from the exterior alone that it had been renovated to a high standard. It had its own front door; the flat above also had a separate entrance. She hadn't been inside an actual classy property before, apart from the mansion where she had been taken to see Zavid.

When Harper opened the front door, she took a deep excitable breath. It was unbelievably perfect. She was met with white gleaming walls and large windows that were dressed in heavy drapes. She walked into a spacious lounge, with soft grey carpet, a large dark-grey sofa with matching armchairs, and two bookcases on either side of the fireplace. Her excitement put a smile on her face. Heading to the room at the back, she was pleasantly surprised. It consisted of a brand-new kitchen and dining area with a contemporary style wooden table and wrought-iron chairs, which she felt finished off the room very well. The French doors opened onto a small garden. She walked back along the narrow corridor and opened the door on the left. 'Bloody hell,' she said, out loud. The bedroom was so swish, she thought she had opened the door into a hotel room at the Ritz, or somewhere fancy like that. The large bed was layered in plush fabrics and cushions, all in muted pinks. The floor was covered in scattered fur rugs, and the bed itself was so plump it reminded her of a marshmallow. She guessed if she lay on it now, she would sleep for a week.

The next room was the same size, with a double bed, high-quality rugs, and a huge black-and-white picture of a jazz player above the bed. It was equally inviting.

Now that she had her ducks in a row, she sat down on the sofa and tipped the contents of her bag onto the floor. Claude's phone was there. She held it in her hand and stared at it.

She recalled the exact time that Pixie had dialled Claude's phone because she remembered glancing up at the clock at that time. It was easy to work out Pixie's phone number from the list of missed calls. There was no doubt it was hers since prior to the call at 1.30 p.m. there had been a string of texts from the same number. Here were all the signs of a desperate woman. She smiled to herself. That was what Pixie or Pasha had called *her* – desperate.

Well, desperate times call for desperate measures, and this Russian gang or wannabe mafia lot were in for a shock. She hadn't stewed inside a prison all that time without learning some old tricks from the best. Fight fire with fucking fire. She knew she didn't have the muscle to take down a whole army. What she would do, though, would be to use her steadily acquired knowledge. While Zavid had seriously dangerous backup, she had Claude's phone, which she now decided could be of real help to her. This would form the basis of her plan. All she had to do was to make sure the plan could never be traced back to her. She would have to spend her time acting the naïve and gobby woman.

The first thing to do was to get Yosef back and safe. She wondered if Claude would text in Russian. Then she realised that Russian letters were not the same as English ones. His phone was a Motorola, and she remembered the passcode – all sixes. Scrolling down at the messages, Harper could see they were in English. A little cryptic but nothing too sophisticated.

As she was about to put the phone in her bag, it buzzed; it was another text from Pixie. ***Where the fuck are you? Zavid is not happy. Call me urgently. Are you with CS???***

Harper guessed she meant Calvin Stuart; the mention of the man's name had obviously got them worried. Now she really would cause mayhem, but first, she needed to talk with Lexi.

***

Harper used the landline phone in the lounge to call a cab. She would make full use of her new flat because one day she could be escorted out in handcuffs or via a black body bag, courtesy of the Russians. The cab arrived and she instructed the driver to take her to the Princess Royal University Hospital. Harper hurried to her sister's ward. She hoped that Lexi was well enough to come home to their new abode.

With her face red and her hands bandaged, Lexi looked so sorry for herself.

‘Hey, Sis, what’s up?’ asked Harper, as she sat on the chair beside the bed.

Lexi peered up and shook her head, her bottom lip quivering.

‘Lex?’

‘Social services came by. They have Yosef.’

Harper twisted her head in confusion. ‘*What?*’

‘They said that Hasad’s sister had no idea that the house had been burned down after she had visited it. She reckons that when she called, she found empty bottles of wine. Mum was drunk and I was out of it on drugs, so she said she took the baby. Now, the social is testing me for drugs. They think I may have lost the plot and need some psychiatric help.’ The tears rolled down her face. ‘Oh God, Harper, why would they do that to me? Why? I’d never drink or take drugs, never ever. I wouldn’t put my baby at risk.’

‘Right,’ said Harper, her muscles tightening in rage. ‘Who is this fucking sister of his?’

Lexi looked around and waved her hand, telling Harper to keep her voice down.

‘Her name is Shabab. She is a few years older than Hasad and a right royal cunt with a fat neck and a moustache. Oh, Harps, I hate her. I’ve never liked the bitch. Always bossing me around and putting me down as a mother.’ She paused, and her eyes narrowed. ‘She didn’t come to the house, the lying cow. It was Hasad. I know it was, and I bet he handed Yosef to her. And then they concocted this bullshit story.’

Harper gritted her teeth. ‘Who sent the box of wine to Mother?’

Lexi shrugged her shoulders, and then a frown of contemplation flickered across her forehead. ‘That wine, I remember now. It came in a crate. Hasad’s brother deals in wine. He buys it by the crate and relabels it for the restaurants. It’s cheap plonk that he serves as good wine.’

‘Where exactly is Yosef now?’

‘With social services, until they can do a full report on me, and what’s worse, now I don’t even have a fucking home. Oh, Sis, I wish I hadn’t left Hasad.’

‘You *do* have a home. It’s a right posh pad, an’ all. Get your gear together. I’ll take you there now. Where’s the nurse? Surely, you’re ready to leave?’ She glanced at her sister’s bandaged hands.

‘The truth is they discharged me early this morning. They gave me an old dressing gown. That’s all I have – a fucking old bit of rag. I was waiting for transport to take me to Erin’s. I had to give the social an address, you see.’

‘Never mind that address. We will call the social services and have them see your new place.’

A sudden torrent of tears flooded Lexi’s cheeks. ‘Harps, I wish I’d never met him, and in a way, I wish I’d never had Yosef. I wouldn’t feel this pain, then.’ She paused and wiped her face. ‘Sorry, Harps, I’m crying like a baby, and it must be worse for you, not having Eddie.’

Harper put her arms around her sister and hugged her. ‘No, my sweetheart, I had years to get used to not having my baby, but you won’t have to because we will get Yosef back, mark my words.’

Lexi smiled, a ray of hope settling in her mind.

‘Now, when we get to my place, I need you to start thinking clearly.’

Lexi frowned. ‘What do you mean?’

‘Let’s just get out of here, first.’

***

As soon as they entered the flat, Lexi threw her bandaged hands to her face. ‘Oh my God, Harps, this is bloody lovely. It’s way better than mine. I mean Hasad’s house. It’s beautiful. All I need is Yosef’s cot and his clothes, and then, once the social realise I’m not on drugs, they can’t have anything to use against me.’

‘That’s right, Lex. Once your tests come back as clear, they will definitely have to let you have him back.’

‘Yeah, but there’s a problem. When my test results are back, then the finger is gonna be pointed at them. And then, they will have me killed. Honestly, Harps, you have no idea how dangerous they are.’

Harper sat in an armchair while Lexi curled her legs up under her on the sofa. ‘Tell me about Hasad’s family, Lex, and leave nothing out. I already know they own the garage in Catford and have a string of takeaways, but I want to know all about their business – their illegal stuff, their names, their addresses. I want to know which fucking hand they wipe their arse with.’

Lexi momentarily chuckled before her face turned serious. ‘I meant it when I said they are dangerous. But Hasad is really the weakest one. His brothers Mehmet and Rifat are both evil. But the father, Mo, is the main man. What he says goes. Harps, if you knew how bad they were, you would probably talk me out of getting Yosef back.’

‘Would I, really? Lex, I fought for you and the others, didn’t I?’ replied Harper, raising her brows.

Lexi nodded. ‘Yes, you kept us safe, unlike Mum, but, Harps, this is different. These people are violent, aggressive men who have no respect for women. It stems from the father, Mo. He beats their mother, and if he knocks her about, what do you think the sons do to their wives? And Mo even encourages it.’

Harper’s blood was boiling. Feeling such a festering anger inside her, she knew that until the Boz family were dealt with, it would continue to burn her from the inside out.

‘And this sister, Shabab?’

Lexi’s eyes welled up with tears. ‘She is a big woman, her father’s princess, but she is probably the sickest of them all. She, she . . .’ The tears tumbled.

‘Tell me, Lex.’

‘I will, if you promise not to go after her. I couldn’t stand it if you went back to prison. I have no one, Harps, only you,’ said Lexi, through her tears.

Harper nodded. ‘I won’t go after her, not without a plan. I swear to God, I’ll have her, though. Lex, tell me, what the fuck have this family done to you?’

Lexi’s eyes were red and heavy. She settled back into the sofa. ‘Can I have a drink first? I’d love a cuppa.’

Harper could see she was tired and in pain. ‘Sorry, o’ course you can, babe.’ Hurrying to the kitchen, she hoped that there were some tea bags, although she’d expected the kitchen cupboards to be empty. Rhea would probably have taken everything with her.

Surprisingly, the cupboards were full, with tins, dried food, tea, and coffee. Even the fridge was packed with fresh products. All healthy food, with no dirty burgers. A sudden uneasy feeling stung her. Perhaps Rhea hadn’t moved out after all. It was quite possible that the Russians had murdered her. Why she felt so shocked was daft. She had already witnessed one brutal killing at their hands.

After putting the kettle on, she entered what would now be her bedroom and pulled open the wardrobe, only to find it bare except for a few old hangers. She then opened a drawer, and to her surprise, inside were new jeans and tops and even underwear, all with the labels still on them. Checking under the bed, Harper found a suitcase with winter clothes inside. And then it hit her. If Claude had gone to clean out Rhea’s flat, then he would have done what a lot of men would and just scooped up the clothes on hangers and bagged them up. But for now, Harper could offer her sister something clean and new to wear. She could also wriggle her own backside into a pair of jeans and wear one of the T-shirts.

As she carried out a more thorough look, she found cabinets and drawers with all kinds of stuff, from make-up and jewellery to tablets and braces.

Teeth braces, she thought, as she held the little plastic container in her hand. Who would have braces except a teenager?

Her heart sank, and her stomach turned over. The reality was slapping her in the face again. She could play happy families in this luxury drum, but, in fact, it was linked to something so much more than she cared to think about.

By the time she returned with a cup of tea and a ham salad baguette, Lexi was dozing. The dressing gown, which she had kept wrapped tightly around her skinny body, was gaping open. Harper almost dropped the tray when she saw the scar. A large patch of Lexi's skin looked like twisted bread dough. She wasn't mistaken: it was the result of a severe burn or scalding.

Harper could feel that rage rising again like molten lava. Wanting to scream, she couldn't move or take her eyes off her sister's hideous-looking skin.

Lexi stirred and opened her eyes. 'Aw, I must have dozed off for a moment.' Then she saw the look of horror on her sister's face and followed her eyeline to her own exposed body. Quickly, she covered herself. 'Don't look at it, Harps.'

Harper couldn't speak for a moment. She was too angry. Placing the plate and cup of tea on the table beside her sister, she took a few deep breaths and sat opposite her. 'Now,' she said, trying to control her livid voice, 'what has been going on? How did that happen? Who did it?'

Lexi took the cup of tea and spotted the two tablets. 'What are they?'

'Only paracetamol, Sis. Don't worry, I wouldn't give you anything more.' She then wondered if Lexi had been drugged before. It wasn't so much what her sister had asked her but how she'd asked the question.

'What happened to you, Lex? And please don't spare me the gory details.'

Lexi's face suddenly lost its innocent charm. Even her voice dropped an octave. 'Once I had Yosef, the whole family controlled me. Shabab told me I had to wear certain clothes. Like covering my arms and legs. She said I mustn't wear any make-up, and I should keep my hair tied back or the men would see me as a whore.'

Harper ran her hands through her hair; she could visualise her sister having to begin a totally controlled existence.

'Shabab explained that since I was part of their family, I could never talk to any boys, even my own family, meaning Teddy. I couldn't say "hello", let alone nod to a man in the street. Then . . .' She paused to regain control of her uneven voice. 'One day, I was out with Yosef. He was a week old. You know what it's like, Sis, showing off the new baby . . .' She looked up; her eyes were wide. 'Oh shit, sorry.'

Harper waved her hands. 'Don't worry, it's fine. Carry on.'

'I was so thrilled to show him off in his new pram, you see. I mean, I never meant to talk to anyone. But I bumped into Frazer from school.' She stopped and stared past Harper as if reliving a memory. 'I loved that boy once, but I didn't know that years ago Hasad had sent him packing, saying that I was his girlfriend. I wasn't, then. Anyway, he said "hello", and I was just caught up in the moment. He was so handsome and sweet, you know, a real gentle boy. Then I saw Mehmet across the road. He wagged his finger at me and walked away.'

Harper swallowed hard. She could guess what had happened next, but she wanted to hear it from her sister's own mouth. 'Go on, Lex.'

'I stood talking for ages. I stupidly thought Mehmet was joking because he smiled before he walked on. Nothing happened between Frazer and me. We just walked and talked. That was all.'

Harper nodded for her to carry on, her breathing intensifying.

'Hasad wasn't home, but his two brothers were, and so was Shabab.'

Lexi's bottom lip quivered as if she was about to cry, but, instead, she straightened herself and lifted her chin. 'They said that if I acted like a slut, they would treat me like one.'

Harper jumped up from her chair. 'Where do they live? I swear to God, I will cut their fucking bollocks off.'

'Sit down, Harper, just sit down. I wish I hadn't told you now.'

Her voice was the firmest Harper had ever heard.

Reluctantly taking her seat, Harper urged her to continue. 'I want to know what they did to you, Lex. Everything, and I *mean* everything.'

'Shabab grabbed the baby from the pram and marched into the kitchen. Mehmet shut the door, and then, literally, he ripped my clothes off. He pinned me down while Rifat raped me.'

Harper had her hand over her mouth. 'Dear God, that's fucking terrible, Lex. The stinking motherfucking bastards.'

'When Rifat had finished, he held me down while Mehmet took me as well. I thought that was the end of it. I was shaking and crying. I had never been so terrified in all my life. I felt so dirty, so humiliated, but I couldn't even fight them. I was so shit-scared. I thought Shabab would help. I really thought she would go mad when she walked into the room, but she didn't. She just laughed, Harps. She fucking laughed at me. Then . . .' She stopped and took a deep breath. 'I saw the kettle in her hand, and the steam leaving the spout. At first, I couldn't work out what the hell they were going to do. Then Mehmet and Rifat gripped me while she poured the boiling water over me.'

Harper jumped up again and pulled Lexi's dressing gown away to see the full extent of the damage. But it was so gruesome she felt vomit rising to the back of her throat, and before she knew it, she was running to the bathroom before she vomited all over the expensive carpet. Her head thumped, and her throat burned. Her whole life, she had tried to protect her sisters, but hearing that horrific story was more than she could bear.

You wait, you evil bastards, I will make you wish you had never been born.

After Harper washed her mouth out and dampened her neck, she returned to the lounge. She could see that Lexi had been crying again.

'I'm sorry, Lex. I just had to see for myself. I had to know what you've been through. Tell me, what did Hasad say?'

'He never knew the truth. I told him I had an accident with the kettle. They warned me that if I ever mentioned what they had done to me to a living soul, they would take my baby and have me sectioned. Their uncle is a doctor, you see, and he could sign the paperwork to have me locked up in a mental hospital.'

The rage was rising again. 'Have you sectioned? Yeah, well, believe me, Lex, *they* will need sectioning by the time I'm done with them. I swear to you, they will wish they had never been born. Now, listen and listen good. As I said earlier, you have to tell me everything you know about them – their business, and anything they do illegally. I mean *everything*. Every tiny detail.'

Lexi drank her tea and nodded. 'If they knew what I was about to tell you, they would string me up. I know more than they think. I hovered around, listening, pretending I was cooking or cleaning or seeing to the baby. I stored it all in me noggin, dreaming that one day I could go to the police and grass them all up. I wanted to hide enough money so that I could do a runner, but I didn't have the chance.'

Harper sat back. 'What's their main business? Is it illegal?'

'Drugs, cocaine, heroin, and prostitutes.'

'Fucking hell, Lex!'

Lexi nodded. 'Yeah, I know. You'd think they would stay straight because the shops rake in enough money. But they're greedy people. They eat too much, drink too much. They do everything to excess. They have property everywhere. And they bring their relatives over from Turkey to work here. It's a big family business. Oh, I nearly forgot. They're into serious money laundering through their shops and garages.'

'So if you went to the police, they would all get locked up, surely?'

'No,' said Lexi. 'I could never prove it. I only overheard conversations. Although the police may question them, I would end up dead, like the other girls who don't do as they're told.'

Harper jolted. '*What?* What other girls?'

'Sis, they run a prostitution racket. You know what prossies are like. They are forever in debt to the pimps, and if they don't pay' – she shrugged her shoulders – 'well, they end up dead, don't they?'

Harper shook her head. 'No, Lex, prossies don't get murdered. A beating, possibly, but, seriously, are you saying they get killed, so this fucking family are murderers too?'

'Oh yeah, but none of them ever go to prison. It just doesn't happen. They probably supply girls to the men in power – judges, MPs – so they get off. It happens everywhere, Sis. I thought you would've known, being inside.'

'No, Lex, because dead girls don't go to prison. Are you telling me that the Boz family men are that big a deal?'

'Yeah, Erin and even Teddy will tell you. They are a family you just don't fuck with.' She ran her hand inside her dressing gown and felt the uneven surface of her scarred skin.

'I'm not trying to be horrible, Lex, but if Hasad and his mob are so wealthy, why were you walking around like the poor relation, then?'

Placing her empty cup on the side table, Lexi smiled in such a sad way that Harper felt a lump in her throat.

'Sis, he never loved me. He *used* me. I gave him a son, but he has other women. The fat fucker slept with me to get me pregnant. I'm a baby machine to him. He doesn't spend any money on me. They won't give me a budget either because I could use it to run away. Honestly, Sis, they watch me like a hawk.'

Harper was utterly shocked but equally amazed. Lexi was telling her everything she needed to know to get revenge. No one was allowed to hurt her sisters and get away with it.

After further conversation, Harper paced the floor. 'I need to make a plan, and you, Lex, may have to help me.'

'I will, Harps, but I need to get Yosef back.'

Harper nodded, but she was staring at Claude's phone; it was pinging with more text messages. *Probably with more evidence that Pixie was desperate to find him*, she thought.

After looking at Claude's previous sent messages, Harper gauged how he would respond, and then slowly, she typed.

Stop texting. I am sorting some business out with the Boz mob. I will be leaving their garage soon. I will speak then.

What came back shocked Harper to the core.

Since when do you deal with the Boz family? Zavid will not be pleased. What are you doing going behind his back?????

'Sis, what is it?' asked Lexi. 'You look like you've just seen a ghost.'

'Do you know of any dealings Hasad or his brothers had with any Russians?'

Looking a little shifty, Lexi chewed her bottom lip. 'Yeah, and I'm not proud of it, either, but honestly, Sis, if I had breathed a word, they would've killed me.'

'Lex, there is a lot of shit I'm not proud of, believe me, but I need you to tell me everything.'

Sensing the urgency in Harper's voice, Lexi nodded. 'I was at the garage. I needed to collect money from Hasad to buy the week's shopping. Anyway, while I was there, a black van drove in. You know, one of those, er . . .' She tutted. 'What are they called? You know, the black vans that carry dead people.'

Harper nodded, hurrying her on.

'Hasad was a little jumpy. He quickly closed the front shutters. Two guys in black suits, dressed like funeral directors, jumped out. I could see something padded underneath them like bulletproof vests. I wondered then if they really were who they pretended to be. When one of the men approached, I could see Hasad was on edge. I'd never seen him like it before. He flicked his head for me to go. Before I left through the side door, I heard a noise, a sound like someone screaming through a gag. I left the door ajar and listened. The funeral directors – or whoever they were – had foreign accents. As I walked away from the garage, I saw another vehicle, a new one and big like a Range Rover type of car, pull up, and the two foreign, maybe Eastern European, men jumped in and shot off.'

'What or who was in the van?'

'Harps, I have no idea. I didn't dare go back. I knew that if I looked, or asked, or found out, then I would have had to go to the police, and, well, I was terrified because I was pregnant with Yosef.'

'Did you ever see that black van again?'

Lexi slowly nodded. 'Harps, I am afraid to think of what the Boz family are really into. Yes, I have seen more than one of them. They come in for a service, but when I heard a girl's muffled screams, that was the first time I had actually seen a driver.'

'Hmm, I wonder if a local funeral company has an account with Hasad's garage?'

'Their cousin – I don't know his name – has a funeral company, or something to do with funerals, but he is in North London.'

Harper's eyes widened. 'So they really do have a wide network of businesses, then?'

Lexi nodded. 'They are a huge family, and Mo runs them all from his armchair.'

Chapter Fourteen

It was mid-afternoon on Tuesday when Lexi woke up. She was not at all surprised to find Harper was still in bed. They had spent hours chatting. Harper had been asking her a million questions regarding the Boz family. Despite all the stress and excitement from the night before, she hadn't slept as soundly since the day Harper had gone to prison. Mindful not to wake her sister, she crept to the bathroom and stared at herself in the mirror. Even though she was a couple of years younger than Harper, right now, she looked considerably older. In the habit of keeping her hair pulled back tightly away from her face, even in bed, she suddenly gripped the band and slid it off her hair, allowing her lank dark locks to fall on either side of her face. Her hair had never been as drab as this; once, it had been full of thick glossy waves. She hadn't worn make-up in years and had forgotten what she looked like with a bit of eyeliner and mascara. Not having had time to study herself in the mirror recently, she hadn't noticed the thin lines that had developed around her lips, which were probably the result of smoking too much. Still, she was a mum, and her baby took priority now. Unravelling the bandages, she sighed. The burns were not as bad as she'd first thought; there were just a few red patches where the skin had peeled away. Gently testing the level of soreness, she ran cold water over her damaged skin and was pleasantly surprised to find the burns didn't hurt as much as she thought they would.

After squeezing toothpaste along her finger, Lexi rubbed it around her teeth, careful not to press too hard on the loose ones. She sloshed water around her mouth before spitting the blood-smeared remnants down the sink.

Then she stared intently into the mirror once more. Opening her mouth as widely as possible, she noticed that two of her side teeth were black and a couple were chipped. She hated Hasad and hoped to God that she wouldn't have to go back to him. Yet in her heart, she knew that if it meant she could keep her son, then she would take the beatings.

Lexi knew she wasn't like Harper; she didn't have the balls that her eldest sister had. Harper would fight anyone, even to the death, if she had to, to save her family.

She adored Harper and only wished that Erin hadn't been so selfish. However, Erin was probably the wild one and had only been kept tame by Harper in her younger days. But Erin was so much like their mother, always going after the forbidden fruit, regardless of the consequences. And regardless of who was hurt along the way. It wasn't so surprising that Erin was the favoured daughter because she and her mother were like two peas in a pod.

Lexi had never understood why Charley hadn't been wanted or loved by their mum. But she wasn't so surprised that Charley hadn't returned after social services took her. A little part of her resented Charley too, for not staying in touch with any of her sisters. Not a single letter to Harper, let alone a prison visit, even when she was old enough. If it hadn't been for their eldest sister, Charley might well have ended up as a victim of a paedophile, and, as a result, she would probably have suffered from severe mental health issues for the rest of her life.

A light rustling sound told Lexi that Harper was awake. Hurrying from the bathroom, she wanted to make her sister a coffee and some scrambled eggs on toast; it was the least she could do. She heard Harper go into the bathroom and take a shower. There would be sufficient time to get the breakfast started. Opening the French doors and laying the table, she felt the most relaxed she had ever been.

'Bloody hell, I didn't realise it was so late. Oh well, I must have needed it. Did you sleep okay, Lex?' asked Harper, thirty minutes later and now standing in the doorway. 'Oh, look at that.' She pointed to the table. 'Blimey, I feel spoilt.'

Lexi beamed, knowing she could at least put a slight smile on her sister's face.

'Lex, I have to go to work today. I probably won't be back until three o'clock in the morning. Okay?'

Lexi sat at the table. 'What do you want me to do? Washing, ironing, cleaning?'

'What? No, Lex, I want you to call social services and get your baby back. I'll leave you some money. Go to Argos to get the baby bits you need. And make your room perfect for Baby Yosef. Oh, yes, and can you buy a phone? Make that two.'

'Bloody hell, Harps, do you have enough money?'

'Let's just say I'm borrowing it from Rhea. She left a few bob in the bottom drawer.'

'Cor, Sis, I bet she's fuming that you've got her flat. She's always hated you. Jealousy, eh?'

'Well, tough luck,' replied Harper, before taking the seat opposite. Sipping the sugary coffee, she winced.

'Too hot, Harps?'

'Babe, I used to have a lot of sugar, but inside, sugar was hard to come by, so I gave it up. Never mind, there's more for you, eh!' She laughed.

Lexi immediately jumped up to make another coffee.

'Hey, Lex, you ain't my fucking slave. Sit down and finish your food. Don't be jumping up for me. I ain't Hasad, you know.'

Lexi sat back down. 'Sorry, Sis.'

'And stop with the "sorry" shit. You, Lexi, are a Kane, and you will not bow down to anyone. Do you hear me?'

A smile lit up Lexi's face. 'I wanted to make you a nice breakfast.' She glanced at the clock. 'Or a nice lunch to say "thank you".'

'Go on, then. No sugar, please. Now, don't forget to find out from social services what the hell was going on. Remember, every little detail counts. And ask social services what the fuck they are gonna do now about this Shabab bitch, who, as I see it, kidnapped your baby.'

Lexi nodded; she didn't want to ask why. If Harper wanted even the tiniest of details, then she would have them.

As Harper got up to leave the table, she looked back at Lexi. 'You do hate Hasad, don't you?'

'With every bit of me, Sis, I hate him *and* his family.'

***

The moment the cab dropped Harper off outside the club, she suddenly felt nervous, which was not a familiar feeling. There were bound to be questions, especially if one of the Russians had gone to check out the Boz family's garage and found Claude's car. She assumed that something had occurred because his phone had stopped pinging around midnight. After turning it off, she had hidden it under a loose floorboard in the bedroom. She couldn't risk having it about her person.

There were no cars around the building, so she felt momentarily relieved, but she knew at some point Pixie or even Zavid would be asking her about Claude.

The smell of floor cleaner hit her, the second she was through the door. The cleaners had been in the club, getting the place ready for opening that evening. *Of course, it was Tuesday.* With all that had gone on, she had completely lost track of time.

The club was spotless but deathly quiet. Harper made her way to the office where she saw a flashing light on the answering machine. She paused before she listened to the message, telling herself that she was the manager, so she should take over the running of every aspect until Vadim returned. She pressed the 'play' button, and it was Vadim himself.

'Hi, hopefully, Harper, you have picked up this message. I will be back in a few days. There are further issues I must deal with here. Please make sure that the stock has been ordered. The file is in the top drawer. If you can't find it, ask Claude. He will know. And please tell Claude to turn on his phone. I cannot get through to him.'

The call ended, leaving Harper thinking about Vadim. His Russian tone was soft in comparison to Zavid's and Claude's. Could she trust him, or was he also involved in this human trafficking circle, which she believed was so much bigger than she could ever have imagined? She would be shocked and gutted if he was. Pushing the thought aside, she got to work checking the stock and reordering what was needed. She dismissed what had gone on in the last few days and acted as if everything was perfectly normal until a cold feeling engulfed her. *The ring. Claude's ring! What had she done with it?*

Leaving the mixers on the bar, she flew into the office, through the side door, and then went up the stairs. Relief came when she saw it on the bed. *How stupid*, she thought. Calming her racing heartbeat, she sat down and looked around. Her clean-up job had been quite a success. Having felt that the rug had completely dried, she closed the window. A nervous chuckle left her lips, but another serious thought gripped her. *The bed sheets. What had she done with them?* Spinning around, she saw the black sacks peeking out on the other side of the bed. Shaking her head, she realised that she could just as easily have set herself up for another stint in stir for murder. For now, she decided they would have to go under the bed. The whole surprise made her feel uneasy again; she couldn't go back to prison, not now she had tasted freedom.

Even by the time the club was ready for opening, she remained on edge. She couldn't shake the feeling off. Taking a few deep breaths, she greeted the girls and ushered them inside. The dancers made their way to the changing room, and the rest of the girls took their places behind the bar. Frenchy was one of the last to arrive.

Her face was pale, but she managed a smile. 'I reckon it's gonna be a quiet one tonight. It normally is on a Tuesday.'

'I think I prefer it busy. The time flies, then,' replied Harper, hoping that Frenchy would spark up a conversation.

'Yeah.' It was all she said.

'Have you seen Pixie?'

Frenchy, who had her back to Harper, spun around. 'No, why? As I said, she doesn't always work. It's more a part-time set-up. Have you seen Claude? He wasn't at the door.'

Harper shrugged her shoulders. 'No, I haven't.'

As they stared at each other, Harper felt as if she was being accused of something. 'What's up, Frenchy? Still pissed off with me, are ya?'

Frenchy frowned. 'Don't know what you mean, Harper. I come here to do a job, take me money, and fuck off. I have no interest in your views on me unless you want to give me the boot.' She looked about. 'But we're short-staffed as it is, so I think if you're smart, then you'll know when you'll need a good hand behind the bar.' She winked. She knew it would piss Harper off.

'Don't think that I can't get staff, love, 'cos I know a whole string of women who would do well here, given half a chance.'

'Ex-cons, yeah?'

'Fucking right, an' all, Frenchy. And ex-cons who would wipe that smirk off your face as soon as look at you. So be careful, or I might just bring one in, who could double up as a bouncer, as well.'

'All right, keep your hair on, and, by the look of it, your false nails, 'cos Vadim don't like ugly fingers.' She glared down at Harper's hand.

Noticing that the false nail from her little finger was missing, Harper felt a sudden bead of sweat trickle down her back. And her throat felt dry. *Where the hell had the nail gone?* She tried to think of the last time she'd looked at her hands. However, because she'd been so intent on getting the blood off them she wouldn't have known if a nail had come off. She recalled using her left hand to hold Claude away from her while searching for the knife. *Oh, fuck! Fuck! Fuck!* Was that nail embedded in his skin? Caught up in the cling film, perhaps? Or in the car? Was it now the evidence the police, or, worse, the Russians needed to pin Claude's murder on her?

As she was about to leave the bar and take a moment for herself in the office, a voice behind her called out, 'Sorry, I'm late again, Harper. Bloody traffic.'

Pixie was back, and it did appear as if the girl had a split personality. Even her voice was remarkably different.

Harper turned around. 'Hi, Pixie, no worries. The place is quiet, as you can see.' Her voice was higher than usual because she really wanted to punch Pixie in the face, but she had to hold off and keep the consequences of such an action in her mind's eye.

When Pixie grinned at her, Harper wondered if it was a knowing grin or a genuine smile. With her nerves on edge, she really wasn't sure of anything right now. A million questions ate away at her brain. Yet the biggest concern was wouldn't Pixie be fuming with Claude for not answering his phone? Worse, wouldn't Pixie be in a terrible state if she'd discovered he'd been murdered and dismembered?

'Anyone lost a fingernail?' Pixie asked, staring straight at Harper.

Panic began to rise, but Harper was desperate to keep herself calm; with her hands clenched into fists, she thought that perhaps she should try to remove her remaining false nails as soon as she was alone and put them into her pocket, so it looked as if she had lost them all.

'Yeah, me, and probably half the scabby tarts in here. Why?' asked Frenchy, laughing.

It was just the distraction Harper needed to walk away to the ladies' changing room, away from Pixie's prying eyes.

A hive of activity made it an excellent place to be. False eye lashes, nails, tits, and wigs were everywhere. Harper saw a packet of French manicure nails on the side; she stealthily grabbed the box and hurried away to her office before any of the girls had a chance to notice she was even there.

Deciding not to remove her remaining false nails after all, she replaced the missing one instead. She then left the office and rejoined the girls at the bar.

'Harper, can I have a private word?' asked Pixie.

Frenchy walked away to serve an annoying punter, who was dressed in a bright polo shirt and wearing a smile that was so full of teeth he could eat an apple through a letterbox.

Following Pixie through to the back, Harper was suddenly gripped by dread. *What did Pixie know?*

'So, what do you want, Pixie? What's the plan?'

The sudden change in expression made Harper's eyes widen.

'Plan? Harper, you do not get to discuss plans. You are here to do as I tell you. Tonight, you must just run the club.'

Harper hated her with a passion. The real Pixie, otherwise known as Pasha, had a dark evilness about her. It wasn't just the dullness in her eyes. It was more the sarcastic smirk and cocky voice that made her so mad she wanted to deck the bitch, there and then, but the thought of her son being collateral damage if she didn't toe the line brought her to her senses.

'Claude is not here tonight, then?' asked Harper.

Pixie glared without blinking. Both stared at each other, reluctant to look away. But when Pixie suddenly laughed, Harper was confused.

'No, he is not. Was that really a question, Harper, or were you just stating the obvious?'

'I wondered if he had left, in which case, Vadim needs a replacement. Is that my job or yours?'

Pixie's eyes narrowed and her face took on a look of spite. 'You mind your own business. I will deal with it. Claude has time off. He has other stuff to attend to. Tuesdays are quiet. Now, you told me that Claude was talking to a man called Calvin Stuart—'

‘No, I said it sounded like Kevin or Calvin or something. I didn’t hear his second name.’

Pixie’s eyes flashed in anger. ‘You distinctly said and I quote, “Calvin Stuart”!’

‘No, I didn’t,’ said Harper, knowing that at that moment Pixie wasn’t paying much attention because she really hadn’t mentioned Calvin’s surname. *So, Pixie, you are not a stickler for detail.*

‘Playing games with me will get you fucking killed,’ hissed Pixie.

‘I’m not playing games. I didn’t say Calvin *Stuart*.’

Harper knew that she was getting up Pixie’s nose by the way her face reddened. She was sure that if Pixie was that confident, she would not have let the matter rest; instead, she just flared her nostrils and angrily looked away.

‘You won’t play me, Harper.’

‘Listen, Pixie, Pasha, or whatever. I am here to do a job. I want my son safe and money in my back pocket. That’s all. So, I don’t have the time, the patience, or the fucking inclination to play games. I served a helluva long time behind bars. I want a peaceful, stress-free life, where I’m secure in the knowledge that my little boy is safe.’

Pixie arched one brow. ‘And your sister, Lexi. Where is she?’

Harper knew then the Russians had got wind of the fact that Lexi was at the flat with her. There was no point in lying about that. ‘Lexi is living with me.’

‘Harper, do you know much about Hasad Boz?’

‘Yes, he’s a Turkish prick, who beat my sister, who I hit with a brick. But you already know that, don’t you? Now, tell me, why do you want to know about him?’

Unexpectedly, Pixie lunged forward and grabbed Harper by the throat, pushing her into the tall freezer.

However, Harper's reaction was not to run but to fight; it had always been that way. In one quick movement, she used her elbow to crack Pixie on the side of the face, sending her off balance. Harper gasped for air for a moment and watched as the anger-fuelled frustration filled Pixie's eyes.

'Now, fucking hold on a minute. I am not a punching bag. If you wanna ruck, we will ruck, but believe me, I can fight, so bring it on.'

Pixie straightened herself. 'You shouldn't have done that.' Her voice lowered.

'I have agreed to your terms for my son's safety, but I'll be fucked if I'm putting up with you getting handy with your fists, just 'cos you're pissed off.'

'We own you, Harper.'

Rolling her eyes, Harper replied, 'No, you *don't* own me. Nobody can own me. We have an agreement, that's all. You may call it what the fuck you like in Russia, but here, it's just an arrangement. Now, I will ask you again. Why are you asking about my sister's ex?'

'I think you know why.'

Harper could feel her stomach churning now; she hoped that it wouldn't start making a noise like a mating donkey. 'No, actually, Pixie, I have no fucking idea why.'

'Your house. It was burned down, was it not? And I hear you think it was your sister's boyfriend.'

There was no point in lying. This Russian firm seemed to have people in all kinds of places. 'Yeah, her ex. I do think it was him. He threatened to do it. So?'

'Did you ask Claude for a favour, Harper? Maybe you decided to pay Hasad a visit and gave him a severe warning using a claw hammer and with the help of some serious backup?' Pixie stepped closer. 'I mean, Claude was here in the club at the same time as you. Are you fucking my bloke?'

As if a ton of bricks had been lifted from her shoulders, Harper wanted to laugh, but she had to think quickly.

'Jesus, is that what you thought?' She sighed. 'Seriously, Pixie, *Claude*? He may be your type, but he certainly ain't mine. He fucking nearly broke my jaw, and you think I would find him attractive? You must be joking.'

'If I find out you're lying, Harper, believe me, I will have your skin stripped, bit by painful bit.'

'He wasn't screwing me, Pixie, but I did hear him talking on the phone to another woman. I think he called her Bibbi or Babab. Not sure.'

'What did he say?'

Harper wanted to smile, but she couldn't; she had to look serious. 'I can't remember. I'm not the type to earwig when someone is practically having sex over the phone.' She turned to walk away.

'Wait, I haven't finished!' screeched Pixie, her tone now like that of a neurotic woman's.

Sensing the hysteria, Harper turned to enjoy the moment. 'What is it, Pixie?'

'If you're lying to me—'

'Yes, Pixie, I heard you. You will have me skinned alive.' She chewed her bottom lip. 'You don't know me at all, but your relationship with Claude has nothing to do with me. I don't care who is fucking who. I have a job to do, so shall I get on with it?'

Like a petulant child, Pixie stormed off, slamming the door behind her.

So, Pixie, you are human after all. You can get wound up, and you are obviously not as cold and heartless as your brother, thought Harper, with a smile on her face. The Russian girl she had served time with would never have reacted like that; she was a hard bitch and no mistake. Any man who did her wrong, she would have cut his bollocks off and dished them up for dinner. In fact, that is exactly what she did.

The club remained quiet for the rest of the evening. She was relieved when the time was approaching midnight. She didn't have to ask the customers to leave; once the last of the dancers finished their turn on the pole, the customers left.

Harper paid all the girls, except Frenchy, a hundred pounds each.

Frenchy was the last to leave. She held out her hands, and Harper slapped a hundred and twenty in them. 'You did well tonight, Frenchy.'

'Cheers, Harper. You scratch my back, girl, and I'll scratch yours.'

Harper wondered if she was referring to the missing fingernail.

Chapter Fifteen

The girls had all gone home, the night air was chilly, and the sky threatened rain. Harper could smell the rain on the sun-beaten path.

It was a reminder of summer holidays with her sisters spent over at the park, where they met the gang, kicked a ball, and played on the swings or on the wooden horse where Teddy had engraved ‘Harper loves Teddy’. He often popped into her mind. She had truly believed he would have stuck by her. Still, she could hardly blame him, really, and who was to say she wouldn’t have gone off with another man, had the shoe been on the other foot?

Dressed in a long red wig, black jeans, and a jacket, she could easily be mistaken for Pixie. They were both tall and slim, and with oversized glasses, who could really tell them apart?

The cab pulled up, and the driver lowered the window. ‘Pixie?’

Harper nodded and climbed in. She felt her nerves return but forced herself to get a grip. If she was ever to get out of this cruel, evil circle, then she had to do stuff she didn’t want to do. Although tonight, if all went well, she might actually feel a little pleasure. Visualising her sister’s scar, her mind travelled back in time to an incident that took place in the prison.

***

She could only imagine the pain the poor girl must have gone through. She remembered seeing one of the inmates, a grass, so they said. She had suffered horrifically in a similar way at the hands of another inmate.

It was a woman they called 'The Boss'. However, she never once called her that; instead, she called her by her name, Remi Davine. They treated each other with mutual respect.

She would have stayed away and kept out of the situation, but the poor kid was on drugs and had no idea what she had said or to whom. This waif of a woman didn't deserve to be tortured by Remi.

Remi was a violent woman with an ABH charge sheet as long as her arm. She had dragged the skinny kid into the laundry room, ripped her top off, and forced half her body into the steamer, pulling the lid down.

She could still hear those screams to this day. It took all of her strength to pull Remi away to release the kid. It wasn't the blistering skin or the screams that disturbed her. It was the look of resignation in the kid's eyes as if she had accepted the torturous burns almost as if it was a premonition of her future inside.

That was the day the whole dynamics changed. She hadn't wanted to be top dog in the prison or anywhere. But when Remi punched her in the face for intervening and then tried to force her arm under the steamer, she saw the red mist descending. She grabbed Remi by her ponytail and dragged her to the floor, smashing her face against the leg of the steam iron. Again and again, she hit her face, until, finally, Remi let out the same blood-curdling scream as the woman she had just tortured.

The screws broke up the fight, and both the little druggie and Remi were stretchered off to the hospital wing, with her carted off down the block.

***

She tapped the cab driver on the shoulder. 'Anywhere here will do,' she said, in a subtle Russian accent. Not that it was part of any plan, but she wanted to ensure that she would not be implicated as a suspect. Who could she trust? She didn't know. Certainly not Pixie, and even Frenchy was becoming a mystery. She had been dead certain that Frenchy was part of the circle, but now, she was not convinced this was the case. Something fishy was going on, unless, of course, Frenchy's comment about the lost fingernail was not about saving her at all.

The grey looming clouds were a godsend since summer evenings rarely got so dark. Wearing a pair of plimsolls on her feet, she quietly walked around the streets, careful to stay among the shadows of the fences. Some of the house numbers were hidden behind bushes that overhung the walls, so it was difficult to find the one she wanted. This particular street consisted of privately owned detached houses on a newly built development. It was so unlike the council estate she grew up in.

Turning the corner, she spotted the house she was looking for. It was number 53. Quickly, she scanned the surroundings. All the neighbouring houses were in total darkness.

Creeping around the perimeter of the property inside the garden wall, she headed for the back door. Not even a sensor light popped on. She reasoned that with their kind of money and Shabab living alone, her father would have put up some sort of security system. But perhaps she hadn't bothered to turn it on. *Ah well, her mistake and my benefit*, she thought.

Carefully, she crept up to the kitchen window, and, instantly, the aroma of cooking spices – garlic and chilli – hit her. She looked closer and saw that the rear window was open just enough for her purposes. Putting on rubber gloves, she eased it open. She had a clear view through the kitchen and into the hallway. It was in total darkness. *Shabab must have gone to bed.*

In seconds, she climbed into the kitchen and listened for any noise. Once the drumming of her own heartbeat quietened, she could hear snoring. She smiled to herself. Lexi had said Shabab was a big bird with no neck. No wonder the father took so long to find the ugly heifer a husband. Apparently, he was due over from Turkey at the end of September for the wedding. She and Lexi had giggled at the fact that Shabab's future husband hadn't seen her yet; it was part of their tradition, yet they both knew that if he saw a photo, he would run for the hills.

Wasting no time, she got to work searching the kitchen for tools to use as weapons. Carefully sliding each drawer open, she was surprised to find not only kitchen knives but skewers. *Of course, Turkish kebabs.* She remembered now. The family owned a kebab shop; in fact, they owned most of the kebab shops in South-East London. She placed the skewers on the worktop and continued rifling through the cabinets and cupboards. Then she decided to look under the sink. *That was where most people kept their cleaning fluids, didn't they?* As she rummaged around, she found a bag and something quite heavy inside. *Fuck!* It was a gun. And a closer look told her it was loaded. The shock compelled her to jump up, but in doing so, she knocked the worktop, and one of the skewers rolled off and hit the tiled floor, making an annoying clanging sound. She froze and listened. The noise had obviously woken the fat bitch because it sounded as if she was walking across the landing wearing diver's boots. *Fuck me, you must be a size.*

'Who's there?' came a croaky voice from upstairs.

Turning the gun over in her hands, she wanted to shout back 'It's me! Harper Kane! Your living nightmare.' But she stayed silent and listened.

'Fucking cat!' yelled Shabab, before stomping back to her room.

She then noticed the cat flap and the cat food on the floor. She knew she would never have made a detective, although, as sisters, they had all wanted to be one, except Erin, of course; she had always wanted to be rich and famous.

Checking that the kettle was full to the brim, she clicked the 'on' switch. Luckily, the kettle boiled quietly.

Gripping the gun, she wandered from the kitchen to the lounge and was surprised to find it immaculate. She had built up a picture of a smelly, ugly slob living there. But it seemed it was just the kitchen that had been left untidy, with messy remnants of an evening meal. The plates were left dripping in some sauce even though there was a dishwasher, right below them. Even the counter tops had specks of rice and the grease marks from the pots and pans. Then she realised, Shabab, the lazy cow, wouldn't have cleaned up after herself. Those dishes were left for the cleaner. *That's what money gets you.*

The lounge was almost minimalist, all cream and red, with a red sofa and curtains and a red rug over the cream carpet. There was a lot of gold as well, a sign of money, probably, in their culture. Not that she knew much about their culture. On the coffee table was a laptop, and it was still open. She knew a bit about IT because she had made sure that she went on every course to prepare herself for the outside world. IT as a subject had not been taught when she was at school.

Taking a seat in the large armchair, she stared at the screen, pleased to find there was no password needed. After clicking on the Microsoft Word icon, she smiled to herself. *Fuck you, Shabab, and all you scummy lot.* Then she began to type, but she had to make a few corrections because the rubber gloves made typing very difficult.

Dear Baba,

I am sorry, I didn't want to disrespect you or Rifat, Mehmet, and Hasad or bring shame on this family, but I love Claude Bolshoi. Please don't be angry. You must understand, I cannot marry Omar. I just can't.

Harper knew that 'father' in Turkish was 'baba'. Lexi had told her that Hasad was constantly pushing Yosef to say it.

Leaving the laptop exactly where she had found it, she returned to the kitchen. She stuck the skewers and a kitchen knife into the waistband of her jeans, held the kettle in one hand, the gun in the other, and wore the Devil's grin on her face.

Careful not to make too much noise, she climbed the stairs and stopped at the first door on the right. She could see the bed and the lump of a woman lying on her back. The snoring was not only loud now but it seemed as though the bed was vibrating as the woman slept. With clammy hands, she continued to grip the gun as she entered the room. Slowly, she approached the bed and leaned over and stared at the woman who was out cold catching flies. She was just as big as her little Lexi had described her. With long black hair and wiry grey strands around her temples, a monobrow, a moustache, and a layer of greasy skin, Shabab looked like a bloke. How the hell could Mo ever call this disgusting human being a princess? And what she had done to Lexi was so cruel that no one could be hated more, right now. With angry revenge on her mind and murder in her heart, she wanted to brutalise the bitch before killing her. Lifting the kettle, she yelled, 'Wakey-wakey!' and poured the boiling contents all over Shabab's face. Nearly every drop went down the woman's throat.

Shabab's piercing screams were deafening.

Clutching her blistering face, she thrashed about in pure agony. Desperate to see who had attacked her, so that she could defend herself, she tried to sit up and focus. But the pain was blinding her. Frantically blinking, she suddenly saw a woman with a smirk on her face and a gun in her hand. But before she could do anything, something shiny and long came at her. Not quick enough to dart out of the way, she felt the sharp thud as the metal object rammed into her shoulder. The sound was sickening as she heard the weapon crunch through her bone. Then the horrific pain followed; it was a burning agony that sucked the breath right out of her.

Shabab's eyes were on stalks, desperately trying to comprehend what the hell was going on.

She gripped her shoulder, only to feel the cold handle of a skewer that was still lodged through her muscles and probably the bone itself. Before she could even think or see clearly, her attacker stabbed her other arm; this time, it must have torn the tendons, ligaments, or nerves because, instantly, she felt her arm flop and couldn't move it.

'Please! Please stop! What do you want? Take anything, anything you want. Please, I have money.'

Harper laughed. 'Really, Shabab? *Anything* I want?'

Shabab was nodding furiously. 'Yes, please, anything, name it.'

'Well, I want your fucking life. I want to take your life. You're an evil, vile fat motherfucking cunt. You hurt my little sister, Lexi. No one hurts my sisters, fucking no one. Now, you're gonna pay.'

With her vision ultimately returning, Shabab could see nothing but pure rage in the woman's eyes.

She knew her life was now at an end. The pain she was suffering from was too horrendous, and she couldn't fight back. The attacker was holding a gun and now a knife.

'Oh God, please don't cut me. I didn't mean to hurt your sister. I swear, it was my brothers who made me. I didn't want to hurt anyone. I had no choice.'

'And I hate liars, an' all. I've a good mind to cut your tongue out.'

Harper paused, soaking in the pure fear on Shabab's face, knowing that her sister had gone through pure agony as well. But this would end differently for Shabab.

Shabab thought she was to be spared any further punishment, when she saw her attacker give her a wink and a smile. That was until the woman plunged the knife into her mouth. She knew it had penetrated the back of her throat. The noise was abhorrent. Realising she was about to die, she glanced up. Her attacker was studying her intently with what looked like a gleeful feeling of satisfaction.

Shabab was coughing and spluttering, horrified that she was bleeding to death. She couldn't breathe because the blood was choking the life out of her.

'My little Lexi didn't do you any harm, but you let your brothers rape her, and you almost boiled her alive, and then you stole her baby, but you never banked on me, did you? Oh, and before you die, just so you know, your dad will be done for your murder. An honour killing, I think they call it.'

Shabab's eyes widened one last time before she closed them for good.

Pulling the ring from her pocket, she placed it over one of Shabab's sausage-like fingers. *Perfect fit! You and Claude would have made an ideal couple.* She took one last satisfied look at the grotesque mess of Shabab's mouth, which had been sliced wide open, like that of a shark's. Even her lips had rolled back, showing her red gums and rotten teeth.

Looking at the skewers sticking out of Shabab's shoulder, she smiled. 'Now, that's what I call a Turkish kebab.'

As soon as she was convinced that Shabab was dead, she looked out of the windows to check that there were no neighbours' lights on. The screams had not penetrated the walls, only her own eardrums.

It was clear that this was simply Shabab's home, and no incriminating evidence was kept here except the gun. Before she left, she washed her face and gloves and checked that there were no speckles of blood. She had already left the knife and remaining skewers on the bed. After wiping the prints clean, she placed the gun back under the sink. Once she was outside and the door was closed behind her, she removed her gloves and checked that all her fingernails were still intact. Again, she hid in the shadows as she walked away from the area and headed towards Bromley, where she managed to hail a London taxi to take her home.

Chapter Sixteen

Harper woke up late again. This time, the flat was empty. She wondered for a moment where Lexi was, and then her mind went dark as images of Shabab came flooding back.

'Shit!' she shouted, when she saw it was midday. *The probation officer. Oh no, she will be ready to sling me back in the irons.*

In a cold sweat, she hurried to the phone to dial Vanessa's number, only to hear the secretary's deep 'I am so bored' voice. 'Who did you want to speak to?' she asked.

'Vanessa.'

'Who's calling, please?'

'Harper Kane.'

'Okay, I will see if she is in.'

Harper knew that meant 'I will see if she wants to talk to you.'

'Harper! Where are you?' came Vanessa's highly strung shrill voice.

'Hi, Vanessa, and how are you today?' asked Harper, sarcastically.

'Harper, you were supposed to have checked in yesterday. You're lucky I didn't recall you back to prison.'

'Yes, I'm sorry, Vanessa, but I had to go into work. There was a spillage. And I've been trying to help my family after the fire. You can imagine how it is.'

'Oh, yes, right, I see. Okay, er, come in tomorrow morning. I need to run through a few things with you. Shall we say, er . . . nine o'clock?'

Harper rolled her eyes. 'I work very late, Vanessa. How about we go to lunch? My treat. I'll meet you at twelve at the offices.'

'Fine.' Vanessa sighed.

Harper sensed that Vanessa seemed somewhat preoccupied. She couldn't put her finger on exactly what it was, but she had this niggling feeling about Vanessa. She cast her mind back. She actually had no recollection of telling the detective where she worked, so Vanessa couldn't have overheard a conversation that never took place. So the question still remained – how did Vanessa know the address?

'Oh, yes, where are you staying? I must have an address and be able to check it out to ensure it's suitable.'

Harper was really taken aback because it was the first thing they needed to have a record of. She reeled off the address and decided to change the plan. 'Hey, why don't you come over at midday tomorrow for lunch?'

'Yes, that's fine,' Vanessa said, again, before rudely cutting the connection.

After making herself a cup of tea, Harper turned on the local radio station, leaned against the open French doors, and admired the small but pretty rear garden. But her attention soon switched to the radio.

Gracie Deeley, a fourteen-year-old, has gone missing from her foster family home in Beckenham. This is the fourth teenager to disappear in the last week. The police are appealing to the public for any information on these girls. The details can be found on our website.

Harper felt her hands shake as she automatically turned off the radio. She couldn't bear to hear any more.

The thought of those poor girls turned her tranquil moment into a feeling of disgust. She tried to tell herself that this flat was part of her job working for Vadim, but the other side of her felt that the disappearance of these girls could be down to the Russian firm. And her heart was telling her that she had to do something more. She wasn't a detective and would probably make a pretty shit one. However, if she could gather some information, then it would be a start.

A banging and crashing coming from the front door had Harper spinning on her heels.

It was Lexi, trying to carry a large box through the hallway. Harper could just make out Lexi's ponytail above the box. And then a voice from behind her. 'Where do you want these bags, love?'

'Just leave them there,' replied Lexi, obviously to a cab driver.

Harper helped her carry the box into the bedroom and quickly paid the driver, who seemed a little puffed, having just lifted the other items that Lexi had bought.

'Here, mate, take an extra tenner. Looks like you've earned it.'

The middle-aged cabbie smiled, but refused the tip. 'No, love, it's yours, for the baby,' he said, before heading back to his cab.

The bags and boxes lining the hallway were all items for the baby. Clothes, a cot, a buggy, and jars of food.

'Lex, come into the kitchen. I want to know what the social services said.'

Lexi was beaming. Her cheeks were rosy as she sat at the table.

'Sis, they were great. All full of apologies. The tests all came back drug and alcohol free. I gave them permission to use the blood taken at the hospital. Anyway, they are bringing Yosef over this afternoon. They have to do the paperwork, but I explained that I have a place, and that's that, really. I can't thank you enough, Harps. I mean—'

‘That’s great news, Lex, but what are they going to do about Shabab? It amounts to kidnapping, surely?’

Lexi was nodding enthusiastically. ‘Yeah, well, they said they will be informing the police because, like you said, it’s a kidnapping. I would love to be a fly on the wall when the police go knocking. I would love to see her face.’

‘It is pretty grotesque,’ mumbled Harper, under her breath.

‘What was that, Harps?’

‘I said, so would I. Tea or coffee, Lex?’

‘Tea, please.’

While Harper made the tea, Lexi returned to the bags and carried them into the bedroom. All except for the last one, she took to the kitchen and started to unpack the items.

‘Baby Yosef will end up as a right porker with all that lot.’

Lexi stopped and looked at her sister. ‘I’m so grateful. Really, I am, Harps.’

Seeing the genuine respect and gratitude in her sister’s eyes, Harper automatically hugged her. ‘It’s nothing, Lex. It’s what families are supposed to do. And besides, you came to see me in the nick and brought me clothes, which allowed me to hold my head up.’

‘Really?’

‘Yes, really. Now I need to talk to you.’

They sat at the table nursing their teas. Lexi was eager to hear what was on Harper’s mind.

‘Lex, do you know what time I got in early this morning?’

A frown crinkled Lexi’s forehead. ‘No, I was in bed by eleven. Why?’

‘Oh, only I heard you stir around 1.30. I thought I may have woken you up.’

Lexi smiled, and Harper could see it was a knowing smile.

‘Yeah, Sis, that’s right. I think you did wake me up. I went to the kitchen for a glass of water after I heard the door close. But that’s okay. I’m a light sleeper.’

Before Harper could say another word, the doorbell rang.

Lexi’s face lit up. ‘That will be Yosef.’ She squealed with excitement, before tearing towards the front door.

The deep voices, coming from the hallway, gave Harper the impression that it wasn’t the social services. Placing her cup on the draining board, she looked to see who was at the door, and right away, she recognised the detective from the night of the fire.

‘What’s up?’

‘May we come in, Ms Kane?’ asked Detective Barrows.

‘Yeah, sure. Come through to the kitchen.’

Barrows and his sidekick, Stephanie Moore, traipsed along the passageway and stood in the kitchen. Both were taking in their surroundings.

‘Nice place.’

Harper knew she shouldn’t speak to a copper unless it was to answer a direct question.

‘Tea, coffee?’

‘No, not for us, thank you,’ said Barrows, before Moore could even open her mouth.

Harper looked her over. She was slight framed with long fair hair tied in a ponytail, and she stood like a man. *Why do all the female coppers seem to strike a masculine pose?* she wondered. *Was it the cut of the trousers?*

‘I’m here about Shabab Boz.’ He turned to face Lexi. ‘Your partner’s sister, I believe.’

Harper noticed how Lexi’s sweet, childlike face suddenly changed. She had become serious, older looking.

‘She is my ex’s sister.’

'Well, we had a call from social services outlining the facts regarding your son being taken by Ms Boz, and when two officers called to bring her in for questioning, they found her dead. Murdered in fact.' He paused and studied her face.

Lexi's eyes widened. '*What?* Dear God, what is this world coming to? How was she murdered?'

The detective continued to stare. 'What was your relationship like with Shabab?'

'*Me?*' Lexi almost shrieked, suddenly looking terrified.

'Whoa, detective,' fumed Harper. 'I hope you are not implicating my sister. When did this murder take place?'

Irritated, Barrows took a deep breath. 'Between two and four this morning.'

'Well, Lexi was at home with me.'

Barrows held his hand up. 'Stop, right there. I didn't say she was implicated. It's just a formality. We believe it is a family issue, but since you, Lexi, are a member or an ex-member of the family, I wanted to ask you about Shabab's relationship with her father and brothers.'

'Please take a seat, detectives,' Harper offered.

Barrows and Moore sat at the table opposite Lexi while Harper leaned on the back of Lexi's chair, letting her know that she had her sister's backing.

'What do you want to know?' asked Lexi, her voice a little calmer.

Barrows took out his notebook. 'The relationship between her father and brothers. And did she have a boyfriend that you may have known about? Anything that she would tell a sister or a friend.'

'We weren't close. They all grew up in a different culture, really, so we didn't have a lot in common.'

'Did you know about the wedding?'

'Yeah, she was getting married in September.'

'Anything else? Her future husband?'

Lexi shook her head. 'Not really.'

Harper turned her back to make some more tea for herself and Lexi.

'Lex, did you say that she didn't want to marry the man? Because they hadn't even met yet, had they?'

Harper hoped that her sister wouldn't pause for too long.

'Oh yeah, it was an arranged marriage. He was coming over from Turkey, but she did say that she wasn't in love with him 'cos she hadn't even met him.'

'Do you think she wanted to go ahead with the marriage?' asked Moore.

Harper was shaking. She so desperately wanted to answer for her sister, but she had to stay schtum. She knew that to anyone else, Lexi could come across as a little weak and dumb, but her sister wasn't like that at all.

'No, definitely not. She wanted no part in it. I kinda got the impression that she had her own interests.'

Harper knew her sister was now getting into the game. When Lexi cottoned on, her brain would click into gear and zoom ahead.

'So Shabab wanted out of the marriage arrangement, then? Have I got that right?' asked Barrows, almost feeding her the lines.

'Shabab wasn't happy. She knew that if she pursued any man who her father and brothers had not chosen, then . . .' She sighed.

'They are that strict, are they?'

Lexi nodded. 'God, yeah. She couldn't date anyone, and she didn't even see a picture of this guy she was going to marry. That was really the only thing she ever kinda spoke to me about. Only because Hasad had a child with me out of wedlock and the men in the Boz family don't have to wed. They didn't want him to marry me anyway. It's only the girls who are forced into it.'

'Did she ever mention a man by the name of Claude Bolshoi?'

Harper could feel her throat closing up.

'No, she didn't mention anyone's name, but there was someone she liked,' Lexi replied.

'Okay, that will do for now,' said Barrows, as he got up to leave.

Harper and Lexi saw them to the door. It was only when Stephanie Moore chirped up that Harper felt uneasy.

'One last thing, Lexi. How did you feel about Shabab practically kidnapping your baby?'

Lexi stretched her neck. 'Feel? How the hell do you think I felt? What a silly question.'

'Angry enough to want her hurt her?' Moore pushed.

'Officer, I left Hasad because I wanted nothing to do with the family. You and I both know that they are a dangerous lot. I'm getting my baby back this afternoon. As I understood it, there was a misunderstanding, and you guys were going to question her about it. All I want is a peaceful life with my baby. I walked away from that family because of all the internal dramas. So, am I angry enough to want to hurt her? No! You have to understand, I am not angry, I'm terrified of them. Do I want *her* hurt? No, because she would have been under her father's instructions, so as far as Shabab is concerned, I felt sorry for her.'

Moore nodded. 'Okay, I think we simply needed to ask that question.'

'Fair enough,' replied Lexi.

As soon as they were out of sight, Harper wanted to clap.

Lexi tiptoed back to the kitchen and sat down. 'I'm only going to ask you one question.' Her voice was serious. 'Did she scream in pain?'

Harper chewed her lip. 'Agonising, blood-curdling screams.'

'Like I did, that day she tortured me, then?'

Harper smiled. 'I should think ten times worse.'

Looking into the remnants of her tea, Lexi turned white and trembled. 'Will this come back to haunt us?'

Harper ruffled her sister's hair. 'No, not us. Me, maybe, but not you.'

Lexi stared off out of the window.

'So, Lex, I need to talk to you—'

'No, Harps. Please, I'm still digesting this. Look, Sis, I'm getting Yosef back today. I really need some kind of normality.'

Seeing the sheer worry in her sister's eyes, Harper decided not to say any more until it would be absolutely necessary.

But before she could even reassure her sister, the doorbell rang again. Lexi gave a compassionate smile and headed for the door. A sudden spring in her step showed Harper that her little sister was excited at the expectation of seeing her baby again.

Harper followed and was surprised to find a man, in his mid-thirties, tall, with ash-blond hair, standing there. He looked out of place, dressed so smartly and holding a dribbling baby. Behind him stood a woman who was laden with bags.

'Ahh, come 'ere, my baby,' said Lexi, putting her arms out to receive Yosef.

He instantly giggled and practically threw himself at her.

The sight brought tears to Harper's eyes. However, it also stirred an angry burning feeling in the pit of her stomach.

The man was stone-faced. There was neither a smidgen of warmth nor even a smile.

Harper felt the hairs on the back of her neck stand on end, and, instantly, she disliked him.

As Lexi bounced Yosef, Harper spotted the pink on his shoulders. 'What's this?' she spat, pointing to the sunburn.

The man's eyes widened. 'Oh, that was there before. We must talk about keeping your baby out of the sun—'

'Hold up a minute. He was never out in the sun before the fire. Whoever has just been looking after him has been careless enough to expose him to the sun without bloody sunscreen. Who looked after him, eh? I wanna give them a piece of my mind.'

The woman behind came closer, offering the bags. 'We have papers for you, Ms Kane, to sign.' She turned to the man. 'Peter, would you get them for me? I left them on your dashboard.'

As Peter went back to his car, Harper took the bags from the woman. 'Oh, is that the Peter who's married to Vanessa?'

The woman smiled. 'Yes, that would be him. Anyway, is it okay if we come in?'

Harper shook her head. 'Lex, take the baby inside.'

'I would like to check over the place. We need to make sure it is suitable. You know how it goes.'

Harper straightened up and crossed her arms. 'Yeah, funnily enough, er . . .'

'Christina Muffat.'

'Well, Christina Muffat, you lot messed up big time, didn't you? You took a baby from its mother, making her do a blood test to prove her innocence, when a woman, Lexi's ex-boyfriend's sister, actually kidnapped Yosef. Am I right?'

Christina swallowed down her nerves. 'Well, yes, but—'

'So Yosef was by no means in any danger with his mother before all of this, then? No history of neglect?'

'No, but—'

'No history of abuse?'

'No—'

'So, no, you cannot start checking to see if Yosef is safe and taken care of. When in your care, he managed to get sunburnt. Shocking, really, love, wouldn't you say?'

'We acted appropriately, given the circumstances.'

Peter approached the doorstep with the papers in his hand and a worried look on his face. 'I have these for Ms Kane to sign. I need to run through a check of the property.'

He attempted to step over the threshold, but Harper stood in his way and glared at Christina.

'Do you want to repeat what I have just said?'

'What's going on here?' asked Peter, his voice now stern.

But Harper detected an edge of worry.

'You have no right, none whatsoever, to check on Yosef's home. You had no need before that woman kidnapped him, and you will be lucky if I don't encourage my sister to take this further, considering the sunburn on that baby's shoulders and the appalling way my sister was treated.'

'Well, we have a job to do, Harper.'

Harper held her hand up. '*Harper?* How do you know my name?'

A glint of pink highlighted his chiselled cheekbones. 'Lexiana must have mentioned it. Anyway, we, as I said—'

'Yes, you made a huge mistake in taking the word of a kidnapper over the child's mother, suggesting she needs a psychiatrist and testing her for drugs, all of which came back clear. So, give me the papers. I will see she signs the appropriate ones, and I will hand them in to your office. It is right opposite probation, is it not?'

'Yes, but—'

'Then, when I pop in to see your missus, I can give them to you. Oh, and I will ask my sister if she mentioned my name. If she didn't, then I assume you got it from somewhere else, your wife, perhaps, or an associate.'

She watched, enjoying him squirm. His cheeks were glowing, and red blotches appeared on his neck.

Unexpectedly, he changed tack. 'Okay, listen, Harper, we do our homework, so, of course, I knew your name. This is just a tick-box exercise, nothing more, and yes, the stupid foster carers forgot the sunblock. So can I just have a quick look? Then, I can leave you in peace. And these papers, they are nothing of real importance. You can see for yourself.'

Harper scrutinised his expression before she nodded for him to come in. 'It doesn't need two of you.' She glared at Christina, who spun on her heel and walked back to the car.

As Harper was about to close the door, she noticed another car besides the one Christina was walking towards, and although the side windows were blacked out, she managed to catch a glimpse of the driver. It was the Russian man who had brought her home the night her mother's place was burned down; she was sure it was him.

While Harper was showing Peter around the flat, she was sizing him up – his new leather shoes, his smart trousers, and his shirt, with the tiny Hugo Boss tag. She wondered if he was actually looking at the suitability of the room, considering the cot wasn't even set up yet. He really didn't seem interested at all.

When he took a seat at the kitchen table, uninvited, Harper felt her hackles rise again, but she kept telling herself that once the papers were signed, he would be out of their hair for good.

Lexi handed the baby over to Harper while she signed the handover documents. Narrowing her eyes at the man, Lexi threw the pen on the table, took her son from Harper, and left the room.

Something still felt very odd to Harper. Peter appeared fidgety, slightly edgy, and a tiny film of sweat coated his top lip while he gathered up his briefcase. Then, for some inexplicable reason, the briefcase slid off his knees and he had to stoop under the table to retrieve it. Once he was sitting down again, having collected the papers, which had ended up strewn over the floor, she noticed his wrist.

‘Nice gold and diamond watch you have there. Being a social worker must pay exceptionally well. And your motor, a new plate no less, much like Vanessa’s.’

Suddenly, he jumped up. ‘Well, that’s all, Harper. Nice to meet you,’ he said, as he hurried to the door with his briefcase under his arm. Before he let himself out, he turned to face her. His expression was one of frustrated fury. He leaned towards her. ‘You are very assured for a woman on probation, considering you could easily be back inside, Msss Kane,’ he hissed, like a snake.

Those words and his tone riled up Harper to a point where she completely forgot herself. ‘And you wanna do your job. It doesn’t look good, does it? All these fourteen-year-old girls going missing and probably under your care, Peter.’

His eyes were on fire, and his lips tightened, but she could see he was lost for words.

‘Bye-bye, Peter.’ She smiled as he threw the door open and stormed off.

There was that car again. *What the fuck is going on?*

Chapter Seventeen

Harper left Lexi to get the baby settled in while she built the cot. She'd always been the one who carried out the practical jobs. Delores was as useless as a knitted condom when it came to building anything. Harper had to learn quickly how to do any maintenance in the house because no one else would. From fixing burst water pipes to putting together an IKEA cabinet, she did it all. She had enjoyed making karts from old pram wheels for her sisters when they were kids. Even though she took care of her siblings, they were all tough in their own way. However, Lexi was a worry at the moment. Maybe the news regarding Shabab was more than she could handle.

Once Lexi managed to put Yosef down to sleep, she began showing Harper how to use her new phone.

Harper laughed. 'Well, I only have one number. Yours.'

'I am sure, Sis, in a few weeks, you will have a shedload. All men, taking a fancy to you.'

A frown of sympathetic concern briefly puckered Harper's brow. 'Listen to me, Lex. I can't reveal to you the whys and wherefores, but you have to trust me with what I'm about to tell you.'

Lexi, lying across the sofa twiddling her toes, suddenly looked up. 'What is it?'

'Do you remember Gayle's dad who lives opposite Mum's?'

'Yeah, of course, I do. Lovely old man. Always asked about you when I saw him. Why?'

Harper hesitated. 'If I don't come home from work or I suddenly go missing, promise me you will take the baby and run to him.'

‘*What?*’ she shrieked. ‘What do you mean?’

‘Listen, you take Yosef, and my boy, and you go there. His place is the last anyone would think to look for you or the kids. That’s all you need to know, but you have to do it, okay? Promise me, Sis.’

Lexi was now sitting upright, as stiff as a board, her eyes wide. ‘What are you caught up in, Harps?’ She pointed around the room. ‘All this ain’t given with a bar job. I knew it was something probably illegal. So tell me. Maybe I can help.’

With a deep breath followed by a heavy sigh, Harper gingerly approached the issue. ‘A Russian gang or mafia, or whatever they are, fucking drugged me, carted me away, and told me I was to do as they said or they would harm you, Yosef, and Eddie.’ She paused and waited for the information to sink in.

Lexi’s hand flew to her mouth, her eyes filled with horror. ‘That’s like a thing you see in the movies. It can’t be real, can it?’

‘Oh, believe me, it’s real, all right. I got the job through Rhea. Well, actually, it was Candy who suggested it. Little did I know it was a set-up. Rhea was the manager, but Vadim, the real owner, sacked her and put me in charge. We kinda had a thing. That’s when it all went wrong.’

‘A thing, Harps? With this Vadim guy? Another Russian?’

Harper waved her hands. ‘Yes, but he is a good guy. Well, at least I think he is. Anyway, the bad Russian called Zavid caused so much trouble back in Russia that Vadim went home. He left me in charge of the club.’

Lexi was confused, and it showed by the bewilderment on her face. ‘So what do you have to do?’

‘Whatever they say.’

‘Yeah, Harps, but *what*?’

‘Well, here’s the thing, they haven’t asked me to do anything, yet. But I know what their business is, and worse, I think so many people are involved, like my probation officer, that social worker Peter, and Hasad.’

‘Your probation officer, the social services?’ She frowned in puzzlement. ‘Sis, you aren’t on drugs, are you? ’Cos I know people get paranoid when they use them.’

‘No, Lex, I’m not on drugs. Do I bloody look like I am?’

Lexi shook her head. ‘So what is the business? Cocaine? Money laundering? What?’

‘Human trafficking, Lex. Bleeding fourteen-year-old girls.’

The gasp from Lexi’s mouth was more than dramatic, and it was a few seconds before she could speak. ‘You have to go to the police, Harps. Tell them everything you know.’

Harper smiled. ‘Lex, with all the information you have on the Boz family, you didn’t go to the police. Why?’

‘’Cos I wasn’t as brave as you.’

‘See, this is the whole issue. I *am* brave, and I would go to the police, if it was just me who would be at risk. But I can’t have these Russians hurt you, Yosef, or Eddie. So you see, I’m in a right shitstorm of a predicament. And they aren’t messing about, Lex. They truly are fucking evil, dangerous people. One even tried to rape me.’ She paused to get her breath. The thought of what she had done to him turned her stomach. The images were hard to wash away.

‘Tried? Oh, thank God. What a bastard. I bet you gave him the kicking of a lifetime.’

‘Kicking?’ An evil smirk spread across her face. ‘I stabbed the great Russian prick a hundred times, removed his limbs, packed him up in his own motor, and took him somewhere.’

Lexi was half laughing, half frowning. ‘You are joking, right?’

‘Sadly not, Lex. I took him for a drive to your ex’s garage. So now you have it.’

Lexi stared at her sister for a moment, too appalled for words.

‘Why did you drive a dead man to Hasad’s garage?’

With a cheeky grin, probably boarding on hysteria, Harper replied, 'I can't fight the Russians with their gun-wielding army, or the Turks with all the family connections they have, so I thought they could fight each other. It's what I call stirring the shitpot with a huge wooden spoon.'

Suddenly, Lexi's eyes bulged. 'Oh Jesus, they *are* involved, aren't they? In the human trafficking, I mean. That black van I told you about. I heard a muffled cry inside it.' She put her hands over her eyes. Feeling a sob building up in her chest, she fruitlessly battled against it.

Harper instantly sat next to her sister on the sofa. 'Listen, Lex, I didn't exactly *ask* to be caught up in all of this. But I am. So, God help me, I will have to do something about it. There is more. I have to carry on working at the club, to find a way to help these girls. I have to find them or bring down the main men. For now, please do as I ask. Like I said, if I go missing, get the kids and run.'

Lexi removed her hands from her tear-stained face and hugged Harper. 'You really have been dealt a crap hand, haven't ya, Sis?'

'No, Lex, I just fell into a lot of shit, but, one day, I will come up smelling of roses, if I ain't pushing up daisies.'

'I promise, Harps, if you don't come home, I think I will go to Teddy's. He has a lot of clout these days. He'll know what to do. But it won't come to that. I get why you have to help those girls. Jesus, what on earth will happen to them? At fourteen, they must be terrified. I just can't imagine what they are going through.' She wiped another tear away from her blotchy pink cheeks. 'I'll take the kids, so at least you'll have peace of mind. It's the very least I can do.'

Hearing that, Harper felt a little more relieved. 'You have to make sure that the Russians don't see or follow you. Teddy will have to be clever about it.'

'Sis, will Teddy listen to me, though?'

Harper nodded. 'You say to him "parsnip".'

Lexi tilted her head in confusion. 'Parsnip?'

'Yeah, we had these little codes when we were kids. One of them was parsnip for "help". Cabbage was for "Let's get out of here."' She laughed. 'We were daft back then.'

'He still loves ya, Sis.'

'Hmmm, well, it's too late now.'

***

At eight o'clock, Harper appeared from the bedroom in a pair of slim-fit blue jeans and a white shirt.

'You look lovely, Harps. I think short hair suits you.' Lexi rose from the sofa, with a small knife in her hand. 'Sis, take this. Have it inside your waistband, please. I need you to stay safe.'

Without arguing, Harper accepted the knife. 'I'm sure it won't come to it. But you know me, Sis. If I'm hitting the deck, then someone's coming down with me.'

The second she slung her bag over her shoulder, the sound of the doorbell ringing followed by the loud knocking at the front door compelled Harper to push her sister into the bedroom.

She knew she had no choice but to open the door because the banging was so loud, the next stage would be the door flying along the hallway.

As she opened it, she was shocked to see Teddy there, his face white and angry. Delores was behind him, looking three sheets to the wind.

'Harps, are they here?'

Stepping aside, Harper let him in. 'Who?' she asked, dreading the answer.

'Erin and Eddie.'

Lexi appeared, holding Yosef. The commotion had obviously woken him up.

'Why would they be here?' asked Harper, her face draining of blood.

‘’Cos where else would she go? She was supposed to take Eddie to school and then come home to see to the decorators, but she didn’t come home, and Eddie ain’t been to school. The fucking bitch has fucked off with him. I swear to God, this nonsense will have to stop.’

Feeling as though her whole body was turning inside out, Harper imagined the worst. The *Russians had discovered that she had killed Claude, and now they had her son. Please, God, don’t let it be true.*

‘Did you have a row? Does she have any reason to want to leave you?’

Teddy paced the hallway, running his hands through his hair. ‘I dunno. She’s got it into her head that I’m planning to get back with you, but she’s always been banging on about it, even before you got out of jail.’

Delores, who had pushed past them all and made her way into the lounge, was more interested in the plush flat. ‘Fucking lovely, this is! What have you been up to, Harper? Sucking off an Arab?’ She laughed as she ran her hands over the sofa. ‘Cor, proper posh, an’ all.’

‘Mum, shut up,’ said Lexi, fuming, knowing how Harper would be going insane with worry.

‘What’s she doing here, Teddy?’ asked Harper, only too aware that her mother had a habit of making matters worse.

‘I dunno. She just tagged along. Anyway, so you haven’t seen or heard from her, have you?’

‘No.’ She glanced at Lexi, her eyes alive with fear. Then, her words flew from her mouth. ‘I have to go. Lex, talk to Teddy about what we’ve said. I haven’t got time. But you, Mother, you can’t stay. Someone call her a cab and send her home, the fucking drunken slob.’

‘Oi, Miss High and Mighty Fancy Pants, I happen to be your mother, so show some respect. This is a family matter. We need to stick together. Now, where’s the brandy? All this worry is rattling my nerves.’

Harper glared while her nostrils flared. 'Lex, call Delores a cab before I physically launch her through the fucking window.' She tried to shuffle past Teddy, desperate to get to the club. 'Look, I have to go.'

'Wow, wait. Where are you going, Harps? Do you know where they are?' asked Teddy, grabbing her arm.

Harper sharply shook him off. 'No, I don't, but please, Teddy, please let me go.'

'No, you tell me what's going on, Harps. Where's our boy?'

'I don't know!' she yelled, her voice high with dread. 'Go home, Teddy, and call me if they turn up. Trust me, Ted. Please, just trust me. Lex has my number.'

Teddy looked her over and nodded. He knew how stubborn Harper could be, but he could be sure that she would do whatever it took to get their boy back. She'd always been the stronger one in the relationship.

'I'll come with you.'

Harper's eyes widened. 'No, no, please, you will make things a whole lot worse. Please, just get that witch out of my house. And how did you even know my address?' she asked, her suspicious mind working overtime.

'Lexi called to give me the new numbers, and I took down the address as well. Surely, Harper, you wouldn't mind?' A wave of tenderness washed over him. 'Erin isn't wrong, though, about you and me. I do love you, Harps.'

Harper didn't reply; she ran along the street towards the main road to the taxi rank. Fear and burning rage pushed her to a state of recklessness. All she wanted was to smash the life out of every Russian in that club, until one of them would tell her where her son was.

The taxi pulled up outside the club, and Harper literally threw the crumpled notes at the driver, before she stormed through the back door. Ready to take down an army, she realised that it was too early for Pixie or anyone else to be there. She made her way to the office and listened to the answering machine. It was Vadim again. 'Hopefully, you will get this message, Harper. I have to delay my return. I will call at eight-thirty. Please pick up then.'

Harper looked at her watch. There were two minutes to go, but what would she say? Could she say 'Please come back. The shit's gone off here big time'? No, of course she couldn't tell him the truth. She would just play it cool. Her heart raced every second she thought of her little boy, and Erin. As much as her sister was a bitch, Erin was still her sister, and she loved her, regardless.

The phone rang, and Harper took a calming breath before she picked up the receiver. 'Hello.'

'Harper, thank you, thank you. I was very concerned, you see. I had no idea if the club was okay. Claude has not answered his phone or returned my calls.' He paused.

'Oh, yes, I haven't seen Claude myself, but the club is fine. I have ordered stock, put the takings in the safe, and . . . Well, that's about it, really. No issues here.'

'Ah, good, good. How are you, Harper? I have not stopped thinking about you. I will be home soon. Just another few days. Are the girls showing you respect? They can get very cheeky sometimes. I must ask a favour. Pixie is Claude's girlfriend. Could you ask her to talk with Claude? It is strange because he would not let me down.'

'I will do, Vadim. I am looking forward to your return as well.'

She heard him chuckle. 'Perhaps we could go away. A short trip. Somewhere hot.'

'Vadim, believe me, I would love that too, but it's sweltering here.'

'I will think of something else, then. Perhaps a cooler climate. I must go now. Remember to tell Pixie.'

The line went dead, and Harper massaged her temples. Then she heard banging on the main entrance door. It snapped her out of her anxious thoughts.

The bouncers had arrived, along with a few of the dancers. One bouncer, a Russian, Claude's buddy, she assumed, a man called Nico, gave her a sideways glance, his eyes beady and narrow. He was massive, and even more imposing than Claude. His corrugated nose and square head made him look vicious, and it was exaggerated by his thick Russian accent.

As the girls hurried past, she flicked her head for him to follow her. They went behind the bar.

'What is it?' he asked, his voice rough and husky.

Out of earshot of the girls, and through gritted teeth, she said, 'Where is Pixie?'

His jaw clenched, looking at Harper's angry expression. 'Why?'

'Never fucking mind why. Where is she?'

Nico raised his brows. 'On her way. She just called to ask if you were here, so she must want to speak with you too.'

***

The instant Pixie stepped in through the back door, dressed in her long wig, black skirt, and white shirt, Harper had a gut feeling that the Russians would be bringing in kids again to be shipped off, once their buyer had made his selection. The thought was boiling her piss and she scanned the room looking for a weapon. She didn't want to use the knife, not just yet, in case she killed her before getting answers. Against the left wall there was a stainless-steel fridge and also a freezer. The opposite wall comprised kitchen cabinets, the cleaning equipment, and the chopping boards, which were used to chop the fruit for cocktails.

In a fighting stance, Pixie pointed her manicured finger at Harper. 'We must speak, Harper!'

The Russian accent cut through the air, sending Harper into a place she never really liked to be. As if all the nerves in her body turned to red hot needles, she grabbed the nearest useful implement to her. It was the marble chopping board. Every ounce of compassion, empathy, and humanity left her body. Only the feeling of rage remained.

'Where's my son?' screamed Harper, gripping the board like a McEnroe two-handed backhand stroke. Swinging it so hard and fast, Pixie had no chance to get out of her way. As the lump of marble cracked Pixie around the head, Harper felt the bones in her own arm vibrate.

The force was so powerful that it literally knocked Pixie off her feet. She slumped to the floor, stunned.

'Where is my son, you fucking whore?' she screamed again, standing over the Russian. 'I swear to God, I will kill you, if you don't tell me where my boy is.' Her rage almost forced the veins in her neck to pop out. And her eyes bulged as she foamed at the mouth.

Reeling from the blow, Pixie took a few moments to come round. All she could see was a ball of fury leaning over her. The blow around the head was brutal enough but it hadn't killed her. *What doesn't kill you makes you stronger,* her father had drummed the Russian equivalent saying into her head. She was resilient compared to most women but not as tough and strong as her brother. She admired Zavid. She loved him, but he always saw her as the weaker sibling. If only he could see her as an equal. Desperate to get to her feet, she had to show Zavid she was worthy of a promotion.

'Where is he?' bellowed Harper.

Pixie held up her hand as she pretended to struggle to get to her feet.

To Harper, Pixie looked pretty much fucked. Her right cheek was swollen, and with her upper body swaying wildly, she was acting as though she was punch-drunk. But Harper wasn't taking any chances. While she scrutinised Pixie, she clocked her hand slowly sliding behind her back. The penny dropped: she had a gun. With the adrenaline now surging around her body, Harper smashed the Russian again with the chopping board. Blood sprayed from Pixie's mouth, and this time her head connected with the back wall.

'I told you, ya Russian bitch, that I will fight ya, but now you have my boy, I will *kill* you, unless you tell me where he is.'

Leaning down, Harper snatched the gun that was poking out of Pixie's waistband and put the chopping board on the counter.

With the gun in her hand, Harper straightened up and stared at the carnage. She really had done a demolition job on Pixie's face. Blood was pouring from her nose and mouth. The whole right side was swollen, and she was coughing the blood from the back of her throat while trying to focus.

But Harper had to admit to herself the girl was hard. Most women would have keeled over. Probably a lot of men too. 'Where is he?'

Pixie shook her head and waved her hand in defeat. 'We don't have him.' Her voice was drowned out by tears and blood.

'Liar!'

'No, we don't have him.' She spat the excess blood from her mouth.

Crouching down, Harper ripped the wig off Pixie's head and grabbed her by her real hair, lifting her up. 'Get Zavid on the phone. I want him to know that I will blow your brains out, if he doesn't hand back my sister and my son.'

Harper let go of Pixie's hair and watched as the woman tried to hold herself up. Her head was wobbling like a nodding dog in a car window. Then Harper's attention turned to Pixie's bag, which had been flung across the room when she had taken the first hit. Still aiming the gun at Pixie, she tipped the contents out and found Pixie's phone.

Sliding it over to her, Harper nodded. 'Go on. Call Zavid. Tell him, I will kill you if necessary. You see, Pixie, when you said I would do anything because I am desperate, you were right. So understand this, you cunt. If I don't get my son back alive, I will put a fucking bullet through your brain. My son is all I have. Without him, I don't wanna live anyway. So, not only am I desperate, Pixie, but I'm fucking dangerous, 'cos I don't give a flying fuck.'

Now that the adrenaline shock, which had been numbing Pixie's face, was wearing off, the pain felt immense. Harper had probably cracked her skull, and she thought both her nose and her jaw were broken. Pressing redial, Pixie stared intently at her.

'Put it on loudspeaker.'

Pixie didn't argue.

The words were in Russian.

'In English, or do not answer at all.'

Pixie nodded. 'Zavid.' Her voice was a level just above a whisper.

She sounded like she was calling from a dentist's chair having just had a load of fillings. 'Talk in Englishhh.'

'What is it, Pasha?'

Harper could sense the irritation in the man's tone. She wondered if perhaps Pixie wasn't such a big shot but a whiney little sister who pulled on her big brother's shirt tails.

Footsteps to the side of her made Harper turn, but she only managed to catch a glimpse of a woman. It was possibly Frenchy. She assumed then that she would have the bouncers storming the room at any moment, so she turned to face the bar, keeping just away from view but having the gun still levelled at Pixie's head.

'Harper thinkssh we have her son.'

'*What?* Why would she think that? We have no reason to hold her son hostage. Tell her she is mistaken.'

Harper wondered for a moment if they were telling the truth. Zavid sounded genuine, but they were Russian gangsters, so what would she really know.

'Tell him I have battered you with a marble board. But I won't stop there if he doesn't tell you where my son is.'

'I can hear you, Harper, remember,' replied Zavid, woodenly. 'My sister is a good fighter. She was trained by the best.'

'Well, she may have been trained by the best, but she went down like a sack of shit. Believe me, she must have come fucking bottom of the class.'

'If you have beaten up my sister, then you must be the stronger woman. If I had your son, I would tell you, or what would be the point? Which makes me wonder, Harper, why you are pointing the finger at me. Have you done something that would force me to take your child?'

'My sister and my boy are missing, and you—'

'You must have another enemy because I have not taken your son.'

The phone connection was cut off, and Harper was left staring at Pixie, who was fast losing consciousness.

Unexpectedly, Harper's phone rang. She was relieved to hear Teddy's voice.

His first words were 'He's safe, Harper. Our boy is okay. Erin has him. She was leaving me, but the daft cow realised she had left her bank card at home. Harps, are you there?'

'Okay,' she replied, in a quiet voice, still with her eyes on Pixie.

'I thought you'd be pleased, Harps. What's—'

'I am. But see that sister of mine? She could have got me . . . Oh, never mind. Go back and play fucking happy families,' she replied, with annoyance and frustration gnawing at her, before ending the call.

Fuck it!

Wrapping the gun in a tea towel, she hid it under the bar. Then she hurried to Nico, ushering him away from the queue of men who were itching to get in.

‘Come with me. You need to take Pixie to the hospital.’

Nico didn’t reply. He hurried to the back room to find Pixie slumped on the floor, her face a train wreck. ‘How the hell?’ He rushed to her side and scooped her up, and then his conniving eyes narrowed once more. ‘Who did this?’

Harper smiled. ‘Me, I did, and now you’d best take her to the hospital because I really don’t think a plaster and a paracetamol will cut it.’

‘Zavid will—’

‘Zavid knows what I did,’ Harper said.

‘You will die for this.’

Harper held her arms out. ‘Well, I’m alive and kicking, and she’ – her face tightened – ‘she is one lucky bitch, so take her to the hospital before I change my mind, and you need a bin liner instead.’

She knew that he wouldn’t argue with her because she’d made him aware that she’d already spoken with Zavid.

As Nico left through the back door, still holding Pixie in his arms, two thoughts lifted the corners of Harper’s lips. Not only was her son safe, but Zavid had no idea where he was, which meant that he didn’t have her boy in his eyeline, as he had previously boasted, after all.

Chapter Eighteen

Noticing the speckles of blood on her white shirt, Harper flitted to the changing room and replaced her soiled top with a fresh one.

The time was approaching ten o'clock, and Harper surmised that if another kid was arriving, they would probably be here by now. She recalled the last two girls had arrived around that time. Hovering around the bar, Harper kept an eye on the front and rear entrances. At 10.30, she thought she heard a bang at the back door and hurried to open it. She had already devised a plan.

Expecting a couple of young schoolgirls, Harper was surprised to find just one girl. She was standing with her hands on her hips and with a cheeky twinkle in her eye. It was hard to speculate the kid's age. She could have been eighteen, but Harper guessed she was nothing like that. Her hair was pretty, in short waves, framing her innocent face. A deep dimple appeared on each cheek when she smiled, and her hazel eyes were laced with thick black lashes. With such a sweet face, the girl seemed to be anything other than candy floss and sugar cane.

'Is Pixie here? I was told I would have a job starting tonight. Me name's Lois,' she said, in between chewing gum and giving Harper the once-over.

Harper wanted to chuckle, slap the girl's backside, and send her home, but God knows who was waiting outside the club. She would play along until the time was ready.

'All right, you can go in. Frenchy will show you the ropes. So, your name's Lois?'

'Yeah, Lois Lane.'

'As in Superman? Right, got ya.' She grabbed the girl's arm. 'So, what's your real name, kid?'

'Louise Brown,' she replied.

'Right, Lois, you will learn how to serve drinks tonight. So, what did, er . . . what's her name . . . ?' she asked, rolling her hand for help with the name. 'The girl who told you about the job.'

'Oh yeah, sorry, Candy.'

'Bloody hell, it was on the tip of my tongue.' Harper laughed.

'Yeah, Candy, she got me the job. I wanna be self-sufficient. I don't need no poxy foster carer, and Candy reckons the job pays well. And I know I would be good at it.'

Harper had to hold back the gasp. *Candy, one of her best mates? Surely not?*

'I got ya. So has Candy cut off that mass of hair yet? She was going to do it for a bet.'

'No, she's got the maddest Afro I've ever seen. A nice woman she is. She's been good to me. She reckons I can get a flat to go with the job, if I do well.'

Harper knew then that it was the same Candy, and her heart sank to the pit of her stomach.

Looking her over, Harper remarked how old she looked for someone who was probably only around fourteen, tops.

The teenager blushed. 'I, er . . . I'm not to disclose my age, but I have tried to look older. Do I pass okay?'

Harper felt her throat constricting. She was about to place the child in danger. 'Yeah, babe, it's fine. So, tell me, Peter, your social worker, does he know you're coming for a job here?' She had to speculate she was on the right track and hope for the best.

'God no, not even that daft Mrs Leonard, me foster carer, knows. But if I do well, then, Candy says I don't have to go back there.'

Harper had to admit that Candy had sent a sweet little thing. But the system that was supposed to be in place to protect her was seriously letting her down. The girl's fake confidence was a transparent attempt to mask her fear. Of course, she would be worried. She was so young. And the flawless face and virgin hair told Harper that although this girl may be in the system, she didn't have that abused look in her eyes. She was probably a real sweetie, who, through no fault of her own, had ended up being taken in by social services.

'So how come you ended up in care?'

'A bit nosey, ain't ya?'

'Yeah, I suppose I am. But I just like to get to know a bit about my staff.' Harper raised a knowing brow.

Louise suddenly straightened up. 'Oh shit. Sorry, I thought, well, I dunno what I thought. Er, yeah, well, I went into care 'cos me mum and dad had a car crash. They were both killed.'

'No aunts or uncles to go to?'

'Nah, and I was the only child. So no big sister either.' Her bottom lip trembled.

Louise's eyes took on a sadness that melted Harper's heart, compelling her to save the child, come what may. *Fuck you, Peter, you disgusting bastard!*

'Okay, Lois Lane, I will walk you through to the bar. Now, if anyone asks if I have been questioning you, you say "no". There is a lot of jealousy in this club, and I have my favourites, and you could be one of them. You see, I hand out the wages.'

Louise nodded and smiled. 'Of course, er . . . What's your name?'

'Harper.'

'Cool name.'

After Harper ushered Louise into the bar, towards Frenchy, she clocked the uncomfortable atmosphere.

Frenchy was on edge. She dropped a glass, and it smashed into a thousand pieces.

'Leave that, Frenchy. This, here, is Lois Lane. You can train her up.'

Harper observed Louise gazing around in wonderment. It was most likely the first time she had set foot in a club, and it would no doubt have been overwhelming. The pole dancers, the music, the lights, were all a spectacle to behold, but seeing the bar staff being handled like pieces of meat would have been shocking to any naïve teenager.

'Er, did she come through the back door?'

Harper nodded. 'Yeah, of course.'

Harper was puzzled by how Frenchy seemed less confident. She kept glancing around the club as if she was waiting for someone. Harper watched as Frenchy guided Louise over to the far end of the bar. She was showing her the mixers and the different glasses for different drinks, but something was off. Harper sensed Frenchy was uncomfortable. Either that or something serious was going down.

Within minutes, Calvin Stuart and another man arrived with two sidekicks. Dressed in suits, the minders stuck out like sore thumbs, considering it was roasting inside the club. The only cool area was the stage. The air con blasted the dancers, preventing them from fainting from the heat. Calvin was dressed more casually in a white polo shirt and chinos. His tanned skin showed up his silver watch and bangle.

Flash fucker, thought Harper.

However, her interest turned to the other man accompanying him. He was slimmer and wore his hair much like Calvin's – dark, long, and sleeked back. His eyebrows were bushy, but his skin was extraordinarily smooth and evenly tanned. Everything about the man, who was probably of a similar age to Calvin, reeked of money. Her mother's words popped into her head. *'Are you sucking off an Arab?'*

He certainly looked like one.

As she stared, mentally summing him up, Calvin shot a glance her way. He nodded and waved his hand for her to come over.

Unexpectedly, and not like her at all, Harper felt nervous, but she offered the men a generous smile and waltzed over.

'What would you like, sir?'

'Harper, I believe.'

Harper felt her skin come alive with goosebumps. Calvin literally made her skin crawl. 'Yes.'

The Arab-looking man stepped closer. 'That girl.' He pointed to Louise.

Harper knew then from his accent that he was from the Middle East. She had been in prison with a girl from the Yemen, a drug mule. He spoke in an almost identical way.

Harper twisted her neck to look back at Louise. 'Yes.'

'*She* must serve me.'

His face beaming, Calvin patted the man's back. Harper could only guess that his expression was one of excitement or anticipation.

Knowing she had to go along with it, Harper smiled sweetly. 'Of course, sir.'

'She's a beauty, Mr Ahmad, wouldn't you say?' whispered Calvin.

But his words weren't discreet enough. Harper heard him.

Against all her moral values, she tapped Louise on the shoulder and asked her to serve the gentleman.

Believing she was put on the spot to impress Harper, not the men, Louise spun around and smiled at Ahmad. 'What can I get for you?'

Harper nudged her. 'Sir.'

'Sorry, what may I get for you, *sir*?'

Harper was aware of the wink Calvin gave her as if she herself was doing a good job. But her stomach muscles knotted, and she bit down on her bottom lip, holding back the urge to stab him in the eye.

'Yes, I would like an apple juice, please.'

'Right away, sir,' said Louise, as she quickly retrieved a bottle of apple juice and poured it into a tall glass. 'Ice with that, sir?'

Ahmad nodded. 'Two cubes.'

Just as Louise plopped the two ice cubes into the glass, she was distracted by the brash, official-sounding voice of Cox.

'Well, hello. I see you're new. Nice arse. I want you to bring my drink over. I'll have a vodka cranberry in a tall glass with lashings of ice.'

His lecherous eyes and crude comments sent Louise into a panic, and she acted like any teenager would. Her eyes welled up with frightened tears, and her face blushed bright red. She looked down at the apple juice and carefully handed it to Ahmad.

To Harper's horror, Ahmad said, 'I think you have a customer who still wants servicing, I mean serving?' He chuckled like any teenage boy.

Harper was seething inside. She desperately wanted to go over and smash Cox in the mouth, but she noticed that Calvin was curiously studying her face. She had no choice other than to play along and pray that the ordeal wouldn't mentally scar the kid.

When Louise looked nervously at Harper for the okay, Harper nodded at her with a compassionate half-smile.

With her hands trembling, Louise filled the glass with far too much vodka and a dash of cranberry. She dropped the ice cubes in, and in the process, she made a mess on the bar.

Surprisingly, Roxy stepped in. 'I'll take this order over, Harper.'

But Harper saw the wag of Calvin's finger. So, she shook her head. 'No, Roxy, Lois will.'

Louise placed the glass on a tray and gingerly crept over to Cox. As she placed his drink on a paper coaster on the low-level table, she was clearly shocked when he slipped his hand up her skirt and attempted to drag her onto his lap. The terror was written all over her face as she tried to pull away, her eyes begging Harper to rescue her.

But Calvin and Ahmad just stood there laughing. To them it was a game but there was a point to their scornful smiles. It was a test to see how innocent the kid really was.

Even though Harper was dying inside, she knew she had to stay calm, but it was hard to hold down that boiling anger and desperation to save Louise.

It was all a bit too much when Harper saw Cox hold the girl down on his lap. His hand ran inside her skirt and down the front of her knickers.

Harper decided to act quickly. 'Stop that! She will be spoiled goods.' It was all she could think to say.

Suddenly, Calvin stopped laughing. 'Stop him.'

Harper flew around the bar and pulled Louise away. 'That's it, Mr Cox. Go on, get out of here.'

Cox looked over at Calvin, who gave him a sharp nod of disapproval. Cox instantly left the bar, weaving his way through the customers.

Seeing Louise visibly trembling, Harper walked her towards the toilets. Before she led the youngster inside, she glanced back at Calvin, who was already on the phone, his face alive and beaming. Then she noticed Ahmad. He was walking out of the club, followed by Calvin's two bodyguards. The deal was obviously done. *Fuck!* They had not only wanted teenage girls, but they'd also wanted the real innocent virgins as well. She swallowed hard, bit her lip, and suppressed the urge to let anger have its way.

Once she closed the door into the ladies' restroom, Harper grabbed Louise's arm.

'Listen to me, babe. Please do as I say.'

Louise was on the verge of a full-blown panic attack. She was gasping for air. 'He put his hands down . . . down . . . my . . . He touched my . . .'

'Shhhh, take a deep breath. Now, listen to me! You have to get a grip, kid, because they will take you away, and believe me, touching your noonie will be the least of your worries.'

'*What?* Oh, please, no. I only wanted a job.'

'Stop with the hysterics. We haven't got the fucking time. Can you climb through that window?'

Louise nodded.

'Good, climb out, and run around to the side of the building. There is a front door there. It looks like an entrance into a flat, but it's actually a cottage. Just go there and wait. Stay in the shadows. Trust me, please.'

Louise nodded again before she crawled out through the small window.

Harper went into one of the toilet cubicles and locked the door before sliding out through the gap underneath. She then left the ladies' restroom and surveyed her surroundings. Frenchy was not in sight. Calvin and his sidekicks, as well as Ahmad, had clearly gone. Harper knew that the kid would be taken, if she didn't act quickly. Bolting into the office before anyone saw her, she locked the door and hurried through the cabinet entrance into the cottage. The second she opened the front door, she whipped Louise inside.

'Did anyone see you?'

Louise was crying. 'No.'

Quietly, they crept up the stairs to the bedroom.

'Louise, please stay here. They will find you and take you away if you try to leave now.'

Before Louise answered, Harper heard the sound of a diesel engine pulling up at the back of the club.

She swiftly returned to the club, via the office, which she left unlocked, and then casually sauntered into the ladies', where she found Frenchy peering under the locked cubicle door and Roxy looking at the window.

'What *are* you both doing? Why aren't you at the bar? It's getting busy.'

'Yeah, in a minute. Where did the girl go?' asked Frenchy.

Harper shrugged her shoulders. 'The last time I saw her, she was in here getting herself straight. I think that ugly old pervert, Cox, gave her a fright. She might be out the back getting some air.'

Frenchy stared silently regarding her with brooding eyes. 'The *back*?'

'Yeah, I'll go and see if she's okay. She was a little bit stressed.'

'No, I'll go,' insisted Frenchy, who didn't even wait for an answer before rushing past Harper.

Harper followed her. When she reached the back door, she found Frenchy outside peering up and down the alley, her face awash with panic.

Harper stood watching with her arms folded.

As soon as Frenchy turned around, she jumped when she saw it was Harper, who was standing there with a cocky attitude.

'Harper, where did she go?'

Harper shrugged her shoulders. 'Like I said, she was in the ladies', the last time I saw her.'

Frenchy was wide-eyed. 'She isn't now. Could she have gone out through the window?'

'Or perhaps whoever was in the vehicle idling outside gave her a lift.'

'What vehicle? Was it a van? A car? What?'

'I didn't see anything. Like I've just said, I only heard a diesel engine idling outside.'

Harper was desperate to ask Frenchy why she appeared so concerned. After all, if any young kid experienced the fright of their life on a job and decided to leave, who would bat an eyelid? Yet she was still unsure of the process of this sick, sordid business, and she sure as hell trusted no one. She still couldn't work Frenchy out. A part of her wanted to believe that Frenchy was on the side of the angels. But if she was, why wasn't she discussing the situation outright? Why all this cloak-and-dagger stuff?

By 1 a.m., the dancers had packed up and were hanging around the bar for their wages. Harper took the money from the till, added it up, and recorded it in the accounts book. It had been a good night's takings. She carefully counted the wages and popped them into the little brown envelopes. She didn't bother sealing them because she had noticed that the girls always checked their money before they left in case they were short. She hurried back and handed the envelopes out. 'Do any of you ladies want a drink before you go? On me.'

It was late, and the girls were eager to get going. Some were 'clucking', so she guessed they would saunter off to the underworld using their money to score a rock.

After the two bouncers escorted the girls outside, ensuring they were safe from loiterers, Frenchy appeared from the back room.

'Oh, I thought you had left with the others,' said Harper.

'I was worried about that girl, so I thought I would have one last look around to see if she was hiding.'

Harper tilted her head to the side and narrowed her eyes. 'And why would she be hiding, Frenchy?'

'I don't know. I was just concerned, that's all.'

'And why is that, Frenchy? Why are you so worried about a new member of staff? You were okay with the other two newbies.'

Frenchy shook her head. 'Oh, never fucking mind. See you later,' she snapped, before she stormed off out of the back door and into the cooler night air.

***

Harper held the door open, breathing in the freshness of a new day's beginnings and exhaling the dirt and disgust of the last few hours. As she enjoyed the breeze, she heard a car pull up. Instantly, her first reaction was to shut the door. She could not lock it because the keys were still in the office. *The office was open. Damn!* She couldn't remember if she had pushed the cabinet across. In a blind panic, she tore off through the bar and into the office. Searching the desk for the keys, she heard a deep voice behind her bellow, 'What are you doing?'

Having noticed immediately the cabinet was closed, Harper could now feel a moment of relief, but then she began to tremble. She was alone, and Nico, the biggest man she had ever met, was in the room with anger in his tone.

Harper pivoted to face him. Pixie's blood had stained his shirt. 'What do you want, Nico?'

'Where is the girl?'

Harper felt the terror lodge in her chest; it was making her breathless. She just hoped he didn't see her fear.

'Lois Lane, the kid who was here earlier, you mean?' asked Harper, trying to maintain her voice on an even keel.

'I don't know her name.' He produced a photo on his phone and shoved it under Harper's nose.

Harper's limbs, which were still trembling up to this point, had now tightened all over. She stared at the girl in a school uniform with no make-up and a smile that defined her sweet dimples. She looked so young. How could she herself turn her grimace into an accommodating smile and go along with this?

The answer was she couldn't. No way was she going to let that kid fall into the clutches of these monsters. So, in as neutral a voice as she could, all she said was, 'Yeah, she was here.'

'Where is she now, Harper?' His eyes bore into hers.

Harper gave an exaggerated frown. 'I thought she left in a van. No?'

Heavy-footed, Nico marched out of the office, clearly alarmed.

Harper heard him on the phone.

'The girl is in the van. They took her.'

Harper couldn't hear who he was speaking to, but Nico's voice was so deep and clear that she heard every word.

'I don't know if she is lying . . . Okay, I will ask her.'

Harper pretended to be checking the week's diary.

When Nico returned, he had his hand over the phone. 'What colour was the van?'

'Black.'

He walked away again, and this time Harper had to strain to hear his words.

'I am shocked that Claude would do this to us. If he thinks that the Turks will cut him in on a deal, he will be mistaken . . . Okay, I will get the men to find Claude and the rest of the Turks. Have faith in me. I will find the girl.'

Harper grinned. Perhaps her plan had worked after all. The Russian obviously thought that Claude had got in with the Turks. Yet she wondered who exactly Nico was talking to because he spoke in English. It crossed her mind that Calvin was higher up the food chain than she had first imagined, and it was probably him, who Nico was talking to.

The minute she heard Nico's car tear away, she ran back to the bedroom in the cottage. Louise was sitting on the bed, her face as white as a sheet, staring into nothing.

Harper sat beside her and gently placed an arm around the girl's shoulders. 'You did good, babe. Now we have to get away from here, so, again, you must trust me.'

Louise's face was so childlike that Harper wanted to cry. *How many kids have these monsters taken?* Well, if she could save one, she would.

After checking the perimeter of the club, Harper called a cab and locked up. She instructed Louise to lie down in the back of the car when it arrived and to stay there until she was told to get out.

Traumatised by the whole ordeal, Louise was past caring if Harper could be trusted or not. She was now in this woman's hands; she only hoped that she was her fairy godmother and not the wicked witch.

The cab stopped opposite Delores's burned-out house.

Harper paid the driver. 'Here, take this fifty.'

'Gawd blimey, love, that's a generous tip. Are you sure?'

'If anyone asks where you dropped me off, it was anywhere but here, and I was alone.'

'For a fifty-quid tip, I'd convince anyone that you were the Queen. Cheers, love. And whatever the trouble, you stay safe now. Take my card, and call me personally, if you need a cab again.'

Harper stared at the man's gentle eyes. She recognised him. 'Thank you. I will. You kindly dropped my sister off and helped her with all her bags.'

'That's right, I remember. Call me Terry. Your sister, Lexi, love her, uses me all the time.'

Harper's eyes widened. 'You know her, then?'

'Yeah, poor cow. Every other Friday, I'd pick her up from the supermarket, laden with food. I bet it's all for him 'cos she looks like she barely nibbles an apple, and him, the tubby lard-arse, he must be going on twenty-odd stone, and she can't be far off seven stone soaking wet.' He stopped for breath, shaking his head. 'I'm sorry, love, but I can't stand her fella. That fucking Hasad. A lazy bastard, he is. He ponces about in that garage of his, and he ain't even a mechanic. I asked him to service the cab once, and he said he was booked up solid for two years.' He let out a chuckle. 'Two years, my arse. Anyway, I like your sister, bless her little heart. I know he beats her up. She's always wearing a bruise on her pretty, dainty face. Anyway, sorry, I'm probably talking out of turn.'

'No, you're okay. I hate the bastard too. Thank you for helping her the other day with her shopping.'

'No worries. I gotta say she was a different girl. All chatty and happy, she was, getting her boy back and staying with you. Trust me, Lexi's sister . . . I've forgotten your name . . .'

'Harper.'

'Yeah, that's it, Harper. Anyway, like I said, you call me if ever you need a lift. There ain't many like you.'

'Like me?'

The chubby middle-aged driver nodded. 'Lexi told me what you went away for. They should never have locked you up. They should have given you a gold medal instead.'

Harper blushed. 'Thanks, Terry. I really appreciate it.'

''Ere, and take this fifty back. I don't need it. I only drive 'cos I'm a sad and lonely old fucker.' He laughed again.

Harper felt the safest she had ever been, being in Terry's company. Out of character, she kissed him on the cheek. 'See you soon, Terry.'

***

Louise stood nervously at the bleak-looking front door to the three-bedroom semi in St Mary Cray.

Harper was anxiously looking about her, before, finally, the door opened, and there, as thin as a rake in his striped pyjamas, stood Morris Baker. He appeared frailer than ever.

He blinked and wiped his eyes. '*Harper?* Is that you, love?'

'Yeah, Mr Baker.'

'Oh, quick, come in.' He ushered them through to the kitchen. His feet padded along as he struggled to loosen his calf muscles.

Once they were in the kitchen, Morris turned the light on. 'It's early hours—'

'I know. I wouldn't have—'

'No worries, my girl. I was about to say it's early hours, so you must need my help, and you know me, Harper. I'd do anything for you.' Slowly, he took a seat. 'So, what's this all about?' He peered up at the young girl, who was staring at the floor.

'A long story, but I have to keep this kid hidden for now.'

'Okay, Harper. Now then, there are two spare rooms upstairs. My Gayle's bedroom, Gawd rest her, and another spare room. There is clean bedding and a set of pyjamas, if you'd like.'

Louise slowly looked up and stared at the old man.

Morris clocked right away that she was afraid. 'It's all right, my darling. Harper will tell you, I don't bite, and I know Harper. I've watched her grow up. And if she feels it's fit for you to stay here for a bit, then you can rest assured you're in safe hands with me.'

Louise sat at the table. 'Can I have a drink? My mouth's bone dry.'

'Harper, see if there's some juice in the fridge, there's a good girl. Me bones ache. I can't keep getting up and down. Now, then, er . . .'

'It's Louise.'

'Louise, eh? Right, have a look through the cupboards, so you know where everything is. I've got tea and coffee.'

Harper opened the fridge. 'And juices, and, blimey, some sponge cake.'

Morris laughed. 'Yeah, I've got a sweet tooth.'

Louise gulped back the orange juice handed to her and wiped her mouth with the back of her hand. 'Thanks.'

'Are you sure you don't mind looking after her for me? She can't go back to social services.'

'Of course, it's fine. She'll be okay with me.'

Louise looked up at Harper and nodded. 'I'll be okay. You do what you need to, and thank you, Harper. Thank you so much.'

Her bottom lip quivered, and Harper knew that if she didn't leave right now, there would be a barrage of tears.

Chapter Nineteen

Harper was shattered by the time she arrived home. As she passed the living room, she heard deep pig-like snoring and knew right away that her mother hadn't gone home. Sighing to herself, Harper headed to bed, not totally surprised that Delores was still here because in reality Lexi had never had the strength to force their mother to do anything.

The soft mattress was like heaven as Harper lay down on her back and soaked up the comforting feeling. It was a stark difference to the thin hard mattress in her cell. She thought about Madeleine and decided not to mention anything about Calvin just yet. She would send her a letter with her new address and ask for a visiting order. Hopefully, she would have some better news to give her friend by then.

How could these teenage girls go missing right under the nose of everyone – parents and school staff? And, worse, through the system? She guessed that if the girls had no relatives, then who, in reality, would kick up a fuss? Her mind turned to Claude. She was puzzled by the fact that no one had mentioned a dead body. There were no televised street wars between the Russians and the Turks. So perhaps what she had conjured up in her head wasn't the way it worked in practice. One thing she had learned was that her son wasn't being watched by the Russians.

It was 10.30 a.m. The alarm went off, and Harper sat bolt upright. She wiped her sleepy eyes and stared at the clock. Suddenly remembering the probation officer was coming to the flat at midday, she knew she would have to get her mother out, or God knows what would fall out of her mouth. The woman simply said all the wrong things, and when she got that look, she would shrug and say 'Well, how was I supposed to know?' And then she would walk off, totally unaware of what she had said.

In her short nightshirt, courtesy of Rhea, Harper waltzed into the kitchen. Yosef was sitting on Delores's lap while Lexi was cooking a huge breakfast. Her sister didn't seem happy, and when she caught sight of Harper, she gave a defeated shrug.

'Morning, Harper. Cor, you look as rough as a badger's arse.' Delores laughed. 'You got home late. I waited up to make sure you were okay.'

'You were supposed to leave *last night*. What are you doing here?' demanded Harper, as Lexi placed a mug of coffee in her hands.

'Well, that's no way to treat your mother. I put you up when you were down on your luck, remember.'

'You have a home with Erin now.'

'I swear sometimes you're a right nasty cow.'

'Yeah, well, I learned it all from you. Anyway, you will have to shift your backside out of here as soon as you've had your breakfast.' She looked her mother over. 'And clean yourself up, for God's sake, because I have someone visiting.'

'Oh yeah? I knew it, Harper. You're selling your fanny! I bet he's an Arab prince or sommat.'

Harper leaned against the worktop and stared at the bacon sizzling in the pan. She didn't look at her mother. 'You know, Delores, you really do think very badly of me, don't you? You honestly think I would become a prossie like you were, don't you?'

Delores looked down at the table. Silently, she stared.

The lack of any form of response had Harper concerned. 'Hey, Mother, I was only kidding.'

Delores looked up, and her face creased in sadness; it was followed by an attempt at a half-smile.

'No, seriously, Mother, I didn't mean that. I was joking.' She felt gutted that she'd actually reduced her mother to silence. That was a first. Her mother never could keep her lips sealed. With a mouth on her, she could outdo the best town crier and have a comeback for any slur.

Even as the three of them ate their full English breakfast, Delores was exceptionally quiet, merely picking at her food. Harper knew then that what she'd said had really got to her mother.

'Listen, Mother, go with Lex to the shops. Get yourself a couple of rig-outs. And while you're there, have your hair done. And you too, Lex. It's on me. But you have to be out of here by quarter to twelve, and, no, Mother, it's not an Arab prince. It's the probation officer.'

Smiling from ear to ear, Lexi gave an excitable little clap. 'Are you sure?'

'Yeah, I'll grab some money.'

She turned to her mother. 'Look, Mother, I don't wanna be hard on you. I know you get on better with Erin, and there isn't a spare room here. I'm sorry.'

While Lexi took the baby off to get him changed, Delores really struggled as she tried to get to her feet.

'Are you okay, Mother?'

Delores nodded. 'Old age, that's all. Thanks for the treat.' Her words were flat and more of a whisper.

'If it's too much for you living with Erin, you can always come over and hang out with Lex and the baby. It's just—'

Delores waved her hand. 'Harper, I understand. I do. I'm not fucking stupid, and I don't blame you.'

Harper made herself another coffee and turned the radio on. 'Do you want another drink?'

Delores was on her feet and straightening her back. 'Oh, go on, then,' she said, as she sat down.

The newsreader, in a serious tone, started with *'A man has been found dead in the back of the boot of his car—'*

‘Two sugars and—’

‘Shush, Mother.’

They both listened to the newsreader.

‘The police believe it was a gang-related murder. They are holding members of the Boz family in custody. Simon Frayer is live in Catford. What can you tell us, Simon?’

‘Hi, so far, we know that the dismembered body of a man, believed to be Claude Bolshoi, was found at 8 a.m. today. It may be connected to the murder of Shabab Boz, the daughter of the businessman Mo Boz. Mo, Rifat Boz, and Mehmet Boz are being held in custody in connection with two other murders. The police are still looking for Hasad Boz and two cousins, who have yet to be named.’

‘Oh my God, they are talking about our Lexi’s fella.’

Lexi was already in the doorway, having heard the news. She glanced at Harper and then turned to her mother. ‘Blimey, lucky I got out of that family quick. How fucking scary.’

Delores nodded. ‘Well, at least you’re safe now, Lexi. So do you reckon they killed their sister?’ asked Delores.

Lexi shrugged her shoulders. ‘If she wasn’t gonna marry that bloke, then, in truth, they might have.’

Delores looked genuinely shocked. ‘So do you think she was having it away with this Russian man, Santa Claus or whatever?’

‘You mean Claude. That was the name mentioned. Anyway, Sis, you keep safe. Don’t you go back to the house. Just stay away. If you need anything, we will get it. Understood?’

Lexi agreed, and the order was settled by Delores’s firm nod.

Just as the newsreader was about to go to the weather, he broke in again. *‘There have been explosions in the area. Police are warning the public to stay clear of the high street in Catford. A chip shop and a kebab shop are on fire. The firefighters are at the scene now. Further explosions were reported from North*

London. Again, it was a chip shop and a kebab shop. We will bring you more news as we get it. Now for the weather.'

The room fell silent the second Harper turned the radio off.

'Well, it's all going on this week, what with ol' Richard Newbury and his brother found murdered.'

'*What?* They were found *dead*? How do you know?' asked Harper, knowing that the Russians would have disposed of the bodies.

'The Ol' Bill came and called in at Erin's. They asked Teddy if he knew anything.'

'And why would Teddy know anything? Surely, he ain't friends with them, not after everything?'

Delores chewed her bottom lip and peered down at the floor. 'His missus, Peggy, said she saw Teddy arrive at Richard's office with a holdall a day or so before the murders. So, naturally, they questioned Teddy. And I heard them say that Richard was charred to a crisp and his brother Larry had been tortured to death. Their bodies were dumped like garbage in their own offices.'

Harper felt the blood pumping in her temples. *Please, God, don't let Teddy be involved as well.*

'Anyway, apparently, they checked all of Richard's calls and found an address. The sly ol' fox had a bird tucked away over London Bridge way, in some posh pad, but, fuck me, when they went in, she was dead, an' all. You couldn't bleedin' make it up. Well, let's hope all this news of these killings dies down. Any more bacon sarnies going?' Delores asked, before popping a small piece of Yosef's crust into her mouth.

'Never mind sarnies, what happened? Why was Teddy there?'

'I dunno. Something about a loan. Apparently, he borrowed a lump from Richard and was returning it.'

'How much?' asked Harper.

Delores glared. 'Listen, my girl, Teddy is a wealthy man, and really stuff like that is his business. I don't like to—'

Harper shut her up by snatching the plate from her hand. 'Mother, how much?'

'Fifty grand. He showed the police his withdrawal from the bank, and he had alibis when the Newburys were murdered.'

Harper felt her heart pounding. She knew right then that Teddy loved her. So he had paid that evil fucker the bounty to keep her alive. She felt a lump lodge in her throat. It was hard, and as much as she told herself she was okay with Erin being with him, deep down, she was suppressing the pain.

***

It was 12.30 p.m. by the time Vanessa arrived, and when she did, Harper was shocked. The usually immaculately groomed woman, with not even a hair out of place, looked bedraggled. Her skin was sunken, her face was gaunt, and her eyes were troubled. Harper clocked the creased skirt, the dirt under the woman's nails, and her lank hair around her face.

'Come in, Vanessa. Can I get you a tea?'

Vanessa nodded, but her eyes were wide and yet lifeless.

Harper turned her back to make the tea while Vanessa sat at the kitchen table and clumsily removed files from her bag.

'There you go. Help yourself to sugar.' Harper pointed to the bowl and sat down at the table.

Vanessa smiled. 'Thank you. Er, I can't stop long. I just need to go over this form. So, is this a long-term lease? If so, what is the rent?' she asked, with her pen poised to the ready.

But Harper could see that not only was her hand trembling but her voice was quivering.

'Are you okay, Vanessa? Is it a little too hot for you?'

With a sudden storm in her eyes, Vanessa flushed. 'A little too hot? What do you know?' Her words flew out like bullets.

Harper smiled and leaned back on the chair, lifting her chin up. 'Actually, Vanessa, I was asking if your *tea* was too hot. I could add a dash of cold water.'

'Oh, I see. Er, yes, it's fine.'

Eager now to wind the woman up, Harper probed further. 'But what did you mean by "What do you know?" Hmm, you seem very flustered. What's going on, Vanessa?' Harper asked, dragging out each word as if she already knew the answer.

'Nothing! Nothing at all.'

'Really, Vanessa? Because I think differently. You don't look yourself. Something is on your mind. Is that it? Could it be your ol' man Peter? Is work getting a little too much? Bitten off more than he can chew, has he?'

'I don't know what you are talking about, Harper. Now, can we get back to filling out this form, or do I have to remind you that you are still on probation and breaking the rules of probation will see you back inside?'

Harper could see she had got beneath Vanessa's skin, just by the way her eyes flashed red.

'You didn't know, then, that Peter was here, in this kitchen, at this very table, spilling the beans. He is another one who gets flustered and finds it hard to hold down his temper,' said Harper, coolly, calling Vanessa's bluff.

She could see from the probation officer's reaction that she was beyond worried. Her eyes flicked from left to right, a string of sweat beads popped above her brow, and red blotches appeared on her neck. Harper looked at the woman's hand holding the pen. It was clearly shaking again.

'Come on, Vanessa, we are both victims in all of this. Don't pretend you don't know what I'm talking about. You, Peter, the Russians, the club . . . the girls.'

Suddenly, it was more than Vanessa could handle. She jumped up. 'Stop it, Harper. You are wrong, so wrong about me. This has nothing to do with me.'

Calmly, Harper remained seated and smiled. 'Sit down, Vanessa. It's all right. Bloody hell, don't get so irate.'

When Vanessa tried to move the chair to get away from the table, she almost tripped, her bag fell out of her hand, and the contents flew across the tiled floor. 'Oh, for God's sake.'

Harper instantly got to her knees to help the woman pack her bag. While Vanessa was collecting the glasses case and her wallet, Harper stealthily grabbed the phone and shoved it in her back pocket.

Oblivious to what Harper had just done, Vanessa sat down again at the table.

'Now, I think me and you need to have a chat, Vanessa. What did you mean when you said "You are wrong, so wrong about me" and "This has nothing to do with me"?'

'Look, Harper, I need to get this form filled out. And let me bloody remind you that you are on probation, so just stop it, and let's get on with it.' She paused before returning to the paperwork, ticking various boxes.

After a brief moment, she peered up at Harper. Her voice was notably different – deeper – with an air of smarminess. 'I can have you recalled at any moment for any reason I fucking choose, and you *will* go back to prison. Do I make myself clear?'

Harper grinned. 'Do I make myself clear?' she repeated, sarcastically. 'Ya know what, Vanessa, you should have been a schoolteacher, the way you just spoke, but, then again, I guess you and your hubby know a lot about schoolgirls, especially the ones with no families. Those poor girls who have no one to notice if they are even there or not – the vulnerable and the trusting.'

Now raging, Vanessa's breathing intensified and her face turned white as she jumped up again. 'Shut up, Harper. You can't prove a damn thing, and you will do as you are told or—'

'I can't prove that your husband is selling the unwanted kids to the Russians, you mean.'

'I can have you back inside, Harper—'

'No, you can't, or rather, no, you *won't.*'

Harper knew now she had the measure of her. Her intuition had been spot on from the moment Vanessa took her to the club having not been told where she worked. Both the probation officer and her husband were in on this human trafficking crime; she was sure now.

'No you won't because the Russians would fucking murder you.'

Suddenly, Vanessa fell back on her chair, exhaling a large lungful of air. 'What do you want, Harper? Because you can't prove anything. You have nothing on me.'

'I guess you love your job because you can literally control someone's freedom. Like you said, you could have me back inside. That power has given you an invisible brace around your neck that holds your head so high that you look down on people. I've seen you brush yourself down after sitting on my mother's sofa and looking around with disgust in your eyes at her worn-out furniture.'

The cockiness went up a level, and Vanessa stared directly into Harper's eyes. 'Like I said, Harper Kane, you have nothing on me.'

'Oh, believe me, darling, I didn't spend the best years of my life behind bars not to pick up a thing or two. Not that you would understand, but all you have inside is time to watch and study. And, believe me, I became the best people-watcher this side of the fucking river.'

With a vast, exaggerated grin, Harper stretched one arm under the table and pulled out a round contraption that looked like a bottle top. She showed it to Vanessa. 'Your old man came here dressed impeccably, but, oddly, he was carrying Yosef, a dribbling baby in his arms. I was surprised, considering he was with a woman who you would've thought would be cradling the baby. Then I realised. He was desperate to get into the house. But even then, I couldn't really fathom why. That was until he purposefully dropped his briefcase and literally got on his hands and knees under the table. I knew then he was up to something. And then I found it. A recording device. He had shoved it under my table.'

Vanessa's eyes widened.

'Now, Vanessa, I have to be honest. I don't know why he did that or who it was for. Himself, perhaps? Or was it for the Russians? But he is a complete bumbling fuckwit. A bit like yourself, Vanessa.'

With her arms snapped tightly across her chest, Vanessa morphed into a deviant child tapping her foot.

'Funny, 'cos when I went away all those years ago, these were gadgets you saw in a James Bond film, and now you can buy them for less than a score. Anyway, tell me, why did he bug my flat?'

Vanessa smiled. 'I have no idea, but I'll give it back to him, shall I?' she replied, holding out her hand.

Harper laughed at Vanessa's sudden cocky tone.

'Oh no, Vanessa, this one isn't his. It's mine. You see, it gave me an idea, and I thought I would tape our conversation . . .' She paused and raised her brow. 'Another cup of tea?'

Vanessa was totally deflated; her feathers had indeed been ruffled.

'What do you want from me?'

'First of all, I want you to understand something. The tables have turned, so don't ever talk down to me again. *You* are the fucking dregs of society, and eventually, love, shit finds its own level. Just so we are clear, if the police have the information that, believe me, I could easily hand over, then you will end up behind bars, as I was. Now, the fucked-up thing is, someone like you – who went to uni 'cos daddy had money and so you probably wanted for nothing – wouldn't last a minute. I'll tell you why: you had a career and money behind you and yet you got greedy and . . . well, let's face it, sugar tits, there's no excuse for what you've done. Unlike you, *real women* nurture. You probably think that you would be safe in prison. The guards will protect you.' She smiled. 'Oh, believe me, Vanessa, they won't. Many are mothers. Sorry to tell you' – she pointed at her – 'but you, darling, will be the punching bag and the main focus of torment. You won't find an ally, and you will never fit in. There will be no visit with your name on it. Who would want to associate with you? I bet even your daddy will turn his back on you in shame.' She paused and watched, enjoying the horror on Vanessa's face. 'Not only will you regret your crime or sin, as I'd call it, but the inmates won't let you forget either. Inside, they will rape you, beat you, and torture you – and fucking daily.'

Vanessa's face turned grey, and for a moment, Harper thought she would faint, but she watched the woman swallow hard and take in a few deep breaths. Surprisingly, Vanessa didn't dispute any of the accusations, so Harper wondered if she was visualising her time inside.

Harper smiled. She was going to milk the bitch for all she was worth before exposing her for what she was – pure evil masked by an innocent-looking face.

'So, what do you want from me, Harper?'

'All in good time, Vanessa, but, remember, you fuck up, and you'll be behind bars, or, worse, a charred corpse.'

Chapter Twenty

Harper sat with a smile on her face turning Peter's listening device over in her hand. She had sussed out what he had done the minute he'd left. Instantly, she'd removed the wires from inside the device. At least Vanessa had left the flat believing that there was a file somewhere with a recording and a few notes ready to be placed in the hands of the police if she didn't do as she was told, or, worse, if she went running to the Russians.

Harper also had the phone that she would have a good look through, to see if she could find anything that would link Vanessa to this trafficking ring. She was sure as hell that the police would love a piece of evidence like that. Either way, she could use it at some point.

It was four o'clock when Lexi and Delores returned, and even Harper was shocked when she saw their transformations.

'Blimey, Lex, you've cut your hair off.'

Lexi gave a twirl and her face beamed with joy. 'I thought because it suited you, Harps, so much, it would suit me too. It gives it more body, eh?'

Harper grinned. 'Lex, you look gorgeous, and yeah, it really suits you. It frames your face, and I love the make-up. Wow, what a stunner you are. You'd stop traffic, that's for sure.'

Delores didn't interrupt; she watched as Harper praised her sister. Harper was everything she wasn't, and she wondered if her eldest actually knew the truth. No one loved the girls more than Harper. She felt a lump in her throat when she saw how Harper pinched her sister's cheek.

'You look like you should – fucking beautiful, Sis. See, you don't need a fella, but any decent man would love to have you on their arm.'

Not used to compliments, Lexi diverted the attention to her mother. 'And what do you think about Mum, eh?'

Delores looked a little embarrassed as she gave a twirl.

'Blonde hair suits you, Mother. They did a right good job on you, an' all. The cut softens your face. And as for your outfit, I wouldn't mind a little number like that meself.'

Delores was near to tears. Had Harper forgiven her?

'Thanks, Harper, I really do appreciate it. It's the start of a new me.'

'Oh yeah? What's this new me all about, then?'

Delores looked at her eldest daughter and smiled. 'I'm packing the drink in, and the fags, and I'm gonna watch my mouth in future.'

'Jesus, you'll end up in a nuthouse, doing all that in one go. Maybe cut down the booze, a bit at a time, eh?'

For the first time ever, Harper saw Delores blush.

'Oh, 'ere, there's a letter for you. The council organised all my mail to go to the post office until it can get redirected to my new address. That is, whenever they get around to rehousing me, while they carry out the work on the old house. Although, I doubt they will put me back there. I'll probably get shoved into a one-bedroom flat. Until then, I'm gonna stay at Erin's, if I can put up with the cow.'

Harper stared at the letter. It had been sent from HMP Bronzefield. Quickly, she ripped open the envelope. It was a VO from Madeleine. *Bingo*, she could go and visit her tomorrow. Tonight, the club was shut, so Harper decided on having a well-deserved night in, with a takeaway pizza and a bottle of wine, and she would even allow her mother to stay over.

When the pizza delivery man arrived, Harper opened the door. As she handed him the money, she saw a black Range Rover with blacked out windows, its engine idling. The second she attempted to get a clearer view, the driver pulled away. Her heart began to pound her chest. *What the hell was going on?* When she closed the door, she bolted it from the inside and did the same to the French doors.

The TV was on, and, true to her word, Delores was holding a large glass of orange juice instead of enjoying a cold glass of wine.

Harper only sipped her drink slowly; she wasn't a drinker.

Lexi wasn't drinking much either because of the baby. Searching for a decent film to watch, the news flashed up, and Hasad's face was on the screen. The newsreader was standing in front of a burning building, spouting off how there had been a spate of fires all connected with the Boz family business. The reporter was saying that Hasad Boz was missing, although it was thought that he may be in Turkey.

'Find another channel,' said Delores. 'It's gonna piss on our chips, and we are all set for a lovely night in.'

Lexi continued searching for a film or a decent documentary when the doorbell rang again.

'Oh, for fuck's sake, tell them to go away,' said Delores, now comfortable that she would be staying the night.

'Open up. I fucking know you're in there, you bastard!'

Harper raised her brow. 'This family, I swear to God, is like a Picasso painting.'

Harper hurried to the door before her sister woke up the baby. Swinging the door wide open, she was taken aback. There was Erin with mascara running down her cheeks. The girl seemed beside herself.

'Where is he, Harper?' she screamed, pushing past to make her way through the flat. Harper followed as her sister aggressively yanked every door open, until, finally, she ended up in the kitchen. 'Open the back doors. I bet the fucking bastard has gone outside. I knew it. I damn well knew it.'

Suddenly, Harper experienced that dreaded feeling again. 'Where's Eddie?'

Erin shrugged as she yanked at the door handle in a temper to open the French doors.

'Where is the boy?' asked Harper again, while she unbolted the latch at the top, allowing Erin to go outside.

Delores leaned against the door frame in the kitchen holding Harper's phone. 'Harper, this was pinging.'

Harper felt a flood of anxiety consume her. Snatching the phone, she stared at the text.

If Erin comes to you, tell her I have gone away with Eddie. She is doing my nut in.

The relief was immense and compelled Harper to let out a giggle; but it was more through a release of tension than anything else.

Erin spun around, almost toppling over in her high heels. 'Where is he, Harper? I know he's with you.' She placed her hands on her hips and growled in anger. 'Playing fucking happy families, are ya? Well, are ya?' she screamed.

'No, Erin. Now, get the fuck out of my flat before your vicious tongue gives Yosef nightmares.'

'You liar, Harper! Where is he?'

Harper threw the phone at Erin. 'Read it yourself.'

Erin glared at the screen. 'And why is he texting *you*?' she demanded, as she threw the phone onto the table.

'Because, Erin, the last time Eddie went missing, I was out of my fucking mind with worry. I guess he knew you would come here accusing me again, and so then, I would wonder where my boy was.'

'*Your* boy? He ain't *your* boy. He's mine!'

Harper sighed. 'Okay, Erin, he's yours now. Would you please leave, or do I have to drag you by your fake hair out of here?'

Lexi pushed past Delores. 'Erin, you come here screaming the odds, but you took *her* fella in the first place. You're so selfish, it's unbelievable! And, by the way, I've not even had a call from you to see how me and Yosef were doing after the fire.'

Erin flicked her hair out of her face and straightened her Marc Jacobs bag that hung over her arm. 'Fuck the lot of ya. I knew the minute you got out of jail, everyone would be jumping through hoops for you, Harper.'

Harper frowned. 'Jumping through hoops? Seriously, Erin, why are you acting like this? You, with all your money?' She pointed at her clothes. 'You didn't even send me a T-shirt! Now, I owe you nothing.' She stepped closer. 'You have my bloke. You have my boy. What more do you want, Erin? Pray, do tell me,' she said, flinging her arms into the air.

Erin's shoulders appeared to slump as she looked down. 'Nothing. I have sod all, now.'

Slowly, as if defeated, she walked past her mother and sister.

Harper called out. 'Wait up, Erin, please. It doesn't have to be like this, ya know. Why don't you stay and join us? You're still me skin and blister. You can tell me all about Eddie, have a glass of wine.'

Erin looked back at Harper with a sneer, and behind clenched teeth, she hissed, 'See, you still have to be the one who everyone looks up to, with your knight-in-shining-armour words.' With a childish voice, she mimicked Harper. 'Why don't you stay and join us? You're still me skin and blister.' Then, she continued in a normal voice. 'You have to come across as the bigger person, the better sister, but you ain't, Harper. I mean, look at you with your stupid short hair and no make-up, like you think you are pretty enough without it. Now, that's what I call vain. So stick your invite up your jacksy. Nah, thanks.'

Harper could see in her sister's eyes that she was truly tormented. But before she could argue the toss, Erin had gone.

'Let the bitch go, Harper. She is obsessed with Teddy,' said Delores.

She stared silently at the front door, thinking about Erin. It was heart-wrenching that after all these years, Erin still hated her. They had been close at one time, so she had thought, but maybe that had been an illusion as far as she was concerned; it was more than likely the case that Erin had followed her around because she had wanted to be more grown-up at the time. Erin had always wanted to be *someone* – like a singer, a model, an actress, or a footballer's wife. She certainly looked like it, dressed in her pink jeans and pink studded leather jacket. She could have stepped out of *TOWIE*, with her pouty lips and tan.

'Yeah, I know she is obsessed with him, but, sadly, she is taking her failings out on me. I must respect that she has brought my boy up. And he goes to a good school, so although she has him, I have to be honest about it – she didn't have to be a mother to him, did she? As I see it, she's done a good job.'

Delores's lips bent into a frown. 'No, you would've done better . . .'

'Oh, come on, Mum, you can't say that.'

The term 'Mum' as opposed to 'Delores' or 'Mother' made Delores raise her brow. She'd never heard it come from Harper's mouth before; it almost brought a tear to her eye.

Guiding her daughter back into the living room, Delores waited for Harper to sit down before she eased herself into an armchair. 'I know you both think I favoured Erin, and you were both right. I did. The reason is 'cos she is so much like me. I used to laugh at her strops, her sneaky ways, and I probably encouraged it. Still, the one thing I do know is that you, Harper, are really the mother of the family. You did what any real mother would do for Charley. I didn't do it. Erin certainly wouldn't have done it either, but you, girl, you did. Look, fair dos, Erin takes care of Eddie's needs. I mean, he is fed and clothed and he has a nice room, but if Teddy wasn't there, he wouldn't be so well cared for. Let's put it that way.'

Harper wondered if her mother was sucking up to her so that she had a place to stay.

'Why did you leave Erin's, Mum?' asked Harper.

Delores huffed loudly. ''Cos the little bitch thinks I'm conspiring with Teddy to get her out of the house to move you in. But truth be told, I've had enough of the fucking hollering and hooting from that girl's vile mouth. I just can't put up with it anymore.'

'Christ, poor Erin. It sounds like she's having a breakdown,' said Harper, wiping her brow with the back of her hand.

'No, she ain't. She's just good at the theatricals. I should have put her in drama school.'

Lexi watched, listened, and marvelled at how much Harper was ready to forgive and forget. She knew she wouldn't have. 'Now you have this flat and a job, are you going to try and get Eddie back?'

Harper bit the glue around her false nail and ripped it clean off. 'No, Teddy was right. What can I really give him?' She listed the points one by one, using her fingers. 'I work in a seedy club, I'm a murderer—'

'You're a mother with a big heart,' interrupted Delores.

It was an early night for the three of them. Delores was more comfortable sleeping in Harper's huge bed so Harper slept on the sofa. It wasn't so bad. The couch was the size of a single bed anyway, and it was certainly more comfortable than the prison mattress.

***

Harper didn't bother to wake her mother or her sister. She heard Yosef grumbling and crept into the bedroom. Gently, she removed him from the cot and kissed his sweaty curls. 'Morning, little man. Let me make you a bottle of milk.'

Yosef naturally tucked his head under Harper's chin and curled into her. She shoehorned him into the high chair and opened the French doors to let in some cool morning air while she made him his bottle. As she watched her nephew tapping a wooden brick onto the tray, she smiled. At least he didn't look like Hasad. That was a blessing. Her finger hovered over the radio button. 'No,' she said, as she looked back at the baby. 'We don't want any nasty thoughts, not today.'

Lexi walked so lightly into the kitchen that she made Harper jump. 'I got a call about two o'clock in the morning from me old neighbour. I texted her yesterday, to see if she fancied lunch. Her baby and mine are the same age. She told me that she saw two men dressed all in black drag Hasad to a car and take him away.'

Harper studied her sister's face. She was glad that Lexi didn't seem bothered.

'He really hurt you, didn't he, Lex?'

Lexi nodded. 'Every day, I must have received a bruise off him. He was always angry, probably 'cos Mo belittled him, and I guess he took it out on me. The only good thing he ever gave me was Yosef.'

***

It was a pleasant journey to Bronzefield Prison. Terry, the cab driver, kept Harper amused all the way to Middlesex. He could talk for England, and he did. Harper could tell he had a soft spot for her sister and herself. He offered to wait for her. He said he would find a café and enjoy a greasy fry-up, place his bets, and read the paper.

The sounds of banging and clanging, as reverberating and bone-shaking as they were, brought Harper back to being inside. And seeing the screws again didn't help matters. Some she had liked and actually respected, but the vast majority she had hated. Now she was free, she knew they couldn't control her, but, somehow, being back here and seeing the uniform, the key chains, and the cold look in their eyes, Harper struggled to feel she was her own woman.

The second the officer bellowed out her name, she almost stood to attention. Then she noticed who it actually was: it was Katharine Swallows, the nasty bitch who had loved to bully her.

She walked through to the next part of the process, the search room. All her belongings had to be placed in a tray, and she had to remove her shoes.

'I thought you of all the inmates would be the last person to return,' gibed Katharine, as she looked archly at Harper.

'Katharine, I don't appreciate you discussing my business in public. You don't have that right. Not a woman in your position to a woman in mine.'

'Ha, I'll give you a year, and you'll be back inside.'

Harper stood unblinkingly as she glared into the woman's eyes. 'And *I'll* give you a year, and I can bet your miserable existence will still be the same.'

Katharine felt the urge to use her baton, but she bit her lip and moved Harper on.

The visiting room was no surprise. The only difference was that Harper could go up to the tuck shop and buy the goodies. She knew Madeleine had a craving for Snickers bars, so before her friend arrived, she bought three Snickers, two coffees, and several packets of cheese and onion crisps, Madeleine's favourite treats.

The smell of onions, cabbage, and sweat faintly permeated the room and reminded her again of being an inmate. It was the one thing that Harper had always detested. The only time she was free of it was in the shower.

Madeleine, and probably purposefully, was the last inmate to enter the visiting room. But she came rushing over and quickly took her seat, an orange plastic seat, which was bolted to the table and the floor. Sporting a black eye and a thick lip, she seemed unperturbed.

'Bloody hell, Maddie, who have you been rucking with?'

Madeleine waved her hands dismissively. 'Two screws and a baton. That's why I was late. I'm down the fucking block for a week. Never mind me, thanks for coming. I wasn't sure if you'd forget me. I'd like to think I can imagine what it's like getting your old life back when you're on the outside.'

'I don't break promises.'

'You look well, Harper, really well. How are things out there?' asked Madeleine, the tears in her eyes welling up.

Harper knew Madeleine would quickly blink those away. She had a reputation to uphold, and crying wasn't a good look in the nick.

'Maddie, I need information—'

Madeleine eagerly jumped in. 'To help find my girl, right?'

Harper looked around and leaned forward. 'No, on Calvin Stuart. I need to know everything you know – where he lives, any holiday homes, his family, the lot.'

'So you believe he killed my husband, then?' she asked, nodding her approval.

'Probably, but listen, Maddie. I could be wrong, but I do believe that bastard is wrapped up in some way, in a human trafficking ring.'

Madeleine drew in a startled breath, leaned back on her chair, and ran her hands through her hair.

Harper could visualise the information whirling around inside Madeleine's head.

Suddenly, Madeleine wrung her hands together in distress. 'Oh God, my girl! Has he got my kid?'

Harper put her finger to her lips. 'Maddie, keep it down, love, please. I don't know the answer to that, but I need everything you have.'

Madeleine nodded, dredging her memory for facts. 'He lives in Chelsea. Fairway Drive, number 15. I think he might have an extravagant holiday home in Brighton as well. It belonged to his late mother. Her name was Clarissa Stuart. I was gonna name our Kera after her. I liked the name.'

'Whereabouts in Brighton?'

Madeleine's face clouded over. 'Oh God, I wish I knew. It's more in the countryside, but I can't remember where exactly. One country lane looks much like another.'

'Okay, so what did she do for a living?'

Madeleine tapped her temple with her index finger, prodding her brain to remember. 'Oh fuck me, yeah, she was the manager of the Grand Brighton, the hotel there. I recall Nicolas joking about going there for a dirty weekend.' She stopped and stared into her coffee. 'It's hard, Harper. I really miss him *and* my Kera. I nearly tied the bed sheets together, ya know.'

Harper's eyes widened. 'No, no, no, listen. I'm trying to find the kids, your girl, all of them.'

Madeleine frowned. 'The kids?'

'Like I said, Calvin is into human trafficking. I'm sure of it. Now, what about the business? Tell me all you know.'

'So, ten years ago, Calvin and Nicolas went into business together. They built it from scratch, and within a year, they had an empire of shipping container depots. They shipped goods all over the world. The business hired, supplied, and stored containers. Since Nicolas was murdered, I have no idea what actually happened to the business. Calvin may have run it into the ground, for all I know.'

'Where is their depot?'

'Depot? They . . . I mean, Calvin, if he is still in business, had lots – Canterbury, Brighton, up north, Christ, everywhere.'

Suddenly, she flew her hands to her face. 'Oh my God, he isn't keeping the girls in those monstrous metal containers, is he?' The blood left her face.

'I don't know, Maddie, but I will do some digging.'

Madeleine couldn't hold back the tears. They tumbled one after the other until she was sobbing.

'Listen, please, Maddie, get a grip, love. I need your help.'

Madeleine wiped her red eyes and sniffed back the snot. 'Harper, a kid could never stand a trip across the sea in one of those things. They are like an oven in the summer and a fridge in the winter. Where would he be shipping them to?'

Harper sighed. 'I don't even know if he is. I just think he is mixed up in it somewhere along the line. Did your husband ever mention a man called Zavid?'

'*Zavid?*' Madeleine's eyes widened as if she had been caught in the headlights.

'Who is he?' asked Harper, convinced now that Madeleine knew him.

'He was doing some business with my husband and Calvin, but one evening, I heard Calvin and Nicolas arguing over the man. I met him a couple of times. We were out for dinner with him. I never liked the Russian twitching twat.'

'He is a very dangerous man, Maddie.'

Madeleine nodded and bit her lip. 'He is a bully. He's a rich Russian who went to university here. His father sent him. Apparently, his father is well known back in Russia. Probably a big shot. And Zavid lives off his father's name. Anyway, Nicolas was arguing with Calvin. He said he wanted rid of Zavid and that they would not be doing any business at all. Something about an Arab market, but that's all I heard.'

'Well, I think there's a right racket going on, and to be honest, Maddie, I have no idea who the fuck I can trust anymore. Either I'm going barmy, or everyone around me is in on it.'

Madeleine sighed heavily. 'Money can buy anything – information, arms, drugs, and girls, 'cos everything and everyone has a price.'

'Not me. I can't be bought.'

'People aren't always bought with money. Some things are more valuable.'

Harper nodded. 'Like my son, my sisters, my family.'

‘How do you think these human traffickers get the girls, women, or whoever, to do as they’re told, eh? Do they threaten to kill their families? Come on, Harper, you must know how it works.’

Harper didn’t feel comfortable admitting that Zavid had threatened to kill her son. For now, she wanted to walk away with the information she’d gained to track down the girls and find a way to destroy the trafficking ring. Because she could never live with it on her conscience.

Madeleine had memorised Harper’s new phone number by the time the bell rang for the visit to be over. She promised to call if she could remember anything else about Calvin or Zavid.

Harper, for her part, pledged to continue to look for Kera. However, just as she was about to leave, she recalled something and spun around. ‘Maddie, have you ever seen a wall with the mosaic of a seahorse?’

Madeleine’s mouth fell open. ‘Yes. At Calvin’s mother’s house.’

‘Time, ladies, please!’ screamed the officer, tapping Madeleine on the arm.

‘How do you know, Harper?’

‘I said, visiting time is over!’

‘Call me, Maddie, or send another VO.’

As Madeleine was being escorted away, she craned her neck to see Harper wave at her.

Chapter Twenty-One

As promised, Terry had parked in the same car park where he had dropped her off. However, as Harper approached, she suddenly froze. Terry's head was slumped forward, and with all the dark and worrying thoughts weighing heavily on her mind, Harper believed that the Russians had killed him.

But as she opened the driver's door, Terry looked up; his eyes were heavy, and a small line of dribble had contoured the crease in his cheek.

Harper put her hand to her chest. 'Oh, for fuck's sake, I thought . . .' Suddenly, she laughed. 'Oh, never mind.'

Terry rolled his eyes. 'Good Gawd, Harpsichord, you didn't think I'd popped me fucking clogs already, did ya?'

Harper laughed again. 'Something like that. I thought you had been shot in the head by the Russian mafia.'

Terry nearly choked, he was laughing so much. 'Cor, Harper, you do remind me of your Aunt Desiree.'

'Who?' asked Harper, as she shuffled into the front seat.

'Your Aunt Desiree! Oh shit, fuck me, did she die? Yeah, she might have, come to think of it,' said Terry, now drifting off to revisit some memory he had of her.

'Terry, I didn't know I had an Aunt Desiree. And, actually, I didn't even know you knew my family.'

Terry pulled away out of the car park. 'Well, I saw ol' Delores when I dropped Lexi off one time. I never spoke much to Lexi about your mum because she was never in the car long enough. Ya know, just to the shops and back. The conversation was usually about her fat fucking fella. I'd listen and let her get it all off her chest, ya see. Oh, and they reckon he has disappeared. You know, I bet he's fucking hiding, the coward. 'Ere, what do you reckon about this Shabab? Do you believe it was one of those honour killings?'

Harper could see that Terry had completely lost his train of thought, jumping from one topic to another. She grinned. She had a real soft spot for Terry and found his ramblings a breath of fresh air.

'Could be, Terry. Going back to me mum, you knew her back then, did you? What was she like in her younger days?'

Terry beamed. 'Ya know what, she was a stunner. I mean a really good-looking film star type of girl. She was always immaculate, with her high heels and a tight frock. I have to admit, she had the curves for it, an' all. She could've given Marilyn Monroe a run for her money. But she was so shy, ya know.'

'Shy?' Harper laughed.

'Oh yeah, she was the quiet one. I used to live over Peckham way. The Kanes lived around the corner. The old man died. I remember he was often drunk, and the old lady, well, I never saw her, if I'm honest. I don't know if she died when they were all kiddies.'

'All?'

'Yeah, your mum had a few brothers and sisters. Then Delores moved away. She was a teenager when she disappeared, so I was surprised to see her in the Cray. No disrespect, but I saw her when you were probably around five or six, and she'd changed a lot, by then. She swore like an ol' fishwife at a car that shot past and covered her in water. She was so different, then. Truth is, I hardly recognised her.'

Harper was quiet; she needed time to think. Her mother had always been reticent about her family. They were simply never mentioned. In fact, growing up, she had been led to believe that Delores was an only child whose parents were dead. She decided to leave it at that. She wasn't going to press him further about her mother. Besides, it wasn't any of her business.

After a few minutes of companionable silence, Harper turned to Terry. 'So you've never married, then, Terry?'

He stared ahead. 'Oh yeah, I did. I was married for thirty-five years. My little Lucy, Gawd rest her soul, died. Cancer. A few years back now.'

'Oh, sorry, Terry.'

'We never had kiddies of our own. She would've loved a big family. I guess I would've too. Anyway, it wasn't meant to be. So, we fostered a few, all colours, all creeds. Loved 'em all, we did. But she got sick, and that was that. So, now, I drive this cab just to have a bit of banter or a good hearty chat. My Lucy said I could rabbit for England.'

Harper was slowly falling in love with Terry. If she'd had a father, she would have wished to have one just like Terry.

Something inside was telling her she could trust him. Up until now, and considering what she had been through, she had found it hard to trust anyone.

'Terry, you are straight up, aren't you?'

Terry shot her a sideways glance and laughed. 'Babe, my little Lucy was sweet, she was caring, and she made a nice home from the money I gave her. She never asked questions, and I never said "no" to her. But I did a few things that I probably shouldn't be proud of, to give my Lucy a lovely home and to put proper classy clothes on her back.'

Harper felt her heart sink, but she had to know. 'What sort of things, Terry?'

Instantly, she could see from his side profile that his face took on a severe expression.

'Ah, well, it was a long time ago. You keep it to yourself though, my girl.'

Harper nodded. 'Of course.'

'I was a smuggler.'

Again, Harper felt her heart sink. 'A people smuggler?'

Terry screeched. '*What?* No, not a fucking people smuggler. Jesus wept, what the hell do you take me for! Blimey O'Reilly. No, only a few ecstasy pills over to Ibiza, back in the day.' He shook his head. 'People smuggling,' he mumbled. 'Those bastards who have sex slaves and do sicko stuff ought to be behind bars. Not the women who pinch a fucking two-quid sandwich to feed their kiddies 'cos their ol' man's spunked the dole money on booze. Or the geezers who end up inside 'cos they knocked ten bells of shit out of a paedo.'

With so much passion behind those words, it was safe for Harper to recognise that Terry could be trusted.

'Terry, I may need your help, but you have to promise me that you will not breathe a word. I know you like to chat, but this cannot be repeated to anyone.'

Terry pulled over and turned to face Harper. With his hands now in his lap and his deadpan expression, he nodded.

Harper relaxed her shoulders. 'I need to find some girls who have been taken, trafficked, smuggled, or whatever you call it.'

Terry just looked at her and nodded, showing he was listening.

'I'm in a right fucking state.' She took a deep breath. 'Okay, I took a job and ended up getting drugged and then beaten up. This Russian lot threatened me, saying that my boy would be killed if I didn't do as they said. They're a really dangerous, violent firm, who told me I must continue managing the club and make sure that when they bring a kid in, basically, I don't throw them out for being underage. It's so mental, I don't understand it. They bring these teenage girls into the club, pretending they have a job, and they have to serve drinks and . . .' She stopped when Terry held up his hand.

'Okay, Harper. As I said, I smuggled ecstasy. But I was also a bit of a fucker. Pavement jobs, robberies, a little bit of violence here and there.' He patted his beer belly. 'I was fit in me younger days, but I know how shit like this works.'

Terry opened the car window to get a breeze through. Then he continued. 'Dirty fucking bastards they are. So, what they do is they get the kid in the bar, in the pretence of a job or a modelling contract or whatever. O' course, the kiddie will just act naturally like any kid would because they aren't kidnapped or in a state of shock. The buyers want to see how innocent the kids really are. They do it by putting the girls into an awkward or compromising position to see their reactions. Now, if the girl reacts to the touchy-feely guy with a pinch of salt, laughs it off, or, worse, flirts for more attention or even gives him a backhander, they're no good and may end up not being sold, so it's a kind of test.'

He looked away and took a deep breath. 'The police told us all about it, ya see. We had to know what these kids had been through, because we were about to foster two of them. Two young orphan girls, Shola and Misty . . .' When he paused and swallowed, Harper could see it was hurting him.

'They were brought to us, late one night. Oh Jesus.' He looked up as if to God. 'They were in a right two and eight.' Tears welled up in his eyes. 'Little Misty, she couldn't speak. She went mute for a year. She had indents around her ankles where she'd had metal cuffs soldered on. Now, she's a grown woman. But, still, she works alone in the pharmacy department at the basement of King's College Hospital, away from the public. She hates men, except me, and it took her a good year before she would even smile my way, love her heart.'

Keeping one eye open for any police car because he had parked in an illegal spot, and another on Harper, who he could see was engrossed in his story, he carried on. 'And then there was Shola. She was from Africa. Beautiful, she was. Her flawless black skin was so smooth. But there wasn't much that was. She had burn scars all across her back, and her eyes were huge, but she was broken. We loved her and tried so hard to help her. Every night she'd scream in terror, and my Lucy would run to her side and cuddle her back to sleep.'

He paused, bit his lip, and blinked away his watery eyes. 'Shy Shola, that's what I called her. She was under the psychiatrist for three years, but after one of her sessions, she took her own life.

My Lucy never really got over it, but I knew that kid was so damaged, no amount of therapy or love could heal her mind. You see, Harper, her horrific memories of her past defined who she was, and she wanted to die. Maybe she's free now from constant torment.'

Harper hadn't realised until now that the whole time Terry was telling his story, tears were cascading down her cheeks. 'Oh my God, Terry, that's so awful. I'm so sorry. I don't know what else to say.'

He looked back and wiped her tears away. 'You tell me everything, Harpsichord, and I will give you my word that I will help you. Driving the cab is getting a bit boring, anyway.'

'They have this hold over me because they showed me footage of my son. They said they will kill him.'

'Where is he now?'

'Teddy, his father, has taken him somewhere, but I don't even know where to.'

'Good, and I fucking bet the Russian mob don't know either.'

'You may have a point because the issue with the Boz family has obviously become serious since it's all over the news. They may be distracted.'

'Oh, I see.' He stared, letting the subtext settle into his brain. So Harper had something to do with the Turks and the feud with the Russians, or even possibly the death of Claude Bolshoi, the Russian found in the boot of his own car. 'Yeah, they will have pooled all their resources, I mean men, to take out the Boz family. Ya see, I know the Russians. They are ruthless bastards. If they thought for a minute that a member of this Boz family had interfered with their cartel, they would take them down. Firebombing is a trademark of theirs.'

'You seem to know a lot about this, Terry.'

'I'm older, wiser, and a nosey bastard. So, girl, I might chat a lot, but I still have my fucking eyes and ears open. I still go for a catch-up with me ol' pals, the naughty ones. Us old bastards sup on a pint and remember when crime did pay and chat over the new wannabe gangsters or the up-and-coming handfuls. My mates like a gossip and the Russian feud with the Turks is on everyone's lips. All the other firms are looking to muscle in, now that this Boz family have been taken out of the picture. So, word has it that with all the businesses literally going up in smoke, this dead Russian and Mo's dead daughter, it's down to one of two things. Either Claude was having it away with Mo's daughter, and so the Boz family's men decided to carry out some ritual killing, or someone from that Turkish family has double-crossed the Russians.'

Harper was intrigued by Terry's summing up.

'Now then, I don't need to know what you've done.' He winked. 'But tell me what you know and leave nothing out, from the club to the Russians to the Boz family. I have a few favours to call in.'

Harper frowned. 'Oh no, don't get anyone else involved. My boy's life could be at risk.'

Terry raised his brow. 'Let me tell you something, my girl. If me and a handful of me pals can take out a whole fucking sex slave campsite, in one night, run by twenty-five or more Lithuanians, love, believe me, I have experience in fucking up the bad guys.'

Harper had to laugh. 'Seriously, Terry, I thought you said . . . Well, you started off by smuggling a bit of ecstasy, then moved on to a few robberies, and now you're telling me you took out twenty-five Lithuanians?' She tilted her head on the side. 'Terry, please, I trusted you with what I know and my predicament, and now, you're taking the piss.'

Terry grinned. 'Babe, let me tell ya. In fact, Harper, let me show you.' He shut the window, checked his rear-view mirror, and pulled away. 'I wouldn't joke about serious heavy shit, babe, believe you me.' His voice softened. 'My story is complex, but I wouldn't lie about stuff like that. Ya see, after my Lucy died, I was left feeling so fucking helpless. Misty was getting on with her life as best she could, and me, well, I kinda wanted to fight the world and its muvver, as you can imagine. So, I cabbed, I listened, and I did my own digging. Eventually, I tracked down a sex trafficking ring. Well, sex slaves. The girls were women, not kiddies. Still, nonetheless, it made no difference, and I knew that the bastards wouldn't spend time in prison where our lads could beat the life out of them. They would just get deported. So, me and a few mates made sure they couldn't enslave another human being . . .' He paused. ''Ere, Harpsichord, you ain't taping this, are ya?'

She laughed; it was more with relief than anything.

All the way back to Kent, Harper told Terry everything she knew from the day she left prison.

Terry didn't interrupt other than nod or say 'yeah', letting her know he was still listening.

***

Terry drove Harper to his home in Farnborough Park.

'Fuck me, Terry. Is this where you live?'

'Yeah, posh, ain't it.'

Harper marvelled at the size of the house and the beautiful front lawn with bright-red roses climbing over the Tudor beams on the exterior of the house.

'Teddy and I always said that when we grow up, we would live in Farnborough or Keston Park. Only because it was gated and made a kind of statement that you have money.'

'Come inside. I wanna show you some newspaper clippings and photos, and I can ping us a couple of microwave dinners, if you fancy one.'

She nudged him before unbuckling her seat belt. 'Are you chatting me up, Terry?'

Terry laughed, his face red. 'Leave off, Harpsichord. I wouldn't know what to do with a young woman now, and besides, I'm old enough to be your farver.'

***

Inside, the large home was immaculate, with not an ornament out of place. It was surprisingly modern and minimalist, particularly in the spacious lounge, where there was a sleek box-shaped sofa and armchairs, glass tables, and mirrored cabinets. An oversized chandelier hung from the lounge ceiling, and the bifold doors at the rear of the house opened up to a long lawned garden with a pergola and two love seats at the far end. To the right, there was a raised koi carp pond, and on the side of a four-foot wall there were mosaic seahorses.

Harper felt a knot in her throat. *Oh, dear God, please don't let Terry be involved.* She stared at the seahorses as the blood drained from her face. Slowly, she turned to see the beaming face on Terry.

'Tea, coffee, love, or a cheeky gin and tonic?'

Harper wanted to shake her head. *Surely, Terry wasn't involved? Besides, it was a pond, so why not have seahorses as decoration.*

'Lovely pond out there.' She pointed in the direction of the garden.

He looked at her sadly then, and when he next spoke, she could hear the pain in his voice. 'Our Shola, she wanted those seahorses. She drew the design herself. Ya see, after she was rescued, she lost a huge part of her memory. The shock and constant sedation had fucked up her mind. But perhaps she thought the seahorses represented something. Who knows, Gawd rest her soul.' Terry suddenly grabbed Harper's elbow. 'You look very white. Take a seat, babe.'

Harper sat in the pale-blue leather armchair. 'Terry, I hate to ask. I know it must be painful, but did Shola ever mention The Grand Brighton Hotel or The Click, a club in Bromley?'

Terry took a seat opposite, his eyes wide. 'Yeah, well, not the club, but definitely a hotel. Well, she said she remembered folding white sheets and making beds in a big posh hotel before being drugged. That was all she recalled. Why? What do you know?'

‘A seahorse mural. It’s in a house now owned by a man called Calvin Stuart. His mother Clarissa managed The Grand in Brighton, and her mansion in Brighton had a wall with a huge seahorse mural. I saw it myself.’

Terry stared at her. ‘Dear Gawd, so do you think this woman, this Clarissa, was taking in the young maids, and then selling them?’

Harper threw her hands into the air. ‘Fuck knows. But she’s dead now, and this Calvin bloke is up to something. But, listen, I need to get home and get changed, ready for work. I can’t not go, or they will think something is up, or, worse, hurt my son.’

Terry shook his head. ‘If Teddy has your son somewhere, tell him to keep your boy there, and I’ll drive Lexi and Yosef to him, to keep them together, and well out of sight, because those fucking Russians are brutal. It’s their culture. After the Cold War and after the Wall came down, they had to learn fast to make a buck, what with their Army and Navy not paying their troops. They had to earn a living, so, as you can imagine, they became your worst kind of gangster. You need to get away as well, Harper. They won’t consider that you’re a woman, believe me. They care about nothing except money. They weed out the weak, so they are only left with the fierce and callous. There is no room for weakness in their firms.’

‘Oh, Terry, I wish to God I could, but I’m in over my head, now. I’m gonna have to carry on as normal and ride out the next couple of days until I can work out a plan.’

‘Okay, but you need a backup plan. Always have a plan B, ’cos no human is predictable.’

Harper chewed her lip. ‘Would you take me home, Terry, please?’

‘Yeah, sure, kitten. I won’t bother you with me trophy photos. Next time, we can go through them, but I can tell that you trust me.’

Harper kissed his ruddy cheek. ‘Yeah, Terry, you are one of a select few, I can tell you that.’

***

The clip-clop of the high-heeled shoes didn't give Kera or the others any reason to get excited; in fact, it filled them with dread. The door opened and in she walked, with a huge beaming grin. 'So today, is the day you get taken to your new homes. First, you must change. We want you looking presentable.' She clicked her fingers, and like two lap dogs, the guards came into the room laden with bags. 'It is imperative that you look clean and tidy and don't make a fuss.' Her voice was firm and spiteful. 'Believe me, if you fight or give my clients any trouble, I will have you dragged back here and whipped to within an inch of your life.' She suddenly smiled sweetly. 'I hope we understand each other, girls.'

Without another word, she spun on her heel and left the room.

The guards placed a bag at the foot of each mattress before they departed. Kera was the first to tip the bag upside down. She stared for a moment at the dress, which was her size, but with a lace collar and with pleats, it looked like a primary school uniform. *Sick bastards*, she said to herself, before reluctantly removing her nightdress and sliding the dress over her head.

'Will they ever let us go, Kera?' asked Lauren, her eyes filled with fear.

'Yeah, 'course they will, one day, Lauren, one day.' She tried to sound upbeat, but who was she really kidding? Their lives were now carved in stone. They would be shipped off to some extremely rich paedophile and end up being disposed of, once they were too old to keep the buyer happy.

Chapter Twenty-Two

It was 6.30 p.m., by the time Harper slipped into the flat. The tantalising smell of shepherd's pie wafted along the hallway, and her stomach rumbled. Harper wondered if she was too late for a helping. She was pleased to find Delores had washed up the breakfast dishes and tidied the bedclothes away in the lounge. And Harper noticed how her mother seemed different; her face was dewier, her eyes wider, and she was smiling as well. *That was it*, thought Harper. *Delores was actually smiling.* Harper was well aware that her mother tended to wear a grimace most of the time, unless, of course, she was grinning sarcastically.

'How's your friend, Harper? Okay, is she?'

Even the questions seemed genuine.

'Not really. She's an innocent woman stuck behind bars, and her little girl has gone missing.' She took a deep breath. 'Anyway, have you had a good day?'

'Me?' Delores asked, seemingly surprised. 'Actually, Harper, I did. I went to the shops and bought some bits for dinner. It's in the oven.'

'Shepherd's pie?'

Delores nodded. 'Your favourite, ain't it?'

Harper smiled. 'Yeah, you could always turn out a really decent shepherd's pie. Shame it was only on special occasions. Still, better than a poke in the eye,' she replied, softly.

'I'm trying, Harper, I'm trying, girl.'

'I know you are, Mum. I know you are.' She held up a cup. 'Fancy a tea? I'm parched meself.'

‘’Ere, you take the weight off your feet, Harper, and *I’ll* make you one.’

Harper gratefully pulled out one of the kitchen chairs and sat down, while Delores, who appeared less slovenly than usual, pottered about making the tea.

‘None of my business, Mum, but can I ask, did you fall out with your family?’

Harper could see Delores freeze in mid-stride. ‘Sorry, never mind. I shouldn’t have asked.’

‘What do you know, Harper?’

‘You know what, Mum? We all have our reasons for saying nothing. Please, just forget I asked.’

She could see her mother’s shoulders physically relax.

‘Where’s Lexi?’

‘Oh yeah, so the police came and took her to the station. She’s not arrested, before you have a meltdown. They just want to talk to her about the Boz family, and, actually, Harper, they asked for you as well, but I said you weren’t in.’

‘And Yosef?’

‘They said she could take him too.’

A deep frown screwed up Harper’s forehead. ‘*What?* I’ve never heard of that before.’

‘They promised me faithfully that she wasn’t in trouble, and everything was fine.’

Harper found it very odd that Lexi was allowed to take Yosef with her. Still, she shrugged it off and sipped her tea. The aroma and the sound of bubbling gravy made Harper’s mouth water. ‘Smells so good, Mum. Any chance I could have some now? Only’ – she looked up at the clock and saw that it was 7 p.m. – ‘I don’t wanna be late for work. I’ve got a cab coming for me at half seven.’

Delores grabbed the oven gloves and carefully lifted the steaming pie from the oven. The cheese potato top was a golden-brown crust with the gravy oozing from the sides, just how she and her daughters liked it.

Harper followed it with her eyes as Delores placed it on a heat mat in the centre of the table.

***

After eating almost too much, Harper struggled to do up the top button on her jeans, and she grinned to herself. That was a first. She'd never eaten anything to excess in prison. The food was jank.

Terry drove into the space directly outside her flat, just as Harper opened her front door. *Great timing*, she thought. The downside was it didn't give her time for a quick fag. But she could have one before she started her shift, unless the eager-beaver bouncers wanted to get inside, ready for opening. Her head was now buzzing with unfinished tasks. She still had a few issues to take care of including getting shot of those bloodstained bed sheets that were still in black bags under the bed. She hoped Nico wouldn't be there. She prayed that he was off firebombing more of the Boz empire. She shuddered at the thought of him, the muscled monster.

'Cooler tonight, eh, Harpsichord.'

Harper smiled, a sudden feeling of nerves making her body tingle. *Was it anticipation or fear?* God knows what the evening would bring, but if another kid came to the club, she knew she would have to rescue her. Poor old Mr Baker could well end up with a houseful. Hearing that Louise was enjoying her stay, filling her face with home-made popcorn and glued to the TV watching copious amounts of old black-and-white movies, put a smile on her face.

'Terry, listen, if anything happens to me, make sure the police know that my probation officer and her husband Peter, the social worker, are in on it, will you. He's using his position to source the vulnerable girls to traffickers. He knows the ones who have no parents or relatives to push for answers when they go missing.'

'Cor, Harper, I'd love to get me hands around the bastard's throat. And, believe me, I would kill him. 'Cos, forget the Russians. This bloke was obviously placed in one of the most trusted positions, looking after the welfare of the young 'uns. Do you know what it says above the Old Bailey?'

Harper shook her head. 'Nah, I haven't got a clue.'

'Well, it says *defend the children of the poor and punish the wrongdoer.'*

'And that's our court's purpose, is it?'

'Yeah,' replied Terry. 'It comes from the Bible. Anyway, those kiddies are poor. Not financially, but orphaned. And that bastard has carried out the worst crime in my eyes, abusing his position of being trusted in that way.'

'Terry, please don't go all vigilante on me.'

'No, no, well, let's see, shall we. I mean, I wouldn't like to bury a geezer alive if he was an innocent in all this.'

Harper gave him a sideways glance and laughed. 'He is no more innocent than I am a nun.'

The outside light that usually lit up the front of the club was off. The side alley that led to the back entrance was also in darkness. She looked at Terry, her temples throbbing with anxiety. As if she had a bad feeling about what was about to happen, she suddenly took out her phone and dialled Teddy's number.

He answered instantly. 'Harps, are you okay?'

'Listen, don't come home. Keep Eddie safe. Where are you now?'

Teddy sensed the panic in her voice. 'I'm in Wales, Pembrokeshire. I've hired a cottage. Me and Eddie can go fishing.'

‘Teddy, can you see your surroundings? Is anyone watching you or Eddie?’

‘I shouldn’t fucking think so. I am literally in the middle of a valley, in the back end of nowhere. You’re lucky that I’ve even got reception. Why, Harper?’

‘Ted, I ain’t got time, but please just keep my baby safe until you hear from me again. And if you don’t, just remember, he was always loved by me.’

‘Harper, what’s going on, babe? Tell me, please.’

‘Trust me, Teddy, you don’t need to know. Just keep him safe, and if you have a gun, keep it on you.’

‘Okay. Listen, Harps, I love ya. I always—’

‘I gotta go.’ She hung up and looked at Terry. ‘Go and take me mum and sister away. Lexi’s at the police station. I guess you were a getaway driver at some point.’

He laughed. ‘How did you guess!’

‘Then, take my family, Terry, and keep ’em safe.’

Terry stared directly into Harper’s eyes. ‘And you, Harpsichord? What about you?’

‘I’ll be okay. I will blow this ring out of the water. You watch me. The second they bring another kid in, I’ll . . .’

‘Do you really know what you’re doing and who you’re up against?’

‘Yeah, I do, Terry, but I can’t sit back and ignore it all. Please help me sister and me mum.’

Terry leaned forward and hugged Harper. It was a real father’s embrace, except he wasn’t her father. But he was still a kind old man with a big heart.

She waved and watched as he drove away. Then she listened. All she could hear was water dripping from somewhere. She knew in her heart that something was not right. But if she called Terry back to take her home, someone would follow, and that would mean she could quite easily be leading them back to her sister and her mum.

Slowly, she walked towards the back door, and was spooked just by the clip-clop of her own shoes. A buzzing seedy club was noisy, yet minutes before it was due to open, it seemed like a derelict building. Why weren't the lights on? Not even the sensor light pinged into action. A cold shiver ran up her spine as she turned the key in the lock. Sliding her other hand into her bag, she fingered the knife. The knife that Lexi had given her. Her heartbeat was so fast, she felt it in her throat. Licking her dry lips in nervous anticipation, she slowly pushed the door open. Had Nico returned with orders from Pixie or Zavid to kill her? What did they know? With so many thoughts racing through her mind, she had to pause and take stock of her options. Her bunch of keys jangled because she shook so much. It was like the day she had walked into the prison kitchen when she knew she would have to fight the most prominent and ugliest inmate with the most violent reputation. That had been a nasty fight, but she'd managed to win it, albeit with the last punch, using her broken hand.

Taking a deep breath, as her heart hammered away inside her chest, she stepped inside. A whiff of something old and damp penetrated her nostrils. It was an old building, and only the living kept the decaying smell away. Then she detected the faint waft of Issey Miyake. She knew the scent. It was one that Teddy had bought for her before she went to prison. *Who would wear that?* she wondered.

As she switched on the light, it pinged and buzzed until the fluorescent tube got its act together and lit up the back room.

A sudden gasp left her mouth. The place had been robbed. The contents of the fridge were strewn all over the floor, the cupboard doors were open, and as she headed to the bar, she saw the cash register was also open. No, they hadn't been burgled, but the place looked as though someone had ransacked it. Dropping her bag onto the counter, she hurried to the office, and when she saw the cabinet pushed to the side, she guessed someone had been to the cottage next door. Fear clawed at her throat when she remembered she hadn't removed the stained sheets, which had been bagged up, from under the bed. As she stood in horror, the sound of hands clapping behind her startled her into spinning around.

There, flapping his gloved hands together like a twitching seal, stood Zavid himself.

'You are a very clever woman. I can understand why Vadim likes you so much.' His tone instantly shot up an octave. 'Now, Harper Kane, where is the girl?'

She could see past Zavid. Three men were standing there, forming a semicircle guard around him. Their hands were folded in front of them as if they were a president's minders. Her nerves made her want to laugh at the absurdity of it all. Christ, she was just an ex-jailbird with not a real pot to piss in, and yet here was Zavid and his minders, all with their attention focused on her.

A sudden sick feeling entrenched her. She had left her bag containing the knife on the counter and Pixie's gun was hidden beneath it. So she had nothing. No weapon at all. And then it dawned on her. She was stupid. As if she could take on this sophisticated gang.

Zavid stepped closer. 'I *said*, where is the girl?'

Harper shrugged. 'I have no idea what you mean.'

'You do. The girl called Louise. Where is she?'

Again, Harper shrugged her shoulders. 'She got freaked out and scarpered, I guess.'

Zavid grinned maliciously. 'You are, how should I say . . . fearless, brave, or, perhaps, even stupid.'

The smell of the perfume tingled the inside of her nose, and struck by fear, she let out a nervous giggle. 'Is that *perfume* you are wearing, Zavid?'

He twitched twice, and his lips pursed in frustration. She tried to picture him not as a very violent, dangerous man, but as a child with an impediment.

'Look, I'm sorry about your sister. Is she okay now?'

Zavid's little-boy-lost look was instantly replaced by a dark, evil expression, just like a dog before it is about to tear your face off.

Her scalp prickled as dread gnawed at her insides.

'Take her!' he bellowed, as he stepped away, as if he'd opened the gates to the lions.

She didn't have time to scarper. The three men grabbed her and handcuffed her wrists behind her back. One even punched her hard at the side of her head to force her into submission.

Silently, she allowed them to push her into the back of a car. There was no point in fighting; she'd never win. Terry's words circled her mind. *Always have a plan B, 'cos no human is predictable.* He wasn't wrong. She hadn't expected Zavid himself to be there. She assumed that they would carry on with the business and bring in another girl. This would give her the chance to do more digging and to enable her to make sure her family were all safe before she could expose this sick and twisted sex trafficking ring. The lack of lights should have forewarned her. And her gut instinct should have been more than enough. However, she hadn't expected the place to look as though it had been robbed; it had caused her to drop her guard.

The car was black, but she had no idea which make or model. Two men got in the front. Sitting next to her in the back was a most odd-looking character; he reminded her of Shrek in the Disney movie.

She saw Zavid climb into the driver's seat of a silver vehicle. Next to him was a woman, but she couldn't see her face.

As they drove away, Harper stared out of the window, and a feeling of sudden panic hit her. She wasn't drugged or blindfolded; she could see where she was being driven. Impending doom thrashed around in her head. She was going to die, to be murdered. It meant she would not be able to tell her mother that she had forgiven her; that after all she had done and had been, her mother was still loved by her. And Lexi, where would Lexi go now? Naturally, the flat would be taken back, and she would be stuck in some high-rise shithole with piss-smelling lifts and druggies for neighbours. Little Eddie popped into her mind – his sweet clean face with his huge innocent eyes. She only wanted a hug, just to smell his hair and feel his soft skin. She shrank back into the seat, helpless and afraid. Gone was the hard girl Harper; now, she was weak with fear.

A feeling of uncertainty poked her in the chest. 'Hey, guys, you haven't covered my eyes. I will know where you are taking me.' She prayed they would suddenly stop the car and see to it.

However, the big Russian, Shrek, with the garlic-smelling breath, who sat with his arms folded over his fifty-inch chest, laughed and threw her an excited look. 'You do not need to have your eyes covered. It doesn't matter if you see where you are going because you are not coming back.'

It was as Harper thought. 'Fair enough, Shrek. That means I don't have to tell you where the girl is.'

He laughed again. 'Oh, you will tell us. Most men twice your size, and – as you English say – tough as old shoes—'

'It's boots, actually. Tough as old boots. But never mind. I've got the gist of it.'

He stared at her, smiling. 'I think it's a waste. Maybe I could find some use for you.' His thick Russian accent was nasal due to his large bulbous nose.

She didn't even bother to respond. Whatever was about to happen to her now had already been decided. Come what may, she was going to be murdered.

Shrek stared again, and this time, he unfolded his arms and slid one across her, feeling her breast.

She knew she was going to die, but the thought of him touching her uninvited made her lose her cool. Even though she was handcuffed, Zavid's men hadn't fastened her seatbelt. Instantly, she sprang up and headbutted him clean across his monstrosity of a nose. It hurt her, and it must have hurt him too, but instead of backing off, he brutally punched her in the guts. The pain shot up to her ribcage, blurred her vision, and sucked the air out of her lungs. She instantly keeled over in agony, coughing and spluttering.

'I will take the front row seat when they burn you alive,' he said, feeling the swelling across the bridge of his nose.

When the younger guard turned around and said something to Shrek in Russian, Harper assumed he was the boss. Then she recognised him. He was the man who drove her to her mother's. There was something soft about him, although Shrek seemed to feel threatened by whatever it was he'd said.

All the way to their final destination, Harper was numb. The throbbing pain in her stomach had been replaced with a knot of primal fear. She breathed through flared nostrils as she watched the miles of fields go by. She assumed they were on their way to Brighton, the place with the seahorse on the wall and where the man had been burned alive in the carport. *Is that where they* take *their disobedient staff, their double-crossers, and their enemies to be mercilessly murdered?* she wondered. Yes, of course, they do, because, unlike her, the Russians probably had a plan A, B, and C, and they had carried out their torturous murders with experience. They were confident in the knowledge that they would get away with it, and she knew by Richard's and Larry's murders that they had. It was the one and only time she wished she was back in prison – even on that hard mattress looking up at the ceiling and dreaming of being at home. At least she had dreams, then; all she had now was dread.

The driveway to the house was long and winding. She hadn't seen the surroundings properly before because she had been drugged on her previous visit. Outside was lit up, but it wasn't as she remembered it, with guards everywhere. Then it dawned on her. She would still have been groggy from the drugs, which would have meant that her mind was wildly being let loose to explore dark thoughts.

They had arrived. There were two cars and a black van. Zavid stepped out of a silver Maserati. He wasn't alone. In the passenger seat was a woman. Harper strained to see who it was, and then her heart sank; it was Frenchy. The other car was a

Porsche. Harper tried to devise a plan, but terror eclipsed her thoughts.

Shrek dragged her from the car and held her up because her legs were giving way. She'd never experienced a feeling where all her limbs felt as though they were filled with lead. *Get a grip, Harper.*

The sound of her footsteps echoed as she slowly walked through the house. It was odd. This house seemed empty; there was nothing in it to absorb noise. She wondered if perhaps they had planned to move out.

Zavid didn't turn around to look at her. He marched on ahead, with his head jerking like a chicken. Harper guessed then that Frenchy had remained in the car.

A door to the right opened, and there inside, on the wall, was the mosaic of a seahorse. Other than a gilt-edged chair in the middle of the rather grand room, there was nothing else. Harper assumed she was supposed to sit there. So instead of waiting to be invited, she shook herself free of Shrek, sat down, and faced Zavid.

Zavid waved his hand, and Shrek left the room, closing the door behind him. Harper watched as Zavid paced the floor, looking at his watch. He stopped abruptly, and with his leather-clad hands, he pointed. 'Now, you will tell me where the girl is.'

Harper shook her head in defiance.

He paced the floor again, his face tight with frustration. It was only when he heard voices outside that he stopped wearing out the floor.

The door opened, and, to Harper's utter surprise, in glided an exquisite woman. She was probably in her sixties. It was apparent that she'd had surgery because although her facial skin was tight, her neck had a few wrinkles. She was fresh out of the hairdresser's chair, with her hair stiff with hairspray and not a strand out of place. Everything about the woman reeked of money, class, and oodles of confidence. In her long emerald-green dress and matching long silk coat edged in gold sequins, she thought she was the bee's knees.

'Get out the garlic,' Harper mumbled, under her breath.

Zavid seemed animated by her arrival. 'This is her. This is Harper Kane.' He spoke with less confidence than before.

The woman's smile slid over Harper as though she was a nothing, a nobody.

If looks could kill. Harper was facing the one woman she wanted to strangle with her bare hands. A woman of her age involved in such a heinous crime was unthinkable. And to make matters worse, she had that conceited look on her face as though she was consistently pissing in the bath and getting away with it.

Whether or not Miss 1970s throwback was smug in her assurance that she could stand there and act like a queen of terror didn't bother Harper. She knew she was going to die anyway, and there was no woman alive who could terrify her. Not after what she'd had to endure in HMP Bronzefield.

'Hello, Clarissa,' said Harper, now with her own version of smugness, guessing that Calvin Stuart's mother wasn't dead after all. There was silence, but Harper watched and enjoyed every inch of confusion as she looked into the eyes of Miss 1970s. It was clear that the woman couldn't pucker up a frown; she was filled with too much muscle-freezing Botox.

'How do you know my name?'

'Look, Ms Stuart, order your men to take these cuffs off and then we can talk.'

Clarissa rolled her eyes and sighed. 'Where is the girl you stole?' Her voice was like the Arctic wind.

If Harper had been sixteen, then the woman might have given her the collywobbles. But not now.

'I didn't steal a girl. I mean, how can you steal a person? You don't own them in the first place.'

Clarissa smirked. 'I see. I was told you were in prison. But you didn't put yourself in there, did you?' She waved her hands. 'Don't bother to answer that. A judge did, though, didn't he? So you were forced to be behind bars. But I bet you didn't think you deserved it. However, that's life, sweetie, you see.'

'They are kids, fucking innocent kids.'

'Hmm, yes, I suppose they are, but they are valuable to me, my clients, and the middleman. They are just a commodity, you see.'

'You are a real sick fucking bitch and yet you're a mother.'

'Yes, dear, I am, and I was lucky to have a son. I never liked girls.'

'Your ol' man ran off with a younger bit of skirt, then, did he?'

'Shut your mouth!' yelled Zavid.

With narrowed eyes and a tight-lipped snarly smirk, Clarissa waved her hand as if she were the Queen, dismissing his input as the subordinate he was.

'I see, so you like to throw insults rather than learn lessons. Prison didn't teach you much, then, did it?'

'Lessons? Pray, tell me, Muvver Earth, what could you possibly teach me that I could ever use in the future? Because, Lady Muck, you're gonna have me killed anyway.'

'That girl you stole, hid, or set free was worth an awful lot of money. Apparently, my men tell me she was highly desired by my buyer. My most prestigious and highly regarded buyer.'

'Oh yeah? You mean that fucking geezer Ahmad, the perverted weasel.'

Clarissa's eyes suddenly widened, as she shot Zavid a look of annoyance. 'How does she know all of this?'

Zavid shrugged. 'I am sorry. I have no idea.'

Harper could see Zavid visibly shrink into himself.

Clarissa glared daringly at Harper. 'Zavid, fetch our new recruit. Let's see what she is made of.' She turned to face Harper. 'I am not here to barter with you. I want the girl back tonight, or you and your family will be dead by the morning.'

Zavid left the room, but he'd forgotten that Harper, although handcuffed, wasn't tied to the chair.

And Clarissa was totally unaware of the fact until Harper stood up and lunged at her.

Lifting her long leg, Harper viciously fly-kicked Clarissa in the chest. The impact was brutal, and Clarissa went down like a bag of bones. Before Zavid and the Shrek monster came back into the room, Harper had managed to kick the woman in the face. The sound of the woman's redefined nose cracking didn't even force a flinch out of Harper. She wanted to go for the kill. Again, she kicked her. This time, the battered woman tried to cover her face, but Harper was relentless and stamped on her head. The blood shot out of Clarissa's nose like paint from a spray gun. 'You evil, subhuman piece of dog shit! Don't you ever threaten my family!'

Hearing the commotion, Zavid tore open the door and screamed in horror. Two men instantly flew into the room. One was Shrek and the other was Calvin Stuart.

'Jesus! Mother! Quick, help me to get her to her room!' he bellowed, trying to help his mother to her feet.

Shrek dragged Harper back to the chair and forced her down.

Breathless through rage, Harper still twisted and wriggled to break free of Shrek's clutches, but he savagely brought his fist back and punched her so hard, she fell off the chair, leaving her stunned. The second punch left her unconscious.

Chapter Twenty-Three

Harper knew she was coming around, but at that moment, between a state of unconsciousness and full awareness of her surroundings, she felt the pain before her brain could understand what had happened. She was being moved – make that dragged – by her arms that were still clamped behind her back. The pain was excruciating as if her feet had been left in boiling water. As her eyes tried to focus, her thoughts rushed to the forefront of her mind. She was in Brighton, she'd given the boss, Clarissa, a good hiding, and now she was being hauled, shoeless, over sharp gravel. The skin had come off her feet. That's why she felt the burning sensation. But there was more. Her face was throbbing and Shrek had obviously continued to beat her even after he'd knocked her out. The evil bastard, all because he had been reprimanded by the young soldier for copping a feel of her tits.

She couldn't struggle because she only had enough fight in her to regain her faculties. Yet, her hearing was superb. Probably it was heightened because her other senses weren't working so well.

'Calvin, my helicopter will be here in two hours, and if I do not leave with that girl, then I will secure my business with another supplier. This is your final chance. You will not be given another one.'

She recognised the Middle Eastern accent of the first voice, followed by Zavid's distinctly subtle Russian accent.

'I understand, Mr Ahmad. Please, please go inside. You don't need to see what we are going to do to this woman. Rest assured, we will find your property, one way or another.'

Harper realised that Shrek or whoever it was who had dragged her had stopped in his tracks. Now they were hoisting her onto a chair. She guessed she was now in the carport. Keeping her eyes closed, she hoped they would believe she was unconscious.

'Frenchy, wake her up!' demanded Zavid.

A crunch of approaching footsteps on the gravel told her that they were probably Frenchy's. That bloody woman; she had never quite been able to suss her out.

Unexpectedly, Harper experienced the worst smell in her life. It was so pungent and gassy that she automatically opened her eyes and then mumbled a curse. The old-fashioned smelling salts, which were in a small bottle, were simply vile.

There was no use in pretending now. She needed to open her eyes to cough and splutter. But as she tried to do so, she found that Shrek had done a right good number on her. It was her swollen cheeks that seemed to be the problem; they were obscuring her vision when she attempted to get a good look at the people around her.

But Calvin was easy to spot dressed in a pair of khaki shorts and a polo shirt, with his collar up, as if he was about to go off sailing with his uni pals. And next to him stood Zavid, who was dressed in black. She was astonished by how alike they looked.

Then Harper took in Frenchy. She was holding the small bottle of smelling salts. Interestingly, she wasn't displaying the same cocky smile that Calvin was. Instead, she appeared to be notably anxious.

When Harper's attention turned to Shrek, as she mentally called him, she couldn't help but notice how small his ears were. In fact, painted green, he could have been Shrek's stunt double.

She needed to keep these players in her eyeline because she'd sussed out where she was, and the last time she was here, she saw a man in a chair in the carport being barbecued. Glancing over at the table to her right, she could see on display an array of torture weapons. It scared the shit out of her. It was only a matter of time before she would be the next victim. So, staring at the living somehow kept her from having to anticipate yet another level of fear.

Zavid stepped forward. 'You have one last chance to die without being tortured. I can easily make that happen once you have told me where that girl is.' He then silently flicked a nod at Shrek.

Harper's eyes widened as the monster approached and freed her wrists from behind her back before he viciously handcuffed her to the arms of the chair, thereby almost pulling her arms out of their sockets in the process. She didn't have the strength to fight. No doubt, she would come off worst and still end up fastened to the chair.

Harper's attempt to talk made her realise that she had more than likely suffered a broken jaw, but she wasn't going to remain silent. 'She musshed have been worth a lot of money, to go to all thissh trouble.' Her words were distinguishable, although not enunciated as she would have liked. As she tried to open her mouth wider, a sudden loud pop and a cracking sound came from her jaw. *It wasn't broken, merely dislocated.* 'I said, she must be worth a lot of money to Mr Ahmad.'

'It is in our blood to make money. All Russians are powered in the same way.' Zavid huffed. 'We didn't grow up playing baseball, like the Italians, or football, like you Brits. We played chess. This means we are masters at strategy. I understand the benefit of keeping our best clients happy, even if I actually want to put a bullet through their eyes. I have a reputation that draws the wealthiest clients my way.' He rubbed his middle finger and thumb together, indicating money. 'And so because I have this reputation, I will not allow someone like you to make me look a fool. So, before we begin with those tools over there, I will ask you again. Where is the girl?' His twitch seemed far worse. There were five spasms in succession.

Harper couldn't feel any pain now because she was numbed by fear and desperate to stay alive. 'Before I decide whether or not to tell you, I am going to negotiate with you.'

Calvin couldn't believe it. He laughed like a girl; it was both high-pitched and dramatic. 'Seriously? You? Bargain with us?' He glanced around, clearly expecting everyone to be laughing with him at Harper's expense. But there was only silence.

Harper guessed he was lower ranked in authority.

Anyone with savvy could tell he was just a poncy mother's boy who was used to getting his own way. It was confirmed when he stamped his foot and glared. 'Where is that girl! Oh, fuck it! Frenchy, or whatever your name is, cut off her finger, and then, perhaps, Harper might be more inclined to tell us.' He walked over to Harper and stared into her eyes, an inch away from her face. 'You *will* tell me.'

Harper could have headbutted him, but she knew she would probably do herself more harm if she did.

Glancing at Frenchy, Harper was puzzled because she appeared uneasy. Her eyes were dancing around, and Harper could see the glistening pearls of sweat, which had just gathered along her top lip.

'So, out of interest, and before you begin to dismember me, tell me this. Why did you think I took the kid? And why didn't you believe me when I told you that she scarpered? I mean, why would I care about a teenager? I have enough shit of my own to take care of.'

'Just cut her finger off, will you, Frenchy. I'm wasting time here,' demanded Calvin, like a spoilt kid.

'Hold up a moment,' said Zavid, as he stepped forward.

'No! Why wait, Zavid? Ahmad is in the house waiting for answers. His helicopter will be here soon, and yet here she is, wanting a fucking conversation.'

'You are my cousin, Calvin, not my boss.'

'Yes!' screamed Calvin, flapping his arms about, almost in tears. 'But the real boss is my mother. And your aunt is nursing a broken nose, and probably concussion, caused by this ugly bitch! Tell me, Zavid, what the fuck do you think your father would do, eh? He wouldn't ask questions before giving her a taste of what was to come, would he?'

Ignoring Calvin's gibes, Zavid placed his hands on his hips. 'You helped her escape, Harper. I know you are a very intelligent woman.' He sighed and wagged his finger. 'But we found the blood-covered bed sheets under the bed. And this.' He held up a small key ring, of a seahorse. 'You killed Claude and . . .' He laughed. 'You cleverly caused unrest between the Turkish community and mine.' He clapped. 'So now I know that you are capable of lying and not just lying but planning and scheming and even murder.'

'Never mind all of that now, Zavid! We have twelve girls in chains, and with one more, that makes the thirteen and completes the order. Just start the process. Forget the finger. Take her fucking hand off. Do it now. We need *answers*!'

Harper felt the contents of her stomach rise and the back of her neck on fire. Sweat dripped from her forehead and stung her eyes.

With her mind in overdrive, she had to go to plan B, which, of course, she didn't have. She'd have to wing it. But, momentarily, she was distracted by Frenchy, who appeared to be nodding with her eyes. *Nodding?* What could that mean? Then it hit her. Frenchy was encouraging her to keep going by talking more.

'So you think that was a clever move of mine, eh? Well, it was actually Calvin's idea.' She looked at Frenchy, who almost seemed to smile with her eyes. Harper hoped it wasn't wishful thinking under the circumstances.

Zavid shot a glare at Calvin, who, in return, shook his head. 'Nice try, Harper, but it won't work, you fool.'

But Harper could see in Zavid's eyes that she had sown a seed. An important one. Now knowing this was the case, she decided to stir the pot, but to do this, she had to rack her brains and recall everything Madeleine had told her.

'Fool? Am I, Calvin? Come on, you hated Claude because he was nosey, and you don't like people who are nosey, do you?

Nicolas, your business partner, went all Inspector Clouseau on you, didn't he? You couldn't have that, could you?' She really hoped she was on the right track. She recalled someone saying *if you say it with enough conviction, then they will believe any shit that leaves your mouth.*

Calvin's laugh wasn't so dramatic this time. 'Come on, acting like you know me? You don't, you slut!'

Harper could imagine Zavid processing the information in his head. However, it seemed from his expression that her bluff wasn't working.

'Frenchy! Cut off her fucking finger!'

Harper glanced at Frenchy, who seemed just as scared, and then her eyes flicked to Calvin with his smug I-am-better-than-you look. It was just like his mother's.

'Wait, Zavid, he is double-crossing you. Please believe me.'

Zavid tapped his chin with his index finger. 'No, Harper, you effectively turned two families against each other. The Boz family were good for business, and you caused a problem, but . . .' He slowly shook his head. 'Calvin is my cousin, and so your plan will not work this time.' He patted Calvin's shoulder. 'He is my blood.'

Frenchy walked slowly over to the table and took her time to pick up the implement that would cleanly remove a finger.

Harper then got the sense that Frenchy was not the up-and-coming soldier anyone thought she was, or perhaps she had her own agenda.

However, before Harper could even contemplate the idea that she was about to have her finger brutally chopped off, Shrek pushed Frenchy out of the way and grabbed the tile snippers. There was no pause, no forewarning, nothing. He simply grabbed Harper's little finger on her right hand, placed the snippers over it, and before she could even catch her breath and brace herself, the finger was off.

The crunching noise echoed the instant pain. The burning, shooting agony shot up her arm and winded her. She couldn't scream or yell, merely gasp violently for breath. Her eyes were wide, ready to pop out of her skull, as she shot a terrified glance at the finger on the plastic sheet. *Plastic sheet? Oh, dear God!* This was going to be one horrible demise. Sweat dripped from every pore and the blood drained from her, leaving her feeling heavy with fear. The throbbing began, but the initial shock slowly subsided, allowing her to breathe more evenly. She had no time to take stock of her injuries. She had to defend the bluff quickly before she lost another finger, or, worse, her entire hand.

Standing a few feet behind Shrek was the younger soldier, the man who had put Shrek in his place while they were in the car. He appeared nervous as his eyes looked up to the sky. Harper thought perhaps he was waiting to guide in Ahmad's helicopter. Because the helicopter pad was behind him. *But wasn't it too soon for the helicopter?* she wondered.

'I can't tell you what I don't know, Zavid, but I can tell you what . . .' She stopped and gasped for air. 'I can tell you what I do know.' Casting a deliberate smile Calvin's way, she continued. 'I trusted you, Calvin. You promised me that you would see me okay, and now this, so—'

Totally unexpectedly, Shrek whacked her jaw with the tile snippers. 'Shut up and tell us what we want to know.'

Harper was stunned. All she could hear was a ringing sound and voices in slow motion. She couldn't control her head as it slumped forward. Her nose poured with blood, warming her lips with its warm stickiness. Detecting the taste of rust invading her mouth, she moved her tongue slowly around until she felt the gap at the back. A tooth had been knocked clean out. Breathing in through her nose, she spat the tooth out before it choked her. As the agony reached an insufferable pitch, she closed her eyes and thought of her Eddie. Yet as quickly as she had been stunned, she was fully conscious again. Obviously, Frenchy had waved the magic potion under her nose.

As she opened her eyes, she saw that Zavid's expression was less than confident.

'*He* has the girl, Zavid,' she managed to say.

'Look, Zavid, time is running out. Ahmad will leave, once that chopper arrives, and we will be left with those twelve girls and no fucking money,' said Calvin, desperate to convince his cousin.

Maybe there was some distrust between them. Harper hoped there was now at least a tiny shadow of doubt.

'He killed Claude because Claude knew too much, and he wanted you to fight the Boz family. He wanted to create a distraction. Ask yourself, why does he need you, Zavid? He has his shipping containers, the means to transport the girls. He even has new suppliers, and all that are left are the buyers. One is sitting in your aunt's mansion. He's probably sipping apple juice, at this very minute.'

Zavid was listening but waving his hands.

Calvin, however, was almost spitting feathers. 'You fucking liar, you stupid bitch! It was *you* who killed Claude.'

Harper scoffed. 'Me? Did you ever see the fucking size of that man? You killed him, Calvin, and planted evidence on me, since I was managing the club. And, of course, you would think I probably knew too much, thanks to your crafty lines of cocaine and whisky chasers, leaving you with a loose tongue.' She paused to take a breath, praying that the bluff would work, but she needed something concrete to entice Zavid to believe her.

'The hotel, the Grand Brighton came in useful, though, didn't it? Go on, Zavid, ask him how I knew about that.' *Please, God, let this work.*

With his eyes suddenly flashing like a serpent, Zavid spun around to face Calvin. 'You told her where the girls are? You fucking fool.' He backed away, staring in disgust. 'You have double-crossed me. *Now* I believe she *is* telling the truth.'

It was then that Harper knew why the oddball Zavid was called 'The Serpent'. His moves were extreme and as fast as a bullet, and yet sleek and sharp, like a snake. She watched as he grabbed Calvin around the throat, lifted him off his feet, and slammed him ruthlessly into the ground. Placing his foot over Calvin's neck, Zavid pressed down, suffocating his cousin. Harper could see the sudden deranged look in Zavid's eyes. There was no question he would murder Calvin. And if he could kill his own flesh and blood, then he would kill anyone.

'Please, Zavid, I didn't tell her anything,' Calvin begged, in a croaky voice.

The sound of a helicopter approaching was much louder than Harper had ever imagined. The glaring lights and the gust of wind from the rotor blades forced Zavid to take his foot off Calvin's neck and step back.

Harper was feeling very light-headed and was fighting to stay conscious. Then everything changed in a split second.

Shrek dropped his smug grin along with his tool and instead tried to release the knife strapped to his leg.

Frenchy, even as small as she was, managed to dive on his back, forcing him to the ground, and within a millisecond, he was handcuffed.

Zavid was rugby tackled by the young soldier. As much as Zavid could fight and was strong for such a slight man, the young soldier had him in a hold with a gun at his head. Another soldier, who appeared from nowhere, pulled Calvin to his feet and handcuffed him.

To her relief, she realised the helicopter wasn't for Ahmad. It was a raid. It seemed to her that a hundred soldiers leaped from the helicopter and scattered like ants in all directions. Each one had a job to do.

Tears filled her eyes and rolled down her swollen cheeks. They were captured. *Dear God, please help them find the girls.* The noise of guns going off, sirens, radios, and flashing lights forced Harper to lean back and let whatever was about to happen play out. She was done.

With her eyes closed, she felt the presence of someone kneeling beside her. 'Hey, I'm so sorry you lost your finger, and . . .'

Harper heard the emotional quiver in the woman's voice, but she didn't care right now. She was exhausted and drained, and now she prayed that the girls were safe.

'I truly am sorry.'

Harper's eyes focused more clearly when she heard the shake in the female officer's voice.

'Will someone get her fucking cuffs off!' she bellowed.

Harper could see Frenchy approaching, merely by the haircut and the way she walked.

With her hands trembling, Frenchy used the keys she'd taken from Shrek and quickly removed the handcuffs. 'I'm so sorry, Harper. So sorry.' Her voice was so different, she didn't sound at all like Frenchy in the club; her voice was educated and quite posh.

'Cheers, Katie. Get the paramedics over here now. See if they can't save her finger.'

Harper watched Frenchy dart off. *So her real name is Katie.*

In seconds, the woman dishing out the orders eased a straw into Harper's mouth. 'Drink, slowly. It's glucose. Let's get you out of here.'

The cool liquid was like instant medicine. Once Harper sucked the pouch empty, she used her good hand to wipe her puffy eyes. Then she felt the woman's hand gently stroke her cheek. 'I'm so sorry, Harps. I didn't realise . . .'

Harper sat up straight. She twisted her head in confusion as she looked at the woman's face. *Harps?*

Those eyes, those sad, troubled, terrified eyes that had haunted her every day, were now staring back at her, but there was no more terror, only confidence.

‘*Charley?*’

‘Yeah, Harps . . .’ Harper heard that quiver again. ‘It’s me, Charley. I am truly sorry you were caught up in all of this, but you have no idea how much you’ve helped us, unwittingly, probably.’

The sob that was caught up in her chest was released, and a silent cry shook Harper’s body until it was smoothed away by her sister’s arms around her.

The paramedics helped her onto the stretcher. They wrapped her in a blanket, ready to take her to the helicopter.

Her sister, still clutching her hand, said, ‘You will be safe with them, Harps. I’ll need to finish up here.’

‘No, Charley, wait, please.’

Charley stopped in her tracks. ‘It’s okay. They will take care of you.’

‘Charley, I need to know where the twelve girls are.’

‘Katie – you know her as Frenchy – had a wire on. We heard what you said, and the police in Brighton have located the girls at the basement of the hotel.’

Harper looked at the radio in her sister’s hand. ‘Do me a favour. Could you find out if one of the girls is called Kera, please?’

‘Yes, I will. I promise,’ she replied, before the paramedics hurried Harper away to the helicopter.

Chapter Twenty-Four

It was the clinical smell and the sound of her name being called from somewhere in the distance that pulled Harper from her sleep. She flicked open her eyes and was surprised to find she was actually in a bed. It took a few moments to process her surroundings before she could make out a man in a white coat holding a clipboard with a stethoscope around his neck. Then, like a huge floor puzzle, she began putting all the pieces together, until it was evident in her mind where she was and who she was and what she had been through. Slowly, her eyes drifted to her right hand, and a surge of excitement sent her skin tingling when she saw a bandage that covered her little finger.

'I am Doctor Watts. We managed to save your finger. It may not move as well as it did before, but we believe the feeling will come back, given time. You also suffered from concussion, so we have kept you sedated for a few days, just to let the swelling in your brain go down. How do you feel?'

Her throat felt dry, and her voice was croaky. 'Okay, I suppose. At least I'm alive.'

The doctor's face came into focus, and she saw him smile and nod.

'Yes, you were fortunate. Although your head injury was life-threatening, I can safely say you are out of the woods, and, in fact, in a day or so, you can go home. There are quite a few visitors in the waiting room. They have been there for some time. Oh, your mum and her friend, Terry, and . . .' He peered down at some notes scribbled on a piece of paper. 'Lexi? I believe they had to go home. They were exhausted, so they said that if they were away when you woke up, we were to let you know that they were all here.' He chuckled. 'I feel like a secretary. You must be popular. Oh, and a chap called Vadim.' He pointed around the room. 'He is covering the cost of this. He said to get well soon. The club won't manage itself. He did send in practically every flower from the local florist, but we cannot allow flowers on the wards, I'm afraid.'

Harper smiled back. 'Well, whoever else is out there, can they come in?' she asked, realising now that she was in a private room.

'Yes, of course. I would suggest one at a time and only for short periods, because you do have a lot of fans.' His smile lit up his soft face and illuminated his pale-blue eyes. It was refreshing to see someone who was genuinely happy for her, after dealing with Calvin, Zavid, and all the Russian brutes.

Charley was barely recognisable, wearing a pink shirt, jeans, and trainers, with her hair pulled back in a ponytail and sunglasses perched on her nose. Since Harper had only met her briefly at the raid, she had wondered if her long-lost sister had, in fact, been a figment of her imagination.

She walked tentatively towards the bed, invited by Harper's outstretched arms. Behind her was the young soldier, who Harper only now recognised because he was dressed in casual clothes, jeans, and a plain T-shirt.

'You saved me, Charley. You bloody well saved me.'

Charley bit her bottom lip and blinked a few times. 'Harps, it was the least I could do.' She pulled a chair over and sat down, with the soldier standing behind her. 'This is Michel. He wanted to say something to you.'

He spoke in Russian, and Harper frowned. Then she heard her sister translate for her.

'He said, you were the bravest woman he'd ever met, and he wanted to intervene so many times, but he couldn't because he had to stay undercover, and sometimes that means seeing and doing things you don't want to do. But it's all been for the greater good.'

Michel continued in Russian, but he was looking at Charley.

'He said . . .' Charley stopped to compose herself. 'He said I am a brave woman and that I must get it from you. He said if he had aborted the mission, then the twelve girls would have been sold to the sex slave industry. We now have in our custody the men we needed to break this ring, and you helped us do that. He said he knows you were dragged into it through no fault of your own and' – she smiled as he placed his hand on her shoulder – 'he said he is proud to call you his sister-in-law.'

Harper's eyes widened. '*What?* . . . You two are *married*? My baby sister married? How lovely. And children?'

Charley shook her head. 'No, not for a while yet.'

'Did you know I was caught up in this?' Harper's voice lost its softness, and for a moment, she felt sad that her sister had used her in this way. It was evident that Charley was some big shot policewoman, by the way she had dished out the orders.

'No, I didn't, Harps. I was heading another project, so I had no involvement in this investigation. That was until I discovered that the two trafficking rings were connected, and then Michel and I had to work together. Still, I orchestrated the raid. That's my job. And when I heard your voice through Katie's wire, I knew it was you. But Michel was right. You didn't just save those twelve girls – and by the way, one of them is outside waiting to see you – but you also saved so many who would have been the next victims. Louise, for instance.'

Harper looked at Michel. 'Thank you for your kind words.'

Michel nodded and left.

Charley held Harper's hand, and once she heard the door close, she allowed the tears to plummet. 'I missed you so much. I cried every day when they sent me away. You should have told the truth, Harps.'

Harper shook her head. 'I had to protect you, Charley. I couldn't let you go to prison, or wherever they sent girls back then. You were a kid. You killed him because he was a wrong 'un, a paedo. Mother should never have let him in our house . . .' She paused, thinking about the past.

Charley was the quiet, weak, sweet sister, and he was a big, overpowering man, and he was drunk that day. He assumed everyone would be out shopping for hours. He hadn't expected her early return. She could still see the bastard, with his trousers down and her little sister's eyes wide with fear. She was shaking, terrified. The knife was in Charley's hand, blood dripping down her wrist. She remembered her instant reaction was to strip her sister, shove her dress and socks in the washing machine, and get her in the shower and into clean clothes. At the time, Charley's whole body was shaking as if she was having convulsions. So she'd bundled her off to Mr Baker's to watch TV and calm down. She then covered herself in the blood and handled the knife before calling the police.

'I went into care, and the psychiatrist and her team tried to rehabilitate me. I guess they could never get to the bottom of why I was angry and violent. I changed my name. I'm Charley Stirling, now.'

'Stirling?'

'I was fostered and then adopted by a couple. Brendan Stirling, his name is, and Maureen, his wife.'

'Were they good to you?'

She nodded. 'Oh yeah, so good. We travelled the world because he worked for the police force, undercover, so we moved around a lot. I decided that I wanted to work in the police force and stop paedophile rings. You know, to crack them, and I worked hard, I trained hard, and I learned to speak Russian, French, and Spanish. I wanted to make you proud of me. I wanted to pay you back in some way.'

Harper laughed. 'So you were the brainbox of the outfit, then.'

The tears in Charley's eyes welled up. 'I feel so guilty now, having seen you again because I should have visited. I should have written, after what you—'

‘Aw, shut up. Listen, Charley. You make me proud. And now, when I think you’re out there saving girls who are victims of the worst crime, a crime that in effect made you who you are now, I feel blessed to have a sister like you.’

Charley nodded. ‘Yeah, I work hard, Harps. I’ve uncovered quite a few paedo rings.’ Her voice was excited. She wanted to show off to her sister like she had done as a child. Harper was the one she’d rushed home from school to, to show her a certificate or a gold star sticker. It was Harper who’d clapped or who’d baked a cake and hugged her tightly, beaming with delight.

‘Charley, what about the probation officer and the social worker?’ She pushed herself up to a seating position and sipped from a glass of water to stop her voice from sounding like a creaky door.

‘You’ve no need to worry. Your friend Terry, he has been a great help. Not only have we arrested your probation officer, but her husband Peter Capshore, the social worker, and two foster carers. Your mate, Candy, who, by the way, I’ve never liked, is also in custody, and she will be made an example of. Her sister Rhea was discovered murdered. That bloody mansion of the Stuarts held many sad facts, ledgers, and records. They were greedy people. Clarissa, we believe, fell down the stairs and died of a brain bleed.’ She winked. ‘And the Boz family will never see the light of day. Their crimes are extensive, so our Lexi will be free of that prick Hasad for the next thirty years.’

‘And Frenchy, I wished she had told me who she was. I would have been less hard on her.’

She paused remembering Frenchy’s odd behaviour when the two little girls went missing. It all made sense now. Frenchy must have been worried the Russians had taken them.

‘Bethany and Victoria? Are they okay?’

‘They were grabbed by another one of our undercover officers, but it panicked Frenchy because apparently it happened so fast, he didn’t have time to give her the okay nod.’

Charley laughed. 'Frenchy, I mean Katie, is the finest undercover officer we have. She will have the best fooled. That girl has taken a bullet rather than blow her cover. You, though, were clever in hiding little Louise. You gave Katie a fright. She thought the Russians had her.'

'Bloody hell, I assumed she was shitting hot bricks because she'd get murdered by the Russians for losing the girl.'

'Like I said, she is the best.' Charley laughed. 'And she had to be careful. She didn't know how much of an alliance you had with the Russians. She reckons you could be a great undercover agent. You have more balls than most.'

Charley rose from her chair. 'Harps, I have to go. I can't see you for a few weeks now. But know this: I love you, with all my heart. You were the only person I kept in my mind's eye, the only person who I focused on when I thought about suicide. I'm fine now, Harps. I hope you understand that I have to stay away, to protect my family, because I could easily put you at risk. It's my job. They can use you all as—'

'I understand,' interrupted Harper. 'I get it. I've been through it. Please stay safe and visit when you can.'

Charley kissed her sister's cheek and swiftly left the room.

Having seen Charley's face, the happy smile was all the thanks Harper needed, really, having experienced what she had been through. She had never wanted much in life, not for herself anyway. She smiled, knowing her family were all safe, and Charley, her baby sister, was a force to be reckoned with, with three more languages to her name and a position high up in some task force. The twelve years behind bars had been worth it.

Sipping more water, Harper stared out of the window at the cityscape. She guessed she was in St Thomas' Hospital, going by the stunning views.

Harper knew it would take a while to get her head around all the developments, but the one thing she was so thrilled by was that the girls were safe. *Oh damn!* She hadn't asked if Kera was one of the girls they found. How could she tell Madeleine that they had found all those girls but not hers? A lump filled her throat as she fought to hold back the tears.

The door creaked open. ‘Knock, knock, may we come in?’ came a recognisable voice.

Harper’s head shot around to see Madeleine *and* presumably Kera. The tears fell like waterfalls. ‘I was just thinking about you both. Oh my God, you’re out. They let you go, then?’ asked Harper, with her arms reaching out to them.

Madeleine hugged her friend, careful not to crush her.

‘Harper Kane, what can I say? How can I ever thank you enough?’

Kera pushed her mum aside. ‘You saved me!’ she cried. ‘And you saved my mum. Please can I give you a hug?’

‘I’m so pleased to meet you, Kera. You’re a little beauty, just like your mum.’

‘Oh, Harper, you have no idea. I mean, a few days ago, I tied those sheets to – well, you know. And last night, I tucked my baby into bed. What a fucking turnaround, eh, and all down to you. I am indebted to you, Harper. Whatever you need or want, you can have. The capture of Calvin and the evidence they had on him was overwhelming. I do believe your sister’s department rushed through my release, and all my husband’s bank accounts were unfrozen, and the business was transferred to my name, so, like I say, anything you want is yours.’

‘Maybe a cup of tea and a chat every so often.’

Madeleine half smiled. Most women, given a chance, would probably have compiled a list of stuff they wanted, but not Harper Kane.

Politely interrupting their visit, the doctor suggested that Harper should rest for a few hours. Her brain still needed to recover, and she couldn’t have too much excitement in one day.

Madeleine and Kera left after a few more hugs and kisses.

Harper felt herself drifting off to sleep again. The doctor's advice was right. She was tired. Relief allowed her to go into a peaceful deep slumber, and by the time she opened her eyes again, she could see from the vast window the millions of red lights littering the buildings of London. Some twinkled, and some glowed. The calmness was soothing. Enjoying the evening backdrop, she heard footsteps, and as she turned to see who was outside the door, she spotted a woman; at first, she assumed it was Delores, but the woman was thinner, and her hair was long. But before Harper could even blink, the woman was gone. For a moment, she wondered if it was Desiree, her mother's sister. Or maybe she herself was still in a dreamlike state. If she'd been a spiritual person, she would have considered the idea that the woman was a ghost. The ghost of Desiree Kane, if the woman was dead.

She sat up, drank more of her water, and sighed. Her thoughts, as they always did, turned to Eddie. At this point in her life, she had to count her blessings. She may not have had the chance to raise him, but at least he was being brought up in a good home with his dad and her sister. Compared to a lot of the girls inside prison, Harper considered herself to be fortunate. Many of them had lost their kids to the social services and would never see them again. Still, it did hurt her to think she couldn't hold him, kiss his cheeks, pat his backside as he ran into school, or stand on the touchline when he played football.

She hadn't noticed that the door was open as she was staring into the evening sky, her mind imagining what the future may hold.

A cough alerted her to someone in the room, and then the smell of aftershave – Hugo Boss – a dead giveaway. She took a deep breath before turning around. 'Teddy.'

'Harps.' He tried to hide his emotions by a cough covering his cracked voice. She could see he was about to cry, but then again, she must have looked a pitiful sight.

'Teddy.'

He suddenly rushed at her, flinging his arms around her. 'Oh Jesus, Harps, what have I done? Fucking hell, I should have waited, I should have—'

'No,' she interrupted, as she gently pushed him away. 'You were young, Teddy. We both were. But you and Erin did good by Eddie, and, well, I was just selfish, I guess. I couldn't ask that you keep him for years and then just hand him back.'

'Harps, I love you, you know that, don't you? And if you would take me back, I'd be back in a shot.'

Out of the corner of her eye, she could see her sister sneaking a peek through the pane of glass set in the door.

Smiling with compassion as her eyes flickered over his handsome face, Harper tried so desperately hard to hold back the tears and swallow down the lump in her throat. With her heart sitting in her chest like a lead brick, Harper whispered, 'We, Teddy, are two very different people. Our paths crossed when we were kids, but now? Now, I'm a different woman.' She tried not to hesitate or show her emotion, but it was like grabbing at a smoke ring.

Her sister's face came into view again, and at that moment, Harper could sense her sister's terror of losing Teddy.

Erin was many things, but she wasn't a bad person.

Harper took another deep breath. 'You and me, Teddy, will always be close, in so much as we had a child together. But other than that, it was the past, and I've moved on. Make my sister happy and Little Eddie too. I probably won't see you again, but that's okay. Just send me a photo of him, so I know my boy's doing okay, will you?'

Teddy nodded, his eyes filled with tears. He coughed. 'Yeah, okay, Harps, sure.'

As he bent over to kiss her goodbye, she felt those warm tears of his land on her cheek.

She wanted so much to grab him, to feel his breath and his warm lips on hers, but she couldn't do it, not to her sister.

When the door closed behind him, Harper allowed herself a moment to feel the pain of heartache. For twelve years, she had yearned to see him, longed to feel his arms around her. She'd also had all that time to get used to it; not that it had got any easier, but she'd managed to cope.

Hearing his footsteps marching down the corridor, she listened again, imagining she would hear the clip-clop of her sister's high heels running after him. Instead, there was nothing. But then the door opened again, and there looking like a wet weekend stood Erin. Her face was devoid of any fake tan, and she wasn't wearing any lipstick or false eyelashes. She was dressed in a modest summer dress and a pair of pumps. Then Harper's eyes drifted to the boy who bustled in behind her.

He was taller than she had expected. And his eyes were bright and his smile so genuine. From ear to ear, he beamed. Harper had forced back the tears from Teddy's visit, but seeing her son was all too much. Her dream of seeing her boy in the flesh had come true. He was there, a foot away from her. She desperately wanted to hold him, to hug him, and to tell him how much he meant to her. But she couldn't; he was Erin's boy now, and she would have to suck it up and fight the tears. She sat up straighter, her eyes unable to leave his. 'Hello, Eddie Bear, I'm your Aunty Harper.' Saying those words ripped her heart right out of her chest and simply crucified her, but they had to be said.

'No, you're not!' he snapped, as he ran to her, flinging his arms around her neck. 'You're my mum. They told me you're my mum! I always knew you were.'

Harper held him close, smelling his hair and kissing his waves of blond curls, as she had done when he was a baby. She looked over at her sister, who was smiling and crying herself.

'He said he always knew,' said Erin, as her bottom lip trembled.

With tears streaming, Harper mouthed the words 'Thank you.'

***

Book two out 2022

Acknowledgements

Once again, this book would not be complete without the loyalty and valuable input of Robert Wood my editor. Even while he was unwell, he continued to work hard on the book ensuring it was ready for the launch date.

Deryl Easton for her constant encouragement and all the members of NotRights book club, who, as always, have supported me every step of the way.

Chrissie Hecquet for her invaluable help.

Robert Wood- www.epworthediting.com